ANGELS

and Awakenings

Illustrated by Warren Chappell

ANGELS AND AWAKENINGS

STORIES OF THE MIRACULOUS

BY

GREAT MODERN WRITERS

EDITED BY
M. CAMERON GREY

To me Sian
Brian —
Christmas
1995

DOUBLEDAY
NEW YORK LONDON TORONTO SYDNEY AUCKLAND

PUBLISHED BY DOUBLEDAY
a division of Bantam Doubleday Dell Publishing Group, Inc.
1540 Broadway, New York, New York 10036

DOUBLEDAY and the portrayal of an anchor with a dolphin are
trademarks of Doubleday, a division of Bantam Doubleday Dell
Publishing Group, Inc.

Library of Congress Cataloging-in-Publication Data
Main entry under title: Angels and awakenings.

1. Short stories.   2. Miracles—Fiction.   3. Angels—Fiction.
I. Grey, M. Cameron.
PZ1.A57277   [PN6120.95.M54]   808.83'1

Library of Congress Catalog Card Number 79-7111

ISBN 0-385-15311-2

Originally published by Doubleday in 1980
This edition is published November 1994

Grateful acknowledgment is made to authors, publishers, and agents for permission to reprint the following copyrighted material:

"The Last Trump," copyright © 1955 by King-Size Publications, Inc., from *Earth Is Room Enough* by Isaac Asimov. Reprinted by permission of Doubleday & Company, Inc.

"The Fire Balloons," copyright 1951, 1961 by Ray Bradbury, from *The Illustrated Man* by Ray Bradbury. Published by Doubleday & Company, Inc. Reprinted by permission of Harold Matson Co., Inc.

"The Angel of the Bridge," copyright © 1961 by John Cheever, first appeared in *The New Yorker*, from *Stories of John Cheever*. Published by Alfred A. Knopf, Inc. Reprinted by permission of the author.

"Mr. Andrews," from *The Eternal Moment & Other Stories* by E. M. Forster. Copyright 1928 by Harcourt Brace Jovanovich, Inc.; copyright © 1956 by E. M. Forster. Reprinted by permission of the publisher.

"The Small Miracle," from *The Small Miracle* by Paul Gallico. Copyright 1950 by Paul Gallico. Reprinted by permission of Doubleday & Company, Inc.

"The Schreuderspitze" by Mark Helprin. Copyright © 1977 The New Yorker Magazine, Inc. Reprinted by permission.

"The Question of Rain" by William Hoffman. Copyright © 1978 by The Atlantic Monthly Company, Boston, Mass. Reprinted by permission of Curtis Brown, Ltd.

FOR
MY MOTHER AND FATHER

Contents

Contents

Contents

Acknowledgments

With special thanks to Pierre DeLattre, Shirley Fisher, Anne Fremantle, Dr. Paul Fussell, Cathleen Jordan, George Lanning, Mavis McIntosh, Dr. William A. Owens, Scott Symon, and Nathan Teitel.

Foreword

IF IT IS the purpose of modern fiction to reflect the modern age, then it would seem hardly possible to collect an anthology of modern stories which imply the presence of a divine intelligence in the world. When life is viewed in terms of scientific cause and effect—*the* theology of the twentieth century—it certainly looks as if human affairs are being played out in a universe with either no God or, worse, a silent and indifferent one. It is no wonder that most serious modern writing is existentialist or absurdist, obsessed with the pain of the world, the gratuitous evil in man's heart, and the ultimate meaninglessness of existence.

The stories here, however, transcend this. Yet they are by writers of integrity, free spirits all; most are the major writers of this century and the turn of the last. One can be sure that their stories, even though about angels and awakenings, Paradise, and divine intervention, will not be predictable or easily sentimental. All of them spring from the intellectual skepticism and sense of spiritual dislocation which characterizes the contemporary Western point of view. But a quality of mind, more implicit than overt, sets these stories apart, a quality which is best described by what Dostoyevsky has called "the real miracle." If, says Ivan Karamazov, we truly are at the mercy of random chance and our own animalistic behavior, then the real miracle is that the idea of a concerned God has occurred to us and that this idea persists in spite of everything.

Persist it does. Even the existentialist Albert Camus, for whom

God is dead, comes to the conclusion that in order to live at all effectively, in order to remain sane in this irrational world, we must act "as if" God existed. It is no doubt symptomatic also that a renewed popular interest in the Devil is taking place—that people wish to see films and read books about God's fallen angel— with the implication that even the triumph of evil is more satisfying, possibly more comforting, than the abyss of no moral order at all.

What was immediately apparent in this search for modern stories about divine intervention is that most great modern writers do have a strong moral sense—sometimes almost in spite of themselves—and that they remain fascinated with the possibility that a moral order and intelligence lies hidden in the mysterious confusion around them. Even Henry James, that master of meticulous ambiguity, finally speaks of his belief in "a visible rule" that "hovers over the mysterious mixture, that bids us will to learn and seek to understand."

In their seeking to understand, it is not surprising that many of the writers in this collection have sidestepped the problems of contemporary credibility by turning to fantasy, allegory, and satire. In fact, almost three quarters of the writers here make use of these literary devices, and for good reason. In this way they are free to take a fresh look at Christianity, at angels and miracles and the promises of Paradise.

Some are indignant over what they find. They attack with humor, and the results are some highly funny and irreverent illuminations. But satire is born of a serious sense of the ideal, and the stories of G. B. Shaw, John Steinbeck, O. Henry, and Mark Twain come from an impatience with easy answers, with the smugness of "goodness," with the limited vision of entrenched, garden variety theologies. Thus Shaw shows us a blithely chaotic Church of England Heaven where the playing fields of the Lord and of Eton are hardly distinguishable; Steinbeck easily canonizes an erstwhile very bad pig; O. Henry's hero is arrested just at the moment he has resolved to go straight; and Twain's good little boy comes to a loud, bad end.

Through their use of fantasy, Ray Bradbury, E. M. Forster, and Isaac Asimov reach beyond the common assumptions of Christian dogma, Bradbury's astronaut missionary asking what will constitute sin in other galaxies, and, if God has revealed himself in man's image, how can this encompass life forms in other universes? Forster, ecumenical before his time, shows a Christian and a Moslem unhappy with their respective Heavens. They leave and join hands in the brotherhood of the "world soul" outside the gates of Paradise. Asimov foresees some knotty problems when the Day of Resurrection arrives—not the least, what the Americans will do about all those slaughtered Indians.

Nor, in their fantasies, have modern writers hesitated to use angels to bring us contemporary messages—even if the message is that the arrival of a real angel would be most annoying, as in Gabriel García Márquez' marvelous and ominous story. Or that the angel who comes may not be what we had in mind; in Bernard Malamud's "Angel Levine," a devout Jew is sent a young black angel who hangs out in Harlem until the Jew can overcome his racism. Even Edgar Allan Poe's hilarious angel in the shape of an angry cask with a thick German accent has a mystical message. Don't be so sure, he tells the drunken hero, that the improbable and the outlandish can't happen over and over again.

The seeming iconoclasm of these stories should not hide the moral seriousness of their intention. They are saying that man's simplistic hopes and demands often do more to obscure the divine presence in the world than to invite it.

More traditionally, Robert Louis Stevenson and Philip Van Doren Stern summon that archetypical figure, the disguised angel, the mysterious stranger who arrives to effect a change of heart —remorse in the heart of Markheim the murderer, a sense of purpose in Stern's potential suicide.

Possibly the strangest story about angels is Arthur Machen's "The Bowmen." It is included because it is the *genesis* of all the rumors and legends of the Angel of Mons in World War I. It was only after Machen published this short, completely fictional tale that St. George and his ghostly Agincourt bowmen were seen in the sky, by the Allied troops, destroying thousands of Germans with their arrows. A baffled Machen insisted he had invented the story, but such was the hunger for the miraculous in that grim "lovely war" that the public did not want to believe him.

Also using fantasy, but with overtones of legend, Leo Tolstoy and Paul Gallico give us relatively straightforward miracles, and both stories reveal that the simplehearted are more likely to receive God's attention. Tolstoy's three ragged old holy men can't remember the words of the Lord's Prayer, which the Bishop so condescendingly teaches them, but they *can* run on water in pursuit of the Bishop's ship. It is significant that both stories are placed slightly at a distance from us, in an age or an atmosphere of faith.

In contrast to these, in H. G. Wells's "The Man Who Could Work Miracles" divine intelligence seems present only by its absence. A young know-it-all in an English pub suddenly has the power to work any miracle he chooses. Ultimately he and a well-meaning vicar accidentally destroy the world. Although this is an amusing, lighthearted tale, Wells, with his well-known gift of foresight, has put his finger on one of our deeper fears in the atomic age: that with our technological capacity to destroy the world, we just might do so—accidentally or through "good" intentions.

In their allegories, "Paradise" and "The City Coat of Arms," both Pär Lagerkvist and Franz Kafka are also concerned with this question of man's technological knowledge and divine intention. Lagerkvist's Lord, in an ironic twist, *urges* mankind to eat of the tree of knowledge. Man does, but so abuses the knowledge that Paradise becomes a mess; now angels with machine guns must stand guard at the gates. Kafka, summing up the agnostic position with chilling concision, tells how humanity's plans to build a tower to Heaven are put off from one generation to another—"because there might be technological breakthroughs" later—until finally the idea becomes "senseless."

The turning point from fantasy to realism in this collection is Wilbur Daniel Steele's fine and passionate story, "The Man Who Saw Through Heaven"—a story which deals dramatically, intensely, with loss of faith. It has been said that we still have not recovered emotionally from the knowledge that the earth is not the center of the universe—that Einstein's vast galaxies extend endlessly beyond the roof/floor of our pre-Copernican Christian Heaven. Steele's fundamentalist missionary, on his way to Africa, is taken by chance to an observatory where his cozy certainties are shattered when he learns the true nature of the cosmos. This knowledge throws him into a new and terrifying world of freedom "where anything is possible," into a world with no one in charge —above all, no one concerned with his soul. How he regains his faith is the rest of this wonderfully imaginative story—for he does rediscover the God who marks the sparrow's fall, whose attention is "intense and static, breathless and eternal all in one." The missionary comes full circle—back to Dostoyevsky's "real miracle," back to a caring God.

The realistic stories which follow Steele's have all the ambivalence and metaphysical sophistication one would expect of writing which comes out of the world of Freud, Einstein, Marx, Skinner. The writers write of experiences which *feel* miraculous but which, at the same time, can safely be interpreted as purely subjective. The miracles become inner miracles, the messages psychic awakenings, and the angels are as subtle of vision as the snowy heron in Eudora Welty's "A Still Moment" or the young father's dead little son in the dream landscape of Mark Helprin's "The Schreuderspitze." Welty's snowy heron is "a single frail yearning" in the whirlwind of human obsessions, when a preacher, a murderer, and the naturalist Audubon converge on the bird feeding in the swamp. God is indeed elusive—*if* the heron is God's intervention which stays the hand of the murderer. But is it? Welty leaves the question open. Helprin is not so ambivalent about the little boy's message. His appearance tells the grieving father that there *is* an afterlife. However, Helprin, in this deeply and so freshly affirmative story, carefully places the message in a dream— possible because, like Poe, he senses that "only in dreams is there certainty."

In contrast, both John Cheever's and William Hoffman's heroes are embarrassed by the possibility of divine intervention. They are each that most familiar of heroes, the modern-day liberal with his informed skepticism—tempered by a discreet dash of spiritual longing. Cheever's angel is actually a flower-child hitch-hiker, her harp no doubt a dulcimer, but she performs her traditional angelic role, delivering the sheepish urbanite from his irrational dread of bridges. In a world of no spiritual beliefs, Cheever's characters "go around and around" in irrational dread of one thing or another. Hoffman's New South minister knows it is highly unwise to pray for rain, yet when his congregation forces him to do so, and it does rain, in torrents, he is left with the ruefully pagan fear that he owes God something, that he will have to pay for the rain.

The antithesis of the liberal's view is Flannery O'Connor's. So harsh are her stories, so perverse her characters, that it is difficult to recognize that she is one of the few great religious writers of contemporary times. Yet divine grace is always crashing in on her characters, forcing awakenings on them, ready or not. "Revelation" is a stunning story of Christ's dictum that "the first shall be last." A smug, hard-working, God-fearing woman is attacked and called "an old wart hog from hell" by a young college girl who suddenly goes berserk in the doctor's waiting room. The woman broods on this for the rest of the day, trying to dismiss it and keep her feelings of moral superiority. But as the evening sun goes down, she has a vision of "a vast horde of souls rumbling toward heaven." Bringing up the end of the procession, way behind the white trash and the lunatics and the freaks and the "niggers," are she and her husband. They alone are marching in step and singing on key. "Yet she could see by their shocked and altered faces that even their virtues were being burned away." Flannery O'Connor's God easily encompasses any caprice or irony the twentieth century has to offer.

In contrast to these realistic stories in which spiritual insights arrive unbidden, only Helprin's hero and possibly Tolstoy's three hermits have the sense of readying, of training themselves for a spiritual awakening which may or may not come. For Helprin's hero, effort, prayer, and meditation are symbolized by his strenuous preparations for climbing the mountain—a training in which all of his softness is beaten away. So that finally on the high peaks he is able to enter "the world of light" . . .

> *The light of things danced and multiplied, again and again, and yet again. It was all there for him to claim. It was alive, and ever would be.*

The words evoke an image of that timeless spiritual space of higher awareness which Pierre Teilhard de Chardin believes the human race must strive to reach if we are to survive at all. And marvelously, unequivocally, Helprin tells us:

> *Although it seemed self-serving, he concluded nonetheless, after a lifetime of adhering to the diffuse principles of a science he did not know, that there was life after death, that the dead rose into a mischievous world of pure light, that something most mysterious lay beyond the enfolding darkness, something wonderful.*

Curious hints, resonances, of this are in Conrad Aiken's "Mr. Arcularis," a harrowing yet beautiful and tender story about death. Aiken too is without the comfort of any Christian doctrine, any surety at all. The dying Mr. Arcularis, although seemingly surrounded by friends, is making a lonely, absolutely new journey. It is cold, the freezing cold of the death of the senses. Yet into this story comes, again, light—that flooding experience of animate light which has illumined mystic visions through the centuries. One is given the feeling that Aiken is describing this light not so much metaphorically as accurately, as accurately as he can. It is the dream of a man who dies on the operating table. Written a number of years ago, the story is oddly prophetic in the way it reflects those experiences of numinousness which patients have reported who feel they died and were brought back to life by the heroic measures of modern medicine.

The last story, "The Marriage Feast" by Pär Lagerkvist, is

almost a miracle in itself. What is missing so much in modern fiction—a sense of the celebratory—is found here in abundance. In a celebration of faith and simple goodness, Lagerkvist makes incarnate, makes so tangible we can feel it, the intertwining of the mystery of love and the love of God. Two overaged, insignificant lovers, Frida, the seamstress, with her false teeth, and Jonas, the humble porter, are married, made one in the eyes of their Creator. Despite the snickerings of the villagers they move through their wedding day dizzy with joy and gratitude. At last, in their marriage bed upstairs, above the still roistering wedding guests, they discover "love speaking, that great, divine love, the incomprehensible miracle which makes everything sacred." They go to sleep . . . "near each other, with burning cheeks, their mouths half-open for a kiss."

One reads this story with a sense of something lost but very near the surface. Nor is it by chance that Lagerkvist gives us love and, yes, the physical act of love (that act which science has now reduced to healthful exercise) as the embodiments of a divine grace at work and available in the world. Before this joyous sacrament, animated by the spirit, rooted in life, the intellect slinks away: "And like a heavenly song of praise, like a hosanna of light . . . the stars rose around their bed in mighty hosts, their numbers increasing with the darkness."

"I believe," Einstein said, "that God is subtle but not malicious." Each of the stories here, in all their wonderings, complexities, questionings, and affirmations, echoes his hope.

M. Cameron Grey

The world will never starve for want of wonders but only for want of wonder.

G. K. Chesterton

Love all God's creation, the whole and every grain of sand in it. Love every leaf, every ray of God's light. Love the animals, love the plants, love everything. If you love everything, you will perceive the divine mystery in things.

Dostoyevsky, *The Brothers Karamazov*

PART I

Messengers from Elsewhere

ANGEL LEVINE

by Bernard Malamud

M ANISCHEVITZ, a tailor, in his fifty-first year suffered many reverses and indignities. Previously a man of comfortable means, he overnight lost all he had, when his establishment caught fire and, after a metal container of cleaning fluid exploded, burned to the ground. Although Manischevitz was insured against fire, damage suits by two customers who had been hurt in the flames deprived him of every penny he had collected. At almost the same time, his son, of much promise, was killed in the war, and his daughter, without so much as a word of warning, married a lout and disappeared with him as off the face of the earth. Thereafter Manischevitz was victimized by excruciating backaches and found himself unable to work even as a presser—the only kind of work available to him—for more than an hour or two daily, because beyond that the pain from standing became maddening. His Fanny, a good wife and mother, who had taken in washing and sewing, began before his eyes to waste away. Suffering shortness of breath, she at last became

3

seriously ill and took to her bed. The doctor, a former customer of Manischevitz, who out of pity treated them, at first had difficulty diagnosing her ailment but later put it down as hardening of the arteries at an advanced stage. He took Manischevitz aside, prescribed complete rest for her, and in whispers gave him to know there was little hope.

Throughout his trials Manischevitz had remained somewhat stoic, almost unbelieving that all this had descended upon his head, as if it were happening, let us say, to an acquaintance or some distant relative; it was in sheer quantity of woe incomprehensible. It was also ridiculous, unjust, and because he had always been a religious man, it was in a way an affront to God. Manischevitz believed this in all his suffering. When his burden had grown too crushingly heavy to be borne he prayed in his chair with shut hollow eyes: "My dear God, sweetheart, did I deserve that this should happen to me?" Then recognizing the worthlessness of it, he put aside the complaint and prayed humbly for assistance: "Give Fanny back her health, and to me for myself that I shouldn't feel pain in every step. Help now or tomorrow is too late. This I don't have to tell you." And Manischevitz wept.

Manischevitz's flat, which he had moved into after the disastrous fire, was a meager one, furnished with a few sticks of chairs, a table, and bed, in one of the poorer sections of the city. There were three rooms: a small, poorly-papered living room; an apology for a kitchen, with a wooden icebox; and the comparatively large bedroom where Fanny lay in a sagging secondhand bed, gasping for breath. The bedroom was the warmest room of the house and it was here, after his outburst to God, that Manischevitz, by the light of two small bulbs overhead, sat reading his Jewish newspaper. He was not truly reading, because his thoughts were everywhere; however the print offered a convenient resting place for his eyes, and a word or two, when he permitted himself to comprehend them, had the momentary effect of helping him forget his troubles. After a short while he discovered, to his surprise, that he was actively scanning the news, searching for an item of great interest to him. Exactly what he thought he would read he couldn't say—until he realized, with some astonishment, that he was expecting to discover something about himself. Manischevitz put his paper down and looked up with the distinct impression that someone had entered the apartment, though he could not remember having heard the sound of the door opening. He looked around: the room was very still, Fanny sleeping, for once, quietly. Half-frightened, he watched her until he was satisfied she wasn't dead; then, still disturbed by the thought of an unannounced visitor, he stumbled into the living room and there had the shock of his life, for at the table sat a Negro reading a newspaper he had folded up to fit into one hand.

"What do you want here?" Manischevitz asked in fright.

The Negro put down the paper and glanced up with a gentle expression. "Good evening." He seemed not to be sure of himself, as if he had got into the wrong house. He was a large man, bonily built, with a heavy head covered by a hard derby, which he made no attempt to remove. His eyes seemed sad, but his lips, above which he wore a slight mustache, sought to smile; he was not otherwise prepossessing. The cuffs of his sleeves, Manischevitz noted, were frayed to the lining and the dark suit was badly fitted. He had very large feet. Recovering from his fright, Manischevitz guessed he had left the door open and was being visited by a case worker from the Welfare Department— some came at night—for he had recently applied for relief. Therefore he lowered himself into a chair opposite the Negro, trying, before the man's uncertain smile, to feel comfortable. The former tailor sat stiffly but patiently at the table, waiting for the investigator to take out his pad and pencil and begin asking questions; but before long he became convinced the man intended to do nothing of the sort.

"Who are you?" Manischevitz at last asked uneasily.

"If I may, insofar as one is able to, identify myself, I bear the name of Alexander Levine."

In spite of all his troubles Manischevitz felt a smile growing on his lips. "You said Levine?" he politely inquired.

The Negro nodded. "That is exactly right."

Carrying the jest farther, Manischevitz asked, "You are maybe Jewish?"

"All my life I was, willingly."

The tailor hesitated. He had heard of black Jews but had never met one. It gave an unusual sensation.

Recognizing in afterthought something odd about the tense of Levine's remark, he said doubtfully, "You ain't Jewish any-more?"

Levine at this point removed his hat, revealing a very white part in his black hair, but quickly replaced it. He replied, "I have recently been disincarnated into an angel. As such, I offer you my humble assistance, if to offer is within my province and ability—in the best sense." He lowered his eyes in apology. "Which calls for added explanation: I am what I am granted to be, and at present the completion is in the future."

"What kind of angel is this?" Manischevitz gravely asked.

"A bona fide angel of God, within prescribed limitations," answered Levine, "not to be confused with the members of any particular sect, order, or organization here on earth operating under a similar name."

Manischevitz was thoroughly disturbed. He had been expecting something but not this. What sort of mockery was it —provided Levine was an angel—of a faithful servant who had from childhood lived in the synagogues, always concerned with the word of God?

To test Levine he asked, "Then where are your wings?"

The Negro blushed as well as he was able. Manischevitz understood this from his changed expression. "Under certain circumstances we lose privileges and prerogatives upon returning to earth, no matter for what purpose, or endeavoring to assist who-soever."

"So tell me," Manischevitz said triumphantly, "how did you get here?"

"I was transmitted."

Still troubled, the tailor said, "If you are a Jew, say the blessing for bread."

Levine recited it in sonorous Hebrew.

Although moved by the familiar words Manischevitz still felt doubt that he was dealing with an angel.

"If you are an angel," he demanded somewhat angrily, "give me the proof."

Levine wet his lips. "Frankly, I cannot perform either miracles or near miracles, due to the fact that I am in a condition of probation. How long that will persist or even consist, I admit, depends on the outcome."

Manischevitz racked his brains for some means of causing Levine positively to reveal his true identity, when the Negro spoke again:

"It was given me to understand that both your wife and you require assistance of a salubrious nature?"

The tailor could not rid himself of the feeling that he was the butt of a jokester. Is this what a Jewish angel looks like? he asked himself. This I am not convinced.

He asked a last question. "So if God sends to me an angel, why a black? Why not a white that there are so many of them?"

"It was my turn to go next," Levine explained.

Manischevitz could not be persuaded. "I think you are a faker."

Levine slowly rose. His eyes showed disappointment and worry. "Mr. Manischevitz," he said tonelessly, "if you should desire me to be of assistance to you any time in the near future, or possibly before, I can be found"—he glanced at his fingernails —"in Harlem."

He was by then gone.

The next day Manischevitz felt some relief from his backache and was able to work four hours at pressing. The day after, he put in six hours; and the third day four again. Fanny sat up a little and asked for some halvah to suck. But on the fourth day the stabbing, breaking ache afflicted his back, and Fanny again lay supine, breathing with blue-lipped difficulty.

Manischevitz was profoundly disappointed at the return of his active pain and suffering. He had hoped for a longer interval of easement, long enough to have some thought other than of himself and his troubles. Day by day, hour by hour, minute after minute, he lived in pain, pain his only memory, questioning the necessity of it, inveighing against it, also, though with affection, against God. Why *so much*, Gottenyu? If He wanted to teach His servant a lesson for some reason, some cause—the nature of His nature—to teach him, say, for reasons of his weakness, his pride, perhaps, during his years of prosperity, his frequent neglect of God—to give him a little lesson, why then any of the tragedies that had happened to him, any *one* would have sufficedto chasten him. But *all together*—the loss of both his children, his means of livelihood, Fanny's health and his—that was too much to ask one frail-boned man to endure. Who, after all, was Manischevitz that he had been given so much to suffer? A tailor. Certainly not a man of talent. Upon him suffering was largely wasted. It went nowhere, into nothing: into more suffering. His pain did not earn him bread, nor fill the cracks in the wall, nor lift, in the middle of the night, the kitchen table; only lay upon him, sleepless, so sharply oppressively that he could many times have cried out yet not heard himself through this thickness of misery

In this mood he gave no thought to Mr. Alexander Levine, but at moments when the pain wavered, slightly diminishing, he sometimes wondered if he had been mistaken to dismiss him. A black Jew and angel to boot—very hard to believe, but suppose he *had* been sent to succor him, and he, Manischevitz, was in his blindness too blind to comprehend? It was this thought that put him on the knife-point of agony

Therefore the tailor, after much self-questioning and continuing doubt, decided he would seek the self-styled angel in Harlem. Of course he had great difficulty, because he had not asked for specific directions, and movement was tedious to him.

9

The subway took him to 116th Street, and from there he wandered in the dark world. It was vast and its lights lit nothing. Everywhere were shadows, often moving. Manischevitz hobbled along with the aid of a cane, and not knowing where to seek in the blackened tenement buildings, looked fruitlessly through store windows. In the stores he saw people and *everybody* was black. It was an amazing thing to observe. When he was too tired, too unhappy to go farther, Manischevitz stopped in front of a tailor's store. Out of familiarity with the appearance of it, with some sadness he entered. The tailor, an old skinny Negro with a mop of woolly gray hair, was sitting cross-legged on his workbench, sewing a pair of full-dress pants that had a razor slit all the way down the seat.

"You'll excuse me, please, gentleman," said Manischevitz, admiring the tailor's deft, thimbled fingerwork, "but you know maybe somebody by the name Alexander Levine?"

The tailor, who Manischevitz thought, seemed a little antagonistic to him, scratched his scalp.

"Cain't say I ever heared dat name."

"Alex-ander Lev-ine," Manischevitz repeated it.

The man shook his head. "Cain't say I heared."

About to depart, Manischevitz remembered to say: "He is an angel, maybe."

"Oh *him*," said the tailor clucking. "He hang out in dat honky tonk down here a ways." He pointed with his skinny finger and returned to the pants.

Manischevitz crossed the street against a red light and was almost run down by a taxi. On the block after the next, the sixth store from the corner was a cabaret, and the name in sparkling lights was Bella's. Ashamed to go in, Manischevitz gazed through the neon-lit window, and when the dancing couples had parted and drifted away, he discovered at a table on the side, towards the rear, Levine.

He was sitting alone, a cigarette butt hanging from the corner of his mouth, playing solitaire with a dirty pack of cards, and Manischevitz felt a touch of pity for him, for Levine had deteriorated in appearance. His derby was dented and had a gray smudge on the side. His ill-fitting suit was shabbier, as if he had been sleeping in it. His shoes and trouser cuffs were muddy, and his face was covered with an impenetrable stubble the color of licorice. Manischevitz, though deeply disappointed, was about to enter, when a big-breasted Negress in a purple evening gown appeared before Levine's table, and with much laughter through many white teeth, broke into a vigorous shimmy. Levine looked straight at Manischevitz with a haunted expression, but the tailor was too paralyzed to move or acknowledge it. As Bella's gyrations continued, Levine rose, his eyes lit in excitement. She embraced him with vigor, both his hands clasped around her big restless buttocks and they tangoed together across the floor, loudly applauded by the noisy customers. She seemed to have lifted Levine off his feet and his large shoes hung limp as they danced. They slid past the windows where Manischevitz, white-faced, stood staring in. Levine winked slyly and the tailor left for home.

Fanny lay at death's door. Through shrunken lips she muttered concerning her childhood, the sorrows of the marriage bed, the loss of her children, yet wept to live. Manischevitz tried not to listen, but even without ears he would have heard. It was not a gift. The doctor panted up the stairs, a broad but bland, unshaven man (it was Sunday) and soon shook his head. A day at most, or two. He left at once, not without pity, to spare himself Manischevitz's multiplied sorrow; the man who never stopped hurting. He would someday get him into a public home.

Manischevitz visited a synagogue and there spoke to God, but God had absented himself. The tailor searched his heart and found no hope. When she died he would live dead. He considered taking his life although he knew he wouldn't. Yet it was something to consider. Considering, you existed. He railed against God— Can you love a rock, a broom, an emptiness? Baring his chest, he smote the naked bones, cursing himself for having believed.

Asleep in a chair that afternoon, he dreamed of Levine. He was standing before a faded mirror, preening small decaying opalescent wings. "This means," mumbled Manischevitz, as he broke out of sleep, "that it is possible he could be an angel." Begging a neighbor lady to look in on Fanny and occasionally wet her lips with a few drops of water, he drew on his thin coat, gripped his walking stick, exchanged some pennies for a subway token, and rode to Harlem. He knew this act was the last desperate one of his woe: to go without belief, seeking a black magician to restore his wife to invalidism. Yet if there was no choice, he did at least what was chosen.

He hobbled to Bella's but the place had changed hands. It was now, as he breathed, a synagogue in a store. In the front, towards him, were several rows of empty wooden benches. In the rear stood the Ark, its portals of rough wood covered with rainbows of sequins; under it a long table on which lay the sacred scroll unrolled, illuminated by the dim light from a bulb on a chain overhead. Around the table, as if frozen to it and the scroll, which they all touched with their fingers, sat four Negroes wearing skullcaps. Now as they read the Holy Word, Manischevitz could, through the plate glass window, hear the singsong chant of their voices. One of them was old, with a gray beard. One was bubble-eyed. One was humpbacked. The fourth was a boy, no older than thirteen. Their heads moved in rhythmic swaying. Touched by this sight from his childhood and youth, Manischevitz entered and stood silent in the rear.

"Neshoma," said bubble eyes, pointing to the word with a stubby finger. "Now what dat mean?"

"That's the word that means soul," said the boy. He wore glasses.

"Let's git on wid de commentary," said the old man.

"Ain't necessary," said the humpback. "Souls is immaterial substance. That's all. The soul is derived in that manner. The immateriality is derived from the substance, and they both, causally an' otherwise, derived from the soul. There can be no higher."

"That's the highest."

"Over de top."

"Wait a minute," said bubble eyes. "I don't see what is dat immaterial substance. How come de one gits hitched up to de odder?" He addressed the humpback.

"Ask me something hard. Because it is substanceless immateriality. It couldn't be closer together, like all the parts of the body under one skin—closer."

"Hear now," said the old man.

"All you done is switched de words."

"It's the primum mobile, the substanceless substance from which comes all things that were incepted in the idea—you, me and everything and body else."

"Now how did all dat happen? Make it sound simple."

"It de speerit," said the old man. "On de face of de water moved de speerit. An' dat was good. It say so in de Book. From de speerit ariz de man."

"But now listen here. How come it become substance if it all de time a spirit?"

"God alone done dat."

"Holy! Holy! Praise His Name."

"But has dis spirit got some kind of a shade or color?" asked bubble eyes, deadpan.

"Man of course not. A spirit is a spirit."

"Then how come we is colored?" he said with a triumphant glare.

"Ain't got nothing to do wid dat."

"I still like to know."

"God put the spirit in all things," answered the boy. "He put it in the green leaves and the yellow flowers. He put it with the gold in the fishes and the blue in the sky. That's how come it came to us."

"Amen."

"Praise Lawd and utter loud His speechless name."

"Blow de bugle till it bust the sky."

They fell silent, intent upon the next word. Manischevitz approached them.

"You'll excuse me," he said. "I am looking for Alexander Levine. You know him maybe?"

"That's the angel," said the boy.

"Oh, *him*," snuffed bubble eyes.

"You'll find him at Bella's. It's the establishment right across the street," the humpback said.

Manischevitz said he was sorry that he could not stay, thanked them, and limped across the street. It was already night. The city was dark and he could barely find his way.

But Bella's was bursting with the blues. Through the window Manischevitz recognized the dancing crowd and among them sought Levine. He was sitting loose-lipped at Bella's side table. They were tippling from an almost empty whiskey fifth. Levine had shed his old clothes, wore a shiny new checkered suit, pearl-gray derby, cigar, and big, two-tone button shoes. To the tailor's dismay, a drunken look had settled upon his formerly dignified face. He leaned toward Bella, tickled her ear lobe with his pinky, while whispering words that sent her into gales of raucous laughter. She fondled his knee.

Manischevitz, girding himself, pushed open the door and was not welcomed.

"This place reserved."

"Beat it, pale puss."

"Exit, Yankel, Semitic trash."

But he moved towards the table where Levine sat, the crowd breaking before him as he hobbled forward.

"Mr. Levine," he spoke in a trembly voice. "Is here Manischevitz."

Levine glared blearily. "Speak yo' piece, son."

Manischevitz shuddered. His back plagued him. Cold tremors tormented his crooked legs. He looked around, everybody was all ears.

"You'll excuse me. I would like to talk to you in a private place."

"Speak, Ah is a private pusson."

Bella laughed piercingly. "Stop it, boy, you killin' me."

Manischevitz, no end disturbed, considered fleeing but Levine addressed him:

"Kindly state the pu'pose of yo' communication with yo's truly."

The tailor wet cracked lips. "You are Jewish. This I am sure."

Levine rose, nostrils flaring. "Anythin' else yo' got to say?"

Manischevitz's tongue lay like stone.

"Speak now or fo'ever hold off."

Tears blinded the tailor's eyes. Was ever man so tried? Should he say he believed a half-drunken Negro to be an angel?

The silence slowly petrified.

Manischevitz was recalling scenes of his youth as a wheel in his mind whirred: believe, do not, yes, no, yes, no. The pointer pointed to yes, to between yes and no, to no, no it was yes. He sighed. It moved but one had still to make a choice.

"I think you are an angel from God." He said it in a broken voice, thinking, If you said it it was said. If you believed it you must say it. If you believed, you believed.

The hush broke. Everybody talked but the music began and they went on dancing. Bella, grown bored, picked up the cards and dealt herself a hand.

Levine burst into tears. "How you have humiliated me."

Manischevitz apologized.

"Wait'll I freshen up." Levine went to the men's room and returned in his old clothes.

No one said goodbye as they left.

They rode to the flat via subway. As they walked up the stairs Manischevitz pointed with his cane at his door.

"That's all been taken care of," Levine said. "You best go in while I take off."

Disappointed that it was so soon over but torn by curiosity, Manischevitz followed the angel up three flights to the roof. When he got there the door was already padlocked.

Luckily he could see through a small broken window. He heard an odd noise, as though of a whirring of wings, and when he strained for a wider view, could have sworn he saw a dark figure borne aloft on a pair of magnificent black wings.

A feather drifted down. Manischevitz gasped as it turned white, but it was only snowing.

He rushed downstairs. In the flat Fanny wielded a dust mop under the bed and then upon the cobwebs on the wall.

"A wonderful thing, Fanny," Manischevitz said. "Believe me, there are Jews everywhere."

THE BOWMEN

by Arthur Machen

IT WAS DURING the retreat of the eighty thousand, and the authority of the censorship is sufficient excuse for not being more explicit. But it was on the most awful day of that awful time, on the day when ruin and disaster came so near that their shadow fell over London far away; and, without any certain news, the hearts of men failed within them and grew faint; as if the agony of the army in the battlefield had entered into their souls.

On this dreadful day, then, when three hundred thousand men in arms with all their artillery swelled like a flood against the little English company, there was one point above all other points in our battle line that was for a time in awful danger, not merely of defeat, but of utter annihilation. With the permission of the censorship and of the military expert, this corner may, perhaps, be described as a salient, and if this angle were crushed and broken, then the English force as a whole would be shattered, the Allied left would be turned, and Sedan would inevitably follow.

All the morning the German guns had thundered and shrieked against this corner, and against the thousand or so of men who held it. The men joked at the shells, and found funny names for them, and had bets about them, and greeted them with scraps of music-hall songs. But the shells came on and burst, and tore good Englishmen limb from limb, and tore brother from brother, and as the heat of the day increased so did the fury of that terrific cannonade. There was no help it seemed. The English artillery was good, but there was not nearly enough of it; it was being steadily battered into scrap iron.

There comes a moment in a storm at sea when people say to one another: "It is at its worst; it can blow no harder," and then there is a blast ten times more fierce than any before it. So it was in these British trenches.

There were no stouter hearts in the whole world than the hearts of these men; but even they were appalled as this seven-times-heated hell of the German cannonade fell upon them and overwhelmed them and destroyed them. And at this very moment they saw from their trenches that a tremendous host was moving against their lines. Five hundred of the thousand remained, and as far as they could see the German infantry was pressing on against them, column upon column, a grey world of men, ten thousand of them, as it appeared afterwards.

There was no hope at all. They shook hands, some of them. One man improvised a new version of the battle-song, *Good-bye, Good-bye to Tipperary,* ending with "And we shan't get there." And they all went on firing steadily. The officers pointed out that such an opportunity for high-class, fancy shooting might never occur again; the Germans dropped line after line; the Tipperary humorist asked: "What price Sidney Street?" And the few machine guns did their best. But everybody knew it was of no use. The dead grey bodies lay in companies and battalions, as others came on and on and on, and they swarmed and stirred and advanced from beyond and beyond.

"World without end. Amen," said one of the British soldiers with some irrelevance as he took aim and fired. And then

he remembered—he says he cannot think why or wherefore—a queer vegetarian restaurant in London where he had once or twice eaten eccentric dishes of cutlets made of lentils and nuts that pretended to be steak. On all the plates in this restaurant there was printed a figure of St. George in blue, with the motto, *Adsit Anglis Sanctus Georgius*—May St. George be a present help to the English. This soldier happened to know Latin and other useless things, and now, as he fired at his man in the grey advancing mass—three hundred yards away—he uttered the pious vegetarian motto. He went on firing to the end, and at last Bill on his right had to clout him cheerfully over the head to make him stop, pointing out as he did so that the King's ammunition cost money and was not lightly to be wasted in drilling funny patterns into dead Germans.

For as the Latin scholar uttered his invocation he felt something between a shudder and an electric shock pass through his body. The roar of the battle died down in his ears to a gentle murmur; instead of it, he says, he heard a great voice and a shout louder than a thunder-peal crying: "Array, array, array!"

His heart grew hot as a burning coal, it grew cold as ice within him, as it seemed to him that a tumult of voices answered to his summons. He heard, or seemed to hear, thousands shouting: "St. George! St. George!"

"Ha! messire; ha sweet Saint, grant us good deliverance!"

"St. George for merry England!"

"Harow! Harow! Monseigneur St. George, succour us."

"Ha! St. George! Ha! St. George! a long bow and a strong bow."

"Heaven's Knight, aid us!"

And as the soldier heard these voices he saw before him, beyond the trench, a long line of shapes, with a shining about them. They were like men who drew the bow, and with another shout their cloud of arrows flew singing and tingling through the air towards the German hosts.

The other men in the trench were firing all the while. They had no hope; but they aimed just as if they had been shooting at Bisley.

Suddenly one of them lifted up his voice in the plainest English.

"Gawd help us!" he bellowed to the man next to him, "but we're blooming marvels! Look at those grey . . . gentlemen, look at them! D'ye see them? They're not going down in dozens, nor in 'undreds; it's thousands, it is. Look! Look! there's a regiment gone while I'm talking to ye."

"Shut it!" the other soldier bellowed, taking aim, "what are ye gassing about?"

But he gulped with astonishment even as he spoke, for, indeed, the grey men were falling by the thousands. The English could hear the guttural scream of the German officers, the crackle of their revolvers as they shot the reluctant; and still line after line crashed to the earth.

All the while the Latin-bred soldier heard the cry:

"Harow! Harow! Monseigneur, dear Saint, quick to our aid! St. George help us!"

"High Chevalier, defend us!"

The singing arrows fled so swift and thick that they darkened the air; the heathen horde melted from before them

"More machine guns!" Bill yelled to Tom.

"Don't hear them," Tom yelled back. "But, thank God, anyway; they've got it in the neck."

In fact, there were ten thousand dead German soldiers left before that salient of the English army, and consequently there was no Sedan. In Germany, a country ruled by scientific principles, the great general staff decided that the contemptible English must have employed shells containing an unknown gas of a poisonous nature, as no wounds were discernible on the bodies of the dead German soldiers. But the man who knew what nuts tasted like when they called themselves steak knew also that St. George had brought his Agincourt bowmen to help the English.

No one can tell you how to pray — you have to learn to pray in your own words
12-28-95

THE THREE HERMITS

by Leo Tolstoy

An Old Legend Current in the Volga District

"And in praying use not vain repetitions, as the Gentiles do: for they think that they shall be heard for their much speaking. Be not therefore like them: for your Father knoweth what things ye have need of, before ye ask Him."

Matthew vi: 7,8.

A BISHOP was sailing from Archangel to the Solovétsk Monastery, and on the same vessel were a number of pilgrims on their way to visit the shrines at that place. The voyage was a smooth one. The wind favorable and the weather fair. The pilgrims lay on deck, eating, or sat in groups talking to one another. The Bishop, too, came on deck, and as he was pacing up and down he noticed a group of men standing near the prow and listening to a fisherman, who was pointing to the sea and telling them something. The Bishop stopped, and looked in the direction in which the man was pointing. He could see nothing, however, but the sea glistening in the sunshine. He drew nearer to listen, but when the man saw him, he took off his cap and

22

was silent. The rest of the people also took off their caps and bowed.

"Do not let me disturb you, friends," said the Bishop. "I came to hear what this good man was saying."

"The fisherman was telling us about the hermits," replied one, a tradesman, rather bolder than the rest.

"What hermits?" asked the Bishop, going to the side of the vessel and seating himself on a box. "Tell me about them. I should like to hear. What were you pointing at?"

"Why, that little island you can just see over there," answered the man, pointing to a spot ahead and a little to the right. "That is the island where the hermits live for the salvation of their souls."

"Where is the island?" asked the Bishop. "I see nothing."

"There, in the distance, if you will please look along my hand. Do you see that little cloud? Below it, and a bit to the left, there is just a faint streak. That is the island."

The Bishop looked carefully, but his unaccustomed eyes could make out nothing but the water shimmering in the sun.

"I cannot see it," he said. "But who are the hermits that live there?"

"They are holy men," answered the fisherman. "I had long heard tell of them, but never chanced to see them myself till the year before last."

And the fisherman related how once, when he was out fishing, he had been stranded at night upon that island, not knowing where he was. In the morning, as he wandered about the island, he came across an earth hut, and met an old man standing near it. Presently two others came out, and after having fed him and dried his things, they helped him mend his boat.

"And what are they like?" asked the Bishop.

"One is a small man and his back is bent. He wears a priest's cassock and is very old; he must be more than a hundred, I should say. He is so old that the white of his beard is taking a greenish tinge, but he is always smiling, and his face is as bright as an angel's from heaven. The second is taller, but he also is very old. He wears a tattered peasant coat. His beard is broad, and of a yellowish grey color. He is a strong man. Before I had time to help him, he turned my boat over as if it were only a pail. He too is kindly and cheerful. The third is tall, and has a beard as white as snow and reaching to his knees. He is stern, with overhanging eyebrows; and he wears nothing but a piece of matting tied round his waist."

"And did they speak to you?" asked the Bishop.

"For the most part they did everything in silence, and spoke but little even to one another. One of them would just give a glance, and the others would understand him. I asked the tallest whether they had lived there long. He frowned, and muttered something as if he were angry; but the oldest one took his hand and smiled, and then the tall one was quiet. The oldest one only said: 'Have mercy upon us,' and smiled."

While the fisherman was talking, the ship had drawn nearer to the island.

"There, now you can see it plainly, if your Lordship will please to look," said the tradesman, pointing with his hand.

The Bishop looked, and now he really saw a dark streak—which was the island. Having looked at it a while, he left the prow of the vessel, and going to the stern, asked the helmsman:

"What island is that?"

"That one," replied the man, "has no name. There are many such in this sea."

"Is it true that there are hermits who live there for the salvation of their souls?"

"So it is said, your Lordship, but I don't know if it's true. Fishermen say they have seen them; but of course they may only be spinning yarns."

"I should like to land on the island and see these men," said the Bishop. "How could I manage it?"

"The ship cannot get close to the island," replied the helmsman, "but you might be rowed there in a boat. You had better speak to the captain."

The captain was sent for and came.

"I should like to see these hermits," said the Bishop. "Could I not be rowed ashore?"

The captain tried to dissuade him.

"Of course it could be done," said he, "but we should lose much time. And if I might venture to say so to your Lordship, the old men are not worth your pains. I have heard say that they are foolish old fellows, who understand nothing, and never speak a word, any more than the fish in the sea."

"I wish to see them," said the Bishop, "and I will pay you for your trouble and loss of time. Please let me have a boat."

There was no help for it; so the order was given. The sailors trimmed the sails, the steersman put up the helm, and the ship's course was set for the island. A chair was placed at the prow for the Bishop, and he sat there, looking ahead. The passengers all collected at the prow, and gazed at the island. Those who had the sharpest eyes could presently make out the rocks on it, and then a mud hut was seen. At last one man saw the hermits themselves. The captain brought a telescope and, after looking through it, handed it to the Bishop.

"It's right enough. There are three men standing on the shore. There, a little to the right of that big rock."

The Bishop took the telescope, got it into position, and he saw the three men: a tall one, a shorter one, and one very small and bent, standing on the shore and holding each other by the hand.

The captain turned to the Bishop.

"The vessel can get no nearer in than this, your Lordship. If you wish to go ashore, we must ask you to go in the boat, while we anchor here."

The cable was quickly let out; the anchor cast, and the sails furled. There was a jerk, and the vessel shook. Then, a boat having been lowered, the oarsmen jumped in, and the Bishop descended the ladder and took his seat. The men pulled at their oars and the boat moved rapidly towards the island. When they came within a stone's throw, they saw three old men: a tall one with only a piece of matting tied round his waist, a shorter one

in a tattered peasant coat, and a very old one bent with age and wearing an old cassock—all three standing hand in hand.

The oarsmen pulled in to the shore, and held on with the boathook while the Bishop got out.

The old men bowed to him, and he gave them his blessing, at which they bowed still lower. Then the Bishop began to speak to them.

"I have heard," he said, "that you, godly men, live here saving your own souls and praying to our Lord Christ for your fellow men. I, an unworthy servant of Christ, am called, by God's mercy, to keep and teach His flock. I wished to see you, servants of God, and to do what I can to teach you, also."

The old men looked at each other smiling, but remained silent.

"Tell me," said the Bishop, "what you are doing to save your souls, and how you serve God on this island."

The second hermit sighed, and looked at the oldest, the very ancient one. The latter smiled, and said:

"We do not know how to serve God. We only serve and support ourselves, servant of God."

"But how do you pray to God?" asked the Bishop.

"We pray in this way," replied the hermit. "Three are ye, three are we, have mercy upon us."

And when the old man said this, all three raised their eyes to heaven, and repeated:

"Three are ye, three are we, have mercy upon us!"

The Bishop smiled.

"You have evidently heard something about the Holy Trinity," said he. "But you do not pray aright. You have won my affection, godly men. I see you wish to please the Lord, but you do not know how to serve Him. That is not the way to pray; but listen to me, and I will teach you. I will teach you, not a way of my own, but the way in which God in the Holy Scriptures has commanded all men to pray to Him."

And the Bishop began explaining to the hermits how God had revealed Himself to men; telling them of God the Father, and God the Son, and God the Holy Ghost.

"God the Son came down on earth," said he, "to save men, and this is how He taught us all to pray. Listen, and repeat after me: 'Our Father.'"

And the first old man repeated after him, "Our Father," and the second said, "Our Father," and the third said, "Our Father."

"Which art in heaven," continued the Bishop.

The first hermit repeated, "Which art in heaven," but the second blundered over the words, and the tall hermit could not say them properly. His hair had grown over his mouth so that he could not speak plainly. The very old hermit, having no teeth, also mumbled indistinctly.

The Bishop repeated the words again, and the old men repeated them after him. The Bishop sat down on a stone, and the old men stood before him, watching his mouth, and repeating the words as he uttered them. And all day long the Bishop labored, saying a word twenty, thirty, a hundred times over, and the old men repeated it after him. They blundered, and he corrected them, and made them begin again.

The Bishop did not leave off till he had taught them the whole of the Lord's Prayer so that they could not only repeat it after him, but could say it by themselves. The middle one was the first to know it, and to repeat the whole of it alone. The Bishop made him say it again and again, and at last the others could say it too.

It was getting dark and the moon was appearing over the water, before the Bishop rose to return to the vessel. When he took leave of the old men they all bowed down to the ground before him. He raised them, and kissed each of them, telling them to pray as he had taught them. Then he got into the boat and returned to the ship.

And as he sat in the boat and was rowed to the ship he

could hear the three voices of the hermits loudly repeating the Lord's Prayer. As the boat drew near the vessel their voices could no longer be heard, but they could still be seen in the moonlight, standing as he had left them on the shore, the shortest in the middle, the tallest on the right, the middle one on the left. As soon as the Bishop had reached the vessel and got on board, the anchor was weighed and the sails unfurled. The wind filled them and the ship sailed away, and the Bishop took a seat in the stern and watched the island they had left. For a time he could still see the hermits, but presently they disappeared from sight, though the island was still visible. At last it too vanished, and only the sea was to be seen, rippling in the moonlight.

The pilgrims lay down to sleep, and all was quiet on deck. The Bishop did not wish to sleep, but sat alone at the stern, gazing at the sea where the island was no longer visible, and thinking of the good old men. He thought how pleased they had been to learn the Lord's Prayer; and he thanked God for having sent him to teach and help such godly men.

So the Bishop sat, thinking, and gazing at the sea where the island had disappeared. And the moonlight flickered before his eyes, sparkling, now here, now there, upon the waves. Suddenly he saw something white and shining, on the bright path which the moon cast across the sea. Was it a seagull, or the little gleaming sail of some small boat? The Bishop fixed his eyes on it, wondering.

"It must be a boat sailing after us," thought he, "but it is overtaking us very rapidly. It was far, far away a minute ago, but now it is much nearer. It cannot be a boat, for I can see no sail; but whatever it may be, it is following us and catching us up."

And he could not make out what it was. Not a boat, nor a bird, nor a fish! It was too large for a man, and besides a man could not be out there in the midst of the sea. The Bishop rose, and said to the helmsman:

"Look there, what is that, my friend? What is it?" the Bishop repeated, though he could now see plainly what it was —the three hermits running upon the water, all gleaming white, their grey beards shining, and approaching the ship as quickly as though it were not moving.

The steersman looked, and let go the helm in terror.

"Oh, Lord! The hermits are running after us on the water as though it were dry land!"

The passengers, hearing him, jumped up and crowded to the stern. They saw the hermits coming along hand in hand, and the two outer ones beckoning the ship to stop. All three were gliding along upon the water without moving their feet. Before the ship could be stopped, the hermits had reached it, and raising their heads, all three as with one voice, began to say:

"We have forgotten your teaching, servant of God. As long as we kept repeating it we remembered, but when we stopped saying it for a time, a word dropped out, and now it has all gone to pieces. We can remember nothing of it. Teach us again."

The Bishop crossed himself, and leaning over the ship's side, said:

"Your own prayer will reach the Lord, men of God. It is not for me to teach you. Pray for us sinners."

And the Bishop bowed low before the old men; and they turned and went back across the sea. And a light shone until daybreak on the spot where they were lost to sight.

THE GREATEST GIFT

by Philip Van Doren Stern

THE LITTLE TOWN straggling up the hill was bright with colored Christmas lights. But George Pratt did not see them. He was leaning over the railing of the iron bridge, staring down moodily at the black water. The current eddied and swirled like liquid glass, and occasionally a bit of ice, detached from the shore, would go gliding downstream to be swallowed up in the shadows under the bridge.

The water looked paralyzingly cold. George wondered how long a man could stay alive in it. The glassy blackness had a strange, hypnotic effect on him. He leaned still farther over the railing . . .

"I wouldn't do that if I were you," a quiet voice beside him said.

George turned resentfully to a little man he had never seen before. He was stout, well past middle age, and his round cheeks were pink in the winter air as though they had just been shaved.

"Wouldn't do what?" George asked sullenly.

"What you were thinking of doing."

"How do you know what I was thinking?"

"Oh, we make it our business to know a lot of things," the stranger said easily.

George wondered what the man's business was. He was a most unremarkable little person, the sort you would pass in a crowd and never notice. Unless you saw his bright blue eyes, that is. You couldn't forget them, for they were the kindest, sharpest eyes you ever saw. Nothing else about him was noteworthy. He wore a moth-eaten old fur cap and a shabby overcoat that was stretched tightly across his paunchy belly. He was carrying a small black satchel. It wasn't a doctor's bag—it was too large for that and not the right shape. It was a salesman's sample kit, George decided distastefully. The fellow was probably some sort of peddler, the kind who would go around poking his sharp little nose into other people's affairs.

"Looks like snow, doesn't it?" the stranger said, glancing up appraisingly at the overcast sky. "It'll be nice to have a white Christmas. They're getting scarce these days—but so are a lot of things." He turned to face George squarely. "You all right now?"

"Of course I'm all right. What made you think I wasn't? I—"

George fell silent before the stranger's quiet gaze.

The little man shook his head. "You know you shouldn't think of such things—and on Christmas Eve of all times! You've got to consider Mary—and your mother too."

George opened his mouth to ask how this stranger could know his wife's name, but the fellow anticipated him. "Don't ask me how I know such things. It's my business to know 'em. That's why I came along this way tonight. Lucky I did too." He glanced down at the dark water and shuddered.

"Well, if you know so much about me," George said, "give me just one good reason why I should be alive."

The little man made a queer chuckling sound. "Come, come, it can't be that bad. You've got your job at the bank. And Mary and the kids. You're healthy, young, and—"

32

"And sick of everything!" George cried. "I'm stuck here in this mudhole for life, doing the same dull work day after day. Other men are leading exciting lives, but I—well, I'm just a small-town bank clerk that even the Army didn't want. I never did anything really useful or interesting, and it looks as if I never will. I might just as well be dead. I might better be dead. Sometimes I wish I were. In fact, I wish I'd never been born!"

The little man stood looking at him in the growing darkness. "What was that you said?" he asked softly.

"I said I wish I'd never been born," George repeated firmly. "And I mean it too."

The stranger's pink cheeks glowed with excitement. "Why that's wonderful! You've solved everything. I was afraid you were going to give me some trouble. But now you've got the solution yourself. You wish you'd never been born. All right! Okay! You haven't!"

"What do you mean?" George growled.

"You haven't been born. Just that. You haven't been born. No one here knows you. You have no responsibilities—no job—no wife—no children. Why, you haven't even a mother. You couldn't have, of course. All your troubles are over. Your wish, I am happy to say, has been granted—officially."

"Nuts!" George snorted and turned away.

The stranger ran after him and caught him by the arm.

"You'd better take this with you," he said, holding out his satchel. "It'll open a lot of doors that might otherwise be slammed in your face."

"What doors in whose face?" George scoffed. "I know everybody in this town. And besides, I'd like to see anybody slam a door in my face."

"Yes, I know," the little man said patiently. "But take this anyway. It can't do any harm and it may help." He opened the satchel and displayed a number of brushes. "You'd be surprised how useful these brushes can be as introduction—especially the free ones. These, I mean." He hauled out a plain little handbrush. "I'll show you how to use it." He thrust the satchel into

George's reluctant hands and began: "When the lady of the house comes to the door you give her this and then talk fast. You say: 'Good evening, Madam. I'm from the World Cleaning Company, and I want to present you with this handsome and useful brush absolutely free—no obligation to purchase anything at all.' After that, of course, it's a cinch. Now you try it." He forced the brush into George's hand.

George promptly dropped the brush into the satchel and fumbled with the catch, finally closing it with an angry snap. "Here," he said, and then stopped abruptly, for there was no one in sight.

The little stranger must have slipped away into the bushes growing along the river bank, George thought. He certainly wasn't going to play hide-and-seek with him. It was nearly dark and getting colder every minute. He shivered and turned up his coat collar.

The street lights had been turned on, and Christmas candles in the windows glowed softly. The little town looked remarkably cheerful. After all, the place you grew up in was the one spot on earth where you could really feel at home. George felt a sudden burst of affection even for crotchety old Hank Biddle whose house he was passing. He remembered the quarrel he had had when his car had scraped a piece of bark out of Hank's big maple tree. George looked up at the vast spread of leafless branches towering over him in the darkness. The tree must have been growing there since Indian times. He felt a sudden twinge of guilt for the damage he had done. He had never stopped to inspect the wound, for he was ordinarily afraid to have Hank catch him even looking at the tree. Now he stepped out boldly into the roadway to examine the huge trunk.

Hank must have repaired the scar or painted it over, for there was no sign of it. George struck a match and bent down to look more closely. He straightened up with an odd, sinking feeling in his stomach. There wasn't any scar. The bark was smooth and undamaged.

He remembered what the little man at the bridge had said.

It was all nonsense, of course, but the non-existent scar bothered him.

When he reached the bank, he saw that something was wrong. The building was dark, and he knew he had turned the vault light on. He noticed, too, that someone had left the window shades up. He ran around to the front. There was a battered old sign fastened on the door. George could just make out the words:

FOR RENT OR SALE
Apply JAMES SILVA, *Real Estate*

Perhaps it was some boys' trick, he thought wildly. Then he saw a pile of ancient leaves and tattered newspapers in the bank's ordinarily immaculate doorway. And the windows looked as though they hadn't been washed in years. A light was still burning across the street in Jim Silva's office. George dashed over and tore the door open.

Jim looked up from his ledgerbook in surprise. "What can I do for you, young man?" he said in the polite voice he reserved for potential customers.

"The bank," George said breathlessly. "What's the matter with it?"

"The old bank building?" Jim Silva turned around and looked out of the window. "Nothing that I can see. Wouldn't like to rent or buy it, would you?"

"You mean—it's out of business?"

"For a good ten years. Went bust. Stranger 'round these parts, ain't you?"

George sagged against the wall. "I was here some time ago," he said weakly. "The bank was all right then. I even knew some of the people who worked there."

"Didn't know a feller named Marty Jenkins, did you?"

"Marty Jenkins! Why, he—" George was about to say that Marty had never worked at the bank—couldn't have, in fact, for when they had both left school they had applied for a job there and George had gotten it. But now, of course, things were different. He would have to be careful. "No, I didn't know him," he said slowly. "Not really, that is. I'd heard of him."

"Then maybe you heard how he skipped out with fifty thousand dollars. That's why the bank went broke. Pretty near ruined everybody around here." Silva was looking at him sharply. "I was hoping for a minute maybe you'd know where he is. I lost plenty in that crash myself. We'd like to get our hands on Marty Jenkins."

"Didn't he have a brother? Seems to me he had a brother named Arthur."

"Art? Oh, sure. But he's all right. He don't know where his brother went. It's had a terrible effect on him, too. Took to drink, he did. It's too bad—and hard on his wife. He married a nice girl."

George felt the sinking feeling in his stomach again. "Who did he marry?" he demanded hoarsely. Both he and Art had courted Mary.

"Girl named Mary Thatcher," Silva said cheerfully. "She lives up on the hill just this side of the church— Hey! Where are you going?"

But George had bolted out of the office. He ran past the empty bank building and turned up the hill. For a moment he thought of going straight to Mary. The house next to the church had been given them by her father as a wedding present. Naturally Art Jenkins would have gotten it if he had married Mary. George wondered whether they had any children. Then he knew he couldn't face Mary—not yet anyway. He decided to visit his parents and find out more about her.

There were candles burning in the windows of the little weather-beaten house on the side street, and a Christmas wreath was hanging on the glass panel of the front door. George raised the gate latch with a loud click. A dark shape on the porch jumped up and began to growl. Then it hurled itself down the steps, barking ferociously.

"Brownie!" George shouted. "Brownie, you old fool, stop that! Don't you know me?" But the dog advanced menacingly and drove him back behind the gate. The porch light snapped on, and George's father stepped outside to call the dog off. The barking subsided to a low, angry growl.

His father held the dog by the collar while George cautiously walked past. He could see that his father did not know him. "Is the lady of the house in?" he asked.

His father waved toward the door. "Go on in," he said cordially. "I'll chain this dog up. She can be mean with strangers."

His mother, who was waiting in the hallway, obviously did not recognize him. George opened his sample kit and grabbed the first brush that came to hand. "Good evening, ma'am," he said politely. "I'm from the World Cleaning Company. We're giving out a free sample brush. I thought you might like to have one. No obligation. No obligation at all . . ." His voice faltered.

His mother smiled at his awkwardness. "I suppose you'll want to sell me something. I'm not really sure I need any brushes."

"No'm. I'm not selling anything," he assured her. "The regular salesman will be around in a few days. This is just— well, just a Christmas present from the company."

"How nice," she said. "You people never gave away such good brushes before."

"This is a special offer," he said. His father entered the hall and closed the door.

"Won't you come in for a while and sit down?" his mother said. "You must be tired walking so much."

"Thank you, ma'am. I don't mind if I do." He entered the little parlor and put his bag down on the floor. The room looked different somehow, although he could not figure out why.

"I used to know this town pretty well," he said to make conversation. "Knew some of the townspeople. I remember a girl named Mary Thatcher. She married Art Jenkins, I heard. You must know them."

"Of course," his mother said. "We know Mary well."

"Any children?" he asked casually.

"Two—a boy and a girl."

George sighed audibly.

"My, you must be tired," his mother said. "Perhaps I can get you a cup of tea."

"No'm, don't bother," he said. "I'll be having supper soon." He looked around the little parlor, trying to find out why it looked different. Over the mantelpiece hung a framed photograph which had been taken on his kid brother Harry's sixteenth birthday. He remembered how they had gone to Potter's studio to be photographed together. There was something queer about the picture. It showed only one figure—Harry's.

"That your son?" he asked.

His mother's face clouded. She nodded but said nothing.

"I think I met him, too," George said hesitantly. "His name's Harry, isn't it?"

His mother turned away, making a strange choking noise in her throat. Her husband put his arm clumsily around her shoulder. His voice, which was always mild and gentle, suddenly became harsh. "You couldn't have met him," he said. "He's been dead a long while. He was drowned the day that picture was taken."

George's mind flew back to the long-ago August afternoon when he and Harry had visited Potter's studio. On their way home they had gone swimming. Harry had been seized with a cramp, he remembered. He had pulled him out of the water and had thought nothing of it. But suppose he hadn't been there!

"I'm sorry," he said miserably. "I guess I'd better go. I hope you like the brush. And I wish you both a very Merry Christmas." There, he had put his foot in it again, wishing them a Merry Christmas when they were thinking about their dead son.

Brownie tugged fiercely at her chain as George went down the porch steps and accompanied his departure with a hostile, rolling growl.

He wanted desperately now to see Mary. He wasn't sure he could stand not being recognized by her, but he had to see her.

The lights were on in the church, and the choir was making

last-minute preparations for Christmas vespers. The organ had been practicing "Holy Night" evening after evening until George had become thoroughly sick of it. But now the music almost tore his heart out.

He stumbled blindly up the path to his own house. The lawn was untidy, and the flower bushes he had kept carefully trimmed were neglected and badly sprouted. Art Jenkins could hardly be expected to care for such things.

When he knocked at the door there was a long silence, followed by the shout of a child. Then Mary came to the door.

At the sight of her, George's voice almost failed him. "Merry Christmas, ma'am," he managed to say at last. His hand shook as he tried to open the satchel.

When George entered the living room, unhappy as he was, he could not help noticing with a secret grin that the too-high-priced blue sofa they often had quarreled over was there. Evidently Mary had gone through the same thing with Art Jenkins and had won the argument with him too.

George got his satchel open. One of the brushes had a bright blue handle and vari-colored bristles. It was obviously a brush not intended to be given away, but George didn't care. He handed it to Mary. "This would be fine for your sofa," he said.

"My, that's a pretty brush," she exclaimed. "You're giving it away free?"

He nodded solemnly. "Special introductory offer. It's one way for the company to keep excess profits down—share them with its friends."

She stroked the sofa gently with the brush, smoothing out the velvety nap. "It *is* a nice brush. Thank you. I—" There was a sudden scream from the kitchen, and two small children rushed in. A little, homely-faced girl flung herself into her mother's arms, sobbing loudly as a boy of seven came running after her, snapping a toy pistol at her head. "Mommy, she won't die," he yelled. "I shot her a hunert times, but she won't die."

He looks just like Art Jenkins, George thought. Acts like him too.

The Greatest Gift

The boy suddenly turned his attention to him. "Who're you?" he demanded belligerently. He pointed his pistol at George and pulled the trigger. "You're dead!" he cried. "You're dead. Why don't you fall down and die?"

There was a heavy step on the porch. The boy looked frightened and backed away. George saw Mary glance apprehensively at the door.

Art Jenkins came in. He stood for a moment in the doorway, clinging to the knob for support. His eyes were glazed, and his face was very red. "Who's this?" he demanded thickly.

"He's a brush salesman," Mary tried to explain. "He gave me this brush."

"Brush salesman!" Art sneered. "Well, tell him to get outa here. We don't want no brushes." Art hiccoughed violently and lurched across the room to the sofa where he sat down suddenly. "An' we don't want no brush salesmen neither."

George looked despairingly at Mary. Her eyes were begging him to go. Art had lifted his feet up on the sofa and was sprawling out on it, muttering unkind things about brush salesmen. George went to the door, followed by Art's son who kept snapping his pistol at him and saying: "You're dead—dead—dead!"

Perhaps the boy was right, George thought when he reached the porch. Maybe he was dead, or maybe this was all a bad dream from which he might eventually awake. He wanted to find the little man on the bridge again and try to persuade him to cancel the whole deal.

He hurried down the hill and broke into a run when he neared the river. George was relieved to see the little stranger standing on the bridge. "I've had enough," he gasped. "Get me out of this—you got me into it."

The stranger raised his eyebrows. "I got you into it! I like that! You were granted your wish. You got everything you asked for. You're the freest man on earth now. You have no ties. You can go anywhere—do anything. What more can you possibly want?"

"Change me back," George pleaded. "Change me back—please. Not just for my sake but for others too. You don't know what a mess this town is in. You don't understand. I've got to get back. They need me here."

"I understand right enough," the stranger said slowly. "I just wanted to make sure you did. You had the greatest gift of all conferred upon you—the gift of life, of being a part of this world and taking a part in it. Yet you denied that gift." As the stranger spoke, the church bell high up on the hill sounded, calling the townspeople to Christmas vespers. Then the downtown church bell started ringing.

"I've got to get back," George said desperately. "You can't cut me off like this. Why, it's murder!"

"Suicide rather, wouldn't you say?" the stranger murmured. "You brought it on yourself. However, since it's Christmas Eve—well, anyway, close your eyes and keep listening to the bells." His voice sank lower. "Keep listening to the bells . . ."

George did as he was told. He felt a cold, wet snowdrop touch his cheek—and then another and another. When he opened his eyes, the snow was falling fast, so fast that it obscured everything around him. The little stranger could not be seen, but then neither could anything else. The snow was so thick that George had to grope for the bridge railing.

As he started toward the village, he thought he heard someone saying: "Merry Christmas," but the bells were drowning out all rival sounds, so he could not be sure.

When he reached Hank Biddle's house he stopped and walked out into the roadway, peering down anxiously at the base of the big maple tree. The scar was there, thank Heaven! He touched the tree affectionately. He'd have to do something about the wound—get a tree surgeon or something. Anyway, he'd evidently been changed back. He was himself again. Maybe it was all a dream, or perhaps he had been hypnotized by the smooth-flowing black water. He had heard of such things.

At the corner of Main and Bridge streets he almost collided with a hurrying figure. It was Jim Silva, the real estate agent.

"Hello, George," Jim said cheerfully. "Late tonight, ain't you? I should think you'd want to be home early on Christmas Eve."

George drew a long breath. "I just wanted to see if the bank is all right. I've got to make sure the vault light is on."

"Sure it's on. I saw it as I went past."

"Let's look, huh?" George said, pulling at Silva's sleeve. He wanted the assurance of a witness. He dragged the surprised real estate dealer around to the front of the bank where the light was gleaming through the falling snow. "I told you it was on," Silva said with some irritation.

"I had to make sure," George mumbled. "Thanks—and Merry Christmas!" Then he was off like a streak, running up the hill.

He was in a hurry to get home, but not in such a hurry that he couldn't stop for a moment at his parents' house, where he wrestled with Brownie until the friendly old bulldog waggled all over with delight. He grasped his startled brother's hand and wrung it frantically, wishing him an almost hysterical Merry Christmas. Then he dashed across the parlor to examine a certain photograph. He kissed his mother, joked with his father, and was out of the house a few seconds later, stumbling and slipping on the newly fallen snow as he ran on up the hill.

The church was bright with light, and the choir and the organ were going full tilt. George flung the door to his home open and called out at the top of his voice: "Mary! Where are you? Mary! Kids!"

His wife came toward him, dressed for going to church, and making gestures to silence him. "I've just put the children to bed," she protested. "Now they'll—" But not another word could she get out of her mouth, for he smothered it with kisses, and then he dragged her up to the children's room, where he violated every tenet of parental behavior by madly embracing his son and his daughter and waking them up thoroughly.

It was not until Mary got him downstairs that he began to be coherent. "I thought I'd lost you. Oh, Mary, I thought I'd lost you!"

"What's the matter, darling?" she asked in bewilderment.

He pulled her down on the sofa and kissed her again. And then, just as he was about to tell her about his queer dream, his fingers came in contact with something lying on the seat of the sofa. His voice froze.

He did not even have to pick the thing up, for he knew what it was. And he knew that it would have a blue handle and vari-colored bristles.

MARKHEIM

by Robert Louis Stevenson

Yes," said the dealer, "our windfalls are of various kinds. Some customers are ignorant, and then I touch a dividend of my superior knowledge. Some are dishonest," and here he held up the candle, so that the light fell strongly on his visitor, "and in that case," he continued, "I profit by my virtue."

Markheim had but just entered from the daylight streets, and his eyes had not yet grown familiar with the mingled shine and darkness in the shop. At these pointed words, and before the near presence of the flame, he blinked painfully and looked aside.

The dealer chuckled. "You come to me on Christmas Day," he resumed, "when you know that I am alone in my house, put up my shutters, and make a point of refusing business. Well, you will have to pay for that; you will have to pay for my loss of time, when I should be balancing my books; you will have to pay, besides, for a kind of manner that I remark in you to-day very strongly. I am the essence of discretion, and ask no awkward questions; but when a customer cannot look me in the eye, he has to pay for it." The dealer once more chuckled; and then, changing to his usual business voice, though still with a note of irony, "You can give, as usual, a clear account of how you came into the possession of the object?" he continued. "Still your uncle's cabinet? A remarkable collector, sir!"

And the little pale, round-shouldered dealer stood almost on tiptoe, looking over the top of his gold spectacles, and nodding his head with every mark of disbelief. Markheim returned his gaze with one of infinite pity, and a touch of horror.

"This time," said he, "you are in error. I have not come to sell, but to buy. I have no curios to dispose of; my uncle's cabinet is bare to the wainscot; even were it still intact, I have done well on the Stock Exchange, and should more likely add to it than otherwise, and my errand to-day is simplicity itself. I seek a Christmas present for a lady," he continued, waxing more fluent as he struck into the speech he had prepared; "and certainly I owe you every excuse for thus disturbing you upon so small a matter. But the thing was neglected yesterday; I must produce my little compliment at dinner; and, as you very well know, a rich marriage is not a thing to be neglected."

There followed a pause, during which the dealer seemed to weigh this statement incredulously. The ticking of many clocks among the curious lumber of the shop, and the faint rushing of the cabs in a near thoroughfare, filled up the interval of silence.

"Well, sir," said the dealer, "be it so. You are an old customer after all; and if, as you say, you have the chance of a good marriage, far be it from me to be an obstacle. Here is a nice thing for a lady now," he went on, "this hand glass—fifteenth century, warranted; comes from a good collection, too; but I reserve the name, in the interests of my customer, who was just like yourself, my dear sir, the nephew and sole heir of a remarkable collector."

The dealer, while he thus ran on in his dry and biting voice, had stooped to take the object from its place; and, as he had done so, a shock had passed through Markheim, a start both of hand and foot, a sudden leap of many tumultuous passions to

the face. It passed as swiftly as it came, and left no trace beyond
a certain trembling of the hand that now received the glass.

"A glass," he said hoarsely, and then paused, and repeated
it more clearly. "A glass? For Christmas? Surely not?"

"And why not?" cried the dealer. "Why not a glass?"

Markheim was looking upon him with an indefinable expression. "You ask me why not?" he said. "Why, look here—
look in it—look at yourself! Do you like to see it? No! nor
I—nor any man."

The little man had jumped back when Markheim had so
suddenly confronted him with the mirror; but now, perceiving
there was nothing worse on hand, he chuckled. "Your future
lady, sir, must be pretty hard favoured," said he.

"I ask you," said Markheim, "for a Christmas present, and
you give me this—this damned reminder of years, and sins and
follies—this hand-conscience! Did you mean it? Had you a
thought in your mind? Tell me. It will be better for you if you
do. Come, tell me about yourself. I hazard a guess now, that you
are in secret a very charitable man?"

The dealer looked closely at his companion. It was very
odd, Markheim did not appear to be laughing; there was something in his face like an eager sparkle of hope, but nothing of
mirth.

"What are you driving at?" the dealer asked.

"Not charitable?" returned the other, gloomily. "Not charitable; not pious; not scrupulous; unloving, unbeloved; a hand to
get money, a safe to keep it. Is that all? Dear God, man, is that
all?"

"I will tell you what it is," began the dealer, with some
sharpness, and then broke off again into a chuckle. "But I see
this is a love match of yours, and you have been drinking the
lady's health."

"Ah!" cried Markheim, with a strange curiosity. "Ah, have
you been in love? Tell me about that."

"I," cried the dealer. "I in love! I never had the time, nor

47

have I the time to-day for all this nonsense. Will you take the glass?"

"Where is the hurry?" returned Markheim. "It is very pleasant to stand here talking; and life is so short and insecure that I would not hurry away from any pleasure—no, not even from so mild a one as this. We should rather cling, cling to what little we can get, like a man at a cliff's edge. Every second is a cliff, if you think upon it—a cliff a mile high—high enough, if we fall, to dash us out of every feature of humanity. Hence it is best to talk pleasantly. Let us talk to each other; why should we wear this mask? Let us be confidential. Who knows, we might become friends?"

"I have just one word to say to you," said the dealer. "Either make your purchase, or walk out of my shop."

"True, true," said Markheim. "Enough fooling. To business. Show me something else."

The dealer stooped once more, this time to replace the glass upon the shelf, his thin blond hair falling over his eyes as he did so. Markheim moved a little nearer, with one hand in the pocket of his great-coat; he drew himself up and filled his lungs; at the same time many different emotions were depicted together on his face—terror, horror, and resolve, fascination and a physical repulsion; and through a haggard lift of his upper lip, his teeth looked out.

"This, perhaps, may suit," observed the dealer; and then, as he began to re-arise, Markheim bounded from behind upon his victim. The long, skewerlike dagger flashed and fell. The dealer struggled like a hen, striking his temple on the shelf, and then tumbled on the floor in a heap.

Time had some score of small voices in that shop, some stately and slow as was becoming to their great age; others garrulous and hurried. All these told out the seconds in an intricate chorus of tickings. Then the passage of a lad's feet, heavily running on the pavement, broke in upon these smaller voices and startled Markheim into the consciousness of his surroundings. He looked about him awfully. The candle stood on the counter, its flame solemnly wagging in a draught; and by that inconsiderable movement, the whole room was filled with noiseless bustle and kept heaving like a sea: the tall shadows nodding, the gross blots of darkness swelling and dwindling as with respiration, the faces of the portraits and the china gods changing and wavering like images in water. The inner door stood ajar, and peered into that leaguer of shadows with a long slit of daylight like a pointing finger.

From these fear-stricken rovings, Markheim's eyes returned to the body of his victim, where it lay both humped and sprawling, incredibly small and strangely meaner than in life. In these poor, miserly clothes, in that ungainly attitude, the dealer lay like so much sawdust. Markheim had feared to see it, and, lo! it was nothing. And yet, as he gazed, this bundle of old clothes and pool of blood began to find eloquent voices. There it must lie; there was none to work the cunning hinges or direct the miracle of locomotion—there it must lie till it was found. Found! ay, and then? Then would this dead flesh lift up a cry that would ring over England, and fill the world with the echoes of pursuit. Ay, dead or not, this was still the enemy. "Time was that when the brains were out," he thought; and the first word struck into his mind. Time, now that the deed was accomplished —time, which had closed for the victim, had become instant and momentous for the slayer.

The thought was yet in his mind, when, first one and then another, with every variety of pace and voice—one deep as the bell from a cathedral turret, another ringing on its treble notes the prelude of a waltz—the clocks began to strike the hour of three in the afternoon.

The sudden outbreak of so many tongues in that dumb chamber staggered him. He began to bestir himself, going to and fro with the candle, beleaguered by moving shadows, and startled to the soul by chance reflections. In many rich mirrors, some of home designs, some from Venice or Amsterdam, he saw his face repeated and repeated, as it were an army of spies; his own eyes met and detected him; and the sound of his own steps, lightly as they fell, vexed the surrounding quiet. And still as he continued to fill his pockets, his mind accused him, with a sickening iteration, of the thousand faults of his design. He should have chosen a more quiet hour; he should have prepared an alibi; he should not have used a knife; he should have been more cautious, and only bound and gagged the dealer, and not killed him; he should have been more bold, and killed the servant also; he should have done all things otherwise; poignant regrets, weary, incessant toiling of the mind to change what was unchangeable, to plan what was now useless, to be the architect of the irrevocable past. Meanwhile, and behind all this activity, brute terrors, like the scurrying of rats in a deserted attic, filled the more remote chambers of his brain with riot; the hand of the constable would fall heavy on his shoulder, and his nerves would jerk like a hooked fish; or he beheld, in galloping defile, the dock, the prison, the gallows, and the black coffin.

Terror of the people in the street sat down before his mind like a besieging army. It was impossible, he thought, but that some rumour of the struggle must have reached their ears and set on edge their curiosity; and now, in all the neighbouring houses, he divined them sitting motionless and with uplifted ear —solitary people, condemned to spend Christmas dwelling alone on memories of the past, and now startlingly recalled from that tender exercise; happy family parties, struck into silence round the table, the mother still with raised finger: every degree and age and humour, but all, by their own hearts, prying and hearkening and weaving the rope that was to hang him. Sometimes it seemed to him he could not move too softly; the clink of the tall Bohemian goblets rang out loudly like a bell; and alarmed by the bigness of the ticking, he was tempted to stop the clocks. And then, again, with a swift transition of his terrors, the very silence of the place appeared a source of peril, and a thing to strike and freeze the passer-by; and he would step more boldly, and bustle aloud among the contents of the shop, and imitate, with elaborate bravado, the movements of a busy man at ease in his own house.

But he was now so pulled about by different alarms that, while one portion of his mind was still alert and cunning, another trembled on the brink of lunacy. One hallucination in particular took a strong hold on his credulity. The neighbour hearkening with white face beside his window, the passer-by arrested by a horrible surmise on the pavement—these could at worst suspect, they could not know; through the brick walls and shuttered windows only sounds could penetrate. But here, within the house, was he alone? He knew he was; he had watched the servant set forth sweethearting, in her poor best, "out for the day" written in every ribbon and smile. Yes, he was alone, of course; and yet, in the bulk of empty house above him, he could surely hear a stir of delicate footing—he was surely conscious, inexplicably conscious of some presence. Ay, surely; to every room and corner of the house his imagination followed it; and now it was a faceless thing, and yet had eyes to see with; and again it was a shadow of himself; and yet again behold the image of the dead dealer, reinspired with cunning and hatred.

At times, with a strong effort, he would glance at the open door which still seemed to repel his eyes. The house was tall, the skylight small and dirty, the day blind with fog; and the light that filtered down to the ground storey was exceedingly faint, and showed dimly on the threshold of the shop. And yet, in that strip of doubtful brightness, did there not hang wavering a shadow?

Suddenly, from the street outside, a very jovial gentleman began to beat with a staff on the shopdoor, accompanying his blows with shouts and railleries in which the dealer was continually called upon by name. Markheim, smitten into ice, glanced at the dead man. But no! he lay quite still; he was fled away far beyond earshot of these blows and shoutings; he was sunk beneath seas of silence; and his name, which would once have caught his notice above the howling of a storm, had become an empty sound. And presently the jovial gentleman desisted from his knocking and departed.

Here was a broad hint to hurry what remained to be done, to get forth from this accusing neighbourhood, to plunge into a bath of London multitudes, and to reach, on the other side of day, that haven of safety and apparent innocence—his bed. One visitor had come: at any moment another might follow and be more obstinate. To have done the deed, and yet not to reap the profit, would be too abhorrent a failure. The money, that was now Markheim's concern; and as a means to that, the keys.

He glanced over his shoulder at the open door, where the shadow was still lingering and shivering; and with no conscious repugnance of the mind, yet with a tremor of the belly, he drew near the body of his victim. The human character had quite departed. Like a suit half stuffed with bran, the limbs lay scattered, the trunk doubled, on the floor; and yet the thing repelled him. Although so dingy and inconsiderable to the eye, he feared it might have more significance to the touch. He took the body by the shoulders, and turned it on its back. It was strangely light and supple, and the limbs, as if they had been broken, fell into the oddest postures. The face was robbed of all expression; but it was as pale as wax, and shockingly smeared with blood about one temple. That was, for Markheim, the one displeasing circumstance. It carried him back, upon the instant, to a certain fair day in a fishers' village: a grey day, a piping wind, a crowd upon the street, the blare of brasses, the booming of drums, the nasal voice of a ballad singer; and a boy going to and fro, buried over head in the crowd and divided between interest and fear, until, coming out upon the chief place of concourse, he beheld a booth and a great screen with pictures, dismally designed, garishly coloured: Brownrigg with her apprentice; the Mannings with their murdered guest; Weare in the death-grip of Thurtell; and a score besides of famous crimes. The thing was as clear as an illusion; he was once again that little boy; he was looking once again, and with the same sense of physical revolt, at these vile pictures; he was still stunned by the thumping of the drums. A bar of that day's music returned upon his memory;

and at that, for the first time, a qualm came over him, a breath of nausea, a sudden weakness of the joints, which he must instantly resist and conquer.

He judged it more prudent to confront than to flee from these considerations; looking the more hardily in the dead face, bending his mind to realise the nature and greatness of his crime. So little a while ago that face had moved with every change of sentiment, that pale mouth had spoken, that body had been all on fire with governable energies; and now, and by his act, that piece of life had been arrested, as the horologist, with interjected finger, arrests the beating of the clock. So he reasoned in vain; he could rise to no more remorseful consciousness; the same heart which had shuddered before the painted effigies of crime, looked on its reality unmoved. At best, he felt a gleam of pity for one who had been endowed in vain with all those faculties that can make the world a garden of enchantment, one who had never lived and who was now dead. But of penitence, no, not a tremor.

With that, shaking himself clear of these considerations, he found the keys and advanced towards the open door of the shop. Outside, it had begun to rain smartly; and the sound of the shower upon the roof had banished silence. Like some dripping cavern, the chambers of the house were haunted by an incessant echoing, which filled the ear and mingled with the ticking of the clocks. And, as Markheim approached the door, he seemed to hear, in answer to his own cautious tread, the steps of another foot withdrawing up the stair. The shadow still palpitated loosely on the threshold. He threw a ton's weight of resolve upon his muscles, and drew back the door.

The faint, foggy daylight glimmered dimly on the bare floor and stairs; on the bright suit of armour posted, halbert in hand, upon the landing; and on the dark wood-carvings, and framed pictures that hung against the yellow panels of the wainscot. So loud was the beating of the rain through all the house that, in Markheim's ears, it began to be distinguished into many different sounds. Footsteps and sighs, the tread of regiments marching in the distance, the chink of money in the counting, and the creaking of doors held stealthily ajar, appeared to mingle with the patter of the drops upon the cupola and the gushing of the water in the pipes. The sense that he was not alone grew upon him to the verge of madness. On every side he was haunted and begirt by presences. He heard them moving in the upper chambers; from the shop, he heard the dead man getting to his legs; and as he began with a great effort to mount the stairs, feet fled quietly before him and followed stealthily behind. If he were but deaf, he thought, how tranquilly he would possess his soul! And then again, and hearkening with ever fresh attention, he blessed himself for that unresting sense which held the outposts and stood a trusty sentinel upon his life. His head turned continually on his neck; his eyes, which seemed starting from their orbits, scouted on every side, and on every side were half rewarded as with the tail of something nameless vanishing. The four-and-twenty steps to the first floor were four-and-twenty agonies.

On that first storey, the doors stood ajar, three of them like three ambushes, shaking his nerves like the throats of cannon. He could never again, he felt, be sufficiently immured and fortified from men's observing eyes; he longed to be home, girt in by walls, buried among bedclothes, and invisible to all but God. And at that thought he wondered a little, recollecting tales of other murderers and the fear they were said to entertain of heavenly avengers. It was not so, at least, with him. He feared the laws of nature, lest, in their callous and immutable procedure, they should preserve some damning evidence of his crime. He feared tenfold more, with a slavish, superstitious terror, some scission in the continuity of man's experience, some wilful illegality of nature. He played a game of skill, depending on the rules, calculating consequence from cause; and what if nature, as the defeated tyrant overthrew the chess-board, should break the mould of their succession? The like had befallen Napoleon (so writers said) when the winter changed the time of its appearance. The like might befall Markheim: the solid walls might become transparent and reveal his doings like those of bees in a glass hive; the stout planks might yield under his foot like quicksands and detain him in their clutch; ay, and there were soberer accidents that might destroy him: if, for instance, the house should fall and imprison him beside the body of his victim; or the house next door should fly on fire, and the firemen invade him from all sides. These things he feared; and, in a sense, these things might be called the hands of God reached forth against sin. But about God himself he was at ease; his act was doubtless exceptional, but so were his excuses, which God knew; it was there, and not among men, that he felt sure of justice.

When he had got safe into the drawing-room, and shut the door behind him, he was aware of a respite from alarms. The room was quite dismantled, uncarpeted besides, and strewn with packing-cases and incongruous furniture; several great pierglasses, in which he beheld himself at various angles, like an actor on a stage; many pictures, framed and unframed, standing, with their faces to the wall; a fine Sheraton sideboard, a cabinet of marquetry, and a great old bed, with tapestry hangings. The windows opened to the floor; but by great good-fortune the lower part of the shutters had been closed, and this concealed him from the neighbours. Here, then, Markheim drew in a packing-case before the cabinet, and began to search among the keys. It was a long business, for there were many; and it was irksome, besides; for, after all, there might be nothing in the cabinet, and time was on the wing. But the closeness of the occupation sobered him. With the tail of his eye he saw the door—even glanced at it from time to time directly, like a besieged commander pleased to verify the good estate of his defences. But in truth he was at peace. The rain falling in the street sounded natural and pleasant. Presently, on the other side, the notes of a piano were wakened to the music of a hymn, and the voices of many children took up the air and words. How stately, how comfortable was the melody! How fresh the youthful voices! Markheim gave ear to it smilingly, as he sorted out the keys; and his mind was thronged with answerable ideas and images;

church-going children and the pealing of the high organ; children afield, bathers by the brookside, ramblers on the brambly common, kite-fliers in the windy and cloud-navigated sky; and then, at another cadence of the hymn, back again to church, and the somnolence of summer Sundays, and the high genteel voice of the parson (which he smiled a little to recall) and the painted Jacobean tombs, and the dim lettering of the Ten Commandments in the chancel.

And as he sat thus, at once busy and absent, he was startled to his feet. A flash of ice, a flash of fire, a bursting gush of blood, went over him, and then he stood transfixed and thrilling. A step mounted the stair slowly and steadily, and presently a hand was laid upon the knob, and the lock clicked, and the door opened.

Fear held Markheim in a vice. What to expect he knew not, whether the dead man walking, or the official ministers of human justice, or some chance witness blindly stumbling in to consign him to the gallows. But when a face was thrust into the aperture, glanced round the room, looked at him, nodded and smiled as if in friendly recognition, and then withdrew again, and the door closed behind it, his fear broke loose from his control in a hoarse cry. At the sound of this the visitant returned.

"Did you call me?" he asked, pleasantly, and with that he entered the room and closed the door behind him.

Markheim stood and gazed at him with all his eyes. Perhaps there was a film upon his sight, but the outlines of the newcomer seemed to change and waver like those of the idols in the wavering candle-light of the shop; and at times he thought he knew him; and at times he thought he bore a likeness to himself; and always, like a lump of living terror, there lay in his bosom the conviction that this thing was not of the earth and not of God.

And yet the creature had a strange air of the commonplace, as he stood looking on Markheim with a smile; and when he added: "You are looking for the money, I believe?" it was in the tones of every-day politeness.

Markheim made no answer.

"I should warn you," resumed the other, "that the maid has left her sweetheart earlier than usual and will soon be here. If Mr. Markheim be found in this house, I need not describe to him the consequences."

"You know me?" cried the murderer.

The visitor smiled. "You have long been a favourite of mine," he said; "and I have long observed and often sought to help you."

"What are you?" cried Markheim: "the devil?"

"What I may be," returned the other, "cannot affect the service I propose to render you."

"It can," cried Markheim; "it does! Be helped by you? No, never, not by you! You do not know me yet; thank God, you do not know me!"

"I know you," replied the visitant, with a sort of kind severity or rather firmness. "I know you to the soul."

"Know me!" cried Markheim. "Who can do so? My life is but a travesty and slander on myself. I have lived to belie my nature. All men do; all men are better than this disguise that grows about and stifles them. You see each dragged away by life, like one whom bravos have seized and muffled in a cloak. If they had their own control—if you could see their faces, they would be altogether different, they would shine out for heroes and saints! I am worse than most; my self is more overlaid; my excuse is known to me and God. But, had I the time, I could disclose myself."

"To me?" inquired the visitant.

"To you before all," returned the murderer. "I supposed you were intelligent. I thought—since you exist—you would prove a reader of the heart. And yet you would propose to judge me by my acts! Think of it; my acts! I was born and I have lived in a land of giants; giants have dragged me by the wrists since I was born out of my mother—the giants of circumstance. And you would judge me by my acts! But can you not look within? Can you not understand that evil is hateful to me? Can you not see within me the clear writing of conscience, never blurred by any wilful sophistry, although too often disregarded? Can you not read me for a thing that surely must be common as humanity—the unwilling sinner?"

"All this is very feelingly expressed," was the reply, "but it regards me not. These points of consistency are beyond my province, and I care not in the least by what compulsion you may have been dragged away, so as you are but carried in the right direction. But time flies; the servant delays, looking in the faces of the crowd and at the pictures on the hoardings, but still she keeps moving nearer; and remember, it is as if the gallows itself was striding towards you through the Christmas streets! Shall I help you; I, who know all? Shall I tell you where to find the money?"

"For what price?" asked Markheim.

"I offer you the service for a Christmas gift," returned the other.

Markheim could not refrain from smiling with a kind of bitter triumph. "No," said he, "I will take nothing at your hands; if I were dying of thirst, and it was your hand that put the pitcher to my lips, I should find the courage to refuse. It may be credulous, but I will do nothing to commit myself to evil."

"I have no objection to a death-bed repentance," observed the visitant.

"Because you disbelieve their efficacy!" Markheim cried.

"I do not say so," returned the other; "but I look on these things from a different side, and when the life is done my interest falls. The man has lived to serve me, to spread black looks under colour of religion, or to sow tares in the wheatfield, as you do, in a course of weak compliance with desire. Now that he draws so near to his deliverance, he can add but one act of service—to repent, to die smiling, and thus to build up in confidence and hope the more timorous of my surviving followers. I am not so hard a master. Try me. Accept my help. Please yourself in life as you have done hitherto; please yourself more amply, spread your elbows at the board; and when the night begins to fall and the curtains to be drawn, I tell you, for your greater comfort, that you will find it even easy to compound your quarrel with your conscience, and to make a truckling peace with God. I came but now from such a deathbed, and the room was full of sincere mourners, listening to the man's last words: and when I looked into that face, which had been set as a flint against mercy, I found it smiling with hope."

"And do you, then, suppose me such a creature?" asked Markheim. "Do you think I have no more generous aspirations than to sin, and sin, and sin, and at last, sneak into heaven? My heart rises at the thought. Is this, then, your experience of mankind? or is it because you find me with red hands that you presume such baseness? and is this crime of murder indeed so impious as to dry up the very springs of good?"

"Murder is to me no special category," replied the other. "All sins are murder, even as all life is war. I behold your race, like starving mariners on a raft, plucking crusts out of the hands of famine and feeding on each other's lives. I follow sins beyond the moment of their acting; I find in all that the last consequence is death; and to my eyes, the pretty maid who thwarts her mother with such taking graces on a question of a ball, drips no less visibly with human gore than such a murderer as yourself. Do I say that I follow sins? I follow virtues also; they differ not by the thickness of a nail, they are both scythes for the reaping angel of Death. Evil, for which I live, consists not in action but in character. The bad man is dear to me; not the bad act, whose fruits, if we could follow them far enough down the hurtling cataract of the ages, might yet be found more blessed than those of the rarest virtues. And it is not because you have killed a dealer, but because you are Markheim, that I offered to forward your escape."

"I will lay my heart open to you," answered Markheim. "This crime on which you find me is my last. On my way to it I have learned many lessons; itself is a lesson, a momentous lesson. Hitherto I have been driven with revolt to what I would not; I was a bond-slave to poverty, driven and scourged. There are robust virtues that can stand in these temptations; mine was not so: I had a thirst of pleasure. But to-day, and out of this deed, I pluck both warning and riches—both the power and a fresh resolve to be myself. I become in all things a free actor in the world; I begin to see myself all changed, these hands the agents of good, this heart at peace. Something comes over me out of the past; something of what I have dreamed on Sabbath evenings to the sound of the church organ, of what I forecast when I shed tears over noble books, or talked, an innocent child, with my mother. There lies my life; I have wandered a few years, but now I see once more my city of destination."

"You are to use this money on the Stock Exchange, I think?" remarked the visitor; "and there, if I mistake not, you have already lost some thousands?"

"Ah," said Markheim, "but this time I have a sure thing."

"This time, again, you will lose," replied the visitor quietly.

"Ah, but I keep back the half!" cried Markheim.

"That also you will lose," said the other.

The sweat started upon Markheim's brow. "Well, then, what matter?" he exclaimed. "Say it be lost, say I am plunged again in poverty, shall one part of me, and that the worst, continue until the end to override the better? Evil and good run strong in me, haling me both ways, I do not love the one thing, I love all. I can conceive great deeds, renunciations, martyrdoms; and though I be fallen to such a crime as murder, pity is no stranger to my thoughts. I pity the poor; who knows their trials better than myself? I pity and help them; I prize love, I love honest laughter; there is no good thing nor true thing on earth but I love it from my heart. And are my vices only to direct my life, and my virtues to lie without effect, like some passive lumber of the mind? Not so; good, also, is a spring of acts."

But the visitant raised his finger. "For six-and-thirty years that you have been in this world," said he, "through many changes of fortune and varieties of humour, I have watched you steadily fall. Fifteen years ago you would have started at a theft. Three years back you would have blenched at the name of murder. Is there any crime, is there any cruelty of meanness, from which you still recoil?—five years from now I shall detect you in the fact! Downward, downward, lies your way; nor can anything but death avail to stop you."

"It is true," Markheim said huskily, "I have in some degree complied with evil. But it is so with all: the very saints, in the mere exercise of living, grow less dainty, and take on the tone of their surroundings."

"I will propound to you one simple question," said the other; "and as you answer, I shall read to you your moral horoscope. You have grown in many things more lax; possibly you do right to be so; and at any account, it is the same with all men. But granting that, are you in any one particular, however trifling, more difficult to please with your own conduct, or do you go in all things with a looser rein?"

"In any one?" repeated Markheim, with an anguish of consideration. "No," he added, with despair, "in none! I have gone down in all."

"Then," said the visitor, "content yourself with what you are, for you will never change; and the words of your part on this stage are irrevocably written down."

Markheim stood for a long while silent, and indeed it was the visitor who first broke the silence. "That being so," he said, "shall I show you the money?"

"And grace?" cried Markheim.

"Have you not tried it?" returned the other. "Two or three years ago, did I not see you on the platform of revival meetings, and was not your voice the loudest in the hymn?"

"It is true," said Markheim; "and I see clearly what remains for me by way of duty. I thank you for these lessons from my soul; my eyes are opened, and I behold myself at last for what I am."

At this moment, the sharp note of the doorbell rang

through the house; and the visitant, as though this were some concerted signal for which he had been waiting, changed at once in his demeanour.

"The maid!" he cried. "She has returned, as I forewarned you, and there is now before you one more difficult passage. Her master, you must say, is ill; you must let her in, with an assured but rather serious countenance—no smiles, no overacting, and I promise you success! Once the girl within, and the door closed, the same dexterity that has already rid you of the dealer will relieve you of this last danger in your path. Thenceforward you have the whole evening—the whole night, if needful—to ransack the treasures of the house and to make good your safety. This is help that comes to you with the mask of danger. Up!" he cried: "up, friend; your life hangs trembling in the scales: up, and act!"

Markheim steadily regarded his counsellor. "If I be condemned to evil acts," he said, "there is still one door of freedom open—I can cease from action. If my life be an ill thing, I can lay it down. Though I be, as you say truly, at the beck of every small temptation, I can yet, by one decisive gesture, place myself beyond the reach of all. My love of good is damned to barrenness; it may, and let it be! But I have still my hatred of evil; and from that, to your galling disappointment, you shall see that I can draw both energy and courage."

The features of the visitor began to undergo a wonderful and lovely change: they brightened and softened with a tender triumph; and, even as they brightened, faded and dislimned. But Markheim did not pause to watch or understand the transformation. He opened the door and went down-stairs very slowly, thinking to himself. His past went soberly before him; he beheld it as it was, ugly and strenuous like a dream, random as chance-medley—a scene of defeat. Life, as he thus reviewed it, tempted him no longer; but on the further side he perceived a quiet haven for his bark. He paused in the passage, and looked into the shop, where the candle still burned by the dead body. It was strangely silent. Thoughts of the dealer swarmed into his mind, as he stood gazing. And then the bell once more broke out into impatient clamour.

He confronted the maid upon the threshold with something like a smile.

"You had better go for the police," said he: "I have killed your master."

THE FIRE BALLOONS

by Ray Bradbury

F IRE EXPLODED over summer night lawns. You saw sparkling
faces of uncles and aunts. Skyrockets fell up in the brown
shining eyes of cousins on the porch, and the cold charred sticks
thumped down in dry meadows far away.

The Very Reverend Father Joseph Daniel Peregrine
opened his eyes. What a dream: he and his cousins with their
fiery play at his grandfather's ancient Ohio home so many years
ago!

He lay listening to the great hollow of the church, the other
cells where other Fathers lay. Had they, too, on the eve of the
flight of the rocket *Crucifix,* lain with memories of the Fourth of
July? Yes. This was like those breathless Independence dawns
when you waited for the first concussion and rushed out on the
dewy sidewalks, your hands full of loud miracles.

So here they were, the Episcopal Fathers, in the breathing
dawn before they pinwheeled off to Mars, leaving their incense
through the velvet cathedral of space.

"Should we go at all?" whispered Father Peregrine.

"Shouldn't we solve our own sins on Earth? Aren't we running from our lives here?"

He arose, his fleshy body, with its rich look of strawberries, milk, and steak, moving heavily.

"Or is it sloth?" he wondered. "Do I dread the journey?"

He stepped into the needle-spray shower.

"But I shall take you to Mars, body." He addressed himself. "Leaving old sins here. And on to Mars to find *new* sins?" A delightful thought, almost. Sins no one had ever thought of. Oh, he himself had written a little book: *The Problem of Sin on Other Worlds,* ignored as somehow not serious enough by his Episcopal brethren.

Only last night, over a final cigar, he and Father Stone had talked of it.

"On Mars sin might appear as virtue. We must guard against virtuous acts there that, later, might be found to be sins!" said Father Peregrine, beaming. "How exciting! It's been centuries since so much adventure has accompanied the prospect of being a missionary!"

"*I* will recognize sin," said Father Stone bluntly, "*even* on Mars."

"Oh, we priests pride ourselves on being litmus paper, changing color in sin's presence," retorted Father Peregrine, "but what if Martian chemistry is such we do not color *at all!* If there are new senses on Mars, you must admit the possibility of unrecognizable sin."

"If there is no malice aforethought, there is no sin or punishment for same—the Lord assures us that," Father Stone replied.

"On Earth, yes. But perhaps a Martian sin might inform the subconscious of its evil, telepathically, leaving the conscious mind of man free to act, seemingly without malice! What *then?*"

"What *could* there be in the way of new sins?"

Father Peregrine leaned heavily forward. "Adam *alone* did not sin. Add Eve and you add temptation. Add a second man and you make adultery possible. With the addition of sex or people, you add sin. If men were armless they could not strangle with their hands. You would not have that particular sin of murder. Add arms, and you add the possibility of a new violence. Amoebas cannot sin because they reproduce by fission. They do not covet wives or murder each other. Add sex to amoebas, add arms and legs, and you would have murder and adultery. Add an arm or leg or person, or take away each, and you add or subtract possible evil. On Mars, what if there are five new senses, organs, invisible limbs we can't conceive of—then mightn't there be five *new sins?*"

Father Stone gasped. "I think you *enjoy* this sort of thing!"

"I keep my mind alive, Father; just alive, is all."

"Your mind's always juggling, isn't it?—mirrors, torches, plates."

"Yes. Because sometimes the Church seems like those posed circus tableaus where the curtain lifts and men, white, zinc-oxide, talcom-powder statues, freeze to represent abstract Beauty. Very wonderful. But I hope there will always be room for me to dart about among the statues, don't you, Father Stone?"

Father Stone had moved away. "I think we'd better go to bed. In a few hours we'll be jumping up to see your *new* sins, Father Peregrine."

The rocket stood ready for the firing.

The Fathers walked from their devotions in the chilly morning, many a fine priest from New York or Chicago or Los Angeles—the Church was sending its best—walking across town to the frosty field. Walking, Father Peregrine remembered the Bishop's words:

"Father Peregrine, you will captain the missionaries, with Father Stone at your side. Having chosen you for this serious task, I find my reasons deplorably obscure, Father, but your pamphlet on planetary sin did not go unread. You are a flexible man. And Mars is like that uncleaned closet we have neglected for millenniums. Sin has collected there like bric-a-brac. Mars is twice Earth's age and has had double the number of Saturday nights, liquor baths, and eye-poppings at women as naked as white seals. When we open that closet door, things will fall on us. We need a quick, flexible man—one whose mind can dodge. Anyone a little too dogmatic might break in two. I feel you'll be resilient. Father, the job is yours."

The Bishop and the Fathers knelt.

The blessing was said and the rocket given a little shower of holy water. Arising, the Bishop addressed them:

"I know you will go with God, to prepare the Martians for the reception of His Truth. I wish you all a *thoughtful* journey."

They filed past the Bishop, twenty men, robes whispering, to deliver their hands into his kind hands before passing into the cleansed projectile.

"I wonder," said Father Peregrine, at the last moment, "if Mars is hell? Only waiting for our arrival before it bursts into brimstone and fire."

"Lord, be with us," said Father Stone.

The rocket moved.

Coming out of space was like coming out of the most beautiful cathedral they had ever seen. Touching Mars was like touching the ordinary pavement outside the church five minutes after having *really* known your love for God.

The Fathers stepped gingerly from the steaming rocket and knelt upon Martian sand while Father Peregrine gave thanks.

"Lord, we thank Thee for the journey through Thy rooms. And, Lord, we have reached a new land, so we must have new eyes. We shall hear new sounds and must needs have new ears. And there will be new sins, for which we ask the gift of better and firmer and purer hearts. Amen."

They arose.

And here was Mars like a sea under which they trudged in the guise of submarine biologists, seeking life. Here the territory of hidden sin. Oh, how carefully they must all balance, like gray feathers, in this new element, afraid that walking *itself* might be sinful; or breathing, or simple fasting!

The Fire Balloons

And here was the mayor of First Town come to meet them with outstretched hand. "What can I do for you, Father Peregrine?"

"We'd like to know about the Martians. For only if we know about them can we plan our church intelligently. Are they ten feet tall? We will build large doors. Are their skins blue or red or green? We must know when we put human figures in the stained glass so we may use the right skin color. Are they heavy? We will build sturdy seats for them."

"Father," said the mayor, "I don't think you should worry about the Martians. There are two races. One of them is pretty well dead. A few are in hiding. And the second race—well, they're not quite human."

"Oh?" Father Peregrine's heart quickened.

"They're round luminous globes of light, Father, living in those hills. Man or beast, who can say? But they act intelligently, I hear." The mayor shrugged. "Of course, they're not men, so I don't think you'll care—"

"On the contrary," said Father Peregrine swiftly. "Intelligent, you say?"

"There's a story. A prospector broke his leg in those hills and would have died there. The blue spheres of light came at him. When he woke, he was down on a highway and didn't know how he got there."

"Drunk," said Father Stone.

"That's the story," said the mayor. "Father Peregrine, with most of the Martians dead, and only these blue spheres, I frankly think you'd be better off in First City. Mars is opening up. It's a frontier now, like in the old days on Earth, out West, and in Alaska. Men are pouring up here. There's a couple thousand black Irish mechanics and miners and day laborers in First Town who need saving, because there're too many wicked women came with them, and too much ten-century-old Martian wine—"

Father Peregrine was gazing into the soft blue hills.

Father Stone cleared his throat. "Well, Father?"

Father Peregrine did not hear. "Spheres of blue *fire?*"

"Yes, Father."

"Ah," Father Peregrine sighed.

"Blue balloons." Father Stone shook his head. "A circus!"

Father Peregrine felt his wrists pounding. He saw the little frontier town with raw, fresh-built sin, and he saw the hills, old with the oldest and yet perhaps an even newer (to him) sin.

"Mayor, could your black Irish laborers cook one more day in hellfire?"

"I'd turn and baste them for you, Father."

Father Peregrine nodded to the hills. "Then that's where we'll go."

There was a murmur from everyone.

"It would be so simple," explained Father Peregrine, "to go into town. I prefer to think that if the Lord walked here and people said, 'Here is the beaten path,' He would reply, 'Show me the weeds. I will *make* a path.'"

"But—"

"Father Stone, think how it would weigh upon us if we passed sinners by and did not extend our hands."

"But globes of fire!"

"I imagine man looked funny to other animals when we first appeared. Yet he has a soul, for all his homeliness. Until we prove otherwise, let us assume that these fiery spheres have souls."

"All right," agreed the mayor, "but you'll be back to town."

"We'll see. First, some breakfast. Then you and I, Father Stone, will walk alone into the hills. I don't want to frighten those fiery Martians with machines or crowds. Shall we have breakfast?"

The Fathers ate in silence.

At nightfall Father Peregrine and Father Stone were high in the hills. They stopped and sat upon a rock to enjoy a moment of relaxation and waiting. The Martians had not as yet appeared and they both felt vaguely disappointed.

"I wonder—" Father Peregrine mopped his face. "Do you think if we called 'Hello!' they might answer?"

"Father Peregrine, won't you ever be serious?"

"Not until the good Lord is. Oh, don't look so terribly shocked, please. The Lord is not serious. In fact, it is a little hard to know just what else He is except loving. And love has to do with humor, doesn't it? For you cannot love someone unless you put up with him, can you? And you cannot put up with someone constantly unless you can laugh at him. Isn't that true? And certainly we are ridiculous little animals wallowing in the fudge bowl, and God must love us all the more because we appeal to His humor."

"*I* never thought of God as humorous," said Father Stone.

"The Creator of the platypus, the camel, the ostrich, and man? Oh, come now!" Father Peregrine laughed.

But at this instant, from among the twilight hills, like a series of blue lamps lit to guide their way, came the Martians.

Father Stone saw them first. "Look!"

Father Peregrine turned and the laughter stopped in his mouth.

The round blue globes of fire hovered among the twinkling stars, distantly trembling.

"Monsters!" Father Stone leaped up. But Father Peregrine caught him. "Wait!"

"We should've gone to town!"

"No, listen, look!" pleaded Father Peregrine.

"I'm afraid!"

"Don't be. This is God's work!"

"The devil's!"

"No, now, quiet!" Father Peregrine gentled him and they crouched with the soft blue light on their upturned faces as the fiery orbs drew near.

And again, Independence Night, thought Father Peregrine,

tremoring. He felt like a child back in those July Fourth evenings, the sky blowing apart, breaking into powdery stars and burning sound, the concussions jingling house windows like the ice on a thousand thin ponds. The aunts, uncles, cousins crying, "Ah!" as to some celestial physician. The summer sky colors. And the Fire Balloons, lit by an indulgent grandfather, steadied in his massively tender hands. Oh, the memory of those lovely Fire Balloons, softly lighted, warmly billowed bits of tissue, like insect wings, lying like folded wasps in boxes and, last of all, after the day of riot and fury, at long last from their boxes, delicately unfolded, blue, red, white, patriotic—the Fire Balloons! He saw the dim faces of dear relatives long dead and mantled with moss as Grandfather lit the tiny candle and let the warm air breathe up to form the balloon plumply luminous in his hands, a shining vision which they held, reluctant to let it go; for, once released, it was yet another year gone from life, another Fourth, another bit of Beauty vanished. And then up, up, still up through the warm summer night constellations, the Fire Balloons had drifted, while red-white-and-blue eyes followed them, wordless, from family porches. Away into deep Illinois country, over night rivers and sleeping mansions the Fire Balloons dwindled, forever gone. . . .

Father Peregrine felt tears in his eyes. Above him the Martians, not one but a *thousand* whispering Fire Balloons, it seemed, hovered. Any moment he might find his long-dead and blessed grandfather at his elbow, staring up at Beauty.

But it was Father Stone.

"Let's go, please, Father!"

"I must speak to them." Father Peregrine rustled forward, not knowing what to say, for what had he ever said to the Fire Balloons of time past except with his mind: *you are beautiful, you are beautiful,* and that was not enough now. He could only lift his heavy arms and call upward, as he had often wished to call after the enchanted Fire Balloons, "Hello!"

But the fiery spheres only burned like images in a dark mirror. They seemed fixed, gaseous, miraculous, forever.

"We come with God," said Father Peregrine to the sky.

"Silly, silly, silly." Father Stone chewed the back of his hand. "In the name of God, Father Peregrine, stop!"

But now the phosphorescent spheres blew away into the hills. In a moment they were gone.

Father Peregrine called again, and the echo of his last cry shook the hills above. Turning, he saw an avalanche shake out dust, pause, and then, with a thunder of stone wheels, crash down the mountain upon them.

"Look what you've done!" cried Father Stone.

Father Peregrine was almost fascinated, then horrified. He turned, knowing they could run only a few feet before the rocks crushed them into ruins. He had time to whisper, *Oh, Lord!* and the rocks fell!

"Father!"

They were separated like chaff from wheat. There was a blue shimmering of globes, a shift of cold stars, a roar, and then they stood upon a ledge two hundred feet away watching the spot where their bodies should have been buried under tons of stone.

The blue light evaporated.

The two Fathers clutched each other. "What happened?"

"The blue fires lifted us!"

"We ran, *that* was it!"

"No, the globes saved us."

"They couldn't!"

"They *did*."

The sky was empty. There was a feel as if a great bell had just stopped tolling. Reverberations lingered in their teeth and marrows.

"Let's get away from here. You'll have us killed."

"I haven't feared death for a good many years, Father Stone."

"We've proved nothing. Those blue lights ran off at the first cry. It's useless."

"No." Father Peregrine was suffused with a stubborn wonder. "Somehow, they saved us. That proves they have souls."

73

"It proves only that they *might* have saved us. Everything was confused. We might have escaped, ourselves."

"They are not animals, Father Stone. Animals do not save lives, especially of strangers. There is mercy and compassion here. Perhaps, tomorrow, we may prove more."

"Prove what? How?" Father Stone was immensely tired now; the outrage to his mind and body showed on his stiff face. "Follow them in helicopters, reading chapter and verse? They're not human. They haven't eyes or ears or bodies like ours."

"But I feel something about them," replied Father Peregrine. "I know a great revelation is at hand. They saved us. They *think*. They had a choice; let us live or die. That proves free will!"

Father Stone set to work building a fire, glaring at the sticks in his hands, choking on the gray smoke. "I myself will open a convent for nursling geese, a monastery for sainted swine, and I shall build a miniature apse in a microscope so that paramecium can attend services and tell their beads with their flagella."

"Oh, Father Stone."

"I'm sorry." Father Stone blinked redly across the fire. "But this is like blessing a crocodile before he chews you up. You're risking the entire missionary expedition. We belong in First Town, washing liquor from men's throats and perfume off their hands!"

"Can't you recognize the human in the inhuman?"

"I'd much rather recognize the inhuman in the human."

"But if I prove these things sin, know sin, know a moral life, have free will and intellect, Father Stone?"

"That will take much convincing."

The night grew rapidly cold and they peered into the fire to find their wildest thoughts, while eating biscuits and berries, and soon they were bundled for sleep under the chiming stars. And just before turning over one last time Father Stone, who had been thinking for many minutes to find something to bother Father Peregrine about, stared into the soft pink charcoal bed and said, "No Adam and Eve on Mars. No original sin. Maybe the

Martians live in a state of God's grace. Then we can go back down to town and start work on the Earthmen."

Father Peregrine reminded himself to say a little prayer for Father Stone, who got so mad and who was now being vindictive, God help him. "Yes, Father Stone, but the Martians killed some of our settlers. That's sinful. There must have been an Original Sin and a Martian Adam and Eve. We'll find them. Men are men, unfortunately, no matter what their shape, and inclined to sin."

But Father Stone was pretending sleep.

Father Peregrine did not shut his eyes.

Of course they couldn't let these Martians go to hell, could they? With a compromise to their consciences, could they go back to the new colonial towns, those towns so full of sinful gullets and women with scintilla eyes and white oyster bodies rollicking in beds with lonely laborers? Wasn't that the place for the Fathers? Wasn't this trek into the hills merely a personal whim? Was he really thinking of God's Church, or was he quenching the thirst of a spongelike curiosity? Those blue round globes of St. Anthony's fire—how they burned in his mind! What a challenge, to find the man behind the mask, the human behind the inhuman. Wouldn't he be proud if he could say, even to his secret self, that he had converted a rolling huge pool table full of fiery spheres! What a sin of pride! Worth doing penance for! But then one did many prideful things out of Love, and he loved the Lord so much and was so happy at it that he wanted everyone else to be happy too.

The last thing he saw before sleep was the return of the blue fires, like a flight of burning angels silently singing him to his worried rest.

The blue round dreams were still there in the sky when Father Peregrine awoke in the early morning.

Father Stone slept like a stiff bundle, quietly. Father Peregrine watched the Martians floating and watching him. They were human—he *knew* it. But he must prove it or face a dry-mouthed, dry-eyed Bishop telling him kindly to step aside.

But how to prove humanity if they hid in the high vaults of the sky? How to bring them nearer and provide answers to the many questions?

"They saved us from the avalanche."

Father Peregrine arose, moved off among the rocks, and began to climb the nearest hill until he came to a place where a cliff dropped sheerly to a floor two hundred feet below. He was choking from his vigorous climb in the frosty air. He stood, getting his breath.

"If I fell from here, it would surely kill me."

He let a pebble drop. Moments later it clicked on the rocks below.

"The Lord would never forgive me."

He tossed another pebble.

"It wouldn't be suicide, would it, if I did it out of Love . . . ?"

He lifted his gaze to the blue spheres. "But first another try." He called to them: "Hello, hello!"

The echoes tumbled upon each other, but the blue fires did not blink or move.

He talked to them for five minutes. When he stopped, he peered down and saw Father Stone, still indignantly asleep, below in the little camp.

"I must prove everything." Father Peregrine stepped to the cliff rim. "I am an old man. I am not afraid. Surely the Lord will understand that I am doing this for Him?"

He drew a deep breath. All his life swam through his eyes and he thought, In a moment shall I die? I am afraid that I love living much too much. But I love other things more.

And, thinking thus, he stepped off the cliff.

He fell.

"Fool!" he cried. He tumbled end over end. "You were wrong!" The rocks rushed up at him and he saw himself dashed on them and sent to glory. "Why did I do this thing?" But he knew the answer, and an instant later was calm as he fell. The wind roared around him and the rocks hurtled to meet him.

And then there was a shift of stars, a glimmering of blue light, and he felt himself surrounded by blueness and suspended. A moment later he was deposited, with a gentle bump, upon the rocks, where he sat a full moment, alive, and touching himself, and looking up at those blue lights that had withdrawn instantly.

"You saved me!" he whispered. "You wouldn't let me die. You knew it was wrong."

He rushed over to Father Stone who still lay quietly asleep. "Father, Father, wake up!" He shook him and brought him round. "Father, they saved me!"

"Who saved you?" Father Stone blinked and sat up.

Father Peregrine related his experience.

"A dream, a nightmare; go back to sleep," said Father Stone irritably. "You and your circus balloons."

"But I was awake!"

"Now, now, Father, calm yourself. There now."

"You don't believe me? Have you a gun? Yes, there, let me have it."

"What are you going to do?" Father Stone handed over the small pistol they had brought along for protection against snakes or other similar and unpredictable animals.

Father Peregrine seized the pistol. "I'll prove it!"

He pointed the pistol at his own hand and fired.

"Stop!"

There was a shimmer of light, and before their eyes the bullet stood upon the air, poised an inch from his open palm. It hung for a moment, surrounded by a blue phosphorescence. Then it fell, hissing, into the dust.

Father Peregrine fired the gun three times—at his hand, at his leg, at his body. The three bullets hovered, glittering, and, like dead insects, fell at their feet.

"You see?" said Father Peregrine, letting his arm fall, and allowing the pistol to drop after the bullets. "They know. They understand. They are not animals. They think and judge and live in a moral climate. What animal would save me from myself like this? There is no animal would do that. Only another man, Father. Now, do you believe?"

Father Stone was watching the sky and the blue lights, and now, silently, he dropped to one knee and picked up the warm bullets and cupped them in his hand. He closed his hand tight.

The sun was rising behind them.

"I think we had better go down to the others and tell them of this and bring them back up here," said Father Peregrine.

By the time the sun was up, they were well on their way back to the rocket.

Father Peregrine drew the round circle in the center of the blackboard.

"This is Christ, the son of the Father."

He pretended not to hear the other Fathers' sharp intake of breath.

"This is Christ, in all his Glory," he continued.

"It looks like a geometry problem," observed Father Stone.

"A fortunate comparison, for we deal with symbols here. Christ is no less Christ, you must admit, in being represented by a circle or a square. For centuries the cross has symbolized his love and agony. So this circle will be the Martian Christ. This is how we shall bring Him to Mars."

The Fathers stirred fretfully and looked at each other.

"You, Brother Mathias, will create, in glass, a replica of this circle, a globe, filled with bright fire. It will stand upon the altar."

"A cheap magic trick," muttered Father Stone.

Father Peregrine went on patiently: "On the contrary. We are giving them God in an understandable image. If Christ had come to us on Earth as an octopus, would we have accepted him readily?" He spread his hands. "Was it then a cheap magic trick of the Lord's to bring us Christ through Jesus, in man's shape?

79

After we bless the church we build here and sanctify its altar and this symbol, do you think Christ would refuse to inhabit the shape before us? You know in your hearts He would not refuse."

"But the body of a soulless animal!" said Brother Mathias.

"We've already gone over that, many times since we returned this morning, Brother Mathias. These creatures saved us from the avalanche. They realized that self-destruction was sinful, and prevented it, time after time. Therefore we must build a church in the hills, live with them, to find their own special ways of sinning, the alien ways, and help them to discover God."

The Fathers did not seem pleased at the prospect.

"Is it because they are so odd to the eye?" wondered Father Peregrine. "But what is a shape? Only a cup for the blazing soul that God provides us all. If tomorrow I found that sea lions suddenly possessed free will, intellect, knew when not to sin, knew what life was and tempered justice with mercy and life with love, then I would build an undersea cathedral. And if the sparrows should, miraculously, with God's will, gain everlasting souls tomorrow, I would freight a church with helium and take after them, for all souls, in any shape, if they have free will and are aware of their sins, will burn in hell unless given their rightful communions. I would not let a Martian sphere burn in hell, either, for it is a sphere only in mine eyes. When I close my eyes it stands before me, an intelligence, a love, a soul—and I must not deny it."

"But that glass globe you wish placed on the altar," protested Father Stone.

"Consider the Chinese," replied Father Peregrine imperturbably. "What sort of Christ do Christian Chinese worship? An oriental Christ, naturally. You've all seen oriental Nativity scenes. How is Christ dressed? In Eastern robes. Where does He walk? In Chinese settings of bamboo and misty mountain and crooked tree. His eyelids taper, His cheekbones rise. Each country, each race adds something to Our Lord. I am reminded of the Virgin of Guadalupe, to whom all Mexico pays its love. Her skin? Have you noticed the paintings of her? A dark skin, like that of her worshipers. Is this blasphemy? Not at all. It is not logical that men should accept a God, no matter how real, of another color. I often wonder why our missionaries do well in Africa, with a snow-white Christ. Perhaps because white is a sacred color, in albino, or any other form, to the African tribes. Given time, mightn't Christ darken there too? The form does not matter. Content is everything. We cannot expect these Martians to accept an alien form. We shall give them Christ in their own image."

"There's a flaw in your reasoning, Father," said Father Stone. "Won't the Martians suspect us of hypocrisy? They will realize that we don't worship a round, globular Christ, but a man with limbs and a head. How do we explain the difference?"

"By showing there is none. Christ will fill any vessel that is offered. Bodies or globes, He is there, and each will worship the same thing in a different guise. What is more, we must *believe* in this globe we give the Martians. We must believe in a shape which is meaningless to us as to form. This spheroid *will* be Christ. And we must remember that we ourselves, and the shape of our Earth Christ would be meaningless, ridiculous, a squander of material to these Martians."

Father Peregrine laid aside his chalk. "Now let us go into the hills and build our church."

The Fathers began to pack their equipment.

The church was not a church but an area cleared of rocks, a plateau on one of the low mountains, its soil smoothed and brushed, and an altar established whereon Brother Mathias placed the fiery globe he had constructed.

At the end of six days of work the "church" was ready.

"What shall we do with this?" Father Stone tapped an iron bell they had brought along. "What does a bell mean to *them?*"

"I imagine I brought it for our own comfort," admitted Father Peregrine. "We need a few familiarities. This church seems so little like a church. And we feel somewhat absurd here —even I; for it is something new, this business of converting the creatures of another world. I feel like a ridiculous play actor at times. And then I pray to God to lend me strength."

"Many of the Fathers are unhappy. Some of them joke about all this, Father Peregrine."

"I know. We'll put this bell in a small tower for their comfort, anyway."

"What about the organ?"

"We'll play it at the first service, tomorrow."

"But, the Martians—"

"I know. But again, I suppose, for our own comfort, our own music. Later we may discover theirs."

They arose very early on Sunday morning and moved through the coldness like pale phantoms, rime tinkling on their habits; covered with chimes they were, shaking down showers of silver water.

"I wonder if it *is* Sunday here on Mars?" mused Father Peregrine, but seeing Father Stone wince, he hastened on, "It might be Tuesday or Thursday—who knows? But no matter. My idle fancy. It's Sunday to *us*. Come."

The Fathers walked into the flat wide area of the "church" and knelt, shivering and blue-lipped.

Father Peregrine said a little prayer and put his cold fingers to the organ keys. The music went up like a flight of pretty birds. He touched the keys like a man moving his hands among the weeds of a wild garden, startling up great soarings of beauty into the hills.

The music calmed the air. It smelled the fresh smell of morning. The music drifted into the mountains and shook down mineral powders in a dusty rain.

The Fathers waited.

"Well, Father Peregrine." Father Stone eyed the empty sky where the sun was rising, furnace-red. "I don't see our friends."

"Let me try again." Father Peregrine was perspiring.

He built an architecture of Bach, stone by exquisite stone, raising a music cathedral so vast that its furthest chancels were

The Fire Balloons

in Nineveh, its furthest dome at St. Peter's left hand. The music stayed and did not crash in ruin when it was over, but partook of a series of white clouds and was carried away among other lands.

The sky was still empty.

"They'll come!" But Father Peregrine felt the panic in his chest, very small, growing. "Let us pray. Let us ask them to come. They read minds; they *know*."

The Fathers lowered themselves yet again, in rustlings and whispers. They prayed.

And to the East, out of the icy mountains of seven o'clock on Sunday morning or perhaps Thursday morning or maybe Monday morning on Mars, came the soft fiery globes.

They hovered and sank and filled the area around the shivering priests. "Thank you; oh, thank you, Lord." Father Peregrine shut his eyes tight and played the music, and when it was done he turned and gazed upon his wondrous congregation.

And a voice touched his mind, and the voice said:

"We have come for a little while."

"You may stay," said Father Peregrine.

"For a little while only," said the voice quietly. "We have come to tell you certain things. We should have spoken sooner. But we had hoped that you might go on your way if left alone."

Father Peregrine started to speak, but the voice hushed him.

"We are the Old Ones," the voice said, and it entered him like a blue gaseous flare and burned in the chambers of his head. "We are the old Martians, who left our marble cities and went into the hills, forsaking the material life we had lived. So very long ago we became these things that we now are. Once we were men, with bodies and legs and arms such as yours. The legend has it that one of us, a good man, discovered a way to free man's soul and intellect, to free him of bodily ills and melancholies, of deaths and transfigurations, of ill humors and senilities, and so we took on the look of lightning and blue fire and have lived in the winds and skies and hills forever after that, neither prideful

83

nor arrogant, neither rich nor poor, passionate nor cold. We have lived apart from those we left behind, those other men of this world, and how we came to be has been forgotten, the process lost; but we shall never die, nor do harm. We have put away the sins of the body and live in God's grace. We covet no other property; we have no property. We do not steal, nor kill, nor lust, nor hate. We live in happiness. We cannot reproduce; we do not eat or drink or make war. All the sensualities and childishnesses and sins of the body were stripped away when our bodies were put aside. We have left sin behind, Father Peregrine, and it is burned like the leaves in the autumn, and it is gone like the soiled snow of an evil winter, and it is gone like the sexual flowers of a red-and-yellow spring, and it is gone like the panting nights of hottest summer, and our season is temperate and our clime is rich in thought.''

Father Peregrine was standing now, for the voice touched him at such a pitch that it almost shook him from his senses. It was an ecstasy and a fire washing through him.

''We wish to tell you that we appreciate your building this place for us, but we have no need of it, for each of us is a temple unto himself and needs no place wherein to cleanse himself. Forgive us for not coming to you sooner, but we are separate and apart and have talked to no one for ten thousand years, nor have we interfered in any way with the life of this planet. It has come into your mind now that we are the lilies of the field; we toil not, neither do we spin. You are right. And so we suggest that you take the parts of this temple into your own new cities and there cleanse others. For, rest assured, we are happy and at peace.''

The Fathers were on their knees in the vast blue light, and Father Peregrine was down, too, and they were weeping, and it did not matter that their time had been wasted; it did not matter to them at all.

The blue spheres murmured and began to rise once more, on a breath of cool air.

''May I''—cried Father Peregrine, not daring to ask, eyes

closed—"may I come again, someday, that I may learn from you?"

The blue fires blazed. The air trembled.

Yes. Someday he might come again. Someday.

And then the Fire Balloons blew away and were gone, and he was like a child, on his knees, tears streaming from his eyes, crying to himself, "Come back, come back!" And at any moment Grandfather might lift him and carry him upstairs to his bedroom in a long-gone Ohio town. . . .

They filed down out of the hills at sunset. Looking back, Father Peregrine saw the blue fires burning. No, he thought, we couldn't build a church for the likes of you. You're Beauty itself. What church could compete with the fireworks of the pure soul?

Father Stone moved in silence beside him. And at last he spoke:

"The way I see it is there's a Truth on every planet. All parts of the Big Truth. On a certain day they'll all fit together like the pieces of jigsaw. This has been a shaking experience. I'll never doubt again, Father Peregrine. For this Truth here is as true as Earth's Truth, and they lie side by side. And we'll go on to other worlds, adding the sum of the parts of the Truth until one day the whole Total will stand before us like the light of a new day."

"That's a lot, coming from you, Father Stone."

"I'm sorry now, in a way, we're going down to the town to handle our own kind. Those blue lights now. When they settled about us, and that *voice* . . ." Father Stone shivered.

Father Peregrine reached out to take the other's arm. They walked together.

"And you know," said Father Stone finally, fixing his eyes on Brother Mathias, who strode ahead with the glass sphere tenderly carried in his arms, that glass sphere with the blue phosphorous light glowing forever inside it, "you know, Father Peregrine, that globe there—"

"Yes?"

"It's Him. It *is* Him, after all."

Father Peregrine smiled, and they walked down out of the hills toward the new town.

THE ANGEL OF THE ODD

by Edgar Allan Poe

An Extravaganza

IT WAS A chilly November afternoon. I had just consummated an unusually hearty dinner, of which the dyspeptic *truffe* formed not the least important item, and was sitting alone in the dining-room, with my feet upon the fender, and at my elbow a small table which I had rolled up to the fire, and upon which were some apologies for dessert, with some miscellaneous bottles of wine, spirit and *liqueur*. In the morning I had been reading Glover's "Leonidas," Wilkie's "Epigoniad," Lamartine's "Pilgrimage," Barlow's "Columbiad," Tuckermann's "Sicily," and Griswold's "Curiosities"; I am willing to confess, therefore, that I now felt a little stupid. I made effort to arouse myself by aid of frequent Lafitte, and, all failing, I betook myself to a stray newspaper in despair. Having carefully perused the column of "houses to let," and the column of "dogs lost," and then the two columns of "wives and apprentices runaway," I attacked with great resolution the editorial matter, and, reading it from beginning to end without understanding a syllable conceived the possibility of its being Chinese, and so re-read it from the end to the beginning, but with no more satisfactory result. I was about throwing away, in disgust,

> *"This folio of four pages, happy work*
> *Which not even poets criticise,"*

when I felt my attention somewhat aroused by the paragraph which follows:

> *"The avenues to death are numerous and strange. A London paper mentions the decease of a person from a singular cause. He was playing at 'puff the dart,' which is played with a long needle inserted in some worsted, and blown at a target through a tin tube. He placed the needle at the wrong end of the tube, and drawing his breath strongly to puff the dart forward with force, drew the needle into his throat. It entered the lungs, and in a few days killed him."*

Upon seeing this I fell into a great rage, without exactly knowing why. "This thing," I exclaimed, "is a contemptible falsehood—a poor hoax—the lees of the invention of some pitiable penny-a-liner—of some wretched concoctor of accidents in Cocaigne. These fellows, knowing the extravagant gullibility of the age, set their wits to work in the imagination of improbable possibilities—of odd accidents, as they term them; but to a reflecting intellect (like mine)," I added, in parentheses, putting my forefinger unconsciously to the side of my nose), "to a contemplative understanding such as I myself possess, it seems evident at once that the marvellous increase of late in these 'odd accidents' is by far the oddest accident of all. For my own part, I intend to believe nothing henceforward that has any thing of the 'singular' about it."

"Mein Gott, den, vat a vool you bees for dat!" replied one of the most remarkable voices I ever heard. At first I took it for a rumbling in my ears—such as a man sometimes experiences when getting very drunk—but, upon second thought, I considered the sound as more nearly resembling that which proceeds from an empty barrel beaten with a big stick; and, in fact, this I should have concluded it to be, but for the articulation of the syllables and words. I am by no means naturally nervous, and the very few glasses of Lafitte which I had sipped served to embolden me a little, so that I felt nothing of trepidation, but merely uplifted my eyes with a leisurely movement, and looked carefully around the room for the intruder. I could not, however, perceive any one at all.

"Humph!" resumed the voice, as I continued my survey, "you mus pe so dronk as de pig, den, for not zee me as I zit here at your zide."

Hereupon I bethought me of looking immediately before my nose, and there, sure enough, confronting me at the table sat a personage nondescript, although not altogether indescribable. His body was a wine-pipe, or a rum-puncheon, or something of that character, and had a truly Falstaffian air. In its nether extremity were inserted two kegs, which seemed to answer all the purposes of legs. For arms there dangled from the upper portion of the carcass two tolerably long bottles, with the necks outward for hands. All the head that I saw the monster possessed of was like a Hessian canteen which resembles a large snuff-box with a hole in the middle of the lid. This canteen (with a funnel on its top, like a cavalier cap slouched over the eyes) was set on edge upon the puncheon, with the hole toward myself; and through this hole, which seemed puckered up like the mouth of a very precise old maid, the creature was emitting certain rumbling and grumbling noises which he evidently intended for intelligible talk.

"I zay," said he, "you mos pe dronk as de pig, vor zit dare and not zee me zit ere; and I zay, doo, you most pe pigger vool as de goose, vor to dispelief vat iz print in de print. 'Tis de troof —dat it iz—eberry vord ob it."

"Who are you, pray?" said I, with much dignity, although

somewhat puzzled; "how did you get here? and what is it you are talking about?"

"As vor ow I com'd ere," replied the figure, "dat iz none of your pizzness; and as vor vat I be talking apout, I be talk apout vat I tink proper; and as vor who I be, vy dat is de very ting I com'd here for to let you zee for yourzelf."

"You are a drunken vagabond," said I, "and I shall ring the bell and order my footman to kick you into the street."

"He! he! he!" said the fellow, "hu! hu! hu! dat you can't do."

"Can't do!" said I, "what do you mean?—I can't do what?"

"Ring de pell," he replied, attempting a grin with his little villainous mouth.

Upon this I made an effort to get up, in order to put my threat into execution; but the ruffian just reached across the table very deliberately, and hitting me a tap on the forehead with the neck of one of the long bottles, knocked me back into the arm-chair from which I had half arisen. I was utterly astounded; and, for a moment, was quite at a loss what to do. In the meantime, he continued his talk.

"You zee," said he, "it iz te bess vor zit still; and now you shall know who I pe. Look at me! zee! I am te *Angel ov te Odd.*"

"And odd enough, too," I ventured to reply; "but I was always under the impression that an angel had wings."

"Te wing!" he cried, highly incensed, "vat I pe do mit te wing? Mein Gott! do you take me vor a shicken?"

"No—oh, no!" I replied, much alarmed, "you are no chicken—certainly not."

"Well, den, zit still and pehabe yourself, or I'll rap you again mid me vist. It iz te shicken ab te wing, und te owl ab te wing, und te imp ab de wing, and te headteuffel ab te wing. Te angel ab *not* te wing, and I am te *Angel ov te Odd.*"

"And your business with me at present is—is—"

"My pizzness!" ejaculated the thing, "vy vot a low-bred

puppy you mos pe vor to ask a gentleman und an angel apout his pizzness!"

This language was rather more than I could bear, even from an angel; so, plucking up courage, I seized a salt-cellar which lay within reach, and hurled it at the head of the intruder. Either he dodged, however, or my aim was inaccurate; for all I accomplished was the demolition of the crystal which protected the dial of the clock upon the mantel-piece. As for the Angel, he evinced his sense of my assault by giving me two or three hard consecutive raps upon the forehead as before. These reduced me at once to submission, and I am almost ashamed to confess that, either through pain or vexation, there came a few tears into my eyes.

"Mein Gott!" said the Angel of the Odd, apparently much softened at my distress; "mein Gott, te man is eder ferry dronk or ferry sorry. You mos not trink it so strong—you mos put de water in te wine. Here, trink dis, like a goot veller, und don't gry now—don't!"

Hereupon the Angel of the Odd replenished my goblet (which was about a third full of Port) with a colorless fluid that he poured from one of his hand bottles. I observed that these bottles had labels about their necks, and that these labels were inscribed "Kirschenwasser."

The considerate kindness of the Angel mollified me in no little measure; and, aided by the water with which he diluted my Port more than once, I at length regained sufficient temper to listen to his very extraordinary discourse. I cannot pretend to recount all that he told me, but I gleaned from what he said that he was the genius who presided over the *contretemps* of mankind, and whose business it was to bring about the *odd accidents* which are continually astonishing the skeptic. Once or twice, upon my venturing to express my total incredulity in respect to his pretensions, he grew very angry indeed, so that at length I considered it the wiser policy to say nothing at all, and let him have his own way. He talked on, therefore, at great length, while I merely leaned back in my chair with my eyes shut, and amused myself with munching raisins and filliping the stems about the room. But, by and by, the Angel suddenly construed this behavior of mine into contempt. He arose in a terrible passion, slouched his funnel down over his eyes, swore a vast oath, uttered a threat of some character which I did not precisely comprehend, and finally made me a low bow and departed, wishing me, in the language of the archbishop in "Gil-Blas," *"beaucoup de bonheur et un peu plus de bon sens."*

His departure afforded me relief. The *very* few glasses of Lafitte that I had sipped had the effect of rendering me drowsy, and I felt inclined to take a nap of some fifteen or twenty minutes, as is my custom after dinner. At six I had an appointment of consequence, which it was quite indispensable that I should keep. The policy of insurance for my dwelling-house had expired the day before; and, some dispute having arisen, it was agreed that, at six, I should meet the board of directors of the company and settle the terms of a renewal. Glancing upward at the clock on the mantel-piece (for I felt too drowsy to take out my watch), I had the pleasure to find that I had still twenty-five minutes to spare. It was half-past five; I could easily walk to the insurance office in five minutes; and my usual siestas had never been known to exceed five and twenty. I felt sufficiently safe, therefore, and composed myself to my slumbers forthwith.

Having completed them to my satisfaction, I again looked toward the time-piece, and was half inclined to believe in the possibility of odd accidents when I found that, instead of my ordinary fifteen or twenty minutes, I had been dozing only three; for it still wanted seven and twenty of the appointed hour. I betook myself again to my nap, and at length a second time awoke, when, to my utter amazement, it *still* wanted twenty-seven minutes of six. I jumped up to examine the clock, and found that it had ceased running. My watch informed me that it was half-past seven; and, of course, having slept two hours, I was too late for my appointment. "It will make no difference," I said; "I can call at the office in the morning and apologize; in the meantime

what can be the matter with the clock?" Upon examining it I discovered that one of the raisin-stems which I had been filliping about the room during the discourse of the Angel of the Odd had flown through the fractured crystal, and lodging, singularly enough, in the key-hole, with an end projecting outward, had thus arrested the revolution of the minute-hand.

"Ah!" said I; "I see how it is. This thing speaks for itself. A natural accident, such as *will* happen now and then!"

I gave the matter no further consideration, and at my usual hour retired to bed. Here, having placed a candle upon a reading-stand at the bed-head, and having made an attempt to peruse some pages of the "Omnipresence of the Deity," I unfortunately fell asleep in less than twenty seconds, leaving the light burning as it was.

My dreams were terrifically disturbed by visions of the Angel of the Odd. Methought he stood at the foot of the couch, drew aside the curtains, and, in the hollow, detestable tones of a rum-puncheon, menaced me with the bitterest vengeance for the contempt with which I had treated him. He concluded a long harangue by taking off his funnel-cap, inserting the tube into my gullet, and thus deluging me with an ocean of Kirschenwasser, which he poured, in a continuous flood, from one of the long-necked bottles that stood him instead of an arm. My agony was at length insufferable, and I awoke just in time to perceive that a rat had run off with the lighted candle from the stand, but *not* in season to prevent his making his escape with it through the hole. Very soon, a strong suffocating odor assailed my nostrils; the house, I clearly perceived, was on fire. In a few minutes the blaze broke forth with violence, and in an incredibly brief period the entire building was wrapped in flames. All egress from my chamber, except through a window, was cut off. The crowd, however, quickly procured and raised a long ladder. By means of this I was descending rapidly, and in apparent safety, when a huge hog, about whose rotund stomach, and indeed about whose whole air and physiognomy, there was something which reminded me of the Angel of the Odd—when this hog, I say, which hitherto had been quietly slumbering in the mud, took it suddenly into his head that his left shoulder needed scratching, and could find no more convenient rubbing-post than that afforded by the foot of the ladder. In an instant I was precipitated, and had the misfortune to fracture my arm.

This accident, with the loss of my insurance, and with the more serious loss of my hair—the whole of which had been singed off by the fire—predisposed me to serious impressions, so that, finally, I made up my mind to take a wife. There was a rich widow disconsolate for the loss of her seventh husband, and to her wounded spirit I offered the balm of my vows. She yielded a reluctant consent to my prayers. I knelt at her feet in gratitude and adoration. She blushed, and bowed her luxuriant tresses into close contact with those supplied me, temporarily, by Grandjean. I know not how the entanglement took place, but so it was. I arose with a shining pate, wigless; she in disdain and wrath, half buried in alien hair. Thus ended my hopes of the widow by an accident which could not have been anticipated, to be sure, but which the natural sequence of events had brought about.

Without despairing, however, I undertook the siege of a less implacable heart. The fates were again propitious for a brief period; but again a trivial incident interfered. Meeting my betrothed in an avenue thronged with the *élite* of the city, I was hastening to greet her with one of my best-considered bows, when a small particle of some foreign matter, lodging in the corner of my eye, rendered me, for the moment, completely blind. Before I could recover my sight, the lady of my love had disappeared—irreparably affronted at what she chose to consider my premeditated rudeness in passing her by ungreeted. While I stood bewildered at the suddenness of this accident (which might have happened, nevertheless, to any one under the sun), and while I still continued incapable of sight, I was accosted by the Angel of the Odd, who proffered me his aid with a civility which I had no reason to expect. He examined my disordered eye with much gentleness and skill, informed me that I had a drop in it, and (whatever a "drop" was) took it out, and afforded me relief.

I now considered it high time to die (since fortune had so determined to persecute me) and accordingly made my way to the nearest river. Here, divesting myself of my clothes (for there is no reason why we cannot die as we were born), I threw myself headlong into the current; the sole witness of my fate being a solitary crow that had been seduced into the eating of brandy-saturated corn, and so had staggered away from his fellows. No sooner had I entered the water than this bird took it into its head to fly away with the most indispensable portion of my apparel. Postponing, therefore, for the present, my suicidal design, I just slipped my nether extremities into the sleeves of my coat, and betook myself to a pursuit of the felon with all the nimbleness which the case required and its circumstances would admit. But my evil destiny attended me still. As I ran at full speed, with my nose up in the atmosphere, and intent only upon the purloiner of my property, I suddenly perceived that my feet rested no longer upon *terra firma;* the fact is, I had thrown myself over a precipice, and should inevitably have been dashed to pieces but for my good fortune in grasping the end of a long guide-rope, which depended from a passing balloon.

As soon as I sufficiently recovered my senses to comprehend the terrific predicament in which I stood or rather hung, I exerted all the power of my lungs to make that predicament known to the aeronaut overhead. But for a long time I exerted myself in vain. Either the fool could not, or the villain would not perceive me. Meantime the machine rapidly soared, while my strength even more rapidly failed. I was soon upon the point of resigning myself to my fate, and dropping quietly into the sea, when my spirits were suddenly revived by hearing a hollow voice from above, which seemed to be lazily humming an opera air. Looking up, I perceived the Angel of the Odd. He was leaning with his arms folded, over the rim of the car; and with a pipe in his mouth, at which he puffed leisurely, seemed to be upon excellent terms with himself and the universe. I was too much exhausted to speak, so I merely regarded him with an imploring air.

For several minutes, although he looked me full in the face, he said nothing. At length removing carefully his meerschaum from the right to the left corner of his mouth, he condescended to speak.

"Who pe you," he asked, "und what der teuffel you pe do dare?"

To this piece of impudence, cruelty, and affectation, I could reply only by ejaculating the monosyllable, "Help!"

"Elp!" echoed the ruffian—"not I. Dare iz te pottle—elp yourself, und pe tam'd!"

With these words he let fall a heavy bottle of Kirschenwasser which, dropping precisely upon the crown of my head, caused me to imagine that my brains were entirely knocked out. Impressed with this idea, I was about to relinquish my hold and give up the ghost with a good grace, when I was arrested by the cry of the Angel, who bade me hold on.

"Old on!" he said; "don't pe in te urry—don't. Will you pe take de odder pottle, or ave you pe got zober yet and come to your zenzes?"

I made haste, hereupon, to nod my head twice—once in the negative, meaning thereby that I would prefer not taking the other bottle at present—and once in the affirmative, intending thus to imply that I *was* sober and *had* positively come to my senses. By these means I somewhat softened the Angel.

"Und you pelief, ten," he inquired, "at te last? You pelief, ten, in te possibility of te odd?"

I again nodded my head in assent.

"Und you ave pelief in *me,* te Angel ov te Odd?"

I nodded again.

"Und you acknowledge tat you pe te blind dronk and te vool?"

I nodded once more.

"Put your right hand into your left hand preeches pocket, ten, in token ov your vull zubmizzion unto te Angel ov te Odd."

This thing, for very obvious reasons, I found it quite impossible to do. In the first place, my left arm had been broken in my fall from the ladder, and, therefore, had I let go my hold with the right hand, I must have let go altogether. In the second place, I could have no breeches until I came across the crow. I was therefore obliged, much to my regret, to shake my head in the negative—intending thus to give the Angel to understand that I found it inconvenient, just at that moment, to comply with his very reasonable demand! No sooner, however, had I ceased shaking my head than—

"Go to der teuffel, ten!" roared the Angel of the Odd.

In pronouncing these words, he drew a sharp knife across the guide-rope by which I was suspended, and as we then happened to be precisely over my own house (which, during my peregrinations, had been handsomely rebuilt), it so occurred that I tumbled headlong down the ample chimney and alit upon the dining-room hearth.

Upon coming to my senses (for the fall had very thoroughly stunned me), I found it about four o'clock in the morning. I lay outstretched where I had fallen from the balloon. My head grovelled in the ashes of an extinguished fire, while my feet reposed upon the wreck of a small table, overthrown, and amid the fragments of a miscellaneous dessert, intermingled with a newspaper, some broken glass and shattered bottles, and an empty jug of the Schiedam Kirschenwasser. Thus revenged himself the Angel of the Odd.

THE SELFISH GIANT

by Oscar Wilde

EVERY AFTERNOON, as they were coming from school, the children used to go and play in the Giant's garden.

It was a large lovely garden, with soft green grass. Here and there over the grass stood beautiful flowers like stars, and there were twelve peach-trees that in the springtime broke out into delicate blossoms of pink and pearl, and in the autumn bore rich fruit. The birds sat on the trees and sang so sweetly that the children used to stop their games in order to listen to them. "How happy we are here!" they cried to each other.

One day the Giant came back. He had been to visit his friend the Cornish ogre, and had stayed with him for seven years. After the seven years were over he had said all that he had to say, for his conversation was limited, and he determined to return to his own castle. When he arrived he saw the children playing in the garden.

"What are you doing there?" he cried in a very gruff voice, and the children ran away.

"My own garden is my own garden," said the Giant; "any

one can understand that, and I will allow nobody to play in it but myself." So he built a high wall all round it, and put up a notice-board:

```
TRESPASSERS
WILL BE
PROSECUTED
```

He was a very selfish giant.

The poor children had now nowhere to play. They tried to play on the road, but the road was very dusty and full of hard stones, and they did not like it. They used to wander round the high wall when their lessons were over, and talk about the beautiful garden inside. "How happy we were there," they said to each other.

Then the spring came, and all over the country there were little blossoms and little birds. Only in the garden of the Selfish Giant it was still winter. The birds did not care to sing in it, as there were no children, and the trees forgot to blossom. Once a beautiful flower put its head out from the grass, but when it saw the notice-board it was so sorry for the children that it slipped back into the ground again, and went off to sleep. The only people who were pleased were the Snow and the Frost. "Spring has forgotten this garden," they cried, "so we will live here all the year round." The Snow covered up the grass with her great white cloak, and the Frost painted all the trees silver. Then they invited the North Wind to stay with them, and he came. He was wrapped in furs, and he roared all day about the garden, and blew the chimney-pots down. "This is a delightful spot," he said; "we must ask the Hail on a visit." So the Hail came. Every day for three hours he rattled on the roof of the castle till he broke most of the slates, and then he ran round and round the garden as fast as he could go. He was dressed in grey, and his breath was like ice.

"I cannot understand why the spring is so late in coming," said the Selfish Giant, as he sat at the window and looked out at his cold white garden; "I hope there will be a change in the weather."

But the spring never came, nor the summer. The autumn gave golden fruit to every garden, but to the Giant's garden she gave none. "He is too selfish," she said. So it was always winter there, and the North Wind, and the Hail, and the Frost, and the Snow danced about through the trees.

One morning the Giant was lying awake in bed when he heard some lovely music. It sounded so sweet to his ears that he thought it must be the King's musicians passing by. It was really only a little linnet singing outside his window, but it was so long since he had heard a bird sing in his garden that it seemed to him to be the most beautiful music in the world. Then the Hail stopped dancing over his head, and the North Wind ceased roaring, and a delicious perfume came to him through the open casement. "I believe the spring has come at last," said the Giant, and he jumped out of bed and looked out.

What did he see?

He saw a most wonderful sight. Through a little hole in the wall the children had crept in, and they were sitting in the branches of the trees. In every tree that he could see there was a little child. And the trees were so glad to have the children back again that they had covered themselves with blossoms, and were waving their arms gently above the children's heads. The birds were flying about and twittering with delight, and the flowers were looking up through the green grass and laughing. It was a lovely scene, only in one corner it was still winter. It was the farthest corner of the garden, and in it was standing a little boy. He was so small that he could not reach up to the branches of the tree, and he was wandering all round it, crying bitterly. The poor tree was still quite covered with frost and snow, and the North Wind was blowing and roaring above it. "Climb up! little boy," said the Tree, and it bent its branches down as low as it could; but the boy was too tiny.

And the Giant's heart melted as he looked out. "How selfish I have been!" he said; "now I know why the spring would not come here. I will put that poor little boy on the top of the tree, and then I will knock down the wall, and my garden shall be the children's play-ground for ever and ever." He was really very sorry for what he had done.

So he crept down-stairs and opened the front door quite softly, and went out into the garden. But when the children saw him they were so frightened that they all ran away, and the garden became winter again. Only the little boy did not run, for his eyes were so full of tears that he did not see the Giant coming. And the Giant strode up behind him and took him gently in his hand, and put him up into the tree. And the tree broke at once into blossom, and the birds came and sang on it, and the little boy stretched out his two arms and flung them round the Giant's neck, and kissed him. And the other children, when they saw that the Giant was not wicked any longer, came running back, and with them came the spring. "It is your garden now, little children," said the Giant, and he took a great axe and knocked down the wall. And when the people were going to market at twelve o'clock they found the Giant playing with the children in the most beautiful garden they had ever seen.

All day long they played, and in the evening they came to the Giant to bid him good-bye.

"But where is your little companion?" he said, "the boy I put into the tree." The Giant loved him the best because he had kissed him.

"We don't know," answered the children; "he has gone away."

"You must tell him to be sure and come here to-morrow," said the Giant. But the children said that they did not know where he lived, and had never seen him before; and the Giant felt very sad.

Every afternoon, when school was over, the children came and played with the Giant. But the little boy whom the Giant loved was never seen again. The Giant was very kind to all the children, yet he longed for his first little friend, and often spoke of him. "How I would like to see him!" he used to say.

Years went over, and the Giant grew very old and feeble. He could not play about any more, so he sat in a huge armchair, and watched the children at their games, and admired his garden. "I have many beautiful flowers," he said; "but the children are the most beautiful flowers of all."

One winter morning he looked out of his window as he was dressing. He did not hate the winter now, for he knew that it was merely spring asleep, and that the flowers were resting.

Suddenly he rubbed his eyes in wonder, and looked and looked. It certainly was a marvellous sight. In the farthest corner of the garden was a tree quite covered with lovely white blossoms. Its branches were all golden, and silver fruit hung down from them, and underneath it stood the little boy he had loved.

Down-stairs ran the Giant in great joy, and out into the garden. He hastened across, and came near to the child. And when he came quite close his face grew red with anger, and he said, "Who hath dared to wound thee?" For on the palms of the child's hands were the prints of two nails, and the prints of two nails were on the little feet.

"Who hath dared to wound thee?" cried the Giant; "tell me, that I may take my big sword and slay him."

"Nay!" answered the child; "but these are the wounds of Love."

"Who art thou?" said the Giant, and a strange awe fell on him, and he knelt before the little child.

And the child smiled on the Giant, and said to him, "You let me play once in your garden; to-day you shall come with me to my garden, which is Paradise."

And when the children ran in that afternoon, they found the Giant lying dead under the tree, all covered with white blossoms.

THE LAST TRUMP

by Isaac Asimov

THE ARCHANGEL Gabriel was quite casual about the whole thing. Idly, he let the tip of one wing graze the planet Mars, which, being of mere matter, was unaffected by the contact.

He said, "It's a settled matter, Etheriel. There's nothing to be done about it now. The Day of Resurrection is due."

Etheriel, a very junior seraph who had been created not quite a thousand years earlier as men counted time, quivered so that distinct vortices appeared in the continuum. Ever since his creation, he had been in immediate charge of Earth and environs. As a job, it was a sinecure, a cubbyhole, a dead end, but through the centuries he had come to take a perverse pride in the world.

"But you'll be disrupting my world without notice."

"Not at all. Not at all. Certain passages occur in the Book of Daniel and in the Apocalypse of St. John which are clear enough."

"They are? Having been copied from scribe to scribe? I wonder if two words in a row are left unchanged."

"There are hints in the Rig-Veda, in the Confucian Analects—"

"Which are the property of isolated cultural groups which exist as a thin aristocracy—"

"The Gilgamesh Chronicle speaks out plainly."

"Much of the Gilgamesh Chronicle was destroyed with the library of Ashurbanipal sixteen hundred years, Earth-style, before my creation."

"There are certain features of the Great Pyramid and a pattern in the inlaid jewels of the Taj Mahal—"

"Which are so subtle that no man has ever rightly interpreted them."

Gabriel said wearily, "If you're going to object to everything, there's no use discussing the matter. In any case, *you* ought to know about it. In matters concerning Earth, you're omniscient."

"Yes, if I choose to be. I've had much to concern me here and investigating the possibilities of Resurrection did not, I confess, occur to me."

"Well, it should have. All the papers involved are in the files of the Council of Ascendants. You could have availed yourself of them at any time."

"I tell you all my time was needed here. You have no idea of the deadly efficiency of the Adversary on this planet. It took all my efforts to curb him, and even so—"

"Why, yes"—Gabriel stroked a comet as it passed—"he does seem to have won his little victories. I note as I let the interlocking factual pattern of this miserable little world flow through me that this is one of those setups with matter-energy equivalence."

"So it is," said Etheriel.

"And they are playing with it."

"I'm afraid so."

"Then what better time for ending the matter?"

"I'll be able to handle it, I assure you. Their nuclear bombs will not destroy them."

"I wonder. Well, now suppose you let me continue, Etheriel. The appointed moment approaches."

The seraph said stubbornly, "I would like to see the documents in the case."

"If you insist." The wording of an Act of Ascendancy appeared in glittering symbols against the deep black of the airless firmament.

Etheriel read aloud: "It is hereby directed by order of Council that the Archangel Gabriel, Serial number etcetera, etcetera (well, that's you, at any rate), will approach Planet, Class A, number G753990, hereinafter known as Earth, and on January 1, 1957, at 12:01 P.M., using local time values—" He finished reading in gloomy silence.

"Satisfied?"

"No, but I'm helpless."

Gabriel smiled. A trumpet appeared in space, in shape like an earthly trumpet, but its burnished gold extended from Earth to sun. It was raised to Gabriel's glittering beautiful lips.

"Can't you let me have a little time to take this up with the Council?" asked Etheriel desperately.

"What good would it do you? The act is countersigned by the Chief, and you know that an act countersigned by the Chief is absolutely irrevocable. And now, if you don't mind, it is almost the stipulated second and I want to be done with this as I have other matters of much greater moment on my mind. Would you step out of my way a little? Thank you."

Gabriel blew, and a clean, thin sound of perfect pitch and crystalline delicacy filled all the universe to the farthest star. As it sounded, there was a tiny moment of stasis as thin as the line separating past from future, and then the fabric of worlds collapsed upon itself and matter was gathered back into the primeval chaos from which it had once sprung at a word. The stars and nebulae were gone, and the cosmic dust, the sun, the planets, the moon; all, all, all except Earth itself, which spun as before in a universe now completely empty.

The Last Trump had sounded.

R. E. Mann (known to all who knew him simply as R.E.) eased himself into the offices of the Billikan Bitsies factory and stared somberly at the tall man (gaunt but with a certain faded elegance about his neat gray mustache) who bent intently over a sheaf of papers on his desk.

R.E. looked at his wristwatch, which still said 7:01, having ceased running at that time. It was Eastern standard time, of course; 12:01 P.M. Greenwich time. His dark brown eyes, staring sharply out over a pair of pronounced cheekbones, caught those of the other.

For a moment, the tall man stared at him blankly. Then he said, "Can I do anything for you?"

"Horatio J. Billikan, I presume? Owner of this place?"

"Yes."

"I'm R. E. Mann and I couldn't help but stop in when I finally found someone at work. Don't you know what today is?"

"Today?"

"It's Resurrection Day."

"Oh, that! I know it. I heard the blast. Fit to wake the dead. . . . That's rather a good one, don't you think?" He chuckled for a moment, then went on. "It woke me at seven in the morning. I nudged my wife. She slept through it, of course. I always said she would. 'It's the Last Trump, dear,' I said. Hortense, that's my wife, said, 'All right,' and went back to sleep. I bathed, shaved, dressed and came to work."

"But why?"

"Why not?"

"None of your workers have come in."

"No, poor souls. They'll take a holiday just at first. You've got to expect that. After all, it isn't every day that the world comes to an end. Frankly, it's just as well. It gives me a chance to straighten out my personal correspondence without interruptions. Telephone hasn't rung once."

He stood up and went to the window. "It's a great improvement. No blinding sun any more and the snow's gone.

The Last Trump

There's a pleasant light and a pleasant warmth. Very good arrangement. . . . But now, if you don't mind, I'm *rather* busy, so if you'll excuse me—"

A great, hoarse voice interrupted with a, "Just a minute, Horatio," and a gentleman, looking remarkably like Billikan in a somewhat craggier way, followed his prominent nose into the office and struck an attitude of offended dignity which was scarcely spoiled by the fact that he was quite naked. "May I ask why you've shut down Bitsies?"

Billikan looked faint. "Good Heavens," he said, "it's Father. Wherever did you come from?"

"From the graveyard," roared Billikan, Senior. "Where on Earth else? They're coming out of the ground there by the dozens. Every one of them naked. Women, too."

Billikan cleared his throat. "I'll get you some clothes, Father. I'll bring them to you from home."

"Never mind that. Business first. Business first."

R.E. came out of his musing. "Is everyone coming out of their graves at the same time, sir?"

He stared curiously at Billikan, Senior, as he spoke. The old man's appearance was one of robust age. His cheeks were furrowed but glowed with health. His age, R.E. decided, was exactly what it was at the moment of his death, but his body was as it should have been at that age if it functioned ideally.

Billikan, Senior, said, "No, sir, they are not. The newer graves are coming up first. Pottersby died five years before me and came up about five minutes after me. Seeing him made me decide to leave. I had had enough of him when . . . And that reminds me." He brought his fist down on the desk, a very solid fist. "There were no taxis, no busses. Telephones weren't working. I had to walk. I had to walk twenty miles."

"Like that?" asked his son in a faint and appalled voice.

Billikan, Senior, looked down upon his bare skin with casual approval. "It's warm. Almost everyone else is naked. . . . Anyway, son, I'm not here to make small talk. Why is the factory shut down?"

"It isn't shut down. It's a special occasion."

"Special occasion, my foot. You call union headquarters and tell them Resurrection Day isn't in the contract. Every worker is being docked for every minute he's off the job."

Billikan's lean face took on a stubborn look as he peered at his father. "I will not. Don't forget, now, you're no longer in charge of this plant. I am."

"Oh, you are? By what right?"

"By your will."

"All right. Now here I am and I void my will."

"You can't, Father. You're dead. You may not look dead, but I have witnesses. I have the doctor's certificate. I have receipted bills from the undertaker. I can get testimony from the pallbearers."

Billikan, Senior, stared at his son, sat down, placed his arm over the back of the chair, crossed his legs and said, "If it comes to that, we're all dead, aren't we? The world's come to an end, hasn't it?"

"But you've been declared legally dead and I haven't."

"Oh, we'll change that, son. There are going to be more of us than of you and votes count."

Billikan, Junior, tapped the desk firmly with the flat of his hand and flushed slightly. "Father, I hate to bring up this particular point, but you force me to. May I remind you that by now I am sure that Mother is sitting at home waiting for you; that she probably had to walk the streets—uh—naked, too; and that she probably isn't in a good humor."

Billikan, Senior, went ludicrously pale. "Good Heavens!"

"And you know she always wanted you to retire."

Billikan, Senior, came to a quick decision. "I'm not going home. Why, this is a nightmare. Aren't there any limits to this Resurrection business? It's—it's—it's sheer anarchy. There's such a thing as overdoing it. I'm just not going home."

At which point, a somewhat rotund gentleman with a smooth, pink face and fluffy white sideburns (much like pictures of Martin Van Buren) stepped in and said coldly, *"Good* day."

"Father," said Billikan, Senior.

"Grandfather," said Billikan, Junior.

Billikan, Grandsenior, looked at Billikan, Junior, with disapproval. "If you are my grandson," he said, "you've aged considerably and the change has not improved you."

Billikan, Junior, smiled with dyspeptic feebleness, and made no answer.

Billikan, Grandsenior, did not seem to require one. He said, "Now if you two will bring me up to date on the business, I will resume my managerial function."

There were two simultaneous answers, and Billikan, Grandsenior's, floridity waxed dangerously as he beat the ground peremptorily with an imaginary cane and barked a retort.

R.E. said, "Gentlemen."

He raised his voice. "Gentlemen!"

He shrieked at full lung-power, "GENTLEMEN!"

Conversation snapped off sharply and all turned to look at him. R.E.'s angular face, his oddly attractive eyes, his sardonic mouth seemed suddenly to dominate the gathering.

He said, "I don't understand this argument. What is it that you manufacture?"

"Bitsies," said Billikan, Junior.

"Which, I take it, are a packaged cereal breakfast food—"

"Teeming with energy in every golden, crispy flake—" cried Billikan, Junior.

"Covered with honey-sweet, crystalline sugar; a confection and a food—" growled Billikan, Senior.

"To tempt the most jaded appetite," roared Billikan, Grandsenior.

"Exactly," said R.E. "What appetite?"

They stared stolidly at him. "I beg your pardon," said Billikan, Junior.

"Are any of you hungry?" asked R.E. "I'm not."

"What is this fool maundering about?" demanded Billikan, Grandsenior, angrily. His invisible cane would have been prodding R.E. in the navel had it (the cane, not the navel) existed.

R.E. said, "I'm trying to tell you that no one will ever eat again. It is the hereafter, and food is unnecessary."

The expressions on the faces of the Billikans needed no interpretation. It was obvious that they had tried their own appetites and found them wanting.

Billikan, Junior, said ashenly, "Ruined!"

Billikan, Grandsenior, pounded the floor heavily and noiselessly with his imaginary cane. "This is confiscation of property without due process of law. I'll sue. I'll sue."

"Quite unconstitutional," agreed Billikan, Senior.

"If you can find anyone to sue, I wish you all good fortune," said R.E. agreeably. "And now if you'll excuse me I think I'll walk toward the graveyard."

He put his hat on his head and walked out the door.

Etheriel, his vortices quivering, stood before the glory of a six-winged cherub.

The cherub said, "If I understand you, your particular universe has been dismantled."

"Exactly."

"Well, surely, now, you don't expect *me* to set it up again?"

"I don't expect you to do anything," said Etheriel, "except to arrange an appointment for me with the Chief."

The cherub gestured his respect instantly at hearing the word. Two wing-tips covered his feet, two his eyes and two his mouth. He restored himself to normal and said, "The Chief is quite busy. There are a myriad score of matters for him to decide."

"Who denies that? I merely point out that if matters stand as they are now, there will have been a universe in which Satan will have won the final victory."

"Satan?"

"It's the Hebrew word for Adversary," said Etheriel impatiently. "I could say Ahriman, which is the Persian word. In any case, I mean the Adversary."

The cherub said, "But what will an interview with the

Chief accomplish? The document authorizing the Last Trump was countersigned by the Chief, and you know that it is irrevocable for that reason. The Chief would never limit his own omnipotence by canceling a word he had spoken in his official capacity."

"Is that final? You will not arrange an appointment?"

"I cannot."

Etheriel said, "In that case, I shall seek out the Chief without one. I will invade the Primum Mobile. If it means my destruction, so be it." He gathered his energies. . . .

The cherub murmured in horror, "Sacrilege!" and there was a faint gathering of thunder as Etheriel sprang upward and was gone.

R. E. Mann passed through the crowding streets and grew used to the sight of people bewildered, disbelieving, apathetic, in makeshift clothing or, usually, none at all.

A girl, who looked about twelve, leaned over an iron gate, one foot on a crossbar, swinging it to and fro, and said as he passed, "Hello, mister."

"Hello," said R.E. The girl was dressed. She was not one of the—uh—returnees.

The girl said, "We got a new baby in our house. She's a sister I once had. Mommy is crying and they sent me here."

R.E. said, "Well, well," passed through the gate and up the paved walk to the house, one with modest pretensions to middle-class gentility. He rang the bell, obtained no answer, opened the door and walked in.

He followed the sound of sobbing and knocked at an inner door. A stout man of about fifty with little hair and a comfortable supply of cheek and chin looked out at him with mingled astonishment and resentment.

"Who are you?"

R.E. removed his hat. "I thought I might be able to help. Your little girl outside—"

A woman looked up at him hopelessly from a chair by a

double bed. Her hair was beginning to gray. Her face was puffed and unsightly with weeping and the veins stood out bluely on the back of her hands. A baby lay on the bed, plump and naked. It kicked its feet languidly and its sightless baby eyes turned aimlessly here and there.

"This is my baby," said the woman. "She was born twenty-three years ago in this house and she died when she was ten days old in this house. I wanted her back so much."

"And now you have her," said R.E.

"But it's too late," cried the woman vehemently. "I've had three other children. My oldest girl is married; my son is in the army. I'm too old to have a baby now. And even if—even if—"

Her features worked in a heroic effort to keep back the tears and failed.

Her husband said with flat tonelessness, "It's not a real baby. It doesn't cry. It doesn't soil itself. It won't take milk. What will we do? It'll never grow. It'll always be a baby."

R.E. shook his head. "I don't know," he said. "I'm afraid I can do nothing to help."

Quietly he left. Quietly he thought of the hospitals. Thousands of babies must be appearing at each one.

Place them in racks, he thought, sardonically. Stack them like cordwood. They need no care. Their little bodies are merely each the custodian of an indestructible spark of life.

He passed two little boys of apparently equal chronological age, perhaps ten. Their voices were shrill. The body of one glistened white in the sunless light so he was a returnee. The other was not. R.E. paused to listen.

The bare one said, "I had scarlet fever."

A spark of envy at the other's claim to notoriety seemed to enter the clothed one's voice. "Gee."

"That's why I died."

"Gee. Did they use pensillun or auromysun?"

"What?"

"They're medicines."

"I never heard of them."

"Boy, you never heard of *much*."

"I know as much as *you*."

"Yeah? Who's President of the United States?"

"Warren Harding, that's who."

"You're crazy. It's Eisenhower."

"Who's he?"

"Ever see television?"

"What's that?"

The clothed boy hooted earsplittingly. "It's something you turn on and see comedians, movies, cowboys, rocket rangers, anything you want."

"Let's see it."

There was a pause and the boy from the present said, "It ain't working."

The other boy shrieked his scorn. "You mean it ain't never worked. You made it all up."

R.E. shrugged and passed on.

The crowds thinned as he left town and neared the cemetery. Those who were left were all walking into town, all were nude.

A man stopped him; a cheerful man with pinkish skin and white hair who had the marks of pince-nez on either side of the bridge of his nose, but no glasses to go with them.

"Greetings, friend."

"Hello," said R.E.

"You're the first man with clothing that I've seen. You were alive when the trumpet blew, I suppose."

"Yes, I was."

"Well, isn't this great? Isn't this joyous and delightful? Come rejoice with me."

"You like this, do you?" said R.E.

"*Like it?* A pure and radiant joy fills me. We are surrounded by the light of the first day; the light that glowed softly and serenely before sun, moon and stars were made. (You know your Genesis, of course.) There is the comfortable warmth that must have been one of the highest blisses of Eden; not enervating heat or assaulting cold. Men and women walk the streets unclothed and are not ashamed. All is well, my friend, all is well."

R.E. said, "Well, it's a fact that I haven't seemed to mind the feminine display all about."

"Naturally not," said the other. "Lust and sin as we remember it in our earthly existence no longer exists. Let me introduce myself, friend, as I was in earthly times. My name on Earth was Winthrop Hester. I was born in 1812 and died in 1884 as we counted time then. Through the last forty years of my life I labored to bring my little flock to the Kingdom and I go now to count the ones I have won."

R.E. regarded the ex-minister solemnly, "Surely there has been no Judgment yet."

"Why not? The Lord sees within a man and in the same instant that all things of the world ceased, all men were judged and we are the saved."

"There must be a great many saved."

"On the contrary, my son, those saved are but as a remnant."

"A pretty large remnant. As near as I can make out, everyone's coming back to life. I've seen some pretty unsavory characters back in town as alive as you are."

"Last-minute repentance—"

"*I* never repented."

"Of what, my son?"

"Of the fact that I never attended church."

Winthrop Hester stepped back hastily. "Were you ever baptized?"

"Not to my knowledge."

Winthrop Hester trembled. "Surely you believe in God?"

"Well," said R.E., "I believed a lot of things about Him that would probably startle you."

Winthrop Hester turned and hurried off in great agitation.

In what remained of his walk to the cemetery (R.E. had no way of estimating time, nor did it occur to him to try) no one else stopped him. He found the cemetery itself all but empty, its trees and grass gone (it occurred to him that there was nothing green in the world; the ground everywhere was a hard, featureless, grainless gray; the sky a luminous white), but its headstones still standing.

On one of these sat a lean and furrowed man with long, black hair on his head and a mat of it, shorter, though more impressive, on his chest and upper arms.

He called out in a deep voice, "Hey, there, you!"

R.E. sat down on a neighboring headstone. "Hello."

Black-hair said, "Your clothes don't look right. What year was it when it happened?"

"1957."

"I died in 1807. Funny! I expected to be one pretty hot boy right about now, with the 'tarnal flames shooting up my innards."

"Aren't you coming along to town?" asked R.E.

"My name's Zeb," said the ancient. "That's short for Zebulon, but Zeb's good enough. What's the town like? Changed some, I reckon?"

"It's got nearly a hundred thousand people in it."

Zeb's mouth yawned somewhat. "Go on. Might nigh bigger'n Philadelphia. . . . You're making fun."

"Philadelphia's got—" R.E. paused. Stating the figure would do him no good. Instead, he said, "The town's grown in a hundred fifty years, you know."

"Country, too?"

"Forty-eight states," said R.E. "All the way to the Pacific."

"No!" Zeb slapped his thigh in delight and then winced at the unexpected absence of rough homespun to take up the worst of the blow. "I'd head out west if I wasn't needed here. Yes, sir." His face grew lowering and his thin lips took on a definite grimness. "I'll stay right here, where I'm needed."

"Why are you needed?"

The explanation came out briefly, bitten off hard. "Injuns!"

"Indians?"

"Millions of 'em. First the tribes we fought and licked and then tribes who ain't never seen a white man. They'll all come back to life. I'll need my old buddies. You city fellers ain't no good at it. . . . Ever seen an Injun?"

R.E. said, "Not around here lately, no."

Zeb looked his contempt, and tried to spit to one side but found no saliva for the purpose. He said, "You better git back to the city, then. After a while, it ain't going to be safe nohow round here. Wish I had my musket."

R.E. rose, thought a moment, shrugged and faced back to the city. The headstone he had been sitting upon collapsed as he rose, falling into a powder of gray stone that melted into the featureless ground. He looked about. Most of the headstones were gone. The rest would not last long. Only the one under Zeb still looked firm and strong.

R.E. began the walk back. Zeb did not turn to look at him. He remained waiting quietly and calmly—for Indians.

Etheriel plunged through the heavens in reckless haste. The eyes of the Ascendants were on him, he knew. From late-born seraph, through cherubs and angels, to the highest archangel, they must be watching.

Already he was higher than any Ascendant, uninvited, had ever been before and he waited for the quiver of the Word that would reduce his vortices to non-existence.

But he did not falter. Through non-space and non-time, he plunged toward union with the Primum Mobile; the seat that encompassed all that Is, Was, Would Be, Had Been, Could Be and Might Be.

And as he thought that, he burst through and was part of it, his being expanding so that momentarily he, too, was part of the All. But then it was mercifully veiled from his senses, and the Chief was a still, small voice within him, yet all the more impressive in its infinity for all that.

"My son," the voice said, "I know why you have come."

"Then help me, if that be your will."

"By my own will," said the Chief, "an act of mine is irrevocable. All your mankind, my son, yearned for life. All feared death. All evolved thoughts and dreams of life unending. No two groups of men; no two single men; evolved the same afterlife, but all wished life. I was petitioned that I might grant the common denominator of all these wishes—life unending. I did so."

"No servant of yours made that request."

"The Adversary did, my son."

Etheriel trailed his feeble glory in dejection and said in a low voice, "I am dust in your sight and unworthy to be in your presence, yet I must ask a question. Is then the Adversary your servant also?"

"Without him I can have no other," said the Chief, "for what then is Good but the eternal fight against Evil?"

And in that fight, thought Etheriel, I have lost.

R.E. paused in sight of town. The buildings were crumbling. Those that were made of wood were already heaps of rubble. R.E. walked to the nearest such heap and found the wooden splinters powdery and dry.

He penetrated deeper into town and found the brick buildings still standing, but there was an ominous roundness to the edges of the bricks, a threatening flakiness.

"They won't last long," said a deep voice, "but there is this consolation, if consolation it be; their collapse can kill no one."

R.E. looked up in surprise and found himself face to face with a cadaverous Don Quixote of a man, lantern-jawed, sunken-cheeked. His eyes were sad and his brown hair was lank and straight. His clothes hung loosely and skin showed clearly through various rents.

"My name," said the man, "is Richard Levine. I was a professor of history once—before this happened."

"You're wearing clothes," said R.E. "You're not one of those resurrected."

"No, but that mark of distinction is vanishing. Clothes are going."

R.E. looked at the throngs that drifted past them, moving slowly and aimlessly like motes in a sunbeam. Vanishingly few wore clothes. He looked down at himself and noticed for the first time that the seam down the length of each trouser leg had parted. He pinched the fabric of his jacket between thumb and forefinger and the wool parted and came away easily.

"I guess you're right," said R.E.

"If you'll notice," went on Levine, "Mellon's Hill is flattening out."

R.E. turned to the north where ordinarily the mansions of the aristocracy (such aristocracy as there was in town) studded the slopes of Mellon's Hill, and found the horizon nearly flat.

Levine said, "Eventually, there'll be nothing but flatness, featurelessness, nothingness—and us."

"And Indians," said R.E. "There's a man outside of town waiting for Indians and wishing he had a musket."

"I imagine," said Levine, "the Indians will give no trouble. There is no pleasure in fighting an enemy that cannot be killed or hurt. And even if that were not so, the lust for battle would be gone, as are all lusts."

"Are you sure?"

"I am positive. Before all this happened, although you may not think it to look at me, I derived much harmless pleasure in a consideration of the female figure. Now, with the unexampled opportunities at my disposal, I find myself irritatingly uninterested. No, that is wrong. I am not even irritated at my uninterest."

R.E. looked up briefly at the passers-by. "I see what you mean."

"The coming of Indians here," said Levine, "is nothing compared with the situation in the Old World. Early during the Resurrection, Hitler and his Wehrmacht must have come back to life and must now be facing and intermingled with Stalin and the Red Army all the way from Berlin to Stalingrad. To complicate the situation, the Kaisers and Czars will arrive. The men at Verdun and the Somme are back in the old battlegrounds. Napoleon and his marshals are scattered over western Europe. And Mohammed must be back to see what following ages have made of Islam, while the Saints and Apostles consider the paths of Christianity. And even the Mongols, poor things, the Khans from Temujin to Aurangzeb, must be wandering the steppes helplessly, longing for their horses."

"As a professor of history," said R.E., "you must long to be there and observe."

"How could I be there? Every man's position on Earth is restricted to the distance he can walk. There are no machines of any kind, and, as I have just mentioned, no horses. And what would I find in Europe anyway? Apathy, I think! As here."

A soft plopping sound caused R.E. to turn around. The wing of a neighboring brick building had collapsed in dust. Portions of bricks lay on either side of him. Some must have hurtled through him without his being aware of it. He looked about. The heaps of rubble were less numerous. Those that remained were smaller in size.

He said, "I met a man who thought we had all been judged and are in Heaven."

"Judged?" said Levine. "Why, yes, I imagine we are. We face eternity now. We have no universe left, no outside phenomena, no emotions, no passions. Nothing but ourselves and thought. We face an eternity of introspection, when all through history we have never known what to do with ourselves on a rainy Sunday."

"You sound as though the situation bothers you."

"It does more than that. The Dantean conceptions of Inferno were childish and unworthy of the Divine imagination: fire and torture. Boredom is much more subtle. The inner torture of a mind unable to escape itself in any way, condemned to fester in its own exuding mental pus for all time, is much more fitting. Oh, yes, my friend, we have been judged, and condemned, too, and this is not Heaven, but hell."

And Levine rose with shoulders drooping dejectedly, and walked away.

R.E. gazed thoughtfully about and nodded his head. He was satisfied.

The self-admission of failure lasted but an instant in Etheriel, and then, quite suddenly, he lifted his being as brightly and highly as he dared in the presence of the Chief and his glory was a tiny dot of light in the infinite Primum Mobile.

"If it be your will, then," he said. "I do not ask you to defeat your will but to fulfill it."

"In what way, my son?"

"The document, approved by the Council of Ascendants and signed by yourself, authorizes the Day of Resurrection at a specific time of a specific day of the year 1957 as Earthmen count time."

"So it did."

"But the year 1957 is unqualified. What then is 1957? To the dominant culture on Earth the year was A.D. 1957. That is true. Yet from the time you breathed existence into Earth and its universe there have passed 5,960 years. Based on the internal evidence you created within that universe, nearly four billion years have passed. Is the year, *unqualified,* then 1957, 5960, or 4000000000?

"Nor is that all," Etheriel went on. "The year A.D. 1957 is the year 7464 of the Byzantine era, 5716 by the Jewish calendar. It is 2708 A.U.C., that is, the 2,708th year since the founding of Rome, if we adopt the Roman calendar. It is the year 1375 in the Mohammedan calendar, and the hundred eightieth year of the independence of the United States.

"Humbly I ask then if it does not seem to you that a year referred to as 1957 alone and without qualification has no meaning."

The Chief's still small voice said, "I have always known this, my son; it was you who had to learn."

"Then," said Etheriel, quivering luminously with joy, "let

the very letter of your will be fulfilled and let the Day of Resurrection fall in 1957, but only when all the inhabitants of Earth unanimously agree that a certain year shall be numbered 1957 and none other."

"So let it be," said the Chief, and this Word re-created Earth and all it contained, together with the sun and moon and all the hosts of Heaven.

It was 7 A.M. on January 1, 1957, when R. E. Mann awoke with a start. The very beginnings of a melodious note that ought to have filled all the universe had sounded and yet had not sounded.

For a moment, he cocked his head as though to allow understanding to flow in, and then a trifle of rage crossed his face to vanish again. It was but another battle.

He sat down at his desk to compose the next plan of action. People already spoke of calendar reform and it would have to be stimulated. A new era must begin with December 2, 1944, and someday a new year 1957 would come; 1957 of the Atomic Era, acknowledged as such by all the world.

A strange light shone on his head as thoughts passed through his more-than-human mind and the shadow of Ahriman on the wall seemed to have small horns at either temple.

A VERY OLD MAN WITH ENORMOUS WINGS

by Gabriel García Márquez

Translated by Gregory Rabassa

A Tale for Children

ON THE THIRD DAY of rain they had killed so many crabs inside the house that Pelayo had to cross his drenched courtyard and throw them into the sea, because the newborn child had a temperature all night and they thought it was due to the stench. The world had been sad since Tuesday. Sea and sky were a single ash-gray thing and the sands of the beach, which on March nights glimmered like powdered light, had become a stew of mud and rotten shellfish. The light was so weak at noon that when Pelayo was coming back to the house after throwing away the crabs, it was hard for him to see what it was that was moving and groaning in the rear of the courtyard. He had to go very close to see that it was an old man, a very old man, lying face down in the mud, who, in spite of his tremendous efforts, couldn't get up, impeded by his enormous wings.

Frightened by that nightmare, Pelayo ran to get Elisenda, his wife, who was putting compresses on the sick child, and he took her to the rear of the courtyard. They both looked at the fallen body with mute stupor. He was dressed like a ragpicker. There were only a few faded hairs left on his bald skull and very few teeth in his mouth, and his pitiful condition of a drenched great-grandfather had taken away any sense of grandeur he might have had. His huge buzzard wings, dirty and half-plucked, were forever entangled in the mud. They looked at him so long and so closely that Pelayo and Elisenda very soon overcame their surprise and in the end found him familiar. Then they dared speak to him, and he answered in an incomprehensible dialect with a strong sailor's voice. That was how they skipped over the inconvenience of the wings and quite intelligently concluded that he was a lonely castaway from some foreign ship wrecked by the storm. And yet, they called in a neighbor woman who knew everything about life and death to see him, and all she needed was one look to show them their mistake.

"He's an angel," she told them. "He must have been coming for the child, but the poor fellow is so old that the rain knocked him down."

On the following day everyone knew that a flesh-and-blood angel was held captive in Pelayo's house. Against the judgment of the wise neighbor woman, for whom angels in those times were the fugitive survivors of a celestial conspiracy, they did not have the heart to club him to death. Pelayo watched over him all afternoon from the kitchen, armed with his bailiff's club, and before going to bed he dragged him out of the mud and locked him up with the hens in the wire chicken coop. In the middle of the night, when the rain stopped, Pelayo and Elisenda were still killing crabs. A short time afterward the child woke up without a fever and with a desire to eat. Then they felt magnanimous and decided to put the angel on a raft with fresh water and pro-

visions for three days and leave him to his fate on the high seas. But when they went out into the courtyard with the first light of dawn, they found the whole neighborhood in front of the chicken coop having fun with the angel, without the slightest reverence, tossing him things to eat through the openings in the wire as if he weren't a supernatural creature but a circus animal.

Father Gonzaga arrived before seven o'clock, alarmed at the strange news. By that time onlookers less frivolous than those at dawn had already arrived and they were making all kinds of conjectures concerning the captive's future. The simplest among them thought that he should be named mayor of the world. Others of sterner mind felt that he should be promoted to the rank of five-star general in order to win all wars. Some visionaries hoped that he could be put to stud in order to implant on earth a race of winged wise men who could take charge of the universe. But Father Gonzaga, before becoming a priest, had been a robust woodcutter. Standing by the wire, he reviewed his catechism in an instant and asked them to open the door so that he could take a close look at that pitiful man who looked more like a huge decrepit hen among the fascinated chickens. He was lying in a corner drying his open wings in the sunlight among the fruit peels and breakfast leftovers that the early risers had thrown him. Alien to the impertinences of the world, he only lifted his antiquarian eyes and murmured something in his dialect when Father Gonzaga went into the chicken coop and said good morning to him in Latin. The parish priest had his first suspicion of an imposter when he saw that he did not understand the language of God or know how to greet His ministers. Then he noticed that seen close up he was much too human: he had an unbearable smell of the outdoors, the back side of his wings was strewn with parasites and his main feathers had been mistreated by terrestrial winds, and nothing about him measured up to the proud dignity of angels. Then he came out of the chicken coop and in a brief sermon warned the curious against the risks of being ingenuous. He reminded them that the devil had the bad habit of making use of carnival tricks in order to confuse the unwary. He argued that if wings were not the essential element in determining the difference between a hawk and an airplane, they were even less so in the recognition of angels. Nevertheless, he promised to write a letter to his bishop so that the latter would write to his primate so that the latter would write to the Supreme Pontiff in order to get the final verdict from the highest courts.

His prudence fell on sterile hearts. The news of the captive angel spread with such rapidity that after a few hours the courtyard had the bustle of a marketplace and they had to call in troops with fixed bayonets to disperse the mob that was about to knock the house down. Elisenda, her spine all twisted from sweeping up so much marketplace trash, then got the idea of fencing in the yard and charging five cents admission to see the angel.

The curious came from far away. A traveling carnival arrived with a flying acrobat who buzzed over the crowd several times, but no one paid any attention to him because his wings were not those of an angel but, rather, those of a sidereal bat. The most unfortunate invalids on earth came in search of health: a poor woman who since childhood had been counting her heartbeats and had run out of numbers; a Portuguese man who couldn't sleep because the noise of the stars disturbed him; a sleepwalker who got up at night to undo the things he had done while awake; and many others with less serious ailments. In the midst of that shipwreck disorder that made the earth tremble, Pelayo and Elisenda were happy with fatigue, for in less than a week they had crammed their rooms with money and the line of pilgrims waiting their turn to enter still reached beyond the horizon.

The angel was the only one who took no part in his own act. He spent his time trying to get comfortable in his borrowed nest, befuddled by the hellish heat of the oil lamps and sacramental candles that had been placed along the wire. At first they tried to make him eat some mothballs, which, according to the wisdom of the wise neighbor woman, were the food prescribed for angels. But he turned them down, just as he turned down the papal lunches that the penitents brought him, and they never found out whether it was because he was an angel or because he was an old man that in the end he ate nothing but eggplant mush. His only supernatural virtue seemed to be patience. Especially during the first days, when the hens pecked at him, searching for the stellar parasites that proliferated in his wings, and the cripples pulled out feathers to touch their defective parts with, and even the most merciful threw stones at him, trying to get him to rise so they could see him standing. The only time they succeeded in arousing him was when they burned his side with an iron for branding steers, for he had been motionless for so many hours that they thought he was dead. He awoke with a start, ranting in his hermetic language and with tears in his eyes, and he flapped his wings a couple of times, which brought on a whirlwind of chicken dung and lunar dust and a gale of panic that did not seem to be of this world. Although many thought that his reaction had been one not of rage but of pain, from then on they were careful not to annoy him, because the majority understood that his passivity was not that of a hero taking his ease but that of a cataclysm in repose.

Father Gonzaga held back the crowd's frivolity with formulas of maidservant inspiration while awaiting the arrival of a final judgment on the nature of the captive. But the mail from Rome showed no sense of urgency. They spent their time finding out if the prisoner had a navel, if his dialect had any connection with Aramaic, how many times he could fit on the head of a pin, or whether he wasn't just a Norwegian with wings. Those meager letters might have come and gone until the end of time if a providential event had not put an end to the priest's tribulations.

It so happened that during those days, among so many other carnival attractions, there arrived in town the traveling show of the woman who had been changed into a spider for having disobeyed her parents. The admission to see her was not only less than the admission to see the angel, but people were permitted to ask her all manner of questions about her absurd state and to examine her up and down so that no one would ever doubt the truth of her horror. She was a frightful tarantula the size of a ram and with the head of a sad maiden. What was most heart-rending, however, was not her outlandish shape but the sincere affliction with which she recounted the details of her misfortune. While still practically a child she had sneaked out of her parents' house to go to a dance, and while she was coming back through the woods after having danced all night without permission, a fearful thunderclap rent the sky in two and through the crack came the lightning bolt of brimstone that changed her into a spider. Her only nourishment came from the meatballs that charitable souls chose to toss into her mouth. A spectacle like that, full of so much human truth and with such a fearful lesson, was bound to defeat without even trying that of a haughty angel who scarcely deigned to look at mortals. Besides, the few miracles attributed to the angel showed a certain mental disorder, like the blind man who didn't recover his sight but grew three new teeth, or the paralytic who didn't get to walk but almost won the lottery, and the leper whose sores sprouted sunflowers. Those consolation miracles, which were more like mocking fun, had already ruined the angel's reputation when the woman who had been changed into a spider finally crushed him completely. That was how Father Gonzaga was cured forever of his insomnia and Pelayo's courtyard went back to being as empty as during the time it had rained for three days and crabs walked through the bedrooms.

The owners of the house had no reason to lament. With the money they saved they built a two-story mansion with balconies and gardens and high netting so that crabs wouldn't get in during the winter, and with iron bars on the windows so that angels wouldn't get in. Pelayo also set up a rabbit warren close to town and gave up his job as bailiff for good, and Elisenda bought some satin pumps with high heels and many dresses of iridescent silk, the kind worn on Sunday by the most desirable women in those times. The chicken coop was the only thing that didn't receive any attention. If they washed it down with creolin and burned tears of myrrh inside it every so often, it was not in homage to the angel but to drive away the dungheap stench that still hung everywhere like a ghost and was turning the new house into an old one. At first, when the child learned to walk, they were careful that he not get too close to the chicken coop. But then they began to lose their fears and got used to the smell, and before the child got his second teeth he'd gone inside the chicken coop to play, where the wires were falling apart. The angel was no less standoffish with him than with other mortals, but he tolerated the most ingenious infamies with the patience of a dog who had no illusions. They both came down with chicken pox at the same time. The doctor who took care of the child couldn't resist the temptation to listen to the angel's heart, and he found so much whistling in the heart and so many sounds in his kidneys that it seemed impossible for him to be alive. What surprised him most, however, was the logic of his wings. They seemed so natural on that completely human organism that he couldn't understand why other men didn't have them too.

When the child began school it had been some time since the sun and rain had caused the collapse of the chicken coop. The angel went dragging himself about here and there like a stray dying man. They would drive him out of the bedroom with a broom and a moment later find him in the kitchen. He seemed to be in so many places at the same time that they grew to think that he'd been duplicated, that he was reproducing himself all through the house, and the exasperated and unhinged Elisenda shouted that it was awful living in that hell full of angels. He could scarcely eat and his antiquarian eyes had also become so foggy that he went about bumping into posts. All he had left were the bare cannulae of his last feathers. Pelayo threw a blanket over him and extended him the charity of letting him sleep in the shed, and only then did they notice that he had a temperature at night, and was delirious with the tongue twisters of an old Norwegian. That was one of the few times they became alarmed, for they thought he was going to die and not even the wise neighbor woman had been able to tell them what to do with dead angels.

And yet he not only survived his worst winter, but seemed improved with the first sunny days. He remained motionless for several days in the farthest corner of the courtyard, where no one would see him, and at the beginning of December some large, stiff feathers began to grow on his wings, the feathers of a scarecrow, which looked more like another misfortune of decrepitude. But he must have known the reason for those changes, for he was quite careful that no one should notice them, that no one should hear the sea chanteys that he sometimes sang under the stars. One morning Elisenda was cutting some bunches of onions for lunch when a wind that seemed to come from the high seas blew into the kitchen. Then she went to the window and caught the angel in his first attempts at flight. They were so clumsy that his fingernails opened a furrow in the vegetable patch and he was on the point of knocking the shed down with the ungainly flapping that slipped on the light and couldn't get a grip on the air. But he did manage to gain altitude. Elisenda let out a sigh of relief, for herself and for him, when she saw him pass over the last houses, holding himself up in some way with the risky flapping of a senile vulture. She kept watching him even when she was through cutting the onions and she kept on watching until it was no longer possible for her to see him, because then he was no longer an annoyance in her life but an imaginary dot on the horizon of the sea.

PART II

Questionings

THE COP AND
THE ANTHEM

by O. Henry

ON HIS BENCH in Madison Square Soapy moved uneasily. When wild geese honk high of nights, and when women without sealskin coats grow kind to their husbands, and when Soapy moves uneasily on his bench in the park, you may know that winter is near at hand.

A dead leaf fell in Soapy's lap. That was Jack Frost's card. Jack is kind to the regular denizens of Madison Square, and gives fair warning of his annual call. At the corners of four streets he hands his pasteboard to the North Wind, footman of the mansion of All Outdoors, so that the inhabitants thereof may make ready.

Soapy's mind became cognizant of the fact that the time had come for him to resolve himself into a singular Committee of Ways and Means to provide against the coming rigor. And therefore he moved uneasily on his bench.

The hibernatorial ambitions of Soapy were not of the

highest. In them were no considerations of Mediterranean cruises, of soporific Southern skies or drifting in the Vesuvian Bay. Three months on the Island was what his soul craved. Three months of assured board and bed and congenial company, safe from Boreas and bluecoats, seemed to Soapy the essence of things desirable.

For years the hospitable Blackwell's had been his winter quarters. Just as his more fortunate fellow New Yorkers had bought their tickets to Palm Beach and the Riviera each winter, so Soapy had made his humble arrangements for his annual hegira to the Island. And now the time was come. On the previous night three Sabbath newspapers, distributed beneath his coat, about his ankles and over his lap, had failed to repulse the cold as he slept on his bench near the spurting fountain in the ancient square. So the Island loomed big and timely in Soapy's mind. He scorned the provisions made in the name of charity for the city's dependents. In Soapy's opinion the Law was more benign than Philanthropy. There was an endless round of institutions, municipal and eleemosynary, on which he might set out and receive lodging and food accordant with the simple life. But to one of Soapy's proud spirit the gifts of charity are encumbered. If not in coin you must pay in humiliation of spirit for every benefit received at the hands of philanthropy. As Cæsar had his Brutus, every bed of charity must have its toll of a bath, every loaf of bread its compensation of a private and personal inquisition. Wherefore it is better to be a guest of the law, which, though conducted by rules, does not meddle unduly with a gentleman's private affairs.

Soapy, having decided to go to the Island, at once set about accomplishing his desire. There were many easy ways of doing this. The pleasantest was to dine luxuriously at some expensive restaurant; and then, after declaring insolvency, be handed over quietly and without uproar to a policeman. An accommodating magistrate would do the rest.

Soapy left his bench and strolled out of the square and across the level sea of asphalt, where Broadway and Fifth Avenue flow together. Up Broadway he turned, and halted at a glittering café, where are gathered together nightly the choicest products of the grape, the silkworm, and the protoplasm.

Soapy had confidence in himself from the lowest button of his vest upward. He was shaven, and his coat was decent and his neat black, ready-tied four-in-hand had been presented to him by a lady missionary on Thanksgiving Day. If he could reach a table in the restaurant unsuspected success would be his. The portion of him that would show above the table would raise no doubt in the waiter's mind. A roasted mallard duck, thought Soapy, would be about the thing—with a bottle of Chablis, and then Camembert, a demi-tasse and a cigar. One dollar for the cigar would be enough. The total would not be so high as to call forth any supreme manifestation of revenge from the café management; and yet the meat would leave him filled and happy for the journey to his winter refuge.

But as Soapy set foot inside the restaurant door the head waiter's eye fell upon his frayed trousers and decadent shoes. Strong and ready hands turned him about and conveyed him in silence and haste to the sidewalk and averted the ignoble fate of the menaced mallard.

Soapy turned off Broadway. It seemed that his route to the coveted Island was not to be an epicurean one. Some other way of entering limbo must be thought of.

At a corner of Sixth Avenue electric lights and cunningly displayed wares behind plate-glass made a shop window conspicuous. Soapy took a cobblestone and dashed it through the glass. People came running around the corner, a policeman in the lead. Soapy stood still, with his hands in his pockets, and smiled at the sight of brass buttons.

"Where's the man that done that?" inquired the officer, excitedly.

"Don't you figure out that I might have had something to do with it?" said Soapy, not without sarcasm, but friendly, as one greets good fortune.

The policeman's mind refused to accept Soapy even as a

clue. Men who smash windows do not remain to parley with the law's minions. They take to their heels. The policeman saw a man halfway down the block running to catch a car. With drawn club he joined in the pursuit. Soapy, with disgust in his heart, loafed along, twice unsuccessful.

On the opposite side of the street was a restaurant of no great pretensions. It catered to large appetites and modest purses. Its crockery and atmosphere were thick; its soup and napery thin. Into this place Soapy took his accusive shoes and telltale trousers without challenge. At a table he sat and consumed beefsteak, flapjacks, doughnuts and pie. And then to the waiter he betrayed the fact that the minutest coin and himself were strangers.

"Now, get busy and call a cop," said Soapy. "And don't keep a gentleman waiting."

"No cop for youse," said the waiter, with a voice like butter cakes and an eye like the cherry in a Manhattan cocktail. "Hey, Con!"

Neatly upon his left ear on the callous pavement two waiters pitched Soapy. He arose joint by joint, as a carpenter's rule opens, and beat the dust from his clothes. Arrest seemed but a rosy dream. The Island seemed very far away. A policeman who stood before a drug store two doors away laughed and walked down the street.

Five blocks Soapy travelled before his courage permitted him to woo capture again. This time the opportunity presented what he fatuously termed to himself a "cinch." A young woman of a modest and pleasing guise was standing before a show window gazing with sprightly interest at its display of shaving mugs and inkstands, and two yards from the window a large policeman of severe demeanor leaned against a water plug.

It was Soapy's design to assume the rôle of the despicable and execrated "masher." The refined and elegant appearance of his victim and the contiguity of the conscientious cop encouraged him to believe that he would soon feel the pleasant official clutch upon his arm that would insure his winter quarters on the right little, tight little isle.

Soapy straightened the lady missionary's ready-made tie, dragged his shrinking cuffs into the open, set his hat at a killing cant and sidled toward the young woman. He made eyes at her, was taken with sudden coughs and "hems," smiled, smirked and went brazenly through the impudent and contemptible litany of the "masher." With half an eye Soapy saw that the policeman was watching him fixedly. The young woman moved away a few steps, and again bestowed her absorbed attention upon the shaving mugs. Soapy followed, boldly stepping to her side, raised his hat and said:

"Ah there, Bedelia! Don't you want to come and play in my yard?"

The policeman was still looking. The persecuted young woman had but to beckon a finger and Soapy would be practically en route for his insular haven. Already he imagined he could feel the cozy warmth of the station-house. The young woman faced him and, stretching out a hand, caught Soapy's coat sleeve.

"Sure, Mike," she said, joyfully, "if you'll blow me to a pail of suds. I'd have spoke to you sooner, but the cop was watching."

With the young woman playing the clinging ivy to his oak Soapy walked past the policeman overcome with gloom. He seemed doomed to liberty.

At the next corner he shook off his companion and ran. He halted in the district where by night are found the lightest streets, hearts, vows and librettos. Women in furs and men in greatcoats moved gaily in the wintry air. A sudden fear seized Soapy that some dreadful enchantment had rendered him immune to arrest. The thought brought a little of panic upon it, and when he came upon another policeman lounging grandly in front of a transplendent theatre he caught at the immediate straw of "disorderly conduct."

On the sidewalk Soapy began to yell drunken gibberish at the top of his harsh voice. He danced, howled, raved, and otherwise disturbed the welkin.

The policeman twirled his club, turned his back to Soapy and remarked to a citizen:

"'Tis one of them Yale lads celebratin' the goose egg they give to the Hartford College. Noisy; but no harm. We've instructions to lave them be."

Disconsolate, Soapy ceased his unavailing racket. Would never a policeman lay hands on him? In his fancy the Island seemed an unattainable Arcadia. He buttoned his thin coat against the chilling wind.

In a cigar store he saw a well-dressed man lighting a cigar at a swinging light. His silk umbrella he had set by the door on entering. Soapy stepped inside, secured the umbrella and sauntered off with it slowly. The man at the cigar light followed hastily.

"My umbrella," he said, sternly.

"Oh, is it?" sneered Soapy, adding insult to petit larceny. "Well, why don't you call a policeman? I took it. Your umbrella! Why don't you call a cop? There stands one on the corner."

The umbrella owner slowed his steps. Soapy did likewise, with a presentiment that luck would again run against him. The policeman looked at the two curiously.

"Of course," said the umbrella man—"that is—well, you know how these mistakes occur—I—if it's your umbrella I hope you'll excuse me—I picked it up this morning in a restaurant— If you recognize it as yours, why—I hope you'll—"

"Of course it's mine," said Soapy, viciously.

The ex-umbrella man retreated. The policeman hurried to assist a tall blonde in an opera cloak across the street in front of a street car that was approaching two blocks away.

Soapy walked eastward through a street damaged by improvements. He hurled the umbrella wrathfully into an excavation. He muttered against the men who wear helmets and carry clubs. Because he wanted to fall into their clutches, they seemed to regard him as a king who could do no wrong.

At length Soapy reached one of the avenues to the east where the glitter and turmoil was but faint. He set his face down this toward Madison Square, for the homing instinct survives even when the home is a park bench.

But on an unusually quiet corner Soapy came to a standstill. Here was an old church, quaint and rambling and gabled. Through one violet-stained window a soft light glowed, where, no doubt, the organist loitered over the keys, making sure of his mastery of the coming Sabbath anthem. For there drifted out to Soapy's ears sweet music that caught and held him transfixed against the convolutions of the iron fence.

The moon was above, lustrous and serene; vehicles and pedestrians were few; sparrows twittered sleepily in the eaves—for a little while the scene might have been a country churchyard. And the anthem that the organist played cemented Soapy to the iron fence, for he had known it well in the days when his life contained such things as mothers and roses and ambitions and friends and immaculate thoughts and collars.

The conjunction of Soapy's receptive state of mind and the influences about the old church wrought a sudden and wonderful change in his soul. He viewed with swift horror the pit into which he had tumbled, the degraded days, unworthy desires, dead hopes, wrecked faculties and base motives that made up his existence.

And also in a moment his heart responded thrillingly to this novel mood. An instantaneous and strong impulse moved him to battle with his desperate fate. He would pull himself out of the mire; he would make a man of himself again; he would conquer the evil that had taken possession of him. There was time; he was comparatively young yet: he would resurrect his old eager ambitions and pursue them without faltering. Those solemn but sweet organ notes had set up a revolution in him. To-morrow he would go into the roaring downtown district and find work. A fur importer had once offered him a place as driver. He would find him to-morrow and ask for the position. He would be some-body in the world. He would—

Soapy felt a hand laid on his arm. He looked quickly around into the broad face of a policeman.

"What are you doin' here?" asked the officer.

"Nothin'," said Soapy.

"Then come along," said the policeman.

"Three months on the Island," said the Magistrate in the Police Court the next morning.

THE STORY OF THE GOOD LITTLE BOY

by Mark Twain

ONCE THERE WAS a good little boy by the name of Jacob Blivens. He always obeyed his parents, no matter how absurd and unreasonable their demands were; and he always learned his book, and never was late at Sabbath-school. He would not play hookey, even when his sober judgment told him it was the most profitable thing he could do. None of the other boys could ever make that boy out, he acted so strangely. He wouldn't lie, no matter how convenient it was. He just said it was wrong to lie, and that was sufficient for him. And he was so honest that he was simply ridiculous. The curious ways that that Jacob had, surpassed everything. He wouldn't play marbles on Sunday, he wouldn't rob birds' nests, he wouldn't give hot pennies to organ-grinders monkeys, he didn't seem to take any interest in any kind of rational amusement. So the other boys used to try to reason it out and come to an understanding of him, but they couldn't arrive at any satisfactory conclusion. As I said before, they could only figure out a sort of vague idea that he was "afflicted," and so they took him under their protection, and never allowed any harm to come to him.

This good little boy read all the Sunday-school books; they were his greatest delight. This was the whole secret of it. He believed in the good little boys they put in the Sunday-school books; he had every confidence in them. He longed to come across one of them alive once; but he never did. They all died before his time, maybe. Whenever he read about a particularly good one he turned over quickly to the end to see what became of him, because he wanted to travel thousands of miles and gaze on him; but it wasn't any use; that good little boy always died in the last chapter, and there was a picture of the funeral, with all his relations and the Sunday-school children standing around the grave in pantaloons that were too short, and bonnets that were too large, and everybody crying into handkerchiefs that had as much as a yard and a half of stuff in them. He was always headed off in this way. He never could see one of those good little boys on account of his always dying in the last chapter.

Jacob had a noble ambition to be put in a Sunday-school book. He wanted to be put in, with pictures representing him gloriously declining to lie to his mother, and her weeping for joy about it; and pictures representing him standing on the doorstep giving a penny to a poor beggar-woman with six children, and telling her to spend it freely, but not to be extravagant, because extravagance is a sin; and pictures of him magnanimously refusing to tell on the bad boy who always lay in wait for him around the corner as he came from school, and welted him over the head with a lath, and then chased him home, saying, "Hi! hi!" as he proceeded. That was the ambition of young Jacob Blivens. He wished to be put in a Sunday-school book. It made him feel a little uncomfortable sometimes when he reflected that the good little boys always died. He loved to live, you know, and this was the most unpleasant feature about being a Sunday-school-book boy. He knew it was not healthy to be good. He knew it was more fatal than consumption to be so supernaturally good as the boys in the books were; he knew that none of them had ever been able to stand it long, and it pained him to think that if they put him in a book he wouldn't ever see it, or even if they did get the book out before he died it wouldn't be popular without any picture of his funeral in the back part of it. It couldn't be much of a Sunday-school book that couldn't tell about the advice he gave to the community when he was dying. So at last, of course, he had to make up his mind to do the best he could under the circumstances—to live right, and hang on as long as he could, and have his dying speech all ready when his time came.

But somehow nothing ever went right with this good little boy; nothing ever turned out with him the way it turned out with the good little boys in the books. They always had a good time, and the bad boys had the broken legs; but in his case there was a screw loose somewhere, and it all happened just the other way. When he found Jim Blake stealing apples, and went under the tree to read to him about the bad little boy who fell out of a neighbor's apple tree and broke his arm, Jim fell out of the tree, too, but he fell on *him* and broke *his* arm, and Jim wasn't hurt at all. Jacob couldn't understand that. There wasn't anything in the books like it.

And once, when some bad boys pushed a blind man over in the mud, and Jacob ran to help him up and receive his blessing, the blind man did not give him any blessing at all, but whacked him over the head with his stick and said he would like to catch him shoving *him* again, and then pretending to help him up. This was not in accordance with any of the books. Jacob looked them all over to see.

One thing that Jacob wanted to do was to find a lame dog that hadn't any place to stay, and was hungry and persecuted, and bring him home and pet him and have that dog's imperishable gratitude. And at last he found one and was happy; and he brought him home and fed him, but when he was going to pet him the dog flew at him and tore all the clothes off him except those that were in front, and made a spectacle of him that was astonishing. He examined authorities, but he could not un-

derstand the matter. It was of the same breed of dogs that was in the books, but it acted very differently. Whatever this boy did he got into trouble. The very things the boys in the books got rewarded for turned out to be about the most unprofitable things he could invest in.

Once, when he was on his way to Sunday-school, he saw some bad boys starting off pleasuring in a sailboat. He was filled with consternation, because he knew from his reading that boys who went sailing on Sunday invariably got drowned. So he ran out on a raft to warn them, but a log turned with him and slid him into the river. A man got him out pretty soon, and the doctor pumped the water out of him, and gave him a fresh start with his bellows, but he caught cold and lay sick abed nine weeks. But the most unaccountable thing about it was that the bad boys in the boat had a good time all day, and then reached home alive and well in the most surprising manner. Jacob Blivens said there was nothing like these things in the books. He was perfectly dumfounded.

When he got well he was a little discouraged, but he resolved to keep on trying anyhow. He knew that so far his experiences wouldn't do to go in a book, but he hadn't yet reached the allotted term of life for good little boys, and he hoped to be able to make a record yet if he could hold on till his time was fully up. If everything else failed he had his dying speech to fall back on.

He examined his authorities, and found that it was now time for him to go to sea as a cabin-boy. He called on a ship-captain and made his application, and when the captain asked for his recommendations he proudly drew out a tract and pointed to the word, "To Jacob Blivens, from his affectionate teacher." But the captain was a coarse, vulgar man, and he said, "Oh, that be blowed! *that* wasn't any proof that he knew how to wash dishes or handle a slush-bucket, and he guessed he didn't want him." This was altogether the most extraordinary thing that ever happened to Jacob in all his life. A compliment from a teacher, on a tract, had never failed to move the tenderest emotions of ship-captains, and open the way to all offices of honor and profit in their gift—it never had in any book that ever *he* had read. He could hardly believe his senses.

This boy always had a hard time of it. Nothing ever came out according to the authorities with him. At last, one day, when he was around hunting up bad little boys to admonish, he found a lot of them in the old iron-foundry fixing up a little joke on fourteen or fifteen dogs, which they had tied together in long procession, and were going to ornament with empty nitroglycerin cans made fast to their tails. Jacob's heart was touched. He sat down on one of those cans (for he never minded grease when duty was before him), and he took hold of the foremost dog by the collar, and turned his reproving eye upon wicked Tom Jones. But just at that moment Alderman McWelter, full of wrath, stepped in. All the bad boys ran away, but Jacob Blivens rose in conscious innocence and began one of those stately little Sunday-school-book speeches which always commence with "Oh, sir!" in dead opposition to the fact that no boy, good or bad, ever starts a remark with "Oh, sir." But the alderman never waited to hear the rest. He took Jacob Blivens by the ear and turned him around, and hit him a whack in the rear with the flat of his hand; and in an instant that good little boy shot out through the roof and soared away toward the sun, with the fragments of those fifteen dogs stringing after him like the tail of a kite. And there wasn't a sign of that alderman or that old iron-foundry left on the face of the earth; and, as for young Jacob Blivens, he never got a chance to make his last dying speech after all his trouble fixing it up, unless he made it to the birds; because, although the bulk of him came down all right in a tree-top in an adjoining county, the rest of him was apportioned around among four townships, and so they had to hold five inquests on him to find out whether he was dead or not, and how it occurred. You never saw a boy scattered so.[1]

---

[1] This glycerin catastrophe is borrowed from a floating newspaper item, whose author's name I would give if I knew it. M.T.

Thus perished the good little boy who did the best he could, but didn't come out according to the books. Every boy who ever did as he did prospered except him. His case is truly remarkable. It will probably never be accounted for.

THE MAN WHO COULD
WORK MIRACLES

by H. G. Wells

A Pantoum in Prose

IT IS DOUBTFUL whether the gift was innate. For my own part, I think it came to him suddenly. Indeed, until he was thirty he was a sceptic, and did not believe in miraculous powers. And here, since it is the most convenient place, I must mention that he was a little man, and had eyes of a hot brown, very erect red hair, a moustache with ends that he twisted up, and freckles. His name was George McWhirter Fotheringay—not the sort of name by any means to lead to any expectation of miracles—and he was a clerk at Gomshott's. He was greatly addicted to assertive argument. It was while he was asserting the impossibility of miracles that he had his first intimation of his extraordinary powers. This particular argument was being held in the bar of the Long Dragon, and Toddy Beamish was conducting the opposition by a monotonous but effective "So *you* say," that drove Mr. Fotheringay to the very limit of his patience.

There were present, besides these two, a very dusty cyclist, landlord Cox, and Miss Maybridge, the perfectly respectable and rather portly barmaid of the Dragon. Miss Maybridge was standing with her back to Mr. Fotheringay, washing glasses; the others were watching him, more or less amused by the present ineffectiveness of the assertive method. Goaded by the Torres Vedras tactics of Mr. Beamish, Mr. Fotheringay determined to make an unusual rhetorical effort. "Looky here, Mr. Beamish," said Mr. Fotheringay. "Let us clearly understand what a miracle is. It's something contrariwise to the course of nature done by power of Will, something what couldn't happen without being specially willed."

"So *you* say," said Mr. Beamish, repulsing him.

Mr. Fotheringay appealed to the cyclist, who had hitherto been a silent auditor, and received his assent—given with a hesitating cough and a glance at Mr. Beamish. The landlord would express no opinion, and Mr. Fotheringay, returning to Mr. Beamish, received the unexpected concession of a qualified assent to his definition of a miracle.

"For instance," said Mr. Fotheringay, greatly encouraged. "Here would be a miracle. That lamp, in the natural course of nature, couldn't burn like that upsy-down, could it, Beamish?"

"*You* say it couldn't," said Beamish.

"And you?" said Fotheringay. "You don't mean to say—eh?"

"No," said Beamish reluctantly. "No, it couldn't."

"Very well," said Mr. Fotheringay. "Then here comes someone, as it might be me, along here, and stands as it might be here, and says to that lamp, as I might do, collecting all my will—'Turn upsy-down without breaking, and go on burning steady,' and—Hullo!"

It was enough to make anyone say "Hullo!" The impossible, the incredible, was visible to them all. The lamp hung inverted in the air, burning quietly with its flame pointing down. It was as solid, as indisputable as ever a lamp was, the prosaic common lamp of the Long Dragon bar.

The Man Who Could Work Miracles

Mr. Fotheringay stood with an extended forefinger and the knitted brows of one anticipating a catastrophic smash. The cyclist, who was sitting next the lamp, ducked and jumped across the bar. Everybody jumped, more or less. Miss Maybridge turned and screamed. For nearly three seconds the lamp remained still. A faint cry of mental distress came from Mr. Fotheringay. "I can't keep it up," he said, "any longer." He staggered back, and the inverted lamp suddenly flared, fell against the corner of the bar, bounced aside, smashed upon the floor, and went out.

It was lucky it had a metal receiver, or the whole place would have been in a blaze. Mr. Cox was the first to speak, and his remark, shorn of needless excrescences, was to the effect that Fotheringay was a fool. Fotheringay was beyond disputing even so fundamental a proposition as that! He was astonished beyond measure at the thing that had occurred. The subsequent conversation threw absolutely no light on the matter so far as Fotheringay was concerned; the general opinion not only followed Mr. Cox very closely but very vehemently. Everyone accused Fotheringay of a silly trick, and presented him to himself as a foolish destroyer of comfort and security. His mind was a tornado of perplexity, he was himself inclined to agree with them, and he made a remarkably ineffectual opposition to the proposal of his departure.

He went home flushed and heated, coat-collar crumpled, eyes smarting, and ears red. He watched each of the ten street lamps nervously as he passed it. It was only when he found himself alone in his little bedroom in Church Row that he was able to grapple seriously with his memories of the occurrence, and ask, "What on earth happened?"

He had removed his coat and boots, and was sitting on the bed with his hands in his pockets repeating the text of his defence for the seventeenth time, "*I* didn't want the confounded thing to upset," when it occurred to him that at the precise moment he had said the commanding words he had inadvertently willed the thing he said, and that when he had seen the lamp in

the air he had felt that it depended on him to maintain it there without being clear how this was to be done. He had not a particularly complex mind, or he might have stuck for a time at that "inadvertently willed," embracing, as it does, the abstrusest problems of voluntary action; but as it was, the idea came to him with a quite acceptable haziness. And from that, following, as I must admit, no clear logical path, he came to the test of experiment.

He pointed resolutely to his candle and collected his mind, though he felt he did a foolish thing. "Be raised up," he said. But in a second that feeling vanished. The candle was raised, hung in the air one giddy moment, and as Mr. Fotheringay gasped, fell with a smash on his toilet-table, leaving him in darkness save for the expiring glow of its wick.

For a time Mr. Fotheringay sat in the darkness, perfectly still. "It did happen, after all," he said. "And 'ow I'm to explain it I *don't* know." He sighed heavily, and began feeling in his pockets for a match. He could find none, and he rose and groped about the toilet-table. "I wish I had a match," he said. He resorted to his coat, and there were none there, and then it dawned upon him that miracles were possible even with matches. He extended a hand and scowled at it in the dark. "Let there be a match in that hand," he said. He felt some light object fall across his palm, and his fingers closed upon a match.

After several ineffectual attempts to light this, he discovered it was a safety-match. He threw it down, and then it occurred to him that he might have willed it lit. He did, and perceived it burning in the midst of his toilet-table mat. He caught it up hastily, and it went out. His perception of possibilities enlarged, and he felt for and replaced the candle in its candle-stick. "Here! *you* be lit," said Mr. Fotheringay, and forthwith the candle was flaring, and he saw a little black hole in the toilet-cover, with a wisp of smoke rising from it. For a time he stared from this to the little flame and back, and then looked up and met his own gaze in the looking-glass. By this help he communed with himself in silence for a time.

"How about miracles now?" said Mr. Fotheringay at last, addressing his reflection.

The subsequent meditations of Mr. Fotheringay were of a severe but confused description. So far as he could see, it was a case of pure willing with him. The nature of his first experiences disinclined him for any further experiments except of the most cautious type. But he lifted a sheet of paper, and turned a glass of water pink and then green, and he created a snail, which he miraculously annihilated, and got himself a miraculous new toothbrush. Somewhen in the small hours he had reached the fact that his will-power must be of a particularly rare and pungent quality, a fact of which he had certainly had inklings before, but no certain assurance. The scare and perplexity of his first discovery were now qualified by pride in this evidence of singularity and by vague intimations of advantage. He became aware that the church clock was striking one, and as it did not occur to him that his daily duties at Gomshott's might be miraculously dispensed with, he resumed undressing, in order to get to bed without further delay. As he struggled to get his shirt over his head he was struck with a brilliant idea. "Let me be in bed," he said, and found himself so. "Undressed," he stipulated; and, finding the sheets cold, added hastily, "and in my nightshirt —no, in a nice soft woollen nightshirt. Ah!" he said with immense enjoyment. "And now let me be comfortably asleep . . ."

He awoke at his usual hour and was pensive all through breakfast-time, wondering whether his overnight experience might not be a particularly vivid dream. At length his mind turned again to cautious experiments. For instance, he had three eggs for breakfast; two his landlady had supplied, good, but shoppy, and one was a delicious fresh goose-egg, laid, cooked, and served by his extraordinary will. He hurried off to Gomshott's in a state of profound but carefully concealed excitement, and only remembered the shell of the third egg when his landlady spoke of it that night. All day he could do no work because of this astonishing new self-knowledge, but this caused him no inconvenience, because he made up for it miraculously in his last ten minutes.

As the day wore on his state of mind passed from wonder to elation, albeit the circumstances of his dismissal from the Long Dragon were still disagreeable to recall, and a garbled account of the matter that had reached his colleagues led to some badinage. It was evident he must be careful how he lifted frangible articles, but in other ways his gift promised more and more as he turned it over in his mind. He intended among other things to increase his personal property by unostentatious acts of creation. He called into existence a pair of very spendid diamond studs, and hastily annihilated them again as young Gomshott came across the counting-house to his desk. He was afraid your Gomshott might wonder how he came by them. He saw quite clearly the gift required caution and watchfulness in its exercise, but so far as he could judge the difficulties attending its mastery would be no greater than those he had already faced in the study of cycling. It was that analogy, perhaps, quite as much as the feeling that he would be unwelcome in the Long Dragon, that drove him out after supper into the lane beyond the gasworks, to rehearse a few miracles in private.

There was possibly a certain want of originality in his attempts, for apart from his will-power Mr. Fotheringay was not a very exceptional man. The miracle of Moses' rod came to his mind, but the night was dark and unfavourable to the proper control of large miraculous snakes. Then he recollected the story of "Tannhäuser" that he had read on the back of the Philharmonic programme. That seemed to him singularly attractive and harmless. He stuck his walking-stick—a very nice Poona-Penang lawyer—into the turf that edged the foot-path, and commanded the dry wood to blossom. The air was immediately full of the scent of roses, and by means of a match he saw for himself that this beautiful miracle was indeed accomplished. His satisfaction was ended by advancing footsteps. Afraid of a premature discovery of his powers, he addressed the blossoming stick hastily: "Go back." What he meant was "Change back"; but of course he was confused. The stick receded at a considerable velocity, and incontinently came a cry of anger and a bad word from the approaching person. "Who are you throwing brambles at, you fool?" cried a voice. "That got me on the shin."

"I'm sorry, old chap," said Mr. Fotheringay, and then realising the awkward nature of the explanation, caught nervously at his moustache. He saw Winch, one of the three Immering constables, advancing.

"What d'yer mean by it?" asked the constable. "Hullo! It's you, is it? The gent that broke the lamp at the Long Dragon!"

"I don't mean anything by it," said Mr. Fotheringay. "Nothing at all."

"What d'yer do it for then?"

"Oh, bother!" said Mr. Fotheringay.

"Bother, indeed? D'yer know that stick hurt? What d'yer do it for, eh?"

For the moment Mr. Fotheringay could not think what he had done it for. His silence seemed to irritate Mr. Winch. "You've been assaulting the police, young man, this time. That's what *you* done!"

"Look here, Mr. Winch," said Mr. Fotheringay, annoyed and confused, "I'm very sorry. The fact is—"

"Well!"

He could think of no way but the truth. "I was working a miracle." He tried to speak in an off-hand way, but try as he would he couldn't.

"Working a—! 'Ere, don't you talk rot. Working a miracle, indeed! Miracle! Well, that's downright funny! Why, you's the chap that don't believe in miracles. . . . Fact is, this is another of your silly conjuring tricks—that's what this is. Now, I tell you—"

But Mr. Fotheringay never heard what Mr. Winch was going to tell him. He realised he had given himself away, flung his valuable secret to all the winds of heaven. A violent gust of irritation swept him to action. He turned on the constable swiftly and fiercely. "Here," he said, "I've had enough of this, I have! I'll show you a silly conjuring trick, I will. Go to Hades! Go, now!"

He was alone!

Mr. Fotheringay performed no more miracles that night nor did he trouble to see what had become of his flowering stick. He returned to the town, scared and very quiet, and went to his bedroom. "Lord!" he said, "it's a powerful gift—an extremely powerful gift! I didn't hardly mean as much as that. Not really. . . . I wonder what Hades is like!"

He sat on the bed taking off his boots. Struck by a happy

thought he transferred the constable to San Francisco, and without any more interference with normal causation went soberly to bed. In the night he dreamt of the anger of Winch.

The next day Mr. Fotheringay heard two interesting items of news. Someone had planted a most beautiful climbing rose against the elder Mr. Gomshott's private house in the Lullaborough Road, and the river as far as Rawling's Mill was to be dragged for Constable Winch.

Mr. Fotheringay was abstracted and thoughtful all that day, and performed no miracles except certain provisions for Winch, and the miracle of completing his day's work with punctual perfection in spite of all the bee-swarm of thoughts that hummed through his mind. And the extraordinary abstraction and meekness of his manner was remarked by several people, and made a matter for jesting. For the most part he was thinking of Winch.

On Sunday evening he went to chapel, and oddly enough, Mr. Maydig, who took a certain interest in occult matters, preached about "things that are not lawful." Mr. Fotheringay was not a regular chapel goer, but the system of assertive scepticism, to which I have already alluded, was now very much shaken. The tenor of the sermon threw an entirely new light on these novel gifts, and he suddenly decided to consult Mr. Maydig immediately after the service. So soon as that was determined, he found himself wondering why he had not done so before.

Mr. Maydig, a lean, excitable man with quite remarkably long wrists and neck, was gratified at a request for a private conversation from a young man whose carelessness in religious matters was a subject for general remark in the town. After a few necessary delays, he conducted him to the study of the Manse, which was contiguous to the chapel, seated him comfortably, and, standing in front of a cheerful fire—his legs threw a Rhodian arch of shadow on the opposite wall—requested Mr. Fotheringay to state his business.

At first Mr. Fotheringay was a little abashed, and found

some difficulty in opening the matter. "You will scarcely believe me, Mr. Maydig, I am afraid"—and so forth for some time. He tried a question at last, and asked Mr. Maydig his opinion of miracles.

Mr. Maydig was still saying "Well" in an extremely judicial tone, when Mr. Fotheringay interrupted again: "You don't believe, I suppose, that some common sort of person—like myself, for instance—as it might be sitting here now, might have some sort of twist inside him that made him able to do things by his will."

"It's possible," said Mr. Maydig. "Something of the sort, perhaps, is possible."

"If I might make free with something here, I think I might show you a sort of experiment," said Mr. Fotheringay. "Now, take that tobacco-jar on the table, for instance. What I want to know is whether what I am going to do with it is a miracle or not. Just half a minute, Mr. Maydig, please."

He knitted his brows, pointed to the tobacco-jar and said: "Be a bowl of vi'lets."

The tobacco-jar did as it was ordered.

Mr. Maydig started violently at the change, and stood looking from the thaumaturgist to the bowl of flowers. He said nothing. Presently he ventured to lean over the table and smell the violets; they were fresh-picked and very fine ones. Then he stared at Mr. Fotheringay again.

"How did you do that?" he asked.

Mr. Fotheringay pulled his moustache. "Just told it—and there you are. Is that a miracle, or is it black art, or what is it? And what do you think's the matter with me? That's what I want to ask."

"It's a most extraordinary occurrence."

"And this day last week I knew no more that I could do things like that than you did. It came quite sudden. It's something odd about my will, I suppose, and that's as far as I can see."

"Is *that*—the only thing? Could you do other things besides that?"

"Lord, yes!" said Mr. Fotheringay. "Just anything." He thought, and suddenly recalled a conjuring entertainment he had seen. "Here!" He pointed. "Change into a bowl of fish—no, not that—change into a glass bowl full of water with goldfish swimming in it. That's better! You see that, Mr. Maydig?"

"It's astonishing. It's incredible. You are either a most extraordinary . . . But no—"

"I could change it into anything," said Mr. Fotheringay. "Just anything. Here! be a pigeon, will you?"

In another moment a blue pigeon was fluttering round the room and making Mr. Maydig duck every time it came near him. "Stop there, will you," said Mr. Fotheringay; and the pigeon hung motionless in the air. "I could change it back to a bowl of flowers," he said, and after replacing the pigeon on the table worked that miracle. "I expect you will want your pipe in a bit," he said, and restored the tobacco-jar.

Mr. Maydig had followed all these later changes in a sort of ejaculatory silence. He stared at Mr. Fotheringay and, in a very gingerly manner, picked up the tobacco-jar, examined it, replaced it on the table, *"Well!"* was the only expression of his feelings.

"Now, after that it's easier to explain what I came about," said Mr. Fotheringay; and proceeded to a lengthy and involved narrative of his strange experiences, beginning with the affair of the lamp in the Long Dragon and complicated by persistent allusions to Winch. As he went on, the transient pride Mr. Maydig's consternation had caused passed away; he became the very ordinary Mr. Fotheringay of everyday intercourse again. Mr. Maydig listened intently, the tobacco-jar in his hand, and his bearing changed also with the course of the narrative. Presently, while Mr. Fotheringay was dealing with the miracle of the third egg, the minister interrupted with a fluttering extended hand—

"It is possible," he said. "It is credible. It is amazing, of course, but it reconciles a number of difficulties. The power to work miracles is a gift—a peculiar quality like genius or second sight—hitherto it has come very rarely and to exceptional people. But in this case . . . I have always wondered at the miracles of Mahomet, and at Yogi's miracles, and the miracles of Madame Blavatsky. But, of course! Yes, it is simply a gift! It carries out so beautifully the arguments of that great thinker"—Mr. Maydig's voice sank—"his Grace the Duke of Argyll. Here we plumb some profounder law—deeper than the ordinary laws of nature. Yes—yes. Go on. Go on!"

Mr. Fotheringay proceeded to tell of his misadventure with Winch, and Mr. Maydig, no longer overawed or scared, began to jerk his limbs about and interject astonishment. "It's this what troubled me most," proceeded Mr. Fotheringay; "it's this I'm most mijitly in want of advice for; of course he's at San Francisco—wherever San Francisco may be—but of course it's awkward for both of us, as you'll see, Mr. Maydig. I don't see how he can understand what has happened, and I dare say he's scared and exasperated something tremendous, and trying to get at me. I dare say he keeps on starting off to come here. I send him back, by a miracle every few hours, when I think of it. And of course, that's a thing he won't be able to understand, and it's bound to annoy him; and, of course, if he takes a ticket every time it will cost him a lot of money. I done the best I could for him, but of course it's difficult for him to put himself in my place. I thought afterwards that his clothes might have got scorched, you know—if Hades is all it's supposed to be—before I shifted him. In that case I suppose they'd have locked him up in San Francisco. Of course I willed him a new suit of clothes on him directly I thought of it. But, you see, I'm already in a deuce of a tangle—"

Mr. Maydig looked serious. "I see you are in a tangle. Yes, it's a difficult position. How you are to end it . . ." He became diffuse and inconclusive.

"However, we'll leave Winch for a little and discuss the

larger question. I don't think this is a case of the black art or anything of the sort. I don't think there is any taint of criminality about it at all, Mr. Fotheringay—none whatever, unless you are suppressing material facts. No, it's miracles—pure miracles—miracles, if I may say so, of the very highest class."

He began to pace the hearthrug and gesticulate, while Mr. Fotheringay sat with his arm on the table and his head on his arm, looking worried. "I don't see how I'm to manage about Winch," he said.

"A gift of working miracles—apparently a very powerful gift," said Mr. Maydig, "will find a way about Winch—never fear. My dear sir, you are a most important man—a man of the most astonishing possibilities. As evidence, for example! And in other ways, the things you may do. . . ."

"Yes, *I've* thought of a thing or two," said Mr. Fotheringay. "But—some of the things came a bit twisty. You saw that fish at first? Wrong sort of bowl and wrong sort of fish. And I thought I'd ask someone."

"A proper course," said Mr. Maydig, "a very proper course—altogether the proper course." He stopped and looked at Mr. Fotheringay. "It's practically an unlimited gift. Let us test your powers, for instance. If they really *are* . . . If they really are all they seem to be."

And so, incredible as it may seem, in the study of the little house behind the Congregational Chapel, on the evening of Sunday, Nov. 10, 1896, Mr. Fotheringay, egged on and inspired by Mr. Maydig, began to work miracles. The reader's attention is specially and definitely called to that date. He will object, probably has already objected, that certain points in this story are improbable, that if any things of the sort already described had indeed occurred, they would have been in all the papers a year ago. The details immediately following he will find particularly hard to accept, because among other things they involve the conclusion that he or she, the reader in question, must have been killed in a violent and unprecedented manner more than a year ago. Now a miracle is nothing if not improbable, and as a matter of fact the reader *was* killed in a violent and unprecedented manner a year ago. In the subsequent course of this story it will become perfectly clear and credible, as every right-minded and reasonable reader will admit. But this is not the place for the end of the story, being but little beyond the hither side of the middle. And at first the miracles worked by Mr. Fotheringay were timid little miracles—little things with the cups and parlour fitments, as feeble as the miracles of Theosophists, and, feeble as they were, they were received with awe by his collaborator. He would have preferred to settle the Winch business out of hand, but Mr. Maydig would not let him. But after they had worked a dozen of these domestic trivialities, their sense of power grew, their imagination began to show signs of stimulation, and their ambition enlarged. Their first larger enterprise was due to hunger and the negligence of Mrs. Minchin, Mr. Maydig's housekeeper. The meal to which the minister conducted Mr. Fotheringay was certainly ill-laid and uninviting as refreshment for two industrious miracle-workers; but they were seated, and Mr. Maydig was descanting in sorrow rather than in anger upon his housekeeper's shortcomings, before it occurred to Mr. Fotheringay that an opportunity lay before him. "Don't you think, Mr. Maydig," he said, "if it isn't a liberty, I—"

"My dear Mr. Fotheringay! Of course! No—I didn't think."

Mr. Fotheringay waved his hand. "What shall we have?" he said, in a large, inclusive spirit, and, at Mr. Maydig's order, revised the supper very thoroughly. "As for me," he said, eyeing Mr. Maydig's selection, "I am always particularly fond of a tankard of stout and a nice Welsh rarebit, and I'll order that. I ain't much given to Burgundy," and forthwith stout and Welsh rarebit promptly appeared at his command. They sat long at their supper, talking like equals, as Mr. Fotheringay presently perceived with a glow of surprise and gratification, of all the miracles they would presently do. "And, by the bye, Mr. Maydig," said Mr. Fotheringay, "I might perhaps be able to help you—in a domestic way."

"Don't quite follow," said Mr. Maydig, pouring out a glass of miraculous old Burgundy.

Mr. Fotheringay helped himself to a second Welsh rarebit out of vacancy, and took a mouthful. "I was thinking," he said, "I might be able (*chum, chum*) to work (*chum, chum*) a miracle with Mrs. Minchin (*chum, chum*)—make her a better woman."

Mr. Maydig put down the glass and looked doubtful. "She's— She strongly objects to interference, you know, Mr. Fotheringay. And—as a matter of fact—it's well past eleven and she's probably in bed and asleep. Do you think, on the whole—"

Mr. Fotheringay considered these objections. "I don't see that it shouldn't be done in her sleep."

For a time Mr. Maydig opposed the idea, and then he yielded. Mr. Fotheringay issued his orders, and a little less at their ease, perhaps, the two gentlemen proceeded with their repast. Mr. Maydig was enlarging on the changes he might expect in his housekeeper next day, with an optimism that seemed even to Mr. Fotheringay's supper senses a little forced and hectic, when a series of confused noises from upstairs began. Their eyes exchanged interrogations, and Mr. Maydig left the room hastily. Mr. Fotheringay heard him calling up to his housekeeper and then his footsteps going softly up to her.

In a minute or so the minister returned, his step light, his face radiant. "Wonderful!" he said, "and touching! Most touching!"

He began pacing the hearthrug. "A repentance—a most touching repentance—through the crack of the door. Poor woman! A most wonderful change! She had got up. She must have got up at once. She had got up out of her sleep to smash a private bottle of brandy in her box. And to confess it, too! . . . But this gives us—it opens—a most amazing vista of possibilities. If we can work this miraculous change in *her* . . ."

"The thing's unlimited seemingly," said Mr. Fotheringay. "And about Mr. Winch—"

"Altogether unlimited." And from the hearthrug Mr. Maydig, waving the Winch difficulty aside, unfolded a series of wonderful proposals—proposals he invented as he went along.

Now what those proposals were does not concern the essentials of this story. Suffice it that they were designed in a spirit of infinite benevolence, the sort of benevolence that used to be called post-prandial. Suffice it, too, that the problem of Winch remained unsolved. Nor is it necessary to describe how far that series got to its fulfillment. There were astonishing changes. The small hours found Mr. Maydig and Mr. Fotheringay careering across the chilly market-square under the still moon, in a sort of ecstasy of thaumaturgy, Mr. Maydig all flap and gesture, Mr. Fotheringay short and bristling, and no longer abashed at his greatness. They had reformed every drunkard in the Parliamentary division, changed all the beer and alcohol to water (Mr. Maydig had overruled Mr. Fotheringay on this point), they had, further, greatly improved the railway communication of the place, drained Flinder's swamp, improved the soil of One Tree Hill, and cured the Vicar's wart. And they were going to see what could be done with the injured pier at South Bridge. "The place," gasped Mr. Maydig, "won't be the same place tomorrow. How surprised and thankful everyone will be!" And just at that moment the church clock struck three.

"I say," said Mr. Fotheringay, "that's three o'clock! I must be getting back. I've got to be at business by eight. And besides, Mrs. Wimms—"

"We're only beginning," said Mr. Maydig, full of the sweetness of unlimited power. "We're only beginning. Think of all the good we're doing. When people wake—"

"But—" said Mr. Fotheringay.

Mr. Maydig gripped his arm suddenly. His eyes were bright and wild. "My dear chap," he said, "there's no hurry. Look"—he pointed to the moon at the zenith—"Joshua!"

"Joshua?" said Mr. Fotheringay.

"Joshua," said Mr. Maydig. "Why not? Stop it."

Mr. Fotheringay looked at the moon.

"That's a bit tall," he said after a pause.

"Why not?" said Mr. Maydig. "Of course it doesn't stop. You stop the rotation of the earth, you know. Time stops. It isn't as if we were doing harm."

"H'm!" said Mr. Fotheringay. "Well." He sighed. "I'll try. Here—"

He buttoned up his jacket and addressed himself to the habitable globe, with as good an assumption of confidence as lay in his power. "Jest stop rotating, will you?" said Mr. Fotheringay.

Incontinently he was flying head over heels through the air at the rate of dozens of miles a minute. In spite of the innumerable circles he was describing per second, he thought; for thought is wonderful—sometimes as sluggish as flowing pitch, sometimes as instantaneous as light. He thought in a second, and willed. "Let me come down safe and sound. Whatever else happens, let me down safe and sound."

He willed it only just in time, for his clothes, heated by his rapid flight through the air, were already beginning to singe. He came down with a forcible but by no means injurious bump in what appeared to be a mound of fresh-turned earth. A large mass of metal and masonry, extraordinarily like the clock-tower in the middle of the market-square, hit the earth near him, ricochetted over him, and flew into stonework, bricks, and masonry, like a bursting bomb. A hurtling cow hit one of the larger blocks and smashed like an egg. There was a crash that made all the most violent crashes of his past life seem like the sound of falling dust, and this was followed by a descending series of lesser crashes. A vast wind roared throughout earth and heaven, so that he could scarcely lift his head to look. For a while he was too breathless and astonished even to see where he was or what had happened. And his first movement was to feel his head and reassure himself that his streaming hair was still his own.

"Lord!" gasped Mr. Fotheringay, scarce able to speak for the gale. "I've had a squeak! What's gone wrong? Storms and thunder. And only a minute ago a fine night. It's Maydig set me on to this sort of thing. *What* a wind! If I go on fooling in this way I'm bound to have a thundering accident!

"Where's Maydig?

"What a confounded mess everything's in!"

He looked about him so far as his flapping jacket would permit. The appearance of things was really extremely strange. "The sky's all right anyhow," said Mr. Fotheringay. "And that's about all that is all right. And even there it looks like a terrific gale coming up. But there's the moon overhead. Just as it was just now. Bright as midday. But as for the rest—Where's the village? Where's—where's anything? And what on earth set this wind a-blowing? *I* didn't order no wind."

Mr. Fotheringay struggled to get to his feet in vain, and after one failure, remained on all fours, holding on. He surveyed the moonlit world to leeward, with the tails of his jacket streaming over his head. "There's something seriously wrong," said Mr. Fotheringay. "And what it is—goodness knows."

Far and wide nothing was visible in the white glare through the haze of dust that drove before a screaming gale but tumbled masses of earth and heaps of inchoate ruins, no trees, no houses, no familiar shapes, only a wilderness of disorder vanishing at last into the darkness beneath the whirling columns and streamers, the lightnings and thunderings of a swiftly rising storm. Near him in the livid glare was something that might once have been an elm-tree, a smashed mass of splinters, shivered from boughs to base, and further a twisted mass of iron girders—only too evidently the viaduct—rose out of the piled confusion.

You see, when Mr. Fotheringay had arrested the rotation of the solid globe, he had made no stipulation concerning the trifling movables upon its surface. And the earth spins so fast that the surface at its equator is traveling at rather more than a thousand miles an hour, and in these latitudes at more than half that pace. So that the village, and Mr. Maydig, and Mr. Fotheringay, and everybody and everything had been jerked violently forward at about nine miles per second that is to say, much more violently than if they had been fired out of a cannon. And every human being, every living creature, every house, and every tree —all the world as we know it—had been so jerked and smashed and utterly destroyed. That was all.

These things Mr. Fotheringay did not, of course, fully appreciate. But he perceived that his miracle had miscarried, and with that a great disgust of miracles came upon him. He was in darkness now, for the clouds had swept together and blotted out his momentary glimpse of the moon, and the air was full of fitful struggling tortured wraiths of hail. A great roaring of wind and waters filled earth and sky, and, peering under his hand through the dust and sleet to windward, he saw by the play of the lightnings a vast wall of water pouring towards him.

"Maydig!" screamed Mr. Fotheringay's feeble voice amid the elemental uproar. "Here!—Maydig!

"Stop!" cried Mr. Fotheringay to the advancing water. "Oh, for goodness' sake, stop!

"Just a moment," said Mr. Fotheringay to the lightnings and thunder. "Stop jest a moment while I collect my thoughts . . . And now what shall I do?" he said. "What *shall* I do? Lord! I wish Maydig was about.

"I know," said Mr. Fotheringay. "And for goodness' sake let's have it right *this* time."

He remained on all fours, leaning against the wind, very intent to have everything right.

"Ah!" he said. "Let nothing what I'm going to order happen until I say 'Off!' . . . Lord! I wish I'd thought of that before!"

He lifted his little voice against the whirlwind, shouting louder and louder in the vain desire to hear himself speak. "Now then!—here goes! Mind about that what I said just now. In the first place, when all I've got to say is done, let me lose my miraculous power, let my will become just like anybody else's will, and all these dangerous miracles be stopped. I don't like them. I'd rather I didn't work 'em. Ever so much. That's the first thing. And the second is—let me be back just before the miracles begin; let everything be just as it was before that blessed lamp turned up. It's a big job, but it's the last. Have you got it? No more miracles, everything as it was—me back in the Long Dragon just before I drank my half-pint. That's it! Yes."

He dug his fingers into the mould, closed his eyes, and said "Off!"

Everything became perfectly still. He perceived that he was standing erect.

"So *you* say," said a voice.

He opened his eyes. He was in the bar of the Long Dragon, arguing about miracles with Toddy Beamish. He had a vague sense of some great thing forgotten that instantaneously passed. You see, except for the loss of his miraculous power, everything was back as it had been; his mind and memory therefore were now just as they had been at the time when this story began. So that he knew absolutely nothing of all that is told here, knows nothing of all that is told here to this day. And among other things, of course, he still did not believe in miracles.

"I tell you that miracles, properly speaking, can't possibly happen," he said, "whatever you like to hold. And I'm prepared to prove it up to the hilt."

"That's what *you* think," said Toddy Beamish, and "Prove it if you can."

"Looky here, Mr. Beamish," said Mr. Fotheringay. "Let us clearly understand what a miracle is. It's something contrariwise to the course of nature done by power of Will. . . ."

PARADISE

by Pär Lagerkvist

AND the Lord said: "Now I have arranged things for you
here as best I can; planted rice, peas and potatoes, many
edible plants which you will find useful, various kinds of grain
for baking bread, cocoanut palms, sugar cane and turnips;
marked out ground suitable for pasture land and gardening;
provided animals that are easy to tame and wild animals for
hunting; laid out plains, valleys and mountainous regions, ter-
races that can well be used for growing grapes and olives; set out
pines, eucalyptus trees and fair acacia groves; devised birch
woods, lotus flowers and breadfruit trees, violet slopes and wild
strawberry patches; invented the sunshine—which you'll find
will please you; put the moon in the heavens so that you'll have
something to go by till you're big enough to get a clock; hung up
the stars to guide you on the sea and lead your thoughts—those
that are not of the earth; seen that there are clouds to give rain
and shade, thought out the seasons and determined their pleasant changing, and one thing and another. I hope you will like it.

"But remember to eat of the tree of knowledge, so that you
will be really sensible and wise."

173

And the first human beings bowed deeply and humbled themselves before their Lord. "Thank you very much," they said.

They began to dig and cultivate the soil, to reap, multiply themselves and fill the whole of paradise, and they liked it very much. They ate freely of the tree of knowledge, as the Lord had told them, but did not grow noticeably sensible. They became very sly and artful and intelligent, and well-informed and excellent in many ways, but they did not become sensible. And this made their existence increasingly complicated and troublesome, and they got into more and more of a muddle.

At last a resolute man appeared who was grieved by the way things were going, and he stepped forward before the Lord and said: "The people are behaving so strangely down there, it seems to me; it's true they grow more intelligent and shrewd every day, but they prefer to turn their cunning and great learning to evil and senseless uses; I don't know, but there must be something wrong with the tree of knowledge."

"What," said the Lord, "something wrong with the tree of knowledge, did you say? Certainly not. It must be like that, don't you see? It's the best I could do. If you think you know what it ought to be like, then please say."

No, he didn't know. But all was not as it should be down there, and however well-thought-out the tree of knowledge might be, it did seem as though eating from it made them a little foolish.

"But the tree cannot be otherwise," the Lord said. "Admittedly, it's rather complicated learning how to eat of it, but it must be complicated; it can't be helped. Some things you must find out for yourselves, or what's the point of your existence? You can't be spoon-fed the whole time. Personally, I think the tree is the finest thing I've created, and if you don't show yourselves worthy of it, human life won't be much to speak of. Tell them that."

And with that answer the man had to be content.

But when he had gone the Lord sat there quite distressed.

If they had found fault with anything else he had made, it wouldn't have mattered so much, but the tree of knowledge was especially dear to his heart, perhaps because it had been so much more difficult to make than the other trees and everything else on the earth. Like the great artist he was, he was thinking at this moment not of his generally recognized achievements but only of this misunderstood work into which he thought he had secretly put his whole soul, without having any joy of it. And just because this very work of his seemed to him so extremely important, he couldn't imagine that humanity could do without it—its real, deep significance.

And perhaps he was right. He was, after all, a great creative spirit and ought to know best himself. He ought to know what he had put his soul into.

He sat thinking that people were ungrateful to him and his most outstanding work.

It is not easy to know how long he sat thus. Perhaps time passes quickly in eternity and the wingbeats of the Lord's thought are perhaps as thousands of years for us. Then a man came again before him, but this time it was the archangel Gabriel himself who came.

"You have no idea what it's like down in paradise," he said. "It is quite incredible. They are trying to destroy everything for you and they think of the worst imaginable deeds of villainy to bring it about. There is a deafening noise and they hurl the hideous fruits of the tree of knowledge at each other so that they burst with a horrible roar, and, worst of all, uproot all the vegetation. They bluster and brag so that it's shameful to hear them and they say they're much cleverer than God himself, for they invent much greater things than you, and they have frightful monsters that shatter everything in their path, everything that you have created, and in the air they have huge imitation birds that vomit fire and devastation. I have never been in hell—I'm glad to say—but that's what it must look like. It is an abomination. And it's all the fault of that tree of knowledge. You should never have given it to them—and come to that, I said so from the outset. Think what you like, but have a look at how things are there!"

And the Lord looked down on to the earth and saw that it was true. Then wrath was kindled in his mighty, pained creator's soul and lightning flashed from his eyes and he sent out his hosts and they drove the people out, together with all their evil and devilish works, into the great desert of Savi, where nothing grows. And he set a fence around paradise, and two angels at its gate, each with his machine gun and flaming sword. And the desert lay right next to paradise and the fence round about.

Inside, life was delightful with its sun and verdure, fresh and springlike now that the people had been driven out; the meadows smelled sweet and the air was full of bird song. And the banished stood looking in between the bars and saw it, but they could not get in.

And the angels—those who were not on guard—retired to rest after the battle and fell asleep, exhausted. But under the best-loved tree in paradise the Lord sat in deep contemplation, and its branches shaded him with their great peace.

SAINT KATY
THE VIRGIN

by John Steinbeck

IN P—— (as the French say), in the year 13—, there lived a bad man who kept a bad pig. He was a bad man because he laughed too much at the wrong times and at the wrong people. He laughed at the good brothers of M—— when they came to the door for a bit of whiskey or a piece of silver, and he laughed at tithe time. When Brother Clement fell in the mill pond and drowned because he would not drop the sack of salt he was carrying, the bad man, Roark, laughed until he had to go to bed for it. When you think of the low, nasty kind of laughter it was, you'll see what a bad man this Roark was, and you'll not be surprised that he didn't pay his tithes and got himself talked about for excommunication. You see, Roark didn't have the proper kind of a face for a laugh to come out of. It was a dark, tight face, and when he laughed it looked as though Roark's leg had just been torn off and his face was getting ready to scream about it. In addition he called people fools, which is

178

unkind and unwise even if they are. Nobody knew what made Roark so bad except that he had been a traveler and seen bad things about the world.

You see the atmosphere the bad pig, Katy, grew up in, and maybe it's no wonder. There are books written how Katy came from a long line of bad pigs; how Katy's father was a chicken eater and everybody knew it, and how Katy's mother would make a meal out of her own litter if she was let. But that isn't true. Katy's mother and father were good modest pigs insofar as nature has provided pigs with equipment for modesty, which isn't far. But still, they had the spirit of modesty as a lot of people have.

Katy's mother had litter after litter of nice red hungry pigs, as normal and decent as you could wish. You must see that the badness of Katy wasn't anything she got by inheritance, so she must have picked it up from the man Roark.

There was Katy lying in the straw with her eyes squinted shut and her pink nose wrinkled, as fine and quiet a piglet as you ever saw, until the day when Roark went out to the sty to name the litter. "You'll be Brigid," he said, "And you're Rory and—turn over you little devil!—you're Katy," and from that minute Katy was a bad pig, the worst pig, in fact, that was ever in the County of P——.

She began by stealing most of the milk; what dugs she couldn't suck on, she put her back against, so that poor Rory and Brigid and the rest turned out runts. Pretty soon, Katy was twice as big as her brothers and sisters and twice as strong. And for badness, can you equal this: one at a time, Katy caught Brigid and Rory and the rest and ate them. With such a start, you might expect almost any kind of a sin out of Katy; and sure enough, it wasn't long before she began eating chickens and ducks, until at last Roark interfered. He put her in a strong sty; at least it was strong on his side. After that, what chickens Katy ate she got from the neighbors.

You should have seen the face of Katy. From the beginning it was a wicked face. The evil yellow eyes of her would frighten you even if you had a stick to knock her on the nose with. She became the terror of the neighborhood. At night, Katy would go stealing out of a hole in her sty to raid hen roosts. Now and then even a child disappeared and was heard of no more. And Roark, who should have been ashamed and sad, grew fonder and fonder of Katy. He said she was the best pig he ever owned, and had more sense than any pig in the county.

After a while the whisper went around that it was a were-pig that wandered about in the night and bit people on the legs and rooted in gardens and ate ducks. Some even went so far as to say it was Roark himself who changed into a pig and stole through the hedges at night. That was the kind of reputation Roark had with his neighbors.

Well, Katy was a big pig now, and it came time for her to be bred. The boar was sterile from that day on and went about with a sad suspicious look on his face and was perplexed and distrustful. But Katy swelled up and swelled up until one night she had her litter. She cleaned them all up and licked them off the way you'd think motherhood had changed her ways. When she got them all dry and clean, she placed them in a row and ate every one of them. It was too much even for a bad man like Roark, for as everyone knows, a sow that will eat her own young is depraved beyond human ability to conceive wickedness.

Reluctantly Roark got ready to slaughter Katy. He was just getting the knife ready when along the path came Brother Colin and Brother Paul on their way collecting tithes. They were sent out from the Monastery of M—— and, while they didn't expect to get anything out of Roark, they thought they'd give him a try anyhow, the way a man will. Brother Paul was a thin, strong man, with a thin strong face and a sharp eye and unconditional piety written all over him, while Brother Colin was a short round man with a wide round face. Brother Paul looked forward to trying the graces of God in Heaven but Brother Colin was all for testing them on earth. The people called Colin a fine man and Paul a good man. They went tithing together, because what Brother Colin couldn't get by persuasion, Brother Paul dug out with threatenings and descriptions of the fires of Hell.

"Roark!" says Brother Paul, "we're out tithing. You won't go pickling your soul in sulphur the way you've been in the habit, will you?"

Roark stopped whetting the knife, and his eyes for evilness might have been Katy's own eyes. He started out to laugh, and then the beginning of it stuck in his throat. He got a look on his face like the look Katy had when she was for eating her litter. "I have a pig for you," said Roark, and he put the knife away.

The Brothers were amazed, for up to that time they'd got nothing out of Roark except the dog sic'd on them, and Roark laughing at the way they tripped over their skirts getting to the gate. "A pig?" said Brother Colin suspiciously. "What kind of a pig?"

"The pig that's in the sty alone there," said Roark, and his eyes seemed to turn yellow.

The Brothers hurried over to the sty and looked in. They noted the size of Katy and the fat on her, and they stared incredulously. Colin could think of nothing but the great hams she had and the bacon she wore about like a top coat. "We'll get a sausage for ourselves from this," he whispered. But Brother Paul was thinking of the praise from Father Benedict when he heard they'd got a pig out of Roark. Paul turned away.

"When will you send this pig over?" he asked.

"I'll bring nothing," Roark cried. "It's your pig there. You take her with you or she will stay here."

The Brothers did not argue. They were too glad to get anything. Paul slipped a cord through the nose-ring of Katy and led her out of the sty; and for a moment Katy followed them as though she were a really good pig. As the three went through the gate, Roark called after them, "Her name is Katy," and the laugh that had been cooped up in his throat so long cackled out.

"It's a fine big sow," Brother Paul remarked uneasily.

Brother Colin was about to answer him, when something

like a wolf trap caught him by the back of the leg. Colin yelled
and spun about. There was Katy contentedly chewing up a piece
of the calf of his leg, and the look on her face like the devil's
own look. Katy chewed slowly and swallowed; then she started
forward to get another piece of Brother Colin, but in that instant
Brother Paul stepped forward and landed a fine big kick on the
end of her snout. If there had been evil in Katy's face before,
there were demons in her eyes then. She braced herself and
growled down deep in her throat; she moved forward snorting
and clicking her teeth like a bulldog. The Brothers didn't wait
for her; they ran to a thorn tree beside the way and up they
climbed with grunts and strainings until at last they were out of
reach of the terrible Katy.

Roark had come down to his gate to see them off, and he
stood there laughing the way they knew they'd get no help from
him. Beneath them, on the ground, Katy paced back and forth;
she pawed the ground and rooted out great pieces of turf to
show her strength. Brother Paul threw a branch at her, and she
tore it to pieces and ground the pieces into the earth under her
sharp hooves, all the time looking up at them with her slanty yellow eyes and grinning to herself.

The two Brothers seated themselves miserably in the tree,
their heads between their shoulders and their robes hugged tight.
"Did you give her a good clout on the nose?" Brother Colin
asked hopefully.

Brother Paul looked down at his foot and then at the tough
leather snout of Katy. "The kick of my foot would knock down
any pig but an elephant," he said.

"You cannot argue with a pig," Brother Colin suggested.

Katy strode ferociously about under the tree. For a long
time the Brothers sat in silence, moodily drawing their robes
about their ankles. Brother Paul studied the problem with a
disfiguring intensity. At last he observed: "You wouldn't say
pigs had much the nature of a lion now, would you?"

"More the nature of the devil," Colin said wearily.

Paul sat straight up and scrutinized Katy with new interest.

Then he held his crucifix out before him, and, in a terrible voice cried, "APAGE SATANAS!"

Katy shuddered as though a strong wind had struck her, but still she came on. "APAGE SATANAS!" Paul cried again and Katy was once more buffeted but unbeaten. A third time Brother Paul hurled the exorcism, but Katy had recovered from the first shock now. It had little effect except to singe a few dried leaves on the ground. Brother Paul turned discouraged eyes to Colin. "Nature of the devil," he announced sadly, "but not the Devil's own self, else that pig would have exploded."

Katy ground her teeth together with horrible pleasure.

"Before I got that idea about exorcising," Paul mused, "I was wondering about Daniel in the lion's den, and would the same thing work on a pig?"

Brother Colin regarded him apprehensively. "There may be some flaws in the nature of a lion," he argued. "Maybe lions are not so heretic as pigs. Every time there's a tight place for a pious man to get out of, there's a lion in it. Look at Daniel, look at Sampson, look at any number of martyrs just to stay in the religious list; and I could name many cases like Androcles that aren't religious at all. No, Brother, the lion is a beast especially made for saintliness and orthodoxy to cope with. If there's a lion in all those stories it must be because of all creatures, the lion is the least impervious to the force of religion. I think the lion must have been created as a kind of object lesson. It is a beast built for parables, surely. But the pig now—there is no record in my memory that a pig recognizes any force but a clout on the nose or a knife in the throat. Pigs in general, and this pig in particular, are the most headstrong and heretic of beasts."

"Still," Brother Paul went on, paying little attention to the lesson, "when you've got ammunition like the church in your hand, it would be a dirty shame not to give it a good try, be it on lion or on pig. The exorcism did not work, and that means nothing." He started to unwind the rope which served him for a girdle. Brother Colin regarded him with horror.

"Paul, lad," he cried, "Brother Paul, for the love of God,

do not go down to that pig." But Paul paid him no attention. He unwound his girdle, and to the end of it tied the chain of his crucifix; then, leaning back until he was hanging by his knees, and the skirts of his robe about his head, Paul lowered the girdle like a fishing line and dangled the iron crucifix toward Katy.

As for Katy, she came forward stamping and champing, ready to snatch it and tread it under her feet. The face of Katy was a tiger's face. Just as she reached the cross, the sharp shadow of it fell on her face, and the cross itself was reflected in her yellow eyes. Katy stopped—paralyzed. The air, the tree, the earth shuddered in an expectant silence, while goodness fought with sin.

Then, slowly, two great tears squeezed out of the eyes of Katy, and before you could think, she was stretched prostrate on the ground, making the sign of the cross with her right hoof and mooing softly in anguish at the realization of her crimes.

Brother Paul dangled the cross a full minute before he hoisted himself back on the limb.

All this time Roark had been watching from his gate. From that day on, he was no longer a bad man; his whole life was changed in a moment. Indeed, he told the story over and over to anyone who would listen. Roark said he had never seen anything so grand and inspiring in his life.

Brother Paul rose and stood on the limb. He drew himself to his full height. Then, using his free hand for gestures, Brother Paul delivered the Sermon on the Mount in beautiful Latin to the groveling, moaning Katy under the tree. When he finished, there was complete and holy silence except for the sobs and sniffles of the repentant pig.

It is doubtful whether Brother Colin had the fiber of a true priest-militant in his nature. "Do—do you think it is safe to go down now?" he stammered.

For answer, Brother Paul broke a limb from the thorn trees and threw it at the recumbent sow. Katy sobbed aloud and raised a tear-stained countenance to them, a face from which all evil had departed; the yellow eyes were golden with repentance and the resulting anguish of grace. The Brothers scrambled out of the tree, put the cord through Katy's nose-ring again, and down the road they trudged with the redeemed pig trotting docilely behind them.

News that they were bringing home a pig from Roark caused such excitement that, on arriving at the gates of the M——, Brothers Paul and Colin found a crowd of monks awaiting them. The Brotherhood squirmed about, feeling the fat sides of Katy and kneading her jowls. Suddenly an opening was broken in the ring, and Father Benedict paced through. His face wore such a smile that Colin was made sure of his sausage and Paul of his praise. Then, to the horror and consternation of everyone present, Katy waddled to a little font beside the chapel door, dipped her right hoof in holy water and crossed herself. It was a moment before anyone spoke. Then Father Benedict's stern voice rang out in anger. "Who was it converted this pig?"

Brother Paul stepped forward. "I did it, Father."

"You are a fool," said the Abbot.

"A fool? I thought you would be pleased, Father."

"You are a fool," Father Benedict repeated. "We can't slaughter this pig. This pig is a Christian."

"There is more rejoicing in heaven—" Brother Paul began to quote.

"Hush!" said the Abbot. "There are plenty of Christians. This year there's a great shortage of pigs."

It would take a whole volume to tell of the thousands of sick beds Katy visited, of the comfort she carried into palaces and cottages. She sat by beds of pain and her dear golden eyes brought relief to the sufferers. For a while it was thought that, because of her sex, she should leave the monastery and enter a nunnery, for the usual ribald tongues caused the usual scandal in the county. But, as the Abbot remarked, one need only look at Katy to be convinced of her purity.

The subsequent life of Katy was one long record of good deeds. It was not until one feast-day morning, however, that the Brothers began to suspect that their community harbored a

saint. On the morning in question, while hymns of joy and thanksgiving sounded from a hundred pious mouths, Katy rose from her seat, strode to the altar, and, with a look of seraphic transport on her face, spun like a top on the tip of her tail for one hour and three-quarters. The assembled Brothers looked on with astonishment and admiration. This was a wonderful example of what a saintly life could accomplish.

From that time on M—— became a place of pilgrimage. Long lines of travelers wound into the valley and stopped at the taverns kept by the good Brothers. Daily at four o'clock, Katy emerged from the gates and blessed the multitudes. If any were afflicted with scrofula or trichina, she touched them and they were healed. Fifty years after her death to a day, she was added to the Calendar of the Elect.

The Proposition was put forward that she should be called Saint Katy the Virgin. However, a minority argued that Katy was not a virgin since she had, in her sinful days, produced a litter. The opposing party retorted that it made no difference at all. Very few virgins, so they said, were virgins.

To keep dissension out of the monastery, a committee presented the problem to a fair-minded and vastly learned barber, agreeing beforehand to be guided by his decision.

"It is a delicate question," said the barber. "You might say there are two kinds of virginity. Some hold that virginity consists in a little bit of tissue. If you have it, you are; if you haven't, you aren't. This definition is a grave danger to the basis of our religion since there is nothing to differentiate between the Grace of God knocking it out from the inside or the wickedness of man from the outside. On the other hand," he continued, "there is virginity by intent, and this definition admits the existence of a great many more virgins than the first does. But here again we get into trouble. When I was a much younger man, I went about in the evenings sometimes with a girl on my arm. Every one of them that ever walked with me was a virgin by intention, and if you take the second definition, you see, they still are."

The committee went away satisfied. Katy had without doubt been a virgin by intent.

In the chapel at M—— there is a gold-bound, jeweled reliquary, and inside, on a bed of crimson satin repose the bones of the Saint. People come great distances to kiss the little box, and such as do, go away leaving their troubles behind them. This holy relic has been found to cure female troubles and ringworm. There is a record left by a woman who visited the chapel to be cured of both. She deposes that she rubbed the reliquary against her cheek, and at the moment her face touched the holy object, a hair mole she had possessed from birth immediately vanished and has never returned.

MR. ANDREWS

by E. M. Forster

THE SOULS of the dead were ascending towards the Judgment Seat and the Gate of Heaven. The world soul pressed them on every side, just as the atmosphere presses upon rising bubbles, striving to vanquish them, to break their thin envelope of personality, to mingle their virtue with its own. But they resisted, remembering their glorious individual life on earth, and hoping for an individual life to come.

Among them ascended the soul of a Mr. Andrews who, after a beneficent and honourable life, had recently deceased at his house in town. He knew himself to be kind, upright and religious, and though he approached his trial with all humility, he could not be doubtful of its result. God was not now a jealous God. He would not deny salvation merely because it was expected. A righteous soul may reasonably be conscious of its own righteousness and Mr. Andrews was conscious of his.

"The way is long," said a voice, "but by pleasant converse the way becomes shorter. Might I travel in your company?"

"Willingly," said Mr. Andrews. He held out his hand, and the two souls floated upward together.

"I was slain fighting the infidel," said the other exultantly, "and I go straight to those joys of which the Prophet speaks."

"Are you not a Christian?" asked Mr. Andrews gravely.

"No, I am a Believer. But you are a Moslem, surely?"

"I am not," said Mr. Andrews. "I am a Believer."

The two souls floated upward in silence, but did not release each other's hands. "I am broad church," he added gently. The word "broad" quavered strangely amid the interspaces.

"Relate to me your career," said the Turk at last.

"I was born of a decent middle-class family, and had my education at Winchester and Oxford. I thought of becoming a missionary, but was offered a post in the Board of Trade, which I accepted. At thirty-two I married, and had four children, two of whom have died. My wife survives me. If I had lived a little longer I should have been knighted."

"Now I will relate my career. I was never sure of my father, and my mother does not signify. I grew up in the slums of Salonika. Then I joined a band and we plundered the villages of the infidel. I prospered and had three wives, all of whom survive me. Had I lived a little longer I should have had a band of my own."

"A son of mine was killed travelling in Macedonia. Perhaps you killed him."

"It is very possible."

The two souls floated upward, hand in hand. Mr. Andrews did not speak again, for he was filled with horror at the approaching tragedy. This man, so godless, so lawless, so cruel, so lustful, believed that he would be admitted into Heaven. And into what a heaven—a place full of the crude pleasures of a ruffian's life on earth! But Mr. Andrews felt neither disgust nor moral indignation. He was only conscious of an immense pity, and his own virtues confronted him not at all. He longed to save the man whose hand he held more tightly, who, he thought, was now holding more tightly on to him. And when he reached the

Gate of Heaven, instead of saying, "Can I enter?" as he had intended, he cried out, "Cannot *he* enter?"

And at the same moment the Turk uttered the same cry. For the same spirit was working in each of them.

From the gateway a voice replied, "Both can enter." They were filled with joy and pressed forward together.

Then the voice said, "In what clothes will you enter?"

"In my best clothes," shouted the Turk, "the ones I stole." And he clad himself in a splendid turban and a waistcoat embroidered with silver, and baggy trousers, and a great belt in which were stuck pipes and pistols and knives.

"And in what clothes will you enter?" said the voice to Mr. Andrews.

Mr. Andrews thought of his best clothes, but he had no wish to wear them again. At last he remembered and said, "Robes."

"Of what colour and fashion?" asked the voice.

Mr. Andrews had never thought about the matter much. He replied, in hesitating tones, "White, I suppose, of some flowing material," and he was immediately given a garment such as he had described. "Do I wear it rightly?" he asked.

"Wear it as it pleases you," replied the voice. "What else do you desire?"

"A harp," suggested Mr. Andrews. "A small one."

A small gold harp was placed in his hand.

"And a palm—no, I cannot have a palm, for it is the reward of martyrdom; my life has been tranquil and happy."

"You can have a palm if you desire it."

But Mr. Andrews refused the palm, and hurried in his white robes after the Turk, who had already entered Heaven. As he passed in at the open gate, a man, dressed like himself, passed out with gestures of despair.

"Why is he not happy?" he asked.

The voice did not reply.

"And who are all those figures, seated inside on thrones and mountains? Why are some of them terrible, and sad, and ugly?"

There was no answer. Mr. Andrews entered, and then he saw that those seated figures were all the gods who were then being worshipped on the earth. A group of souls stood around each, singing his praises. But the gods paid no heed, for they were listening to the prayers of living men, which alone brought them nourishment. Sometimes a faith would grow weak, and then the god of that faith also drooped and dwindled and fainted for his daily portion of incense. And sometimes, owing to a revivalist movement, or to a great commemoration, or to some other cause, a faith would grow strong, and the god of that faith grow strong also. And, more frequently still, a faith would alter, so that the features of its god altered and became contradictory, and passed from ecstasy to respectability, or from mildness and universal love to the ferocity of battle. And at times a god would divide into two gods, or three, or more, each with his own ritual and precarious supply of prayer.

Mr. Andrews saw Buddha, and Vishnu, and Allah, and Jehovah, and the Elohim. He saw little ugly determined gods who were worshipped by a few savages in the same way. He saw the vast shadowy outlines of the neo-pagan Zeus. There were cruel gods, and coarse gods, and tortured gods, and, worse still, there were gods who were peevish, or deceitful, or vulgar. No aspiration of humanity was unfulfilled. There was even an intermediate state for those who wished it, and for the Christian Scientists a place where they could demonstrate that they had not died.

He did not play his harp for long, but hunted vainly for one of his dead friends. And though souls were continually entering Heaven, it still seemed curiously empty. Though he had all that he expected, he was conscious of no great happiness, no mystic contemplation of beauty, no mystic union with good. There was nothing to compare with that moment outside the gate, when he prayed that the Turk might enter and heard the Turk uttering the same prayer for him. And when at last he saw his companion, he hailed him with a cry of human joy.

The Turk was seated in thought, and round him, by sevens, sat the virgins who are promised in the Koran.

"Oh, my dear friend!" he called out. "Come here, and we will never be parted, and such as my pleasures are, they shall be yours also. Where are my other friends? Where are the men whom I love, or whom I have killed?"

"I, too, have only found you," said Mr. Andrews. He sat down by the Turk, and the virgins, who were all exactly alike, ogled them with coal black eyes.

"Though I have all that I expected," said the Turk, "I am conscious of no great happiness. There is nothing to compare with that moment outside the gate when I prayed that you might enter, and heard you uttering the same prayer for me. These virgins are as beautiful and good as I had fashioned, yet I could wish that they were better."

As he wished, the forms of the virgins became more rounded, and their eyes grew larger and blacker than before. And Mr. Andrews, by a wish similar in kind, increased the purity and softness of his garment and the glitter of his harp. For in that place their expectations were fulfilled, but not their hopes.

"I am going," said Mr. Andrews at last. "We desire infinity and we cannot imagine it. How can we expect it to be granted? I have never imagined anything infinitely good or beautiful excepting in my dreams."

"I am going with you," said the other.

Together they sought the entrance gate, and the Turk parted with his virgins and his best clothes, and Mr. Andrews cast away his robes and his harp.

"Can we depart?" they asked.

"You can both depart if you wish," said the voice, "but remember what lies outside."

As soon as they passed the gate, they felt again the pressure of the world soul. For a moment they stood hand in hand resisting it. Then they suffered it to break in upon them, and they, and all the experience they had gained, and all the love and wisdom they had generated, passed into it, and made it better.

THE SMALL MIRACLE
by Paul Gallico

APPROACHING Assisi via the chalky, dusty road that twists its way up Monte Subasio, now revealing, now concealing the exquisite little town, as it winds its way through olive and cypress groves, you eventually reach a division where your choice lies between an upper and a lower route.

If you select the latter, you soon find yourself entering Assisi through the twelfth-century archway of the denticulated door of St. Francis. But if, seduced by the clear air, the wish to mount even closer to the canopy of blue Italian sky and expose still more of the delectable view of the rich Umbrian valley below, you choose the upper way, you and your vehicle eventually become inextricably entangled in the welter of humanity, oxen, goats, bawling calves, mules, fowl, children, pigs, booths and carts gathered at the market place outside the walls.

It is here you would be most likely to encounter Pepino, with his donkey Violetta, hard at work, turning his hand to anything whereby a small boy and a strong, willing beast of burden could win for themselves the crumpled ten and twenty lira notes needed to buy food and pay for lodging in the barn of Niccolo the stableman.

Pepino and Violetta were everything to each other. They were a familiar sight about Assisi and its immediate environs— the thin brown boy, ragged and barefooted, with the enormous dark eyes, large ears, and close-cropped, upstanding hair, and the dust-colored little donkey with the Mona Lisa smile.

Pepino was ten years old and an orphan, his father, mother and near relatives having been killed in the war. In self-reliance, wisdom and demeanor he was, of course, much older, a circumstance aided by his independence, for Pepino was an unusual orphan in that having a heritage he need rely on no one. Pepino's heritage was Violetta.

She was a good, useful and docile donkey, alike as any other with friendly, gentle eyes, soft taupe-colored muzzle, and long, pointed brown ears, with one exception that distinguished her. Violetta had a curious expression about the corners of her mouth, as though she was smiling gently over something that amused or pleased her. Thus, no matter what kind of work, or how much she was asked to do, she always appeared to be performing it with a smile of quiet satisfaction. The combination of Pepino's dark lustrous eyes and Violetta's smile was so harmonious that people favored them and they were able not only to earn enough for their keep but, aided and advised by Father Damico, the priest of their parish, to save a little as well.

There were all kinds of things they could do—carry loads of wood or water, deliver purchases carried in the panniers that thumped against Violetta's sides, hire out to help pull a cart mired in the mud, aid in the olive harvest, and even, occasionally, help some citizen who was too encumbered with wine to reach his home on foot, by means of a four-footed taxi with Pepino walking beside to see that the drunkard did not fall off.

But this was not the only reason for the love that existed between boy and donkey, for Violetta was more than just the means of his livelihood. She was mother to him, and father, brother, playmate, companion, and comfort. At night, in the straw of Niccolo's stable, Pepino slept curled up close to her when it was cold, his head pillowed on her neck.

Since the mountainside was a rough world for a small boy, he was sometimes beaten or injured, and then he could creep to her for comfort and Violetta would gently nuzzle his bruises. When there was joy in his heart, he shouted songs into her waving ears; when he was lonely and hurt, he could lean his head against her soft, warm flank and cry out his tears.

On his part, he fed her, watered her, searched her for ticks and parasites, picked stones from her hoofs, scratched and groomed and curried her, lavished affection on her, particularly when they were alone, while in public he never beat her with the donkey stick more than was necessary. For this treatment Violetta made a god of Pepino, and repaid him with loyalty, obedience and affection.

Thus, when one day in the early spring Violetta fell ill, it was the most serious thing that had ever happened to Pepino. It began first with an unusual lethargy that would respond neither to stick nor caresses, nor the young, strident voice urging her on. Later Pepino observed other symptoms and a visible loss of weight. Her ribs, once so well padded, began to show through her sides. But most distressing, either through a change in the conformation of her head, due to growing thinner, or because of the distress of the illness, Violetta lost her enchanting and lovable smile.

Drawing upon his carefully hoarded reserves of lira notes and parting with several of the impressive denomination of a hundred, Pepino called in Dr. Bartoli, the vet.

The vet examined her in good faith, dosed her, and tried his best; but she did not improve and, instead, continued to lose weight and grow weaker. He hummed and hawed then and said, "Well, now, it is hard to say. It might be one thing, such as the bite of a fly new to this district, or another, such as a germ settling in the intestine." Either way, how could one tell? There had been a similar case in Foligno and another in a far-away town. He recommended resting the beast and feeding her lightly.

If the illness passed from her and God willed, she might live. Otherwise, she would surely die and there would be an end to her suffering.

After he had gone away, Pepino put his cropped head on Violetta's heaving flank and wept unrestrainedly. But then, when the storm, induced by the fear of losing his only companion in the world, had subsided, he knew what he must do. If there was no help for Violetta on earth, the appeal must be registered above. His plan was nothing less than to take Violetta into the crypt beneath the lower church of the Basilica of St. Francis, where rested the remains of the Saint who had so dearly loved God's creations, including all the feathered and the four-footed brothers and sisters who served Him. There he would beg St. Francis to heal her. Pepino had no doubt that the Saint would do so when he saw Violetta.

These things Pepino knew from Father Damico, who had a way of talking about St. Francis as though he were a living person who might still be encountered in his frayed cowl, bound with a hemp cord at the middle, merely by turning a corner of the Main Square in Assisi or by walking down one of the narrow, cobbled streets.

And besides, there was a precedent. Giani, his friend, the son of Niccolo the stableman, had taken his sick kitten into the crypt and asked St. Francis to heal her, and the cat had got well —at least half well, anyway, for her hind legs still dragged a little; but at least she had not died. Pepino felt that if Violetta were to die, it would be the end of everything for him.

Thereupon, with considerable difficulty, he persuaded the sick and shaky donkey to rise, and with urgings and caresses and minimum use of the stick drove her through the crooked streets of Assisi and up the hill to the Basilica of St. Francis. At the beautiful twin portal of the lower church he respectfully asked Fra Bernard, who was on duty there, for permission to take Violetta down to St. Francis, so that she might be made well again.

Fra Bernard was a new monk, and, calling Pepino a young

and impious scoundrel, ordered him and his donkey to be off. It was strictly forbidden to bring livestock into the church, and even to think of taking an ass into the crypt of St. Francis was a desecration. And besides, how did he imagine she would get down there when the narrow, winding staircase was barely wide enough to accommodate humans in single file, much less four-footed animals? Pepino must be a fool as well as a shiftless rascal.

As ordered, Pepino retreated from the portal, his arm about Violetta's neck, and bethought himself of what he must do next to succeed in his purpose, for while he was disappointed at the rebuff he had received, he was not at all discouraged.

Despite the tragedy that had struck Pepino's early life and robbed him of his family, he really considered himself a most fortunate boy, compared with many, since he had acquired not only a heritage to aid him in earning a living but also an important precept by which to live.

This maxim, the golden key to success, had been left with Pepino, together with bars of chocolate, chewing gum, peanut brittle, soap, and other delights, by a corporal in the United States Army who had, in the six months he had been stationed in the vicinity of Assisi, been Pepino's demigod and hero. His name was Francis Xavier O'Halloran, and what he told Pepino before he departed out of this life forever was, "If you want to get ahead in this world, kid, don't never take no for an answer. Get it?" Pepino never forgot this important advice.

He thought now that his next step was clear; nevertheless, he went first to his friend and adviser, Father Damico, for confirmation.

Father Damico, who had a broad head, lustrous eyes, and shoulders shaped as though they had been especially designed to support the burdens laid upon them by his parishioners, said, "You are within your rights, my son, in taking your request to the lay Supervisor and it lies within his power to grant or refuse it."

There was no malice in the encouragement he thus gave

Pepino, but it was also true that he was not loath to see the Supervisor brought face to face with an example of pure and innocent faith. For in his private opinion that worthy man was too much concerned with the twin churches that formed the Basilica and the crypt as a tourist attraction. He, Father Damico, could not see why the child should not have his wish, but, of course, it was out of his jurisdiction. He was, however, curious about how the Supervisor would react, even though he thought he knew in advance.

However, he did not impart his fears to Pepino and merely called after him as he was leaving, "And if the little one cannot be got in from above, there is another entrance from below, through the old church, only it has been walled up for a hundred years. But it could be opened. You might remind the Supervisor when you see him. He knows where it is."

Pepino thanked him and went back alone to the Basilica and the monastery attached to it and asked permission to see the Supervisor.

This personage was an accessible man, and even though he was engaged in a conversation with the Bishop, he sent for Pepino, who walked into the cloister gardens where he waited respectfully for the two great men to finish.

The two dignitaries were walking up and down, and Pepino wished it were the Bishop who was to say yea or nay to his request, as he looked the kindlier of the two, the Supervisor appearing to have more the expression of a merchant. The boy pricked up his ears, because, as it happened, they were speaking of St. Francis, and the Bishop was just remarking with a sigh, "He has been gone too long from this earth. The lesson of his life is plain to all who can read. But who in these times will pause to do so?"

The Supervisor said, "His tomb in the crypt attracts many to Assisi. But in a Holy Year, relics are even better. If we but had the tongue of the Saint, or a lock of his hair, or a fingernail."

The Small Miracle

The Bishop had a far-away look in his eyes, and he was shaking his head gently. "It is a message we are in need of, my dear Supervisor, a message from a great heart that would speak to us across the gap of seven centuries to remind us of The Way." And here he paused and coughed, for he was a polite man and noticed that Pepino was waiting.

The Supervisor turned also and said, "Ah yes, my son, what is it that I can do for you?"

Pepino said, "Please, sir, my donkey Violetta is very sick. The Doctor Bartoli has said he can do nothing more and perhaps she will die. Please, I would like permission to take her into the tomb of St. Francis and ask him to cure her. He loved all animals, and particularly little donkeys. I am sure he will make her well."

The Supervisor looked shocked. "A donkey. In the crypt. However did you come to that idea?"

Pepino explained about Giani and his sick kitten, while the Bishop turned away to hide a smile.

But the Supervisor was not smiling. He asked, "How did this Giani succeed in smuggling a kitten into the tomb?"

Since it was all over, Pepino saw no reason for not telling, and replied, "Under his coat, sir."

The Supervisor made a mental note to warn the brothers to keep a sharper eye out for small boys or other persons with suspicious-looking lumps under their outer clothing.

"Of course we can have no such goings on," he said. "The next thing you know, everyone would be coming, bringing a sick dog, or an ox, or a goat, or even a pig. And then where should we end up? A veritable sty."

"But, sir," Pepino pleaded, "no one need know. We would come and go so very quickly."

The Supervisor's mind played. There was something touching about the boy—the bullet head, the enormous eyes, the jug-handle ears. And yet, what if he permitted it and the donkey then died, as seemed most likely if Dr. Bartoli had said there was no further hope? Word was sure to get about, and the shrine would suffer from it. He wondered what the Bishop was thinking and how *he* would solve the problem.

He equivocated: "And besides, even if we were to allow it, you would never be able to get your donkey around the turn at the bottom of the stairs. So, you see, it is quite impossible."

"But there is another entrance," Pepino said. "From the old church. It has not been used for a long time, but it could be opened just this once—couldn't it?"

The Supervisor was indignant. "What are you saying—destroy church property? The entrance has been walled up for over a century, ever since the new crypt was built."

The Bishop thought he saw a way out and said gently to the boy, "Why do you not go home and pray to St. Francis to assist you? If you open your heart to him and have faith, he will surely hear you."

"But it wouldn't be the same," Pepino cried, and his voice was shaking with the sobs that wanted to come. "I must take her where St. Francis can see her. She isn't like any other old donkey —Violetta has the sweetest smile. She does not smile any more since she has been so ill. But perhaps she would, just once more for St. Francis. And when he saw it he would not be able to resist her, and he would make her well. I know he would!"

The Supervisor knew his ground now. He said, "I am sorry, my son, but the answer is no."

But even through his despair and the bitter tears he shed as he went away, Pepino knew that if Violetta was to live he must not take no for an answer.

"Who is there, then?" Pepino asked of Father Damico later. "Who is above the Supervisor and my lord the Bishop who might tell them to let me take Violetta into the crypt?"

Father Damico's stomach felt cold as he thought of the dizzying hierarchy between Assisi and Rome. Nevertheless, he explained as best he could, concluding with, "And at the top is His Holiness, the Pope himself. Surely his heart would be touched by what has happened if you were able to tell him, for he is a great and good man. But he is busy with important weighty affairs, Pepino, and it would be impossible for him to see you."

Pepino went back to Niccolo's stable, where he ministered to Violetta, fed and watered her and rubbed her muzzle a hundred times. Then he withdrew his money from the stone jar buried under the straw and counted it. He had almost three hundred lire. A hundred of it he set aside and promised to his friend Giani if he would look after Violetta, while Pepino was gone, as if she were his own. Then he patted her once more, brushed away the tears that had started again at the sight of how thin she was, put on his jacket, and went out on the high road, where, using his thumb as he had learned from Corporal Francis Xavier O'Halloran, he got a lift in a lorry going to Foligno and the main road. He was on his way to Rome to see the Holy Father.

Never had any small boy looked quite so infinitesimal and forlorn as Pepino standing in the boundless and almost deserted, since it was early in the morning, St. Peter's Square. Everything towered over him—the massive dome of St. Peter's, the obelisk of Caligula, the Bernini colonnades. Everything contrived to make him look pinched and miserable in his bare feet, torn trousers, and ragged jacket. Never was a boy more overpowered, lonely, and frightened, or carried a greater burden of unhappiness in his heart.

For now that he was at last in Rome, the gigantic proportions of the buildings and monuments, their awe and majesty, began to sap his courage, and he seemed to have a glimpse into the utter futility and hopelessness of his mission. And then there would arise in his mind a picture of the sad little donkey who did not smile any more, her heaving flanks and clouded eyes, and who would surely die unless he could find help for her. It was thoughts like these that enabled him finally to cross the piazza and timidly approach one of the smaller side entrances to the Vatican.

The Swiss guard, in his slashed red, yellow, and blue uniform, with his long halberd, looked enormous and forbidding. Nevertheless, Pepino edged up to him and said, "Please, will you take me to see the Pope? I wish to speak to him about my donkey Violetta, who is very ill and may die unless the Pope will help me."

The guard smiled, not unkindly, for he was used to these ignorant and innocent requests, and the fact that it came from a dirty, ragged little boy, with eyes like ink pools and a round head from which the ears stood out like the handles on a cream jug, made it all the more harmless. But, nevertheless, he was shaking his head as he smiled, and then said that His Holiness was a very busy man and could not be seen. And the guard grounded his halberd with a thud and let it fall slantwise across the door to show that he meant business.

Pepino backed away. What good was his precept in the face of such power and majesty? And yet the memory of what Corporal O'Halloran had said told him that he must return to the Vatican yet once again.

At the side of the piazza he saw an old woman sitting under an umbrella, selling little bouquets and nosegays of spring flowers —daffodils and jonquils, snowdrops and white narcissus, Parma violets and lilies of the valley, vari-colored carnations, pansies, and tiny sweetheart roses. Some of the people visiting St. Peter's liked to place these on the altar of their favorite saint. The flowers were crisp and fresh from the market, and many of them had glistening drops of water still clinging to their petals.

Looking at them made Pepino think of home and Father Damico and what he had said of the love St. Francis had for flowers. Father Damico had the gift of making everything he thought and said sound like poetry. And Pepino came to the conclusion that if St. Francis, who had been a holy man, had been so fond of flowers, perhaps the Pope, who according to his position was even holier, would love them, too.

For fifty lire he bought a tiny bouquet in which a spray of lilies of the valley rose from a bed of dark violets and small red roses crowded next to yellow pansies all tied about with leaf and feather fern and paper lace.

From a stall where postcards and souvenirs were sold, he begged pencil and paper, and laboriously composed a note:

Dear and most sacred Holy Father:
These flowers are for you. Please let me see you and tell you about my donkey Violetta who is dying, and they will not let me take her to see St. Francis so that he may cure her. I live in the town of Assisi, but I have come all the way here to see you.
Your loving Pepino.

Thereupon, he returned to the door, placed the bouquet and the note in the hand of the Swiss guard, and begged, "Please take these up to the Pope. I am sure he will see me when he receives the flowers and reads what I have written."

The guard had not expected this. The child and the flowers had suddenly placed him in a dilemma from which he could not extricate himself in the presence of those large and trusting eyes. However, he was not without experience in handling such matters. He had only to place a colleague at his post, go to the Guard Room, throw the flowers and the note into the wastepaper basket, absent himself for a sufficient length of time, and then return to tell the boy that His Holiness thanked him for the gift of the flowers and regretted that press of important business made it impossible for him to grant him an audience.

This little subterfuge the guard put into motion at once; but when he came to completing the next-to-last act in it, he found to his amazement that somehow he could not bring himself to do it. There was the wastepaper basket, yawning to receive the offering, but the little nosegay seemed to be glued to his fingers. How gay, sweet, and cool the flowers were. What thoughts they brought to his mind of spring in the green valleys of his far-off canton of Luzern. He saw again the snow-capped mountains of his youth, the little gingerbread houses, the gray, soft-eyed cattle grazing in the blossom-carpeted meadows, and he heard the heart-warming tinkling of their bells.

Dazed by what had happened to him, he left the Guard Room and wandered through the corridors, for he did not know where to go or what to do with his burden. He was eventually encountered by a busy little Monsignor, one of the vast army of clerks and secretaries employed in the Vatican, who paused, astonished at the sight of the burly guard helplessly contemplating a tiny posy.

And thus occurred the minor miracle whereby Pepino's plea and offering crossed the boundary in the palace that divided the mundane from the spiritual, the lay from the ecclesiastical.

For to the great relief of the guard, the Monsignor took over the burning articles that he had been unable to relinquish; and this priest they touched, too, as it is the peculiar power of flowers that while they are universal and spread their species over the world, they invoke in each beholder the dearest and most cherished memories.

In this manner, the little bouquet passed on and upward from hand to hand, pausing briefly in the possession of the clerk of the Apostolic Chamber, the Privy Almoner, the Papal Sacristan, the Master of the Sacred Palaces, the Papal Chamberlain. The dew vanished from the flowers; they began to lose their freshness and to wilt, passing from hand to hand. And yet they retained their magic, the message of love and memories that rendered it impossible for any of these intermediaries to dispose of them.

Eventually, then, they were deposited with the missive that accompanied them on the desk of the man for whom they had been destined. He read the note and then sat there silently contemplating the blossoms. He closed his eyes for a moment, the better to entertain the picture that arose in his mind of himself as a small Roman boy taken on a Sunday into the Alban Hills, where for the first time he saw violets growing wild.

When he opened his eyes at last, he said to his secretary, "Let the child be brought here. I will see him."

Thus it was that Pepino at last came into the presence of the Pope, seated at his desk in his office. Perched on the edge of a chair next to him, Pepino told the whole story about Violetta, his need to take her into the tomb of St. Francis, about the Supervisor who was preventing him, and all about Father Damico, too, and the second entrance to the crypt, Violetta's smile, and his love for her—everything, in fact, that was in his heart and that now poured forth to the sympathetic man sitting quietly behind the desk.

And when, at the end of half an hour, he was ushered from the presence, he was quite sure he was the happiest boy in the world. For he had not only the blessing of the Pope, but also, under his jacket, two letters, one addressed to the lay Supervisor of the Monastery of Assisi and the other to Father Damico. No longer did he feel small and overwhelmed when he stepped out on to the square again past the astonished but delighted Swiss guard. He felt as though he could give one leap and a bound and fly back to his Violetta's side.

Nevertheless, he had to give heed to the more practical side of transportation. He enquired his way to a bus that took him to where the Via Flaminia became a country road stretching to the north, then plied his thumb backed by his eloquent eyes, and before nightfall of that day, with good luck, was home in Assisi.

After a visit to Violetta had assured him that she had been well looked after and at least was no worse than she had been before his departure, Pepino proudly went to Father Damico and presented his letters as he had been instructed to do.

The Father fingered the envelope for the Supervisor and then, with a great surge of warmth and happiness, read the one addressed to himself. He said to Pepino, "Tomorrow we will take the Supervisor's letter to him. He will summon masons and the old door will be broken down and you will be able to take Violetta into the tomb and pray there for her recovery. The Pope himself has approved it."

The Pope, of course, had not written the letters personally. They had been composed with considerable delight and satisfaction by the Cardinal-Secretary, backed by Papal authority, who said in his missive to Father Damico:

Surely the Supervisor must know that in his lifetime the blessed St. Francis was accompanied to chapel by a little lamb that used to follow him about Assisi. Is an asinus any less created by God because his coat is rougher and his ears longer?

And he wrote also of another matter, which Father Damico imparted to Pepino in his own way.

He said, "Pepino, there is something you must understand before we go to see the Abbot. It is your hope that because of your faith in St. Francis he will help you and heal your donkey. But had you thought, perhaps, that he who dearly cared for all of God's creatures might come to love Violetta so greatly that he would wish to have her at his side in Eternity?"

A cold terror gripped Pepino as he listened. He managed to say, "No, Father, I had not thought—" The priest continued: "Will you go to the crypt only to ask, Pepino, or will you also, if necessary, be prepared to give?"

Everything in Pepino cried out against the possibility of losing Violetta, even to someone as beloved as St. Francis. Yet when he raised his stricken face and looked into the lustrous eyes of Father Damico, there was something in their depths that gave him the courage to whisper, "I will give—if I must. But, oh, I hope he will let her stay with me just a little longer."

The clink of the stonemason's pick rang again and again through the vaulted chamber of the lower church, where the walled-up door of the passageway leading to the crypt was being removed. Nearby waited the Supervisor and his friend the Bishop, Father Damico, and Pepino, large-eyed, pale, and silent. The boy kept his arms about the neck of Violetta and his face pressed to hers. The little donkey was very shaky on her legs and could barely stand.

The Supervisor watched humbly and impassively while broken bricks and clods of mortar fell as the breach widened and the freed current of air from the passage swirled the plaster dust in clouds. He was a just man for all his weakness and had invited the Bishop to witness his rebuke.

A portion of the wall proved obstinate. The mason attacked the archway at the side to weaken its support. Then the loosened masonry began to tumble again. A narrow passageway was effected, and through the opening they could see the distant flicker of the candles placed at the altar wherein rested the remains of St. Francis.

Pepino stirred towards the opening. Or was it Violetta who had moved nervously, frightened by the unaccustomed place and noises? Father Damico said, "Wait," and Pepino held her; but the donkey's uncertain feet slipped on the rubble and then lashed out in panic, striking the side of the archway where it had been weakened. A brick fell out. A crack appeared.

Father Damico leaped and pulled boy and animal out of the way as, with a roar, the side of the arch collapsed, laying bare a piece of the old wall and the hollow behind it before everything vanished in a cloud of dust.

But when the dust settled, the Bishop, his eyes starting from his head, was pointing to something that rested in a niche of the hollow just revealed. It was a small, gray, leaden box. Even from there they could see the year 1226, when St. Francis died, engraved on the side, and the large initial "F."

The Bishop's breath came out like a sigh. "Ah, could it be? The legacy of St. Francis! Fra Leo mentions it. It was hidden away centuries ago, and no one had ever been able to find it since."

The Supervisor said hoarsely, "The contents! Let us see what is inside—it may be valuable!"

The Bishop hesitated. "Perhaps we had best wait. For this is in itself a miracle, this finding."

But Father Damico, who was a poet and to whom St. Francis was a living spirit, cried, "Open it, I beg of you! All who are here are humble. Surely Heaven's plan has guided us to it."

The Abbot held the lantern. The mason with his careful, honest workman's hands deftly loosed the bindings and pried the lid of the airtight box. It opened with an ancient creaking of its hinge and revealed what had been placed there more than seven centuries before.

There was a piece of hempen cord, knotted as though, perhaps, once it had been worn about the waist. Caught in the knot, as fresh as though it had grown but yesterday, was a single sprig of wheat. Dried and preserved, there lay, too, the stem and starry flower of a mountain primrose and, next to it, one downy feather from a tiny meadow bird.

Silently the men stared at these objects from the past to try to read their meaning, and Father Damico wept, for to him they brought the vivid figure of the Saint, half-blinded, worn and fragile, the cord knotted at his waist, singing, striding through a field of wheat. The flower might have been the first discovered by him after a winter's snow, and addressed as "Sister Cowslip," and praised for her tenderness and beauty. As though he were transported there, Father Damico saw the little field bird fly trustingly to Francis' shoulder and chirrup and nestle there and leave a feather in his hand. His heart was so full he thought he could not bear it.

The Bishop, too, was close to tears as, in his own way, he interpreted what they had found. "Ah, what could be clearer than the message of the Saint? Poverty, love, and faith. This is his bequest to all of us."

Pepino said, "Please, lords and sirs, may Violetta and I go into the crypt now?"

They had forgotten him. Now they started up from their contemplation of the touching relics.

Father Damico cleared the tears from his eyes. The doorway was freed now, and there was room for boy and donkey to pass. "Ah, yes," he said. "Yes, Pepino. You may enter now. And may God go with you."

The hoofs of the donkey went sharply *clip-clop, clip-clop* on the ancient flagging of the passageway. Pepino did not support her now, but walked beside, hand just resting lightly and lovingly on her neck. His round, cropped head with the outstanding ears was held high, and his shoulders were bravely squared.

And to Father Damico it seemed, as they passed, whether because of the uneven light and the dancing shadows, or because he wished it so, that the ghost, the merest wisp, the barest suspicion of a smile had returned to the mouth of Violetta.

Thus the watchers saw boy and donkey silhouetted against the flickering oil lamps and altar candles of the crypt as they went forward to complete their pilgrimage of faith.

THE CITY
COAT OF ARMS

by Franz Kafka

AT FIRST all the arrangements for building the Tower of Babel were characterized by fairly good order, indeed the order was perhaps too perfect, too much thought was taken for guides, interpreters, accommodation for the workmen and roads of communication, as if there were centuries before one to do the work in. In fact the general opinion at that time was that one simply could not build too slowly; a very little insistence on this would have sufficed to make one hesitate to lay the foundations at all. People argued in this way: The essential thing in the whole business is the idea of building a tower that will reach to heaven. In comparison with that idea everything else is secondary. The idea, once seized in its magnitude, can never vanish again; so long as there are men on the earth there will be also the irresistible desire to complete the building. That being so, however, one need have no anxiety about the future; on the contrary, human knowledge is increasing, the art of building has

made progress and will make further progress, a piece of work which takes us a year may perhaps be done in half the time in another hundred years, and better done, too, more enduringly. So why exert oneself to the limit of one's present powers? There would be some sense in doing that only if it were likely that the tower could be completed in one generation. But that is beyond all hope. It is far more likely that the next generation with their perfected knowledge will find the work of their predecessors bad, and tear down what has been built so as to begin anew. Such thoughts paralysed people's powers, and so they troubled less about the tower than the construction of a city for the workmen. Every nationality wanted the finest quarter for itself, and this gave rise to disputes, which developed into bloody conflicts. These conflicts never came to an end; to the leaders they were a new proof that, in the absence of the necessary unity, the building of the tower must be done very slowly, or indeed preferably postponed until universal peace was declared. But the time was spent not only in conflict; the town was embellished in the intervals, and this unfortunately enough evoked fresh envy and fresh conflict. In this fashion the age of the first generation went past, but none of the succeeding ones showed any difference; except that technical skill increased and with it occasion for conflict. To this must be added that the second or third generation had already recognized the senselessness of building a heaven-reaching tower; but by that time everybody was too deeply involved to leave the city. All the legends and songs that came to birth in that city are filled with longing for a prophesied day when the city would be destroyed by five successive blows from a giant fist. It is for that reason too that the city has a closed fist on its coat of arms.

AERIAL FOOTBALL: THE NEW GAME

by George Bernard Shaw

Is she dead?" said the motor bus driver, looking very sick, as the medical student from the Free Hospital picked up Mrs. Hairns in the Gray's Inn Road.

"She smells frightfully of your petrol," said the student.

The driver sniffed at her. "That's not petrol," he said. "It's methylated spirit. She's been drinking. You'll bear me witness that she smells of drink."

"Don't you know all you've done yet?" said the policeman. "You've killed his lordship."

"What lordship?" said the driver, changing from tallow colour to green.

"The back end of the bus swung right into the carriage," panted the footman. "I heard his lordship's neck crack." The footman wept, not because he loved his late employer, but because sudden death affected him that way.

Aerial Football: The New Game

"The Bishop of St. Pancras," said a boy, in explanation.

"Oh, my good Lord!" said the motorman, in great trouble. "How could I help it?" he added, after wiping his brow, appealing to the crowd, which seemed to have been in solution in the air, so suddenly had it precipitated round the accident. "The bus skidded."

"So would any bus skid in this mud, going at that rate," said an indignant bystander.

And immediately the crowd began to dispute as to whether the bus had been going too fast or not, with the motorman passionately maintaining the negative against the affirmative of the whole Gray's Inn Road.

Mrs. Hairns certainly did smell of drink. She had done so more or less for forty years whenever she had twopence to spare. She had never been a nice looking woman nor a cleanly dressed one; and the passage of the crowded motor bus over her ribs had made surprisingly little difference in her appearance. A little more mud ground into her garments could make them no worse than they were; and the change from being drunk and able to shuffle home and being drunk and incapable was not startling.

As to the bishop, there was not a scratch nor a speck of mud on him. He had not been touched. He had been boyishly proud of being a bishop, and had expressed his pride by holding his neck very stiff. Consequently it broke when the carriage was stopped suddenly by the swinging round of the tail of the bus.

Mrs. Hairns was taken aback when the bus suddenly swooped round at her. That made no difference, because no presence of mind on her part could have saved her. It did not hurt her at all. A single broken rib touching a lung is painful; but when an overwhelming shock annihilates your nerves, and an overwhelming weight makes bone dust of all your ribs, and wraps them up in a squash with your heart and lungs, sympathy becomes ridiculous. The game is up. The remediable has become irremediable: the temporal, eternal. A really flexible mind accepts the situation and thinks a great deal about it before there is time even to die. The suddenest death is a long business compared with the lightning work of imagining an experience of, say, a thousand years.

Mrs. Hairns was squashed clean out of the Gray's Inn Road on to the foot of a hill with a city on the top. It was rather like Orvieto, of which city there was a photograph in the drawing room of the Vicar of St. Pancras, who employed Mrs. Hairns as a charwoman whenever he attempted to reclaim her, and was beaten every time by her acquired taste for methylated spirits, which enabled her to drink furniture polish with avidity, though you could trust her with untold dozens of mere hock. Beyond getting the photograph focussed on her retina occasionally whilst dusting, Mrs. Hairns knew nothing about Orvieto. A place so unlike Pentonville Hill suggested dread and discomfort to her. She felt sure it must be almost as bad as heaven, which she associated with teetotalism, cleanliness, self-control, being particular, and all sorts of horrors. Now that she found herself actually on the road to it, she looked up at it with the utmost misgiving until a superior voice behind her made her start and attempt a shambling curtsey. It was the bishop.

"Can I obtain a conveyance anywhere here," he said, "to take me up to the gate?"

"I can't say, I'm sure, sir," said Mrs. Hairns: "I'm a stranger here."

The bishop passed on the moment she said "can't say," taking no further interest in her, and resigned himself to walk up.

There was a horse grazing a little way off. As Mrs. Hairns noticed it, a faint ray of heavenly comfort stole into her soul. Though for many years—ever since the passing away of the last rays of her youth at twenty-four or thereabouts—she had been interested in nothing but methylated alcohol, she had been born with an unaccountable fancy, not for horses exactly, but, as she put it, for a horse. It was an unintelligent and innocent fancy; but it had won her hand in marriage for the late Alfred Hairns, normally and by economic necessity a carman, but by natural vocation a poacher. This rude fancier of the equine was too poor to afford a horse. But after all he was too poor to afford a residence in London, or a double bed, or even a suit of clothes. Yet he always had a London address; he never appeared in the streets naked; and neither he nor Mrs. Hairns slept on the floor. Society had convinced him that the lodging, the bed, and the clothes were indispensable, whether he could afford them or not: accordingly, he had them. The conviction that a horse was equally indispensable was idiosyncratic with him; so he always kept a horse, even when he could by no means afford to keep himself, maintaining that a horse made no difference—that it even paid its way. The same view has been taken of 80 h.p. motor cars.

Bonavia Banks was attracted by his idiosyncrasy, which was also her own. She easily persuaded him that a wife was as indispensable as a horse, and equally made no difference. She became Mrs. Alfred Hairns, and bore thirteen children, of whom eleven died in infancy owing to the malversation of their parental care by the horse. Finally the horse died; and the heartbroken Hairns was tempted to buy a magnificent thoroughbred for four pounds from the widow of a gentleman who had paid two hundred and thirty for him only three days before. Hairns, whilst leading his bargain home, was savaged by him so that he died of lockjaw the day after the horse was shot. Thus perished miserably Alfred Hairns, the victim of the bond between man and beast which proclaims that all life is one.

The horse raised its muzzle from the grass; looked at Mrs. Hairns carelessly; switched its tail; moved on a few steps to an uncropped patch of verdure; and was about to continue its repast when, as if some fibre of memory had suddenly vibrated, it erected its ears; raised its neck; and looked more attentively at her. Finally it came to her, stopping only once on the way absent-mindedly to graze, and said, "Don't you remember me?"

"Chipper!" exclaimed Mrs. Hairns. "It can't be."

"It *is*," said Chipper.

Chipper conversed after the manner of Balaam's ass. That is, Mrs. Hairns knew what he was saying too well to notice that

he did not actually utter any sound. But for the matter of that neither did she, though she did not notice that also. Conversation in this Orvietan region was wholly telepathic.

"Have I got to walk up that hill, Chipper?" said Mrs. Hairns.

"Yes," said Chipper, "unless I carry you."

"Would you mind?" said Mrs. Hairns shyly.

"Not at all," said Chipper.

"Ain't there a vehicle?" said Mrs. Hairns. "I can't ride barebacked. Not that I can ride anyhow."

"Then you must walk," said Chipper. "Hold on to my mane; and I'll help you up."

They got up somehow, and were close to the gate before it occurred to Mrs. Hairns to ask what place it was, and to ask herself why she was going there.

"It's heaven," said Chipper.

"Oh Lord!" said Mrs. Hairns, stopping dead. "Why didn't you tell me before? I never done anything to get me into heaven."

"True," said Chipper. "Would you rather go to hell?"

"Don't be so silly, Chipper," said Mrs. Hairns. "Ain't there nothin' between hell and heaven? We ain't all saints; but then we ain't all devils neither. Surely to gracious there must be a place for everyday sort of people that don't set up to be too particular."

"This is the only place I know," said Chipper; "and it's certainly heaven."

"Belike there might be some kitchens in it," said Mrs. Hairns. "You won't let on that I used to get a bit overcome once in a way, Chipper, will you?"

Chipper snuffed up a noseful of Mrs. Hairns's aura. "I should keep on the lee side of St. Peter," he said. "That's Peter," he added jerking his head in the direction of an elderly gentleman with a pair of keys of XII century design.

The keys were more for ornament than use, apparently; for the gate stood wide open; and a stone placed against it to keep it from blowing-to was covered with moss, and had evidently not been moved for centuries. This surprised Mrs. Hairns, because it had been strongly impressed on her in her childhood on earth that the gates of heaven were always shut tight, and that it was no end of a business to get them opened.

A group of angels stood in the carriage way. Their wings, purple and gold, heliotrope and silver, amber and black, and all sorts of fine colours, struck Mrs. Hairns as lovely. One of them had a sword with a blade of lambent garnet-coloured flame. Another, with one leg naked from the knee down, and a wading boot on the other, had a straight slender trumpet, which seemed long enough to reach to the horizon and yet was as handy as an umbrella. Through the first floor window of one of the turrets of the gate Mrs. Hairns saw Matthew, Mark, Luke, and John in bed with their breeches on according to the old rhyme. Seeing that, she knew this was really the gate of heaven. Nothing else would have quite convinced her.

Chipper addressed himself to Peter. "This woman is drunk," said Chipper.

"So I see," said St. Peter.

"Ow Chipper!" said Mrs. Hairns reproachfully. "How could you?" They all looked at her; and she began to cry. The angel with the sword of flame drew it across her eyes and dried her tears. The flame did not hurt, and was wonderfully reviving.

"I'm afraid she's hopeless," said Chipper. "Her own children will have nothing to do with her."

"Which planet?" said the angel with the trumpet.

"Tellus," answered Chipper.

"What am I to tell them?" said Mrs. Hairns.

The angels laughed. Peter roared. "Come!" said the trumpet angel: "she can make puns. What's wrong with her?"

"She's a liar and a thief," said Chipper.

"All the inhabitants of Tellus are liars and thieves," said the trumpet angel.

"I mean she is what even they call a liar and a thief," said Chipper.

"Oh!" said the sword angel, looking very grave.

"I'm only making it easy for you," said Chipper to Mrs. Hairns; "so that they shan't expect too much." Then, to Peter, "I brought her up because she once got out and walked on a hot Sunday when I was dragging her up a hill with her husband, three of his friends, their wives, eight children, a baby, and three dozen of beer."

"Fancy your remembering!" said Mrs. Hairns. "Did I really?"

"It was so unlike you, if I may say so," said Chipper, "that I have never forgotten it."

"I dessay it *was* silly of me," said Mrs. Hairns apologetically.

Just then the bishop arrived. He had been energetically climbing the hill by the little foot tracks which cut across the zigzags of the road, and had consequently been overtaken by Chipper, who knew better.

"Is this the gate of heaven?" said the bishop.

"It is," said Peter.

"The *front* gate?" said the bishop suspiciously. "You are sure it is not the tradesman's entrance?"

"It is everybody's entrance," said Peter.

"An unusual arrangement, and in my opinion an inconvenient one," said the bishop. He turned from Peter to the angels, "Gentlemen," he said. "I am the Bishop of St. Pancras."

"If you come to that," said a youth in a dalmatic, putting his head out of one of the turret windows, "I am St. Pancras himself."

"As your bishop, I am glad to meet you," said the bishop, "I take a personal interest in every member of my flock. But for the moment I must ask you to excuse me, as I have pressing business at court. By your leave, gentlemen"—and he shouldered his way firmly through the group of angels into heaven and trotted sturdily up the street. He turned only once, for a moment, to say, "Better announce me," and went his way. The angels stared after him quite dumbfounded. Then the trumpet angel made a post horn of his trumpet, and first root-a-tooted at the sky, and then swept the trumpet downwards like the ray of a searchlight. It reached along the street to the bishop's coat tails; and the next blast swept him like a dry leaf clean round a corner and out of sight.

The angels smiled a beautifully grave smile. Mrs. Hairns could not help laughing. "Ain't he a tease!" she said to Chipper, indicating the trumpet angel.

"Hadn't you better follow the bishop in?" said Chipper.

Mrs. Hairns looked apprehensively at Peter (she was not afraid of the angels), and asked him might she go in.

"Anybody may go in," said Peter. "What do you suppose the gate is for?"

"I didn't understand, sir," said Mrs. Hairns. And she was approaching the threshold timidly when the bishop came back, flushed and indignant.

"I have been through the whole city in a very high wind," said the bishop; "and I cannot find it. I question whether this is really heaven at all."

"Find what?" said Peter.

"The Throne, sir," said the bishop severely.

"*This* is the throne," said St. Pancras, who was still looking out of the window, with his cheeks on his palms and his palms propped on his elbows.

"*This!*" said the bishop. "Which?"

"The city," said St. Pancras.

"But—but—where is He?" said the bishop.

"Here, of course," said the sword angel.

"*Here!* Where?" said the bishop hurriedly, lowering his voice and looking apprehensively round from one to the other until he finished with the trumpet angel, who had sat down to take off his wading boot and shake a stone out of it.

"He is the presence in which we live," said the sword angel, speaking very harmoniously.

"That is why they are angels," St. Pancras explained.

"What are you looking about for?" said the trumpet angel,

standing up with his boot comfortable again. "Did you expect to see somebody in a shovel hat and apron, with a nose, and a handkerchief to blow it with?"

The bishop reddened. "Sir," he said, "you are profane. You are blasphemous. You are even wanting in good taste. But for the charity my profession imposes on me I should be tempted to question whether you are in the truest sense of the word a gentleman. Good morning." And he shook the dust of heaven from his feet and walked away.

"Ain't he a cure!" said Mrs. Hairns. "But I'm glad there's no throne, nor nobody, nor nothin'. It'll be more like King's Cross." She looked at them rather desolately; for something in the sword angel's voice had made her feel very humble and even ashamed of being drunk. They all looked back at her gravely; and she would have cried again, only she knew it would be of no use after the sword had touched her eyes: her tears were dried for ever. She twisted a corner of her jacket—a deplorable jacket —in her restless fingers; and there was a silence, unbroken until the snoring of Matthew, Mark, Luke, and John became painfully audible, and made her look forlornly up at their common little wooden beds, and at the flyblown illuminated text on the wall above them: "A broken and a contrite heart, O Lord, thou wilt not despise."

"I wonder," she said, "would one of you gentlemen say a prayer for a poor drunken old charwoman that has buried eleven, and nobody's enemy but her own, before I offer to go in."

Suddenly she sat down stunned in the middle of the way; for every angel threw up his hands and wings with an amazing outcry; the sword flamed all over the sky; the trumpet searched the corners of the horizon and filled the universe with ringing notes; and the stars became visible in broad daylight and sent back an echo which affected Mrs. Hairns like an enormous draught of some new and delightful sort of methylated spirit.

"Oh, not such a fuss about me, gentlemen," she said. "They'll think it's a queen or a lady from Tavistock Square or the like." And she felt shyer than ever about going in. The sword angel smiled, and was going to speak to her when the bishop came back, pegging along more sturdily than ever.

"Gentlemen," he said: "I have been thinking over what passed just now; and whilst my reason tells me that I was entirely justified in acting and speaking as I did, still, your point of view may be a tenable one, and your method of expressing it, however unbecoming, effective for its purpose. I also find myself the victim of an uncontrollable impulse to act in a manner which I cannot excuse, though refraint is unfortunately beyond my powers of self-inhibition."

And with that speech he snatched off his apron; made a ball of it; stuffed it into his shovel hat; and kicked the hat into space. Before it could descend, the sword angel, with a single cut of his wings, sprang into the air whooping with ecstasy, and kicked it a mile higher. St. Pancras, who had no wings, but shot up by mere levitation, was on it in a second and was shooting off with it when the trumpet angel collared him and passed it to the amber and black angel. By that time Matthew, Mark, Luke, and John were out of bed and after Peter into the blue vault above, where a football match was already in full swing between the angels and the saints, with Sirius for one goal and the sun for the other. The bishop looked in amazement for a moment at the flying scrum; then, with a yell, sprang into the air and actually got up nearly fifty feet, but was falling from that dangerous height when the saint he patronized swooped and caught him up into the game. Twenty seconds later his hat was halfway to the moon; and the exultant shouts of the angels had dwindled to mere curlew pipings, whilst the celestial players looked smaller than swifts circling over Rome in summer.

Now was Mrs. Hairns's opportunity to creep in through the gate unnoticed. As her foot approached the threshold the houses of the heavenly street shone friendly in the sunshine before her; and the mosaics in the pavement glowed like flower beds of jewels.

"She's dead," said the student from the Free Hospital. "I think there was a spark left when I took hold of her to straighten her out; but it was only a spark. She's dead now all right enough — I mean poor woman!"

PART III

Revelations and Celebrations

THE MAN WHO SAW
THROUGH HEAVEN

by Wilbur Daniel Steele

P EOPLE have wondered (there being obviously no question of
romance involved) how I could ever have allowed myself to
be let in for the East African adventure of Mrs. Diana in search of
her husband. There were several reasons. To begin with, the time
and effort and money weren't mine; they were the property of
the wheel of which I was but a cog, the Society through which
Diana's life had been insured, along with the rest of that job lot
of missionaries. The "letting in" was the firm's. In the second
place, the wonderers have not counted on Mrs. Diana's capacity
for getting things done for her. Meek and helpless. Yes, but God
was on her side. Too meek, too helpless to move mountains herself, if those who happened to be handy didn't move them for
her then her God would know the reasons why. Having dedicated
her all to makeing straight the Way, why should her neighbor
cavil at giving a little? The writer for one, a colonial governor-
general for another, railway magnates, insurance managers,

safari leaders, the ostrich farmer of Ndua, all these and a dozen others in their turns have felt the hundred-ton weight of her thin-lipped meekness—have seen her in metaphor sitting grimly on the doorsteps of their souls.

A third reason lay in my own troubled conscience. Though I did it in innocence, I can never forget that it was I who personally conducted Diana's party to the Observatory on that fatal night in Boston before it sailed. Had it not been for that kindly intentioned "hunch" of mine, the astounded eye of the Reverend Hubert Diana would never have gazed through the floor of Heaven, and he would never have undertaken to measure the Infinite with the foot rule of his mind.

It all started so simply. My boss at the shipping-and-insurance office gave me the word in the morning. "Bunch of missionaries for the *Platonic* tomorrow. They're on our hands in a way. Show 'em the town." It wasn't so easy when you think of it: one male and seven females on their way to the heathen; though it was easier in Boston than it might have been in some other towns. The evening looked the simplest. My friend Krum was at the Observatory that semester; there at least I was sure their sensibilities would come to no harm.

On the way out in the street car, seated opposite to Diana and having to make conversation, I talked of Krum and of what I knew of his work with the spiral nebulae. Having to appear to listen, Diana did so (as all day long) with a vaguely indulgent smile. He really hadn't time for me. That night his life was exalted as it had never been, and would perhaps never be again. Tomorrow's sailing, the actual fact of leaving all to follow Him, held his imagination in thrall. Moreover, he was a bridegroom of three days with his bride beside him, his nerves at once assuaged and thrilled. No, but more. As if a bride were not enough, arrived in Boston, he had found himself surrounded by a very galaxy of womanhood gathered from the four corners; already within hours one felt the chaste tentacles of their feminine dependence curling about the party's unique man; already their contacts with the world of their new lives began to be made

through him; already they saw in part through his eyes. I wonder what he would have said if I had told him he was a little
drunk.

In the course of the day I think I had got him fairly well.
As concerned his Church he was at once an asset and a liability.
He believed its dogma as few still did, with a simplicity, "the
old-time religion." He was born that kind. Of the stuff of the fanatic, the reason he was not a fanatic was that, curiously impervious to little questionings, he had never been aware that his
faith was anywhere attacked. A self-educated man, he had accepted the necessary smattering facts of science with a serene in-
dulgence, as simply so much further proof of what the Creator
could do when He put His Hand to it. Nor was he conscious of
any conflict between these facts and the fact that there existed a
substantial Heaven, geographically up, and a substantial Hot
Place, geographically down.

So, for his Church, he was an asset in these days. And so,
and for the same reason, he was a liability. The Church must
after all keep abreast of the times. For home consumption, with
modern congregations, especially urban ones, a certain streak of
"healthy" scepticism is no longer amiss in the pulpit; it makes
people who read at all more comfortable in their pews. A man
like Hubert Diana is more for the cause than a hundred. But
what to do with him? Well, such things arrange themselves.
There's the Foreign Field. The blacker the heathen the whiter
the light they'll want, and the solider the conception of a God the
Father enthroned in a Heaven of which the sky above them is
the visible floor.

And that, at bottom, was what Hubert Diana believed. Accept as he would with the top of his brain the fact of a spherical
earth zooming through space, deep in his heart he knew that the
world lay flat from modern Illinois to ancient Palestine, and that
the sky above it, blue by day and by night festooned with guiding stars for wise men, was the nether side of a floor on which
the resurrected trod.

I shall never forget the expression of his face when he realized he was looking straight through it that night. In the quiet dark of the dome I saw him remove his eye from the eyepiece of the telescope up there on the staging and turn it, in the ray of a hooded bulb, on the demon's keeper, Krum.

"What's that, Mr. Krum? I didn't get you!"

"I say, that particular cluster you're looking at—"

"This star, you mean?"

"You'd have to count awhile to count the stars describing their orbits in that 'star,' Mr. Diana. But what I was saying—have you ever had the wish I used to have as a boy—that you could actually look back into the past? With your own two eyes?"

Diana spoke slowly. He didn't know it, but it had already begun to happen; he was already caught. "I have often wished, Mr. Krum, that I might actually look back into the time of our Lord. Actually. Yes."

Krum grunted. He was young. "We'd have to pick a nearer neighbor than *Messier 79* then. The event you see when you put your eye to that lens is happening much too far in the past. The lightwaves thrown off by that particular cluster on the day, say, of the Crucifixion—*you* won't live to see them. They've hardly started yet—a mere twenty centuries on their way—leaving them something like eight hundred and thirty centuries yet to come before they reach the earth."

Diana laughed the queerest catch of a laugh. "And—and there—there won't be any earth here, then, to welcome them."

"*What?*" It was Krum's turn to look startled. So for a moment the two faces remained in confrontation, the one, as I say, startled, the other exuding visibly little sea-green globules of sweat. It was Diana that caved in first, his voice hardly louder than a whisper.

"W-w-will there?"

None of us suspected the enormousness of the thing that had happened in Diana's brain. Krum shrugged his shoulders and snapped his fingers. Deliberately. *Snap!* "What's a thousand centuries or so in the cosmic reckoning?" He chuckled. "We're just beginning to get out among 'em with *Messier,* you know. In the print room, Mr. Diana, I can show you photographs of clusters to which, if you cared to go, traveling at the speed of light—"

The voice ran on; but Diana's eye had gone back to the eyepiece, and his affrighted soul had re-entered the big black tube sticking its snout out of the slit in the iron hemisphere. . . . "At the speed of light!" . . . That unsuspected, that wildly chance-found chink in the armor of his philosophy! The body is resurrected and it ascends to Heaven instantaneously. At what speed must it be borne to reach instantaneously that city beyond the ceiling of the sky? At a speed inconceivable, mystical. At, say (as he had often said to himself), *the speed of light.* . . . And now, hunched there in the trap that had caught him, black rods, infernal levers and wheels, he was aware of his own eye passing vividly through unpartitioned emptiness, *eight hundred and fifty centuries at the speed of light!*

"And still beyond these," Krum was heard, "we begin to come into the regions of the spiral nebulae. We've some interesting photographs in the print room, if you've the time."

The ladies below were tired of waiting. One had "lots of packing to do." The bride said, "Yes, I do think we should be getting along, Hubert, dear; if you're ready—"

The fellow actually jumped. It's lucky he didn't break anything. His face looked greener and dewier than ever amid the contraptions above. "If you—you and the ladies, Cora—wouldn't mind—if Mr.—Mr.—(he'd mislaid my name) would see you back to the hotel—" Meeting silence, he began to expostulate. "I feel that this is a rich experience. I'll follow shortly; I know the way."

In the car going back into the city Mrs. Diana set at rest the flutterings of six hearts. Being unmarried they couldn't understand men as she did. When I think of that face of hers, to which I was destined to grow only too accustomed in the weary, itchy days of the trek into Kavirondoland, with its slightly tilted nose, its irregular pigmentation, its easily inflamed lids, and long moist cheeks, like those of a hunting dog, glorying in weariness, it seems incredible that a light of coyness could have found lodgment there. But that night it did. She sat serene among her virgins.

"You don't know Bert. You wait; he'll get a perfectly wonderful sermon out of all that tonight, Bert will."

Krum was having a grand time with his neophyte. He would have stayed up all night. Immured in the little print room crowded with files and redolent of acids, he conducted his disciple "glassy-eyed" through the dim frontiers of space, holding before him one after another the likenesses of universes sister to our own, islanded in immeasurable vacancy, curled like glimmering crullers on their private Milky Ways, and hiding in their wombs their myriad "coal-pockets," star-dust foetuses of which—their quadrillion years accomplished—their litters of new suns would be born, to bear their planets, to bear their moons in turn.

"And beyond these?"

Always, after each new feat of distance, it was the same. "And beyond?" Given an ell, Diana surrendered to a pop-eyed lust for nothing less than light-years. "And still beyond?"

"Who knows?"

"The mind quits. For if there's no end to these nebulae—"

"But supposing there is?"

"An end? But, Mr. Krum, in the very idea of an ending—"

"An end to what we might call this particular category of magnitudes. Eh?"

"I don't get that."

"Well, take this—take the opal in your ring there. The numbers and distances inside that stone may conceivably be to themselves as staggering as ours to us in our own system. Come! that's not so far-fetched. What are we learning about the structure of the atom? A nucleus (call it a sun) revolved about in eternal orbits by electrons (call them planets, worlds). Infinitesimal; but after all what are bigness and littleness but matters of comparison? To eyes on one of those electrons (don't be too sure there aren't any) its tutelary sun may flame its way across a heaven a comparative ninety million miles away. Impossible for them to conceive of a boundary to their billions of atomic systems, molecular universes. In that category of magnitudes its diameter is infinity; once it has made the leap into our category and become an opal it is merely a quarter of an inch. That's right, Mr. Diana, you may well stare at it: between *now* and *now* ten thousand histories may have come and gone down there. . . . And just so the diameter of our own cluster of universes, going over into another category, may be—"

"May be a—a ring—a little stone—in a—a—a—ring."

Krum was tickled by the way the man's imagination jumped and engulfed it.

"Why not? That's as good a guess as the next. A ring, let's say, worn carelessly on the—well, say the tentacle—of some vast organism—some inchoate creature hobnobbing with its cloudy kind in another system of universes—which in turn—"

It is curious that none of them realized next day that they were dealing with a stranger, a changed man. Why he carried on, why he capped that night of cosmic debauch by shaving, eating an unremarkable breakfast, packing his terrestrial toothbrush and collars, and going up the gangplank in tow of his excited convoy to sail away, is beyond explanation—unless it was simply that he was in a daze.

It wasn't until four years later that I was allowed to know what had happened on that ship, and even then the tale was so disjointed, warped, and opinionated, so darkly seen in the mirror of Mrs. Diana's orthodoxy, that I had almost to guess what it was *really* all about.

"When Hubert turned irreligious . . ." That phrase, recurrent on her tongue in the meanderings of the East African quest to which we were by then committed, will serve to measure her understanding. Irreligious! Good Lord! But from that sort of thing I had to reconstruct the drama. Evening after evening beside her camp fire (appended to the Mineral Survey Expedition Toward Uganda through the kindness—actually the worn-down surrender—of the Protectorate government) I lingered awhile before joining the merrier engineers, watched with fascination the bumps growing under the mosquitoes on her forehead, and listened to the jargon of her mortified meekness and her scandalized faith.

There had been a fatal circumstance, it seems, at the very outset. If Diana could but have been seasick, as the rest of them were (horribly), all might still have been well. In the misery of desired death, along with the other contents of a heaving midriff, he might have brought up the assorted universes of which he had been led too rashly to partake. But he wasn't. As if his wife's theory was right, as if Satan was looking out for him, he was spared to prowl the swooping decks immune. Four days and nights alone. Time enough to digest and assimilate into his being beyond remedy that lump of whirling magnitudes and to feel himself surrendering with a strange new ecstasy to the drunkenness of liberty.

Such liberty! Given Diana's type, it is hard to imagine it adequately. The abrupt, complete removal of the toils of reward and punishment; the withdrawal of the surveillance of an all-seeing, all-knowing Eye; the windy assurance of being responsible for nothing, important to no one, no longer (as the police say) "wanted"! It must have been beautiful in those few days of its first purity, before it began to be discolored by his contemptuous pity for others, the mask of his inevitable loneliness and his growing fright.

The first any of them knew of it—even his wife—was in mid-voyage, the day the sea went down and the seven who had been sick came up. There seemed an especial Providence in the calming of the waters; it was Sunday morning and Diana had been asked to conduct the services.

He preached on the text: "For of such is the kingdom of Heaven."

"If our concept of God means anything it means a God *all*-mighty, Creator of *all* that exists, Director of the *infinite,* cherishing in His Heaven the saved souls of *all space and all time.*"

Of course; amen. And wasn't it nice to feel like humans

again, and real sunshine pouring up through the lounge ports from an ocean suddenly grown kind? . . . But—then—*what* was Diana *saying?*

Mrs. Diana couldn't tell about it coherently even after a lapse of fifty months. Even in a setting as remote from that steamer's lounge as the equatorial bush, the ember-reddened canopy of thorn trees, the meandering camp fires, the chant and tramp somewhere away of Kikuyu porters dancing in honor of an especial largesse of fat zebra meat—even here her memory of that impious outburst was too vivid, too aghast.

"It was Hubert's look! The way he stared at us! As if you'd said he was licking his chops! . . . That '*Heaven*' of his!"

It seems they hadn't waked up to what he was about until he had the dimensions of his sardonic Paradise irreparably drawn in. The final haven of all right souls. Not alone the souls released from this our own tiny earth. In the millions of solar systems we see as stars how many millions of satellites must there be upon which at some time in their histories conditions suited to organic life subsist? Uncounted hordes of wheeling populations! Of Men? God's creatures at all events, a portion of them reasoning. Weirdly shaped perhaps, but what of that? And that's only to speak of our own inconsiderable cluster of universes. That's to say nothing of other systems of magnitudes, where God's creatures are to our world what we are to the worlds in the atoms in our finger rings. (He had shaken *his,* here, in their astounded faces.) And all these, all the generations of these enormous and microscopic beings harvested through a time beside which the life span of our earth is as a second in a million centuries: all these brought to rest for an eternity to which time itself is a watch tick—all crowded to rest pellmell, thronged, serried, packed, packed to suffocation in layers unnumbered light-years deep. This must needs be our concept of Heaven if God is the God of the Whole. If, on the other hand—

The other hand was the hand of the second officer, the captain's delegate at divine worship that Sabbath day. He at last had "come to."

I don't know whether it was the same day or the next; Mrs.

Diana was too vague. But here's the picture. Seven women huddled in the large stateroom on B-deck, conferring in whispers, aghast, searching one another's eye obliquely even as they bowed their heads in prayer for some light—and of a sudden the putting back of the door and the in-marching of the Reverend Hubert. . . .

As Mrs. Diana tried to tell me, "You understand, don't you, he had just taken a bath? And he hadn't—he had forgotten to—"

Adam-innocent there he stood. Not a stitch. But I don't believe for a minute it was a matter of forgetting. In the high intoxication of his soul release, already crossed (by the second officer) and beginning to show his zealot claws, he needed some gesture stunning enough to witness to his separation, his unique rightness, his contempt of match-flare civilizations and infinitesimal taboos.

But I can imagine that stateroom scene: the gasps, the heads colliding in aversion, and Diana's six weedy feet of birthday suit towering in the shadows, and ready to sink through the deck I'll warrant, now the act was irrevocable, but still grimly carrying it off.

"And if, on the other hand, you ask me to bow down before a God peculiar to this one earth, this one grain of dust lost among the giants of space, watching its sparrows fall, profoundly interested in a speck called Palestine no bigger than the quadrillionth part of one of the atoms in the ring here on my finger—"

Really scared by this time, one of the virgins shrieked. It was altogether too close quarters with a madman.

Mad? Of course there was the presumption: "Crazy as a loon." Even legally it was so adjudged at the *Platonic*'s first port of call, Algiers, where, when Diana escaped ashore and wouldn't come back again, he had to be given over to the workings of the French Law. I talked with the magistrate myself some forty months later, when, "let in" for the business as I have told, I stopped there on my way out.

"But what would you?" were his words. "We must live in

the world as the world lives, is it not? Sanity? Sanity is what? Is it, for example, an intellectual clarity, a balanced perception of the realities? Naturally, speaking out of court, your friend was of a sanity—of a sanity, sir—" Here the magistrate made with thumb and fingers the gesture only the French can make for a thing that is matchless, a beauty, a transcendent instance of any kind. He himself was Gallic, rational. Then, with a lift of shoulder: "But what would you? We must live in the world that seems."

Diana, impounded in Algiers for deportation, escaped. What after all are the locks and keys of this pinchbeck category of magnitudes? More remarkable still, there in Arab Africa, he succeeded in vanishing from the knowledge and pursuit of men. And of women. His bride, now that their particular mission had fallen through, was left to decide whether to return to America or to go on with two of the company, the Misses Brookhart and Smutts, who were bound for a school in Smyrna. In the end she followed the latter course. It was there, nearly four years later, that I was sent to join her by an exasperated and worn-out Firm.

By that time she knew again where her husband-errant was —or where at least, from time to time in his starry dartings over this our mote of dust, he had been heard of, spoken to, seen.

Could we but have a written history of those years of his apostolic vagabondage, a record of the towns in which he was jailed or from which he was kicked out, of the ports in which he starved, of the ships on which he stowed away, presently to reveal himself in proselyting ardor, denouncing the earthlings, the fatelings, the dupes of bugaboo, meeting scoff with scoff, preaching the new revelation red-eyed, like an angry prophet. Or was it, more simply, like a man afraid?

Was that the secret, after all of his prodigious restlessness? Had it anything in common with the swarming of those pale worms that flee the Eye of the Infinite around the curves of the stone you pick up in a field? Talk of the man without a country! What of the man without a universe?

It is curious that I never suspected his soul's dilemma until I saw the first of his mud-sculptures in the native village of Ndua in the province of Kasuma in British East. Here it was, our objective attained, we parted company with the government *safari* and shifted the burden of Way-straightening to the shoulders of Major Wyeside, the ostrich farmer of the neighborhood.

While still on the *safari* I had put to Mrs. Diana a question that had bothered me: "Why on earth should your husband ever have chosen this particular neck of the woods to land up in? Why Kavirondoland?"

"It was here we were coming at the time Hubert turned irreligious, to found a mission. It's a coincidence, isn't it?"

And yet I would have sworn Diana hadn't a sense of humor about him anywhere. But perhaps it *wasn't* an ironic act. Perhaps it was simply that, giving up the struggle with a society blinded by "a little learning" and casting about for a virgin field, he had remembered this.

"I supposed he was a missionary," Major Wyeside told us with a flavor of indignation. "I went on that. I let him live here —six or seven months of it—while he was learning the tongue. I was a bit nonplussed, to put it mildly, when I discovered what he was up to."

What things Diana had been up to the Major showed us in one of the huts in the native kraal—a round dozen of them, modeled in mud and baked. Blackened blobs of mud, that's all. Likenesses of nothing under the sun, fortuitous masses sprouting haphazard tentacles, only two among them showing postules that might have been experimental heads. . . . The ostrich farmer saw our faces.

"Rum, eh? Of course I realized the chap was anything but fit. A walking skeleton. Nevertheless, whatever it is about these beasties, there's not a nigger in the village has dared set foot inside this hut since Diana left. You can see for yourselves it's about to crash. There's another like it he left at Suki, above here. Taboo, no end!"

So Diana's "hunch" had been right. He had found his virgin field, indeed, fit soil for his cosmic fright. A religion in the making, here before our eyes.

"This was at the very last before he left," Wyeside explained. "He took to making these mud pies quite of a sudden; the whole lot within a fortnight's time. Before that he had simply talked, harangued. He would sit here in the doorway of an evening with the niggers squatted around and harangue 'em by the hour. I knew something of it through my house-boys. The most amazing rot. All about the stars to begin with, as if these black baboons could half grasp *astronomy!* But that seemed all proper. Then there was talk about a something a hundred times as big and powerful as the world, sun, moon, and stars put together—some perfectly enormous stupendous awful being—but knowing how mixed the boys can get, it still seemed all regular—simply the parson's way of getting at the notion of an Almighty God. But no, they insisted, there wasn't any God. That's the point, they said; there *is no* God. . . . Well, that impressed me as a go. That's when I decided to come down and get the rights of this star-swallowing monstrosity the beggar was feeding my labor on. And here he sat in the doorway with one of these beasties—here it is, this one—waving it furiously in the niggers' benighted faces. And do you know what he'd done?—you can see the mark here still on this wabble-leg, this tentacle-business—he had taken off a ring he had and screwed it on just here. His finger ring, my word of honor! And still, if you'll believe it, I didn't realize he was just daft. Not until he spoke to me. 'I find,' he was good enough to enlighten me, 'I find I have to make it somehow concrete.' . . . 'Make what?' . . . 'Our wearer.' 'Our *what, where?*' . . . 'In the following category.' . . . His actual words, honor bright. I was going to have him sent down-country where he could be looked after. He got ahead of me though. He cleared out. When I heard he'd turned up at Suki I ought, I suppose, to have attended to it. But I was having trouble with leopards. And you know how things go."

From there we went to Suki, the Major accompanying. It was as like Ndua as one flea to its brother, a stockade enclosing round houses of mud, wattles, and thatch, and full of naked heathen. The Kavirondo are the nakedest of all African peoples and, it is said, the most moral. It put a great strain on Mrs. Diana; all that whole difficult anxious time, as it were detachedly, I could see her itching to get them into Mother Hubbard and cast-off Iowa pants.

Here too, as the Major had promised, we found a holy of holies, rather a dreadful of dreadfuls, "taboo no end," its shadows cluttered with the hurlothrumbos of Diana's artistry. What puzzled me was their number. Why this appetite for experimentation? There was an uncertainty; one would think its effect on potential converts would be bad. Here, as in Ndua, Diana had contented himself at first with words and skyward gesticulations. Not for so long however. Feeling the need of giving his concept of the cosmic "wearer" a substance much earlier, he had shut himself in with the work, literally—a fever of creation. We counted seventeen of the nameless "blobs," all done, we were told, in the seven days and nights before their maker had again cleared out. The villagers would hardly speak of him; only after spitting to protect themselves, their eyes averted, and in an undertone, would they mention him: "He of the Ring." Thereafter we were to hear of him only as "He of the Ring."

Leaving Suki, Major Wyeside turned us over (thankfully, I warrant) to a native who told us his name was Charlie Kamba. He had spent some years in Nairobi, running for an Indian outfitter, and spoke English remarkably well. It was from him we learned, quite casually, when our modest eight-load *safari* was some miles on its way, that the primary object of our coming was nonexistent. Hubert Diana was dead.

Dead nearly five weeks—a moon and a little—and buried in the mission church at Tara Hill.

Mission church! There was a poser for us. *Mission church?*

Well then, Charlie Kamba gave us to know that he was paraphrasing in a large way suitable to our habits of thought. We wouldn't have understood *his* informant's "wizard house" or "house of the effigy."

I will say for Mrs. Diana that in the course of our halt of lugubrious amazement she shed tears. That some of them were not tears of unrealized relief it would be hardly natural to believe. She had desired loyally to find her husband, but when she should have found him—what? This problem, sturdily ignored so long, was now removed.

Turn back? Never! Now it would seem the necessity for pressing forward was doubled. In the scrub-fringed ravine of our halt the porters resumed their loads, the dust stood up again, the same caravan moved on. But how far it was now from being the same.

From that moment it took on, for me at least, a new character. It wasn't the news especially; the fact that Diana was dead had little to do with it. Perhaps it was simply that the new sense of something aimfully and cumulatively dramatic in our progress had to have a beginning, and that moment would do as well as the next.

Six villages: M'nann, Leika, Leikapo, Shamba, Little Tara, and Tara, culminating in the apotheosis of Tara Hill. Six stops for the night on the road it had cost Diana as many months to cover in his singular pilgrimage to his inevitable goal. Or in his flight to it. Yes, his stampede. Now the pipers at that four-day orgy of liberty on the *Platonic*'s decks were at his heels for their pay. Now that his strength was failing, the hosts of loneliness were after him, creeping out of their dreadful magnitudes, the hounds of space. Over all that ground it seemed to me we were following him not by the word of hearsay but, as one follows a wounded animal making for its earth, by the droppings of his blood.

Our progress had taken on a pattern; it built itself with a dramatic artistry; it gathered suspense. As though it were a story at its most breathless places "continued in our next," and I a reader forgetting the road's weariness, the dust, the torment of insects never escaped, the inadequate food, I found myself hardly able to keep from running on ahead to reach the evening's village, to search out the inevitable repository of images left by the white stranger who had come and tarried there awhile and gone again.

More concrete and ever more concrete. The immemorial compromise with the human hunger for a symbol to see with the eyes, touch with the hands. Hierarchy after hierarchy of little mud effigies—one could see the necessity pushing the man. Out of the protoplasmic blobs of Ndua, Suki, even M'nann, at Leikapo Diana's concept of infinity (so pure in that halcyon epoch at sea), of categories nested within categories like Japanese boxes, of an over-creature wearing our cosmos like a trinket, unawares, had become a mass with legs to stand on and a real head. The shards scattered about in the filth of the hut there (as if in violence of despair) were still monstrosities, but with a sudden stride of concession their monstrousness was the monstrousness of lizard and turtle and crocodile. At Shamba there were dozens of huge-footed birds.

It is hard to be sure in retrospect, but I do believe that by the time we reached Little Tara I began to see the thing as a whole—the foetus, working out slowly, blindly, but surely, its evolution in the womb of fright. At Little Tara there was a change in the character of the exhibits; their numbers had diminished, their size had grown. There was a boar with tusks and a bull the size of a dog with horns, and on a tusk and on a horn an indentation left by a ring.

I don't believe Mrs. Diana got the thing at all. Toward the last she wasn't interested in the huts of relics; at Little Tara she wouldn't go near the place; she was "too tired." It must have been pretty awful, when you think of it, even if all she saw in them was the mud-pie play of a man reverted to a child.

There was another thing at Little Tara quite as momentous as the jump to boar and bull. Here at last a mask had been thrown aside. Here there had been no pretense of proselyting, no astronomical lectures, no doorway harangues. Straightway he had arrived (a fabulous figure already, long heralded), he had commandeered a house and shut himself up in it and there, mysterious, assiduous, he had remained three days and nights, eating nothing, but drinking gallons of the foul water they left in gourds outside his curtain of reeds. No one in the village had ever seen what he had done and left there. Now, candidly, those labors were for himself alone.

Here at last in Tara the moment of that confession had overtaken the fugitive. It was he, ill with fever and dying of nostalgia—not these naked black baboon men seen now as little more than blurs—who had to give the Beast of the Infinite a name and a shape. And more and more, not only a shape, but a *shapeliness*. From the instant when, no longer able to live alone with nothingness, he had given it a likeness in Ndua mud, and perceived that it was intolerable and fled its face, the turtles and distorted crocodiles of Leikapo and the birds of Shamba had become inevitable, and no less inevitable the Little Tara boar and bull. Another thing grows plain in retrospect: the reason why, done to death (as all the way they reported him) he couldn't die. He didn't dare to. Didn't dare to close his eyes.

It was at Little Tara we first heard of him as "Father Witch," a name come back, we were told, from Tara, where he had gone. I had heard it pronounced several times before it suddenly obtruded from the native context as actually two English words. That was what made it queer. It was something they must have picked up by rote, uncomprehending; something then they could have had from no lips but his own. When I repeated it after them with a better accent they pointed up toward the north, saying "Tara! Tara!"—their eagerness mingled with awe.

I shall never forget Tara as we saw it, after our last blistering scramble up a gorge, situated in the clear air on a slope belted with cedars. A mid-African stockade left by some blunder in an honest Colorado landscape, or a newer and bigger Vermont. Here at the top of our journey, black savages, their untidy *shambas,* the very Equator, all these seemed as incongruous as a Gothic cathedral in a Congo marsh. I wonder if Hubert Diana knew whither his instinct was guiding him on the long road of his journey here to die. . . .

The Man Who Saw Through Heaven

He had died and he was buried, not in the village, but about half a mile distant, on the ridge; this we were given to know almost before we had arrived. There was no need to announce ourselves, the word of our coming had outrun us; the populace was at the gates.

"Our Father Witch! Our Father Witch!" They knew what we were after; the funny parrot-wise English stood out from the clack and clatter of their excited speech. "Our Father Witch! Ay! Ay!" With a common eagerness they gesticulated at the hill-top beyond the cedars.

Certainly here was a change. No longer the propitiatory spitting, the averted eyes, the uneasy whispering allusion to him who had passed that way: here in Tara they would shout him from the housetops, with a kind of civic pride.

We learned the reason for this on our way up the hill. It was because they were his chosen, the initiate.

We made the ascent immediately, against the village's advice. It was near evening; the return would be in the dark; it was a bad country for goblins; wouldn't tomorrow morning do? . . . No, it wouldn't do the widow. Her face was set. . . . And so, since we were resolved to go, the village went with us, armed with rattles and drums. Charlie Kamba walked beside us, sifting the information a hundred were eager to give.

These people were proud, he said, because their wizard was more powerful than all the wizards of all the other villages "in the everywhere together." If he cared to he could easily knock down all the other villages in the "everywhere," destroying all the people and all the cattle. If he cared to he could open his mouth and swallow the sky and the stars. But Tara he had chosen. Tara he would protect. He made their mealies to grow and their cattle to multiply.

I protested, "But he is *dead* now!"

Charlie Kamba made signs of deprecation. I discerned that he was far from being clear about the thing himself.

Yes, he temporized, this Father Witch was dead, quite

dead. On the other hand he was up there. On the other hand he would never die. He was longer than forever. Yes, quite true, he was dead and buried under the pot.

I gave it up. "How did he die?"

Well, he came to this village of Tara very suffering, very sick. The dead man who walked. His face was very sad. Very eaten. Very frightened. He came to this hill. So he lived here for two full moons, very hot, very eaten, very dead. These men made him a house as he commanded them, also a stockade. In the house he was very quiet, very dead, making magic two full moons. Then he came out and they that were waiting saw him. He had made the magic, and the magic had made him well. His face was kind. He happy. He was full fed. He was full fed, these men said, without any eating. Yes, they carried up to him very fine food, because they were full of wonder and some fear, but he did not eat any of it. Some water he drank. So, for two days and the night between them, he continued sitting in the gate of the stockade, very happy, very full fed. He told these people very much about their wizard, who is bigger than every-where and longer than forever and can, if he cares to, swallow the sky and stars. From time to time however, ceasing to talk to these people, he got to his knees and talked in his own strange tongue to Our Father Witch, his eyes held shut. When he had done this just at sunset of the second day he fell forward on his face. So he remained that night. The next day these men took him into the house and buried him under the pot. On the other hand Our Father Witch is longer than forever. He remains there still. . . .

The first thing I saw in the hut's interior was the earthen pot at the northern end, wrong-side-up on the ground. I was glad I had preceded Mrs. Diana. I walked across and sat down on it carelessly, hoping so that her afflicted curiosity might be led astray. It gave me the oddest feeling, though, to think of what was there beneath my nonchalant sitting-portion—aware as I was of the Kavirondo burial of a great man—up to the neck in mother earth, and the rest of him left out in the dark of the pot for the undertakings of the ants. I hoped his widow wouldn't wonder about that inverted vessel of clay.

I needn't have worried. Her attention was arrested other-wheres. I shall not forget the look of her face, caught above me in the red shaft of sundown entering the western door, as she gazed at the last and the largest of the Reverend Hubert Diana's gods. That long, long cheek of hers, buffeted by sorrow, startled now and mortified. Not till that moment, I believe, had she comprehended the steps of mud-images she had been following for what they were, the steps of idolatry.

For my part, I wasn't startled. Even before we started up the hill, knowing that her husband had dared to die here, I could have told her pretty much what she would find.

This overlord of the cosmic categories that he had fash-ioned (at last) in his own image sat at the other end of the red-streaked house upon a bench—a throne?—of mud. Diana had been no artist. An ovoid two-eyed head, a cylindrical trunk, two arms, two legs, that's all. But indubitably man, man-size. Only one finger of one of the hands had been done with much care. It wore an opal, a two-dollar stone from Mexico, set in a silver ring. This was the hand that was lifted, and over it the head was bent.

I've said Diana was no artist. I'll take back the words. The figure was crudeness itself, but in the relation between that bent head and that lifted hand there was something which was some-thing else. A sense of scrutiny one would have said no genius of mud could ever have conveyed. An attitude of interest centered in that bauble, intense and static, breathless and eternal all in one—penetrating to its bottom atom, to the last electron, to a hill upon it, and to a two-legged mite about to die. Marking (yes, I'll swear to the incredible) the sparrow's fall.

The magic was made. The road that had commenced with the blobs of Ndua—the same that commenced with our hairy ancestors listening to the night-wind in their caves—was run.

And from here Diana, of a sudden happy, of a sudden looked after, "full fed," had walked out—

But no; I couldn't stand that mortified sorrow on the widow's face any longer. She had to be made to see what she wanted to see. I said it aloud:

"From here, Mrs. Diana, your husband walked out—"

"He had sunk to idolatry. *Idolatry!*"

"To the bottom, yes. And come up its whole history again. And from here he walked out into the sunshine to kneel and talk with 'Our Father Which—'"

She got it. She caught it. I wish you could have seen the light going up those long, long cheeks as she got it:

"Our Father which art in Heaven, Hallowed be Thy Name!"

We went down hill in the darkness, protected against goblins by a vast rattling of gourds and beating of goat-hide drums.

A STILL MOMENT

by Eudora Welty

Lorenzo Dow rode the Old Natchez Trace at top speed upon
a race horse, and the cry of the intinerant Man of God, "I
must have souls! And souls I must have!" rang in his own windy
ears. He rode as if never to stop, toward his night's appointment.

It was the hour of sunset. All the souls that he had saved
and all those he had not took dusky shapes in the mist that hung
between the high banks, and seemed by their great number and
density to block his way, and showed no signs of melting or
changing back into mist, so that he feared his passage was to be
difficult forever. The poor souls that were not saved were darker
and more pitiful than those that were, and still there was not
any of the radiance he would have hoped to see in such a congregation.

"Light up, in God's name!" he called, in the pain of his
disappointment.

Then a whole swarm of fireflies instantly flickered all around
him, up and down, back and forth, first one golden light and
then another, flashing without any of the weariness that had held

back the souls. These were the signs sent from God that he had not seen the accumulated radiance of saved souls because he was not able, and that his eyes were more able to see the fireflies of the Lord than His blessed souls.

"Lord, give me the strength to see the angels when I am in Paradise," he said. "Do not let my eyes remain in this failing proportion to my loving heart always."

He gasped and held on. It was that day's complexity of horse-trading that had left him in the end with a Spanish race horse for which he was bound to send money in November from Georgia. Riding faster on the beast and still faster until he felt as if he were flying he sent thoughts of love with matching speed to his wife Peggy in Massachusetts. He found it effortless to love at a distance. He could look at the flowering trees and love Peggy in fullness, just as he could see his visions and love God. And Peggy, to whom he had not spoken until he could speak fateful words ("Would she accept of such an object as him?"), Peggy, the bride, with whom he had spent a few hours of time, showing of herself a small round handwriting, declared all in one letter, her first, that she felt the same as he, and that the fear was never of separation, but only of death.

Lorenzo well knew that it was Death that opened underfoot, that rippled by at night, that was the silence the birds did their singing in. He was close to death, closer than any animal or bird. On the back of one horse after another, winding them all, he was always riding toward it or away from it, and the Lord sent him directions with protection in His mind.

Just then he rode into a thicket of Indians taking aim with their new guns. One stepped out and took the horse by the bridle, it stopped at a touch, and the rest made a closing circle. The guns pointed.

"Incline!" The inner voice spoke sternly and with its customary lightning-quickness.

Lorenzo inclined all the way forward and put his head to the horse's silky mane, his body to its body, until a bullet meant for him would endanger the horse and make his death of no value. Prone he rode out through the circle of Indians, his obedience to the voice leaving him almost fearless, almost careless with joy.

But as he straightened and pressed ahead, care caught up with him again. Turning half-beast and half-divine, dividing himself like a heathen Centaur, he had escaped his death once more. But was it to be always by some metamorphosis of himself that he escaped, some humiliation of his faith, some admission to strength and argumentation and not frailty? Each time when he acted so it was at the command of an instinct that he took at once as the word of an angel, until too late, when he knew it was the word of the devil. He had roared like a tiger at Indians, he had submerged himself in water blowing the savage bubbles of the alligator, and they skirted him by. He had prostrated himself to appear dead, and deceived bears. But all the time God would have protected him in His own way, less hurried, more divine.

Even now he saw a serpent crossing the Trace, giving out knowing glances.

He cried, "I know you now!", and the serpent gave him one look out of which all the fire had been taken, and went away in two darts into the tangle.

He rode on, all expectation, and the voices in the throats of the wild beasts went, almost without his noticing when, into words. "Praise God," they said. "Deliver us from one another." Birds especially sang of divine love which was the one ceaseless protection. "Peace, in peace," were their words so many times when they spoke from the briars, in a courteous sort of inflection, and he turned his countenance toward all perched creatures with a benevolence striving to match their own.

He rode on past the little intersecting trails, letting himself be guided by voices and by lights. It was battlesounds he heard most, sending him on, but sometimes ocean sounds, that long beat of waves that would make his heart pound and retreat as heavily as they, and he despaired again in his failure in Ireland when he took a voyage and persuaded with the Catholics with his back against the door, and then ran away to their cries of

"Mind the white hat!" But when he heard singing it was not the militant and sharp sound of Wesley's hymns, but a soft, tireless and tender air that had no beginning and no end, and the softness of distance, and he had pleaded with the Lord to find out if all this meant that it was wicked, but no answer had come.

Soon night would descend, and a camp-meeting ground ahead would fill with its sinners like the sky with its stars. How he hungered for them! He looked in prescience with a longing of love over the throng that waited while the flames of the torches threw change, change, change over their faces. How could he bring them enough, if it were not divine love and sufficient warning of all that could threaten them? He rode on faster. He was a filler of appointments, and he filled more and more, until his journeys up and down creation were nothing but a shuttle, driving back and forth upon the rich expanse of his vision. He was homeless by his own choice, he must be everywhere at some time, and somewhere soon. There hastening in the wilderness on his flying horse he gave the night's torch-lit crowd a premature benediction, he could not wait. He spread his arms out, one at a time for safety, and he wished, when they would all be gathered in by his tin horn blasts and the inspired words would go out over their heads, to brood above the entire and passionate life of the wide world, to become its rightful part.

He peered ahead. "Inhabitants of Time! The wilderness is your souls on earth!" he shouted ahead into the treetops. "Look about you, if you would view the conditions of your spirit, put here by the good Lord to show you and afright you. These wild places and these trails of awesome loneliness lie nowhere, nowhere, but in your heart."

A dark man, who was James Murrell the outlaw, rode his horse out of a cane brake and began going along beside Lorenzo without looking at him. He had the alternately proud and aggrieved look of a man believing himself to be an instrument in the hands of a power, and when he was young he said at once to strangers that he was being used by Evil, or sometimes he stopped a traveler by shouting, "Stop! I'm the Devil!" He rode along now talking and drawing out his talk, by some deep control of the voice gradually slowing the speed of Lorenzo's horse down until both the horses were softly trotting. He would have wondered that nothing he said was heard, not knowing that Lorenzo listened only to voices of whose heavenly origin he was more certain.

Murrell riding along with his victim-to-be, Murrell riding, was Murrell talking. He told away at his long tales, with always a distance and a long length of time flowing through them, and all centered about a silent man. In each the silent man would have done a piece of evil, a robbery or a murder, in a place of long ago, and it was all made for the revelation in the end that the silent man was Murrell himself, and the long story had happened yesterday, and the place *here*—the Natchez Trace. It would only take one dawning look for the victim to see that all of this was another story and he himself had listened his way into it, and that he too was about to recede in time (to where the dread was forgotten) for some listener and to live for a listener in the long ago. Destroy the present!—that must have been the first thing that was whispered in Murrell's heart—the living moment and the man that lives in it must die before you can go on. It was his habit to bring the journey—which might even take days—to a close with a kind of ceremony. Turning his face at last into the face of the victim, for he had never seen him before now, he would tower up with the sudden height of a man no longer the tale teller but the speechless protagonist, silent at last, one degree nearer the hero. Then he would murder the man.

But it would always start over. This man going forward was going backward with talk. He saw nothing, observed no world at all. The two ends of his journey pulled at him always and held him in a nowhere, half asleep, smiling and witty, dangling his predicament. He was a murderer whose final stroke was over-long postponed, who had to bring himself through the greatest tedium to act, as if the whole wilderness, where he was born, were his impediment. But behind him and before him he kept in sight a victim, he saw a man fixed and stayed at the point of death—no matter how the man's eyes denied it, a victim, hands spreading to reach as if for the first time for life. Contempt! That is what Murrell gave that man.

Lorenzo might have understood, if he had not been in haste, that Murrell in laying hold of a man meant to solve his mystery of being. It was as if other men, all but himself, would lighten their hold on the secret, upon assault, and let it fly free at death. In his violence he was only treating of enigma. The violence shook his own body first, like a force gathering, and now he turned in the saddle.

Lorenzo's despair had to be kindled as well as his ecstasy, and could not come without that kindling. Before the awe-filled moment when the faces were turned up under the flares, as though an angel hand tipped their chins, he had no way of telling whether he would enter the sermon by sorrow or by joy. But at this moment the face of Murrell was turned toward him, turning at last, all solitary, in its full, and Lorenzo would have seized the man at once by his black coat and shaken him like prey for a lost soul, so instantly was he certain that the false fire was in his heart instead of the true fire. But Murrell, quick when he was quick, had put his own hand out, a restraining hand, and laid it on the wavelike flesh of the Spanish race horse, which quivered and shuddered at the touch.

They had come to a great live-oak tree at the edge of a low marshland. The burning sun hung low, like a head lowered on folded arms, and over the long reaches of violet trees the evening seemed still with thought. Lorenzo knew the place from having seen it among many in dreams, and he stopped readily and willingly. He drew rein, and Murrell drew rein, he dismounted and Murrell dismounted, he took a step, and Murrell was there too; and Lorenzo was not surprised at the closeness, how Murrell in his long dark coat and over it his dark face darkening still, stood beside him like a brother seeking light.

But in that moment instead of two men coming to stop by the great forked tree, there were three.

A Still Moment

From far away, a student, Audubon, had been approaching lightly on the wilderness floor, disturbing nothing in his lightness. The long day of beauty had led him this certain distance. A flock of purple finches that he tried for the first moment to count went over his head. He made a spelling of the soft *pet* of the ivory-billed woodpecker. He told himself always: remember.

Coming upon the Trace, he looked at the high cedars, azure and still as distant smoke overhead, with their silver roots trailing down on either side like the veins of deepness in this place, and he noted some fact to his memory—this earth that wears but will not crumble or slide or turn to dust, they say it exists in one other spot in the world, Egypt—and then forgot it. He walked quietly. All life used this Trace, and he liked to see the animals move along it in direct, oblivious journeys, for they had begun it and made it, the buffalo and deer and the small running creatures before man ever knew where he wanted to go, and birds flew a great mirrored course above. Walking beneath them Audubon remembered how in the cities he had seen these very birds in his imagination, calling them up whenever he wished, even in the hard and glittering outer parlors where if an artist were humble enough to wait, some idle hand held up promised money. He walked lightly and he went as carefully as he had started at two that morning, crayon and paper, a gun, and a small bottle of spirits disposed about his body. (*Note: "The mocking birds so gentle that they would scarcely move out of the way."*) He looked with care; great abundance had ceased to startle him, and he could see things one by one. In Natchez they had told him of many strange and marvelous birds that were to be found here. Their descriptions had been exact, complete, and wildly varying, and he took them for inventions and believed that like all the worldly things that came out of Natchez, they would be disposed of and shamed by any man's excursion into the reality of Nature.

In the valley he appeared under the tree, a sure man, very sure and tender, as if the touch of all the earth rubbed upon him and the stains of the flowery swamp had made him so.

Lorenzo welcomed him and turned fond eyes upon him. To transmute a man into an angel was the hope that drove him all over the world and never let him flinch from a meeting or withhold good-byes for long. This hope insistently divided his life into only two parts, journey and rest. There could be no night and day and love and despair and longing and satisfaction to make partitions in the single ecstasy of this alternation. All things were speech.

"God created the world," said Lorenzo, "and it exists to give testimony. Life is the tongue: speak."

But instead of speech there happened a moment of deepest silence.

Audubon said nothing because he had gone without speaking a word for days. He did not regard his thoughts for the birds and animals as susceptible, in their first change, to words. His long playing on the flute was not in its origin a talking to himself. Rather than speak to order or describe, he would always draw a deer with a stroke across it to communicate his need of venison to an Indian. He had only found words when he discovered that there is much otherwise lost that can be noted down each item in its own day, and he wrote often now in a journal, not wanting anything to be lost the way it had been, all the past, and he would write about a day, "Only sorry that the Sun Sets."

Murrell, his cheated hand hiding the gun, could only continue to smile at Lorenzo, but he remembered in malice that he had disguised himself once as an Evangelist, and his final words to this victim would have been, "One of my disguises was what you are."

Then in Murrell Audubon saw what he thought of as "acquired sorrow"—that cumbrousness and darkness from which the naked Indian, coming just as he was made from God's hand, was so lightly freed. He noted the eyes—the dark kind that loved to look through chinks, and saw neither closeness nor distance, light nor shade, wonder nor familiarity. They were narrowed to contract the heart, narrowed to make an averting plan. Audubon knew the finest-drawn tendons of the body and the working of their power, for he had touched them, and he supposed then that in man the enlargement of the eye to see started a motion in the hands to make or do, and that the narrowing of the eye stopped the hand and contracted the heart. Now Murrell's eyes followed an ant on a blade of grass, up the blade and down, many times in the single moment. Audubon had examined the Cave-In Rock where one robber had lived his hiding life, and the air in the cave was the cavelike air that enclosed this man, the same odor, flinty and dark. O secret life, he thought—is it true that the secret is withdrawn from the true disclosure, that man is a cave man, and that the openness I see, the ways through forests, the rivers brimming light, the wide arches where the birds fly, are dreams of freedom? If my origin is withheld from me, is my end to be unknown too? Is the radiance I see closed into an interval between two darks, or can it not illuminate them both and discover at last, though it cannot be spoken, what was thought hidden and lost?

In that quiet moment a solitary snowy heron flew down not far away and began to feed beside the marsh water.

At the single streak of flight, the ears of the race horse lifted, and the eyes of both horses filled with the soft lights of sunset, which in the next instant were reflected in the eyes of the men too as they all looked into the west toward the heron, and all eyes seemed infused with a sort of wildness.

Lorenzo gave the bird a triumphant look, such as a man may bestow upon his own vision, and thought, Nearness is near, lighted in a marshland, feeding at sunset. Praise God, His love has come visible.

Murrell, in suspicion pursuing all glances, blinking into a haze, saw only whiteness ensconced in darkness, as if it were a little luminous shell that drew in and held the eyesight. When he shaded his eyes, the brand "H.T." on his thumb thrust itself into his own vision, and he looked at the bird with the whole plan of the Mystic Rebellion darting from him as if in rays of the bright reflected light, and he stood looking proudly, leader as he was bound to become of the slaves, the brigands and outcasts of the

entire Natchez country, with plans, dates, maps burning like a brand into his brain, and he saw himself proudly in a moment of prophecy going down rank after rank of successively bowing slaves to unroll and flaunt an awesome great picture of the Devil colored on a banner.

Audubon's eyes embraced the object in the distance and he could see it as carefully as if he held it in his hand. It was a snowy heron alone out of its flock. He watched it steadily, in his care noting the exact inevitable things. When it feeds it muddies the water with its foot. . . . It was as if each detail about the heron happened slowly in time, and only once. He felt again the old stab of wonder—what structure of life bridged the reptile's scale and the heron's feather? That knowledge too had been lost. He watched without moving. The bird was defenseless in the world except for the intensity of its life, and he wondered, how can heat of blood and speed of heart defend it? Then he thought, as always as if it were new and unbelievable, it has nothing in space or time to prevent its flight. And he waited, knowing that some birds will wait for a sense of their presence to travel to men before they will fly away from them.

Fixed in its pure white profile it stood in the precipitous moment, a plumicorn on its head, its breeding dress extended in rays, eating steadily the little water creatures. There was a little space between each man and the others, where they stood overwhelmed. No one could say the three had ever met, or that this moment of intersection had ever come in their lives, or its promise fulfilled. But before them the white heron rested in the grasses with the evening all around it, lighter and more serene than the evening, flight closed in its body, the circuit of its beauty closed, a bird seen and a bird still, its motion calm as if it were offered: Take my flight. . . .

What each of them had wanted was simply *all*. To save all souls, to destroy all men, to see and to record all life that filled this world—all, all—but now a single frail yearning seemed to go out of the three of them for a moment and to stretch toward

this one snowy, shy bird in the marshes. It was as if three whirl-
winds had drawn together at some center, to find there feeding
in peace a snowy heron. Its own slow spiral of flight could take it
away in its own time, but for a little it held them still, it laid
quiet over them, and they stood for a moment unburdened. . . .

Murrell wore no mask, for his face was that, a face that
was aware while he was somnolent, a face that watched for him,
and listened for him, alert and nearly brutal, the guard of a
planner. He was quick without that he might be slow within, he
staved off time, he wandered and plotted, and yet his whole
desire mounted in him toward the end (was this the end—the
sight of a bird feeding at dusk?), toward the instant of confession. His incessant deeds were thick in his heart now, and flinging
himself to the ground he thought wearily, when all these trees
are cut down, and the Trace lost, then my Conspiracy that is yet
to spread itself will be disclosed, and all the stone-loaded bodies
of murdered men will be pulled up, and all everywhere will
know poor Murrell. His look pressed upon Lorenzo, who stared
upward, and Audubon, who was taking out his gun, and his eyes
squinted up to them in pleading, as if to say, "How soon may I
speak, and how soon will you pity me?" Then he looked back to
the bird, and he thought if it would look at him a dread pene-
tration would fill and gratify his heart.

Audubon in each act of life was aware of the mysterious origin he half-concealed and half-sought for. People along the
way asked him in their kindness or their rudeness if it were true,
that he was born a prince, and was the Lost Dauphin, and some
said it was his secret, and some said that that was what he
wished to find out before he died. But if it was his identity that
he wished to discover, or if it was what a man had to seize beyond that, the way for him was by endless examination, by the
care for every bird that flew in his path and every serpent that
shone underfoot. Not one was enough; he looked deeper and
deeper, on and on, as if for a particular beast or some legendary
bird. Some men's eyes persisted in looking outward when they
opened to look inward, and to their delight, there outflung was

the astonishing world under the sky. When a man at last brought himself to face some mirror-surface he still saw the world looking back at him, and if he continued to look, to look closer and closer, what then? The gaze that looks outward must be trained without rest, to be indomitable. It must see as slowly as Murrell's ant in the grass, as exhaustively as Lorenzo's angel of God, and then, Audubon dreamed, with his mind going to his pointed brush, it must see like this, and he tightened his hand on the trigger of the gun and pulled it, and his eyes went closed. In memory the heron was all its solitude, its total beauty. All its whiteness could be seen from all sides at once, its pure feathers were as if counted and known and their array one upon the other would never be lost. But it was not from that memory that he could paint.

His opening eyes met Lorenzo's, close and flashing, and it was on seeing horror deep in them, like fires in abysses, that he recognized it for the first time. He had never seen horror in its purity and clarity until now, in bright blue eyes. He went and picked up the bird. He had thought it to be a female, just as one sees the moon as female; and so it was. He put it in his bag, and started away. But Lorenzo had already gone on, leaning a-tilt on the horse which went slowly.

Murrell was left behind, but he was proud of the dispersal, as if he had done it, as if he had always known that three men in simply being together and doing a thing can, by their obstinacy, take the pride out of one another. Each must go away alone, each send the others away alone. He himself had purposely kept to the wildest country in the world, and would have sought it out, the loneliest road. He looked about with satisfaction, and hid. Travelers were forever innocent, he believed: that was his faith. He lay in wait; his faith was in innocence and his knowledge was of ruin; and had these things been shaken? Now, what could possibly be outside his grasp? Churning all about him like a cloud about the sun was the great folding descent of his thought. Plans of deeds made his thoughts, and they rolled and mingled about his ears as if he heard a dark voice that rose up to overcome the wilderness voice, or was one with it. The night would soon come; and he had gone through the day.

Audubon, splattered and wet, turned back into the wilderness with the heron warm under his hand, his head still light in a kind of trance. It was undeniable, on some Sunday mornings, when he turned over and over his drawings they seemed beautiful to him, through what was dramatic in the conflict of life, or what was exact. What he would draw, and what he had seen, became for a moment one to him then. Yet soon enough, and it seemed to come in that same moment, like Lorenzo's horror and the gun's firing, he knew that even the sight of the heron which surely he alone had appreciated, had not been all his belonging, and that never could any vision, even any simple sight, belong to him or to any man. He knew that the best he could make would be, after it was apart from his hand, a dead thing and not a live thing, never the essence, only a sum of parts; and that it would always meet with a stranger's sight, and never be one with the beauty in any other man's head in the world. As he had seen the bird most purely at its moment of death, in some fatal way, in his care for looking outward, he saw his long labor most revealingly at the point where it met its limit. Still carefully, for he was trained to see well in the dark, he walked on into the deeper woods, noting all sights, all sounds, and was gentler than they as he went.

In the woods that echoed yet in his ears, Lorenzo riding slowly looked back. The hair rose on his head and his hands began to shake with cold, and suddenly it seemed to him that God Himself, just now, thought of the Idea of Separateness. For surely He had never thought of it before, when the little white heron was flying down to feed. He could understand God's giving Separateness first and then giving Love to follow and heal in its wonder; but God had reversed this, and given Love first and then Separateness, as though it did not matter to Him which came first. Perhaps it was that God never counted the moments of Time; Lorenzo did that, among his tasks of love. Time did not occur to God. Therefore—did He even know of it? How to explain Time and Separateness back to God, Who had never thought of them, Who could let the whole world come to grief in a scattering moment?

Lorenzo brought his cold hands together in a clasp and stared through the distance at the place where the bird had been as if he saw it still; as if nothing could really take away what had happened to him, the beautiful little vision of the feeding bird. Its beauty had been greater than he could account for. The sweat of rapture poured down from his forehead, and then he shouted into the marshes.

"Tempter!"

He whirled forward in the saddle and began to hurry the horse to its high speed. His camp ground was far away still, though even now they must be lighting the torches and gathering in the multitudes, so that at the appointed time he would duly appear in their midst, to deliver his address on the subject of "In that day when all hearts shall be disclosed."

Then the sun dropped below the trees, and the new moon, slender and white, hung shyly in the west.

267

THE ANGEL OF
THE BRIDGE

by John Cheever

You may have seen my mother waltzing on ice skates in
Rockefeller Center. She's seventy-eight years old now but
very wiry, and she wears a red velvet costume with a short skirt.
Her tights are flesh-colored, and she wears spectacles and a red
ribbon in her white hair, and she waltzes with one of the rink attendants. I don't know why I should find the fact that she
waltzes on ice skates so disconcerting, but I do. I avoid that
neighborhood whenever I can during the winter months, and I
never lunch in the restaurants on the rink. Once when I was
passing that way, a total stranger took me by the arm and,
pointing to Mother, said, "Look at that crazy old dame." I was
very embarrassed. I suppose I should be grateful for the fact that
she amuses herself and is not a burden to me, but I sincerely
wish she had hit on some less conspicuous recreation. Whenever
I see gracious old ladies arranging chrysanthemums and pouring
tea, I think of my own mother, dressed like a hat-check girl,

pushing some paid rink attendant around the ice, in the middle of the third biggest city in the world.

My mother learned to figure-skate in the little New England village of St. Botolphs, where we come from, and her waltzing is an expression of her attachment to the past. The older she grows, the more she longs for the vanishing and provincial world of her youth. She is a hardy woman, as you can imagine, but she does not relish change. I arranged one summer for her to fly to Toledo and visit friends. I drove her to the Newark airport. She seemed troubled by the airport waiting room, with its illuminated advertisements, vaulted ceiling, and touching and painful scenes of separation played out to an uproar of continuous tango music. She did not seem to find it in any way interesting or beautiful, and compared to the railroad station in St. Botolphs—whistles, steam, the smell of coal gas, and the noise of the telegraph—it was indeed a strange background against which to take one's departure. The flight was delayed for an hour, and we sat in the waiting room. Mother looked tired and old. When we had been waiting half an hour, she began to have some noticeable difficulty in breathing. She spread a hand over the front of her dress and began to gasp deeply, as if she was in pain. Her face got mottled and red. I pretended not to notice this. When the plane was announced, she got to her feet and exclaimed, "I want to go home! If I have to die suddenly, I don't want to die in a flying machine." I cashed in her ticket and drove her back to her apartment, and I have never mentioned this seizure to her or to anyone, but her capricious, or perhaps neurotic, fear of dying in a plane crash was the first insight I had into how, as she grew older, her way was strewn with invisible rocks and lions and how eccentric were the paths she took, as the world seemed to change its boundaries and become less and less comprehensible.

At the time of which I'm writing, I flew a great deal myself. My business was in Rome, New York, San Francisco, and Los Angeles, and I sometimes travelled as often as once a month between these cities. I liked the flying. I liked the incandescence of the sky at high altitudes. I liked all eastward flights where you can see from the ports the edge of night move over the continent and where, when it is four o'clock by your California watch, the housewives of Garden City are washing up the supper dishes and the stewardess in the plane is passing a second round of drinks. Toward the end of the flight, the air is stale. You are tired. The gold thread in the upholstery scratches your cheek, and there is a momentary feeling of forlornness, a sulky and childish sense of estrangement. You find good companions, of course, and bores, but most of the errands we run at such high altitudes are humble and terrestrial. That old lady, flying over the North Pole, is taking a jar of calf's-foot jelly to her sister in Paris, and the man beside her sells imitation-leather inner soles. Flying westward one dark night—we had crossed the Continental Divide, but we were still an hour out of Los Angeles and had not begun our descent, and were at such an altitude that the sense of houses, cities, and people below us was lost—I saw a formation, a trace of light, like the lights that burn along a shore. There was no shore in that part of the world, and I knew I would never know if the edge of the desert or some bluff or mountain accounted for this hoop of light, but it seemed, in its obscurity—and at that velocity and height—like the emergence of a new world, a gentle hint at my own obsolescence, the lateness of my time of life, and my inability to understand the things I often see. It was a pleasant feeling, completely free of regret, of being caught in some observable midpassage, the farther reaches of which might be understood by my sons.

I liked to fly, as I say, and had none of my mother's anxieties. It was my older brother—her darling—who was to inherit her resoluteness, her stubbornness, her table silver, and some of her eccentricities. One evening, my brother—I had not seen him for a year or so—called and asked if he could come for dinner. I was happy to invite him. We live on the eleventh floor of an apartment house, and at seven-thirty he telephoned from the lobby and asked me to come down. I thought he must have something to tell me privately, but when we met in the lobby he got into the automatic elevator with me and we started up. As soon as the doors closed, he showed the same symptoms of fear I had seen in my mother. Sweat stood out on his forehead, and he gasped like a runner.

"What in the world is the matter?" I asked.

"I'm afraid of elevators," he said miserably.

"But what are you afraid of?"

"I'm afraid the building will fall down."

I laughed—cruelly, I guess. For it all seemed terribly funny, his vision of the buildings of New York banging against one another like ninepins as they fell to the earth. There has always been a strain of jealousy in our feelings about one another, and I am aware, at some obscure level, that he makes more money and has more of everything than I, and to see him humiliated—crushed—saddened me but at the same time and in spite of myself made me feel that I had taken a stunning lead in the race for honors that is at the bottom of our relationship. He is the older, he is the favorite, but watching his misery in the elevator I felt that he was merely my poor old brother, overtaken by his worries. He stopped in the hallway to recover his composure, and explained that he had been suffering from this phobia for over a year. He was going to a psychiatrist, he said. I couldn't see that it had done him any good. He was all right once he got out of the elevator, but I noticed that he stayed away from the windows. When it was time to go, I walked him out to the corridor. I was curious. When the elevator reached our floor, he turned to me and said, "I'm afraid I'll have to take the stairs." I led him to the stairway, and we climbed slowly down the eleven flights. He clung to the railing. We said goodbye in the lobby, and I went up in the elevator, and told my wife about his fear that the building might fall down. It seemed strange and sad to her, and it did to me, too, but it also seemed terribly funny.

It wasn't terribly funny when, a month later, the firm he worked for moved to the fifty-second floor of a new office building and he had to resign. I don't know what reasons he gave. It was another six months before he could find a job in a third-floor office. I once saw him on a winter dusk at the corner of Madison Avenue and Fifty-ninth Street, waiting for the light to change. He appeared to be an intelligent, civilized, and well-dressed man, and I wondered how many of the men waiting with him to cross the street made their way as he did through a ruin of absurd delusions, in which the street might appear to be a torrent and the approaching cab driven by the angel of death.

He was quite all right on the ground. My wife and I went to his house in New Jersey, with the children, for a weekend, and he looked healthy and well. I didn't ask about his phobia. We drove back to New York on Sunday afternoon. As we approached the George Washington Bridge, I saw a thunderstorm over the city. A strong wind struck the car the moment we were on the bridge, and nearly took the wheel out of my hand. It seemed to me that I could feel the huge structure swing. Halfway across the bridge, I thought I felt the roadway begin to give. I could see no signs of a collapse, and yet I was convinced that in another minute the bridge would split in two and hurl the long lines of Sunday traffic into the dark water below us. This imagined disaster was terrifying. My legs got so weak that I was not sure I could brake the car if I needed to. Then it became difficult for me to breathe. Only by opening my mouth and gasping did I seem able to take in any air. My blood pressure was affected and I began to feel a darkening of my vision. Fear has always seemed to me to run a course, and at its climax the body and perhaps the spirit defend themselves by drawing on some new and fresh source of strength. Once over the center of the bridge, my pain and terror began to diminish. My wife and the children were admiring the storm, and they did not seem to have noticed my spasm. I was afraid both that the bridge would fall down and that they might observe my panic.

I thought back over the weekend for some incident that might account for my preposterous fear that the George Washington Bridge would blow away in a thunderstorm, but it had been a pleasant weekend, and even under the most exaggerated scrutiny I couldn't uncover any source of morbid nervousness or anxiety. Later in the week, I had to drive to Albany, and although the day was clear and windless, the memory of my first attack was too keen; I hugged the east bank of the river as far north as Troy, where I found a small, old-fashioned bridge that I could cross comfortably. This meant going fifteen or twenty miles out of my way, and it is humiliating to have your travels obstructed by barriers that are senseless and invisible. I drove back from Albany by the same route, and next morning I went to the family doctor and told him I was afraid of bridges.

He laughed. "You, of all people," he said scornfully. "You'd better take hold of yourself."

"But Mother is afraid of airplanes," I said. "And Brother hates elevators."

"Your mother is past seventy," he said, "and one of the most remarkable women I've ever known. I wouldn't bring *her* into this. What *you* need is a little more backbone."

This was all he had to say, and I asked him to recommend an analyst. He does not include psychoanalysis in medical science, and told me I would be wasting my time and money, but, yielding to his obligation to be helpful, he gave me the name and address of a psychiatrist, who told me that my fear of bridges was the surface manifestation of a deep-seated anxiety and that I would have to have a full analysis. I didn't have the time, or the money, or, above all, the confidence in the doctor's methods to put myself in his hands, and I said I would try and muddle through.

There are obviously areas of true and false pain, and my pain was meretricious, but how could I convince my lights and vitals of this? My youth and childhood had their deeply troubled and their jubilant years, and could some repercussions from this past account for my fear of heights? The thought of a life determined by hidden obstacles was unacceptable, and I decided to take the advice of the family doctor and ask more of myself. I had to go to Idlewild later in the week, and, rather than take a bus or a taxi, I drove the car myself. I nearly lost consciousness on the Triborough Bridge. When I got to the airport I ordered a cup of coffee, but my hand was shaking so I spilled the coffee on the counter. The man beside me was amused and said that I must have put in quite a night. How could I tell him that I had gone to bed early and sober but that I was afraid of bridges?

I flew to Los Angeles late that afternoon. It was one o'clock by my watch when we landed. It was only ten o'clock in California. I was tired and took a taxi to the hotel where I always stay, but I couldn't sleep. Outside my hotel window was a monumental statue of a young woman, advertising a Las Vegas night club. She revolves slowly in a beam of light. At 2 A.M. the light is extinguished, but she goes on restlessly turning all through the night. I have never seen her cease her turning, and I wondered, that night, when they greased her axle and washed her shoulders. I felt some affection for her, since neither of us could rest, and I wondered if she had a family—a stage mother, perhaps, and a compromised and broken-spirited father who drove a municipal bus on the West Pico line? There was a restaurant across the street, and I watched a drunken woman in a sable cape being led out to a car. She twice nearly fell. The crosslights from the open door, the lateness, her drunkenness, and the solicitude of the man with her made the scene, I thought, worried and lonely. Then two cars that seemed to be racing down Sunset Boulevard pulled up at a traffic light under my window. Three men piled out of each car and began to slug one another. You could hear the blows land on bone and cartilage. When the light changed, they got back into their cars and raced off. The fight, like the hoop of light I had seen from the plane, seemed like the signs of a new world, but in this case an emergence of brutality and chaos. Then I remembered that I was to go to San Francisco on Thursday, and was expected in Berkeley for lunch. This meant crossing the San Francisco-Oakland Bay Bridge, and I reminded myself to take a cab both ways and leave the car I rented in San Francisco in the hotel garage. I tried again to reason out my fear that the bridge would fall. Was I the victim of some sexual dislocation? My life has been promiscuous, care-

The Angel of the Bridge

free, and a source of immense pleasure, but was there some secret here that would have to be mined by a professional? Were all my pleasures impostures and evasions, and was I really in love with my old mother in her skating costume?

Looking at Sunset Boulevard at three in the morning, I felt that my terror of bridges was an expression of my clumsily concealed horror of what is becoming of the world. I can drive with composure through the outskirts of Cleveland and Toledo—past the birthplace of the Polish Hot Dog, the Buffalo Burger stands, the used-car lots, and the architectural monotony. I claim to enjoy walking down Hollywood Boulevard on a Sunday afternoon. I have cheerfully praised the evening sky hanging beyond the dishevelled and expatriated palm trees on Doheny Boulevard, stuck up against the incandescence, like rank upon rank of wet mops. Duluth and East Seneca are charming, and if they aren't, just look away. The hideousness of the road between San Francisco and Palo Alto is nothing more than the search of honest men and women for a decent place to live. The same thing goes for San Pedro and all that coast. But the height of bridges seemed to be one link I could not forge or fasten in this hypocritical chain of acceptances. The truth is, I hate freeways and Buffalo Burgers. Expatriated palm trees and monotonous housing developments depress me. The continuous music on special-fare trains exacerbates my feelings. I detest the destruction of familiar landmarks, I am deeply troubled by the misery and drunkenness I find among my friends, I abhor the dishonest practices I see. And it was at the highest point in the arc of a bridge that I became aware suddenly of the depth and the bitterness of my feelings about modern life, and the profoundness of my yearning for a more vivid, simple, and peaceable world.

But I couldn't reform Sunset Boulevard, and until I could, I couldn't drive across the San Francisco-Oakland Bay Bridge. What *could* I do? Go back to St. Botolphs, wear a Norfolk jacket, and play cribbage in the firehouse? There was only one bridge in the village, and you could throw a stone across the river there.

I got home from San Francisco on Saturday, and found my daughter back from school for the weekend. On Sunday morning, she asked me to drive her to the convent school in Jersey where she is a student. She had to be back in time for nine o'clock Mass, and we left our apartment in the city a little after seven. We were talking and laughing, and I had approached and was in fact on the George Washington Bridge without having remembered my weakness. There were no preliminaries this time. The seizure came with a rush. The strength went out of my legs, I gasped for breath, and felt the terrifying loss of sight. I was, at the same time, determined to conceal these symptoms from my daughter. I made the other side of the bridge, but I was violently shaken. My daughter didn't seem to have noticed. I got her to school in time, kissed her goodbye, and started home. There was no question of my crossing the George Washington Bridge again, and I decided to drive north to Nyack and cross on the Tappan Zee Bridge. It seemed, in my memory, more gradual and more securely anchored to its shores. Driving up the parkway on the west shore, I decided that oxygen was what I needed, and I opened all the windows of the car. The fresh air seemed to help, but only momentarily. I could feel my sense of reality ebbing. The roadside and the car itself seemed to have less substance than a dream. I had some friends in the neighborhood, and I thought of stopping and asking them for a drink, but it was only a little after nine in the morning, and I could not face the embarrassment of asking for a drink so early in the day, and of explaining that I was afraid of bridges. I thought I might feel better if I talked to someone, and I stopped at a gas station and bought some gas, but the attendant was laconic and sleepy, and I couldn't explain to him that his conversation might make the difference between life and death. I had got onto the Thruway by then, and I wondered what alternatives I had if I couldn't cross the bridge. I could call my wife and ask her to make some arrangements for removing me, but our relationship involves so much self-esteem and face that to admit openly to this foolishness might damage our married hap-

piness. I could call the garage we use and ask them to send up a man to chauffeur me home. I could park the car and wait until one o'clock, when the bars opened, and fill up on whiskey, but I had spent the last of my money for gasoline. I decided to take a chance, and turned onto the approach to the bridge.

All the symptoms returned, and this time they were much worse than ever. The wind was knocked out of my lungs as by a blow. My equilibrium was so shaken that the car swerved from one lane into another. I drove to the side and pulled on the hand brake. The loneliness of my predicament was harrowing. If I had been miserable with romantic love, racked with sickness, or beastly drunk, it would have seemed more dignified. I remembered my brother's face, sallow and greasy with sweat in the elevator, and my mother in her red skirt, one leg held gracefully aloft as she coasted backward in the arms of a rink attendant, and it seemed to me that we were all three characters in some bitter and sordid tragedy, carrying impossible burdens and separated from the rest of mankind by our misfortunes. My life was over, and it would never come back, everything that I loved—blue-sky courage, lustiness, the natural grasp of things. It would never come back. I would end up in the psychiatric ward of the county hospital, screaming that the bridges, all the bridges in the world, were falling down.

Then a young girl opened the door of the car and got in. "I didn't think anyone would pick me up on the bridge," she said. She carried a cardboard suitcase and—believe me—a small harp in a cracked waterproof. Her straight light-brown hair was brushed and brushed and grained with blondness and spread in a kind of cape over her shoulders. Her face seemed full and merry.

"Are you hitchhiking?" I asked.

"Yes."

"But isn't it dangerous for a girl your age?"

"Not at all."

"Do you travel much?"

"All the time. I sing a little. I play the coffeehouses."

"What do you sing?"

"Oh, folk music, mostly. And some old things—Purcell and Dowland. But mostly folk music. . . . 'I gave my love a cherry that had no stone,'" she sang in a true and pretty voice. "'I gave my love a chicken that had no bone/I told my love a story that had no end/I gave my love a baby with no cryin'.'"

She sang me across a bridge that seemed to be an astonishingly sensible, durable, and even beautiful construction designed by intelligent men to simplify my travels, and the water of the Hudson below us was charming and tranquil. It all came back—blue-sky courage, the high spirits of lustiness, an ecstatic sereneness. Her song ended as we got to the toll station on the east bank, and she thanked me, said goodbye, and got out of the car. I offered to take her wherever she wanted to go, but she shook her head and walked away, and I drove on toward the city through a world that, having been restored to me, seemed marvellous and fair. When I got home, I thought of calling my brother and telling him what had happened, on the chance that there was also an angel of the elevator banks, but the harp—that single detail—threatened to make me seem ridiculous or mad, and I didn't call.

I wish I could say that I am convinced that there will always be some merciful intercession to help me with my worries, but I don't believe in rushing my luck, so I still stay off the George Washington Bridge, although I can cross the Triborough and the Tappan Zee with ease. My brother is still afraid of elevators, and my mother, although she's grown quite stiff, still goes around and around and around on the ice.

THE QUESTION
OF RAIN

by William Hoffman

THE REQUEST came from an unexpected source during the
dusty, choking summer. Wayland was in the back yard of
the white frame manse. His wife, Mims, called through the
kitchen screen door that Alex Bradner was on the way out. Oh
damn, Wayland thought, because he believed he had at last
educated his congregation not to bother him on Mondays except
for illness or death.

Alex Bradner owned knitting mills, cinder-block plants
which manufactured textured polyesters and spun down a fine,
almost invisible lint over the flat Virginia town. When the mills
worked three shifts, a person could look out at the early morning
grass and believe it was frosted even in July.

"We might have to close unless it rains," Alex said to
Wayland.

Alex was a hard-driving man in his mid-fifties, his impatience held in check only by his breeding. Even sitting in a lawn

chair, Alex seemed in motion, about to leap up to do a job, to wrench the world to the shape his hands desired.

"I didn't know you used that much water," Wayland said.

"It's the dye," Alex explained. "We need water for our dyeing process, and if the river runs low, the discharge concentration is increased to where the Water Control Board in Richmond can shut us down. I'd like you to pray for rain."

Wayland almost smiled, because Alex Bradner had little spiritual depth. He was generous with his pocketbook, but not himself. During services, rather than sing the hymns, he studied them as if they were corporate reports. He never recited The Apostles' Creed.

"Well, of course, I'll be happy to pray," Wayland said, the smile twitching at his lips. "Would you like to right now, you and I together?"

"I think it ought to be in the church," Alex said. His green eyes were speckled and seemed lidless, they were so unblinking.

"All right, we'll walk over," Wayland said, prepared to stand. "Though I don't think it's necessary. I'm certain our prayers can be heard just as well from a back yard."

"I don't mean just us," Alex said. "I think you ought to make this Sunday a Special Prayer Day for Rain."

Wayland said nothing. He looked at Alex to see how serious he was. Alex wasn't frowning, but his face perpetually verged upon it.

"I don't think I'd care to alter our regular service," Wayland said.

"But wouldn't it be better?" Alex asked. "The more people we gather, the whole congregation, and in the church, would appear to make praying more productive."

Alex Bradner was playing divine odds. Four was better than two, a crowd more powerful than an individual. Wayland hoped he didn't sound peevish.

"God hears each of us," he said. "Efficacy doesn't require massing."

"I believe in covering all bases," Alex said.

"God knows our needs," Wayland explained. "He meets them out of His love for us. We don't pray to ask favors as if He's a rich uncle, but to have fellowship with Him, to achieve a feeling that we are close and in His care."

"Would it hurt to try?" Alex asked, pragmatic and relentless.

"I don't suppose it could hurt anything," Wayland said. "The question is whether or not our regular worship service ought to be used. I don't object to rain as part of the general prayer, but to make rain the point of an entire service not only might set a precedent whereby people would soon request snow on Christmas or cooling breezes in August, but would also presume on God's plans for us and this world. Loving and seeking Him is the great prayer, and He will order affairs so that we want nothing in any essential way."

"You won't do it, then?" Alex asked, and tightened his broad freckled hands on the aluminum chair arms to stand.

"I'm not speaking that strongly," Wayland said. "As I pray for the sick and the lost, I'll pray for rain, but not use the entire service."

"A lot of people are going to be out of work," Alex said.

Alex's visit soured the day for Wayland. He capped his paints, cleaned his brushes, and talked with Mims in the kitchen. She was thirty-three, four years younger than he, a small, fair-skinned woman with brown eyes and reddish-brown hair.

"But what can superdealer do?" she asked. She smelled of vinegar and linseed oil from her work of refinishing a pine washstand she had bought at a farm auction.

"I don't know, but I can tell you Alex won't let go," Wayland said.

On Tuesday night, as Wayland was about to close the deacons' meeting with a prayer, Harlan Henderson spoke. Harlan was chairman of the group, a weathered, square-jawed man who was the county agent.

"Are you going to take any action on the rain?" Harlan asked.

"You mean me personally?" Wayland asked, and got a laugh.

"There's sentiment among the congregation for a special day," Harlan persisted.

"I've winded that sentiment," Wayland said. "I have to tell you frankly I don't like the idea."

"We could sure God use a rain," Nelson Dunnavant said. Nelson had only one arm. He had lost the other to the claws of a mechanical corn picker. He owned both a dairy farm and a John Deere dealership.

"I want rain as much as anyone, but my feeling is rain is a lesser need," Wayland said. "If we're going to unite our voices, we should ask for grateful hearts, not put in a special order. I hope you see the distinction."

He looked into their faces, good faces, good men, his friends and helpers, men he loved and could rely on, but he observed that they did not see any distinction. They reminded him of cattle staring motionless in a pasture.

"I suggest some things have to be left to the minister's judgment," Wayland said.

As he walked home through the dry, abrasive darkness, he slapped at mosquitoes. Seared grass crackled under his shoes. Mims sat in the manse parlor playing the black upright piano. Barefoot, wearing white shorts and a blue halter, she was practicing hymns to be sung at Sunday School.

"You heard a weather report?" he asked.

"Rain?" she asked, brightening. Her fingers were still curved to the keys.

"I was hoping you'd listened and could tell me," he said.

"Sorry there, fellow. Failed once again by your trifling, weak-minded wife."

He laughed, crossed to sit by her on the piano bench, and kissed her neck, ear, and mouth. She wore perfume, but he still smelled the vinegar.

"Keep this up and you'll have to race me to the bedroom," she said.

When, on Wednesday morning, he walked to the post

office, heat quivered above the gummy asphalt street. Lawns were a pale, kinky brown, scorched right to the soil. The soil itself had cracks in it, as if the earth would give up its dead. No flowers bloomed, no sprinklers spun.

Beyond the iron bridge over the shallow, dust-filmed river, cars were leaving the fenced parking lot at the mill. He first thought ten-forty was a strange time for a shift change. Then he understood that the men had been let go.

As he walked through the listless, sun-glazed town, he believed people were eyeing him. He might be imagining it. Ministers developed persecution feelings. The most intent eyes might be his own, peering at himself from within.

"Hear about the plant closings?" Spud Hogge, cashier and a member of the congregation, asked when Wayland stopped by the Planters & Merchants Bank to deposit his bimonthly salary check.

"Terrible for the men," Wayland said. Was he being criticized?

"Rough to have no beans for your family," Spud said, his lumpy face set. When the bell mechanism had broken in the church steeple, Spud had climbed through rafters and been stung by wasps in order to find the trouble and fix it.

"Spud, are you sending me a message?" Wayland asked, smiling.

"I think everybody has his Christian duty to help all he can in tight times," Spud said, his chin raised as if facing wind.

Wayland walked home, changed into shorts, and sat in his study. He intended to preach this Sunday on the sacrament of baptism. He would soon, obviously, have to work up a sermon on prayer, its nature.

Despite the open windows, no air moved in his study. It wasn't air at all, but a tormenting pressure which galled the skin. The mimosa, which stirred with even the slightest breeze, was immobile against a citrine sky, its dusty, drooping fronds tinged with yellow. No bird flew, no cloud floated. It would not rain today.

In this week's sermon he would emphasize that a man's

being sprinkled or immersed symbolized drowning and the death of an old life and the emergence of a new person to a new life. It occurred to him that the subject of baptism might cause the congregation to think all the more about water and drought. He imagined some wag remarking that there wasn't enough river left to baptize even a dainty Episcopalian.

He was conscious of the weltering locusts, their chirring warping over the parched town. He scratched a bare shoulder. He switched on a radio which sat in his bookshelf. The Town Council was asking citizens to take as few baths as possible. His routine called for two showers a day. He considered which to deny himself.

He wrote pell-mell, having no thought for jarring transitions or even scriptural relevance, but just trying to get something on paper to work with. Afterward it would be polish, polish, polish until Saturday, when he taped the sermon in order that he and Mims could listen and judge how it would play in Peoria.

The ladies arrived at four, rang the bell—Bess Blakley, Ellen Boswer, and Caroline Devereaux, each an officer in the Women of the Church. Mims seated them in the parlor and came for Wayland. She rolled her eyes.

There was no way he could go past them and up the steps to change his clothes without being seen. He did pull on his red tank top and apologize for his bare feet. Caroline Devereaux looked at his legs, which were hairy and slightly bowed. Aware of his skin and the ladies' finery, he sat on a leatherette ottoman.

"I guess we're a delegation," Bess Blakley said. Oldest of the three, she had bluish-white hair. "The Women of the Church have gone on record as being in favor of a Special Prayer Day for Rain to end the drought."

Wayland almost sighed openly. The ladies were nearly always the problem. He loved, indeed honored them for being the most devout laborers in Christ's vineyard, but they also became too easily aroused and were regimental in their causes.

"Bess, to repeat my position, let me state that I'm strongly

in favor of prayer, but I feel what people really want is a medicine man, and I never rattle bones, do a rain dance, or wear chicken feathers."

"All people want is for you to try," Caroline Devereaux said. She was a tanned, short-haired blond who annually won the town tennis tournament. She also taught the majorettes at the high school.

"Caroline, we can't twist God's arm," he explained. "All we have is given us by His grace, and we are undeserving of that."

"We could fill the church," said Ellen Boswer, the wife of Jamerson Boswer, the mayor, who was also in the tobacco export business. Ellen was tiny, hardly five feet tall, yet she had mothered six robust, rowdy children.

"Well, I'm sure we could, but the service would be a sideshow," Wayland said. "Somebody might suggest we serve popcorn and play bingo."

His sarcasm offended them. They had come to him with serious spiritual business, even if misguided, and he should have been patient and loving.

"It doesn't have to be a sideshow," Bess Blakley said. "I don't see why you and all of us couldn't pray with dignity."

"You're right, Bess, and I'm sorry," he said. "What I'm trying to tell you is, we can't force God's hand even with our most fervent prayers. In praying we shouldn't be talking at all, making demands, but listening, feeling, and receiving Him."

"Then you won't," Caroline Devereaux said. "We heard you were against it."

"Against it, not you," he said. "Refusing you ladies anything distresses me. I'd rather suffer toads and boils. Yet I know you wouldn't want me to do something I consider wrong for myself and the church."

They fidgeted, glanced at each other, and drew their pocketbooks higher on their laps. He walked them to the door, where Ellen Boswer turned to him.

"I hear cattle lowing," she said tearfully. "They sound hurt and mournful. They have no water or pasture. They stand by dry holes looking pitiful. I'd think a minister would be touched by that."

"Believe me, Ellen, I'm not in favor of pain and suffering," Wayland said, and for a moment he felt very near despair at the gap between them, their lives on one side of the theological divide, his life on the other, and so little possibility of ever reaching across and joining hands.

When they were gone, he walked musing to his study. He sat discouraged. He began to pray. Depression, rooted in self-pity, he considered a sin. To the Lord he gave thanks for tribulation, as the Epistle of James suggested. All things truly worked for good to those who loved God. And Wayland did love God. When he lifted his head, Mims, hands folded, waited beyond the doorway.

"There wasn't time to warn you," she said. "I had to invite them in."

"It's okay," he said. "I'll be all right now. At least I hope I will."

"You'll feel better after your shower," she said.

"I'm not showering this afternoon," he said.

That night he had a telephone call from Henry Porter of the Danville *Bee*. Henry was nearly inactive in the church, a Christmas Christian.

"Richmond called me," Henry said. "They want a story about this Special Prayer Day for Rain."

"Wait just a second," Wayland said. "How would anybody in Richmond know?"

"I can't answer you," Henry said. "I can tell you they might send a reporter. You want to make a statement?"

"I'm definitely not holding a Special Prayer Day for Rain," Wayland said. "I'm having my regular Sunday service, though I will pray for rain in my pastoral prayer."

Wayland had trouble sleeping. He worried, and the heat chafed him. The locusts didn't cease their chirring until after ten o'clock. Then dogs started a monotonous, unrelieved barking. He attempted to lie still so as not to disturb Mims, but he sensed she wasn't sleeping either.

Finally, when he had nearly dropped off, the telephone rang. He snatched it from the night table.

" 'O ye of little faith!' " a male voice said.

"What?" Wayland asked. "Who is this?"

But the person hung up. Wayland looked at Mims, who lay uncovered in the pearly glow from the bathroom night-light. Her dark eyes were open.

"I heard it," she said.

"Who'd do that to me?" Wayland asked. He lay beside her and held her moist hand.

"So many people have become irritable in this weather," she said. "The call could've come from a tavern."

He was up early Thursday to work on his sermon during the slight morning coolness. There was no dampness on the withered grass. He stayed at his desk until ten. He then drove his Plymouth to the community hospital, a modern brick and glass structure built on the town's only rise of ground. Stone visitor's benches were placed under shriveled locust and willow trees.

As he made his rounds to the sick and suffering, a voice calling his name echoed along the waxy, metallic corridor. The voice belonged to Lee Gordon, a young doctor whom Wayland had spoken the marriage vows over this past April.

"Margo tells me the phone lines are smoking," Lee said. Margo was his sultry Georgia wife. Lee laughed. "She tells me you're expected to perform miracles."

Slim and athletic, Lee, who had played for the Duke team, was a prowling shark on the golf course. He wore a starched white smock, wine slacks, and perforated black and white kilties. His good-humored assumption that he and Wayland were far more sophisticated about God and religion than anybody else in town disturbed Wayland.

"Miracles happen," Wayland said. "Even today they can happen." He did believe that, didn't he?

"But you wouldn't want to put your chips on the line, would you?" Lee asked, his outsized teeth gritted in a grin. "I mean right up there in front of everybody in church, to put your chips on the line for a miracle?"

How to make Lee and people understand it wasn't a question of chips on the line? God in His omnipotence could change the course of history by merely willing it, but the question was whether or not God was careless and ran the universe by whim and the seat of His divine trousers.

"Maybe you ought to break over and have a beer," Mims said that afternoon when Wayland, dejected, slumped in his study. She kept a few cans for him. Buying it was dangerous, never done locally, but only while she shopped in Danville or South Hill.

The telephone call came at ten minutes after five, not anonymous, but from Fred Pepper, chairman of the Board of Elders. They were holding a special meeting. Wayland had drunk two beers and was relaxed. He was forced to hurry his eating of Mims's cool shrimp salad and follow it with Listerine. He fought anger.

There were five elders, veteran Christians, important to the church and to the community. Fred Pepper owned a department store, yet was a man of the cross, always willing to attend presbytery and quick to reach for the check.

"We've been receiving calls," Fred said. He and the other elders sat on the same folding wooden chairs the diaconate used, chairs in a Sunday School room with a view of the thirsting cemetery. Fred wore a seersucker suit, a white shirt, and a narrow black tie. His gray hair had deep comb furrows in it.

"The ladies are in an uproar," Chap Bonney said. Chap, at least a hundred pounds overweight, was an attorney and on the board at the bank. "Do anything, face storms and earthquakes, lions and tigers, but not the fury of the aroused human female."

Wayland laughed with the others.

"Just what is the problem?" Reid Poindexter asked, slim,

precise, mathematical Reid, a dispatcher for the Norfolk & Western Railroad.

"The problem with rain is, I'm in sales, not management," Wayland said.

That too got a laugh, though he still had to go through his explanation for refusing to hold the Special Prayer Day for Rain. He had given his reasons so many times he felt he was becoming practiced, smooth, like a sermon repeated until it possessed momentum of its own.

"It's God's world to do with what He will, and it falls to us to glorify His use of it," Wayland said.

"I thought the world belonged to Satan," Gaston Fervier said. Gaston was a tobacco planter and even now tightened his lip over a dip of snuff, though he was washed and handsome with his white hair, pale blue Palm Beach suit, and polished black shoes. If there was elder trouble, it usually came from Gaston, not because he intended to start it or was mischievous, but because Gaston had his own peculiar manner of seeing everything, including Scriptures.

"God created the world good," Wayland said. "When man sinned through pride, the world was wounded and broken, just as man himself, Adam, was wounded and broken in his relationship to God. In the end, however, all things are still God's to do with as He wills."

Gaston stared, his long face not hostile but serious, a trader calculating percentages.

"Maybe it's His will to have us meeting here tonight," Gaston said. "Maybe it's part of His plan to make us have a Special Prayer Day for Rain."

"Suppose it's not God's purpose to have rain at this time, for reasons we can't fathom?" Wayland said, seeing before them the endless convolutions of predestination, which Gaston loved. "Then it won't rain no matter how hard we pray. We'll have held the church and ourselves up to ridicule."

They were silent. When one spoke, it was Carson Puckett, a former superintendent of schools, now in his late seventies, bald, wasting, a deliberate, pious man, pious in the best sense of that misused word.

"Are we afraid to put our faith to the test?" Carson asked. "I believe the Lord will give us rain if we ask for it. He'll find a way."

Wayland hadn't expected it from Carson, a person he greatly respected. He knew the depths of Carson's spirituality. Carson was an Old Testament figure, a patriarch who could strike a rock for water, tread unravished among beasts, and stand unsinged in the fiery furnace. For the first time Wayland felt unsure, even shaken.

"And if we fail?" Wayland asked Carson.

"Then it's us, not God, who've failed," Carson said. "I think it ought to be tried. Pastor, I wish you'd at least consider it."

"I'll of course do that," Wayland said.

Walking home, he felt light-headed. Mims sat fanning herself on the screened porch. In the refrigerator was a glass of iced tea she had fixed for him.

"Maybe I'm wrong," Wayland said. "I could be behaving like one of these slick modern ministers who act as if Scriptures were private property. I've become so professional I've lost sight of the power of simple belief."

Early in the morning he drove to Richmond to see Dr. Hans Koppman, his friend and former teacher, at Union Theological. Dr. Koppman was a brusque and powerful man, one who, unlike many lecturers at the seminary, heaped work on his students because he believed the ministry was life's highest calling and more should be expected of those who aspired to it. He stormed around his classroom asking questions which were snares. He loved parable and paradox.

Dr. Koppman was in his office. From his ponderous head his graying black hair grew into tangled ovals, and hair curled from his porous nose. He whooped, laughed loudly, and repeatedly slapped his desk.

"Oh, brother, I'm glad it's you, not me!" he shouted. "I'd rather be roasted over hot coals. Lord, deliver my heifers from the drought!"

"Somehow it's not funny to me," Wayland said.

"So you've come to a foolish professor in a preacher factory and want him to tell you what to do," Dr. Koppman said. "Listen, the understanding of faith is not in the seminaries. Faith exists in the recesses of that mad place, the heart, and who knows the labyrinthine corridors of the heart?"

As Dr. Koppman discoursed, Wayland gazed out the mullioned window at tennis players, at the nets and lines on the green courts, at the patterns of white and green, the perfect little world of games. He longed for the certainty of rules.

"I'm reminded of the story about a holy young man who doubted the strength of his belief," Dr. Koppman said. "The young man thought that if he were really strong in the faith, he could walk on water. He traveled to the land's edge. Trembling, he set foot on the stormy depths. Lo, the waters held him! Joy welled in him as he walked over the thrashing waters like a tottering child, glorious, mind-blowing joy. He was fired by the ecstasy of knowing he was favored by God."

"Is that all the story?" Wayland asked.

"Not quite," Dr. Koppman said, his thick brows wagging. "In running for joy, he crossed a highway without due care, heard the blast of an air horn, looked up, and saw a bread truck which rolled over and killed him. His last vision was one of loaves."

Dr. Koppman laughed and laughed. Wayland drove home more muddled than ever. He sat in his study and stared at the yellowing mimosa and his desiccated rock garden. He slipped to his knees, rested his elbows on the swivel chair, and raised his face.

"Father, open me to Thy will so that what I do may be for Thy glory," he prayed.

Again he gave up his evening shower. After dinner he was unable to stop himself from studying the weather map in the Danville *Bee*. There was no mention of rain in the entire nation.

He returned to his study to work on the baptism sermon. The words wouldn't flow. He watched twilight settle like gauze over the dusty yard. He became fearful. Suppose his indecision indicated some mortal chink in his theological armor?

Scratching at his hot skin, he roamed the manse. In the kitchen Mims was pinching her rings from the windowsill where she always set them while washing dishes.

"I feel everybody in the country's taking a bite out of me," Wayland said.

"On suffocating days like these, people aren't themselves," she said.

"Who are they?" he asked. He saw she was tired—more than tired, worn.

"We can't expect them to be more than human," she said. Wilted, sweaty, carrying his worries as well as her own, she touched her forehead with the limp back of a hand. It was a beautiful gesture: patient, feminine, long-suffering. And then she served him up a smile to encourage him.

He was so moved he could only nod. Oh, he loved her! And her words, such simple, ordinary words, but there it was, the whole truth of prayer really, stripped of theology and man's encrustments. To plead when troubled, to go to one's father, was human. God knew our needs, sure, but He wouldn't expect anyone, not even a minister, to be more than human—just as no father would expect a son or daughter to be other than a child.

For an instant Wayland was tormented that he hadn't seen the truth, yet grateful that he saw it now.

"Would you consider your husband a weak, spineless creature if he reversed himself and decided to hold a rain service?" Wayland asked.

"Oh, I'd be so glad!" she said.

"You would?" he asked. He had believed she wholly supported his ideas on prayer.

"My husband, the good shepherd, wants to feed his flock," she said.

The Question of Rain

So Saturday he worked late writing and mimeographing a service for the Special Prayer Day, and on Sunday morning the church was full even to the balconies. Wayland had composed a responsive liturgy in order that the congregation might have a role. He spoke his part over the reverent, upturned faces.

"As Your children we come to ask of You," he intoned.

"Lord, bring us rain," the congregation responded.

After the service Wayland's fingers became sore from shaking hands. Men pawed his shoulder. The ladies were gracious, and he and Mims received seven invitations to dinner. Only Gaston Fervier annoyed him.

"I see you didn't bring your umbrella," Gaston said. Gaston had his.

At the manse Mims fixed Wayland a sandwich. She was happy about the service, but he felt emptied. He lay down for a nap.

He would not anticipate. Rain wasn't necessary. He and the congregation had acknowledged God's fathership, which was the main thing. He turned his back to the window so he wouldn't be tempted to judge the quality of the afternoon sunlight edging the drawn shade.

Yet he felt a stillness, the absolute hush of the day. Even the locusts were silent. A distant rumble had to be a truck. He stood, went downstairs, and walked out onto the screened porch where Mims sat. She wore her lavender church dress in case of visitors, but had pushed off her white pumps so that her heels were free.

The expression on her clean face was strange as she gazed upward. He looked at the sky and, tingling, saw the dazzling cloud growing, building rapidly into a thunderhead, the underside purplish, the crown of radiant whiteness seething as it mounted into a cathedral of a cloud. People came from their houses to stare. Then Wayland felt a coolness, a nudge of air, and knew rain must be close.

In wonder Mims watched the sky. Wayland's amazement gave way to rapture as the majestic thunderhead conquered the heavens. He realized his mouth had opened as if to catch the rain on his lips. The pressure of gratitude brought him near to weeping.

During the slashing, luminous rain, he put on his shorts to walk in the yard. With his face uplifted, he gave thanks. Children, despite lightning, ran in the streets and across glossy lawns. Adults too splashed through puddles. The artificial pond in his rock garden overflowed. The telephone rang so often that Mims, now wearing her pink bathing suit, took it off the hook.

Only later, during the wet night when he and Mims lay together, did he think of the holy young man who had walked on water. The story had to be just another of Dr. Koppman's pranks, but the truth is that for days Wayland not only looked in both directions with extreme care before crossing streets, even the least traveled ones, but also peered at ceilings, floors, the ground, tree limbs, and into shadows, as if something waited for him.

REVELATION

by Flannery O'Connor

THE DOCTOR's waiting room, which was very small, was almost full when the Turpins entered and Mrs. Turpin, who was very large, made it look even smaller by her presence. She stood looming at the head of the magazine table set in the center of it, a living demonstration that the room was inadequate and ridiculous. Her little bright black eyes took in all the patients as she sized up the seating situation. There was one vacant chair and a place on the sofa occupied by a blond child in a dirty blue romper who should have been told to move over and make room for the lady. He was five or six, but Mrs. Turpin saw at once that no one was going to tell him to move over. He was slumped down in the seat, his arms idle at his sides and his eyes idle in his head; his nose ran unchecked.

Mrs. Turpin put a firm hand on Claud's shoulder and said in a voice that included anyone who wanted to listen, "Claud, you sit in that chair there," and gave him a push down into the vacant one. Claud was florid and bald and sturdy, somewhat shorter than Mrs. Turpin, but he sat down as if he were accustomed to doing what she told him to.

Mrs. Turpin remained standing. The only man in the room besides Claud was a lean stringy old fellow with a rusty hand spread out on each knee, whose eyes were closed as if he were asleep or dead or pretending to be so as not to get up and offer her his seat. Her gaze settled agreeably on a well-dressed grey-haired lady whose eyes met hers and whose expression said: if that child belonged to me, he would have some manners and move over—there's plenty of room there for you and him too.

Claud looked up with a sigh and made as if to rise.

"Sit down," Mrs. Turpin said. "You know you're not supposed to stand on that leg. He has an ulcer on his leg," she explained.

Claud lifted his foot onto the magazine table and rolled his trouser leg up to reveal a purple swelling on a plump marble-white calf.

"My!" the pleasant lady said. "How did you do that?"

"A cow kicked him," Mrs. Turpin said.

"Goodness!" said the lady.

Claud rolled his trouser leg down.

"Maybe the little boy would move over," the lady suggested, but the child did not stir.

"Somebody will be leaving in a minute," Mrs. Turpin said. She could not understand why a doctor—with as much money as they made charging five dollars a day to just stick their head in the hospital door and look at you—couldn't afford a decent-sized waiting room. This one was hardly bigger than a garage. The table was cluttered with limp-looking magazines and at one end of it there was a big green glass ash tray full of cigaret butts and cotton wads with little blood spots on them. If she had had anything to do with the running of the place, that would have been emptied every so often. There were no chairs against the wall at the head of the room. It had a rectangular-shaped panel in it that permitted a view of the office where the nurse came and went and the secretary listened to the radio. A plastic fern in a gold pot sat in the opening and trailed its fronds down almost to the floor. The radio was softly playing gospel music.

Revelation

Just then the inner door opened and a nurse with the highest stack of yellow hair Mrs. Turpin had ever seen put her face in the crack and called for the next patient. The woman sitting beside Claud grasped the two arms of her chair and hoisted herself up; she pulled her dress free from her legs and lumbered through the door where the nurse had disappeared.

Mrs. Turpin eased into the vacant chair, which held her tight as a corset. "I wish I could reduce," she said, and rolled her eyes and gave a comic sigh.

"Oh, *you* aren't fat," the stylish lady said.

"Ooooo I am too," Mrs. Turpin said. "Claud he eats all he wants to and never weighs over one hundred and seventy-five pounds, but me I just look at something good to eat and I gain some weight," and her stomach and shoulders shook with laughter. "You can eat all you want to, can't you, Claud?" she asked, turning to him.

Claud only grinned.

"Well, as long as you have such a good disposition," the stylish lady said, "I don't think it makes a bit of difference what size you are. You just can't beat a good disposition."

Next to her was a fat girl of eighteen or nineteen, scowling into a thick blue book which Mrs. Turpin saw was entitled *Human Development*. The girl raised her head and directed her scowl at Mrs. Turpin as if she did not like her looks. She appeared annoyed that anyone should speak while she tried to read. The poor girl's face was blue with acne and Mrs. Turpin thought how pitiful it was to have a face like that at that age. She gave the girl a friendly smile but the girl only scowled the harder. Mrs. Turpin herself was fat but she had always had good skin, and, though she was forty-seven years old, there was not a wrinkle in her face except around her eyes from laughing too much.

Next to the ugly girl was the child, still in exactly the same position, and next to him was a thin leathery old woman in a cotton print dress. She and Claud had three sacks of chicken feed in their pump house that was in the same print. She had

seen from the first that the child belonged with the old woman. She could tell by the way they sat—kind of vacant and white-trashy, as if they would sit there until Doomsday if nobody called and told them to get up. And at right angles but next to the well-dressed pleasant lady was a lank-faced woman who was certainly the child's mother. She had on a yellow sweat shirt and wine-colored slacks, both gritty-looking, and the rims of her lips were stained with snuff. Her dirty yellow hair was tied behind with a little piece of red paper ribbon. Worse than niggers any day, Mrs. Turpin thought.

The gospel hymn playing was, "When I looked up and He looked down," and Mrs. Turpin, who knew it, supplied the last line mentally, "And wona these days I know I'll we-eara crown."

Without appearing to, Mrs. Turpin always noticed people's feet. The well-dressed lady had on red and grey suede shoes to match her dress. Mrs. Turpin had on her good black patent leather pumps. The ugly girl had on Girl Scout shoes and heavy socks. The old woman had on tennis shoes and the white-trashy mother had on what appeared to be bedroom slippers, black straw with gold braid threaded through them—exactly what you would have expected her to have on.

Sometimes at night when she couldn't go to sleep, Mrs. Turpin would occupy herself with the question of who she would have chosen to be if she couldn't have been herself. If Jesus had said to her before he made her, "There's only two places available for you. You can either be a nigger or white-trash," what would she have said? "Please, Jesus, please," she would have said, "just let me wait until there's another place available," and he would have said, "No, you have to go right now and I have only those two places so make up your mind." She would have wiggled and squirmed and begged and pleaded but it would have been no use and finally she would have said, "All right, make me a nigger then—but that don't mean a trashy one." And he would have made her a neat clean respectable Negro woman, herself but black.

Next to the child's mother was a red-headed youngish woman, reading one of the magazines and working a piece of chewing gum, hell for leather, as Claud would say. Mrs. Turpin could not see the woman's feet. She was not white-trash, just common. Sometimes Mrs. Turpin occupied herself at night naming the classes of people. On the bottom of the heap were most colored people, not the kind she would have been if she had been one, but most of them; then next to them—not above, just away from—were the white-trash; then above them were the home-owners, and above them the home-and-land owners, to which she and Claud belonged. Above she and Claud were people with a lot of money and much bigger houses and much more land. But here the complexity of it would begin to bear in on her, for some of the people with a lot of money were common and ought to be below she and Claud and some of the people who had good blood had lost their money and had to rent and then there were colored people who owned their homes and land as well. There was a colored dentist in town who had two red Lincolns and a swimming pool and a farm with registered white-face cattle on it. Usually by the time she had fallen asleep all the classes of people were moiling and roiling around in her head, and she would dream they were all crammed in together in a box car, being ridden off to be put in a gas oven.

"That's a beautiful clock," she said and nodded to her right. It was a big wall clock, the face encased in a brass sunburst.

"Yes, it's very pretty," the stylish lady said agreeably. "And right on the dot too," she added, glancing at her watch.

The ugly girl beside her cast an eye upward at the clock, smirked, then looked directly at Mrs. Turpin and smirked again. Then she returned her eyes to her book. She was obviously the lady's daughter because, although they didn't look anything alike as to disposition, they both had the same shape of face and the same blue eyes. On the lady they sparkled pleasantly but in the girl's seared face they appeared alternately to smolder and to blaze.

What if Jesus had said, "All right, you can be white-trash or a nigger or ugly!"

Mrs. Turpin felt an awful pity for the girl, though she thought it was one thing to be ugly and another to act ugly.

The woman with the snuff-stained lips turned around in her chair and looked up at the clock. Then she turned back and appeared to look a little to the side of Mrs. Turpin. There was a cast in one of her eyes. "You want to know wher you can get you one of themther clocks?" she asked in a loud voice.

"No, I already have a nice clock," Mrs. Turpin said. Once somebody like her got a leg in the conversation, she would be all over it.

"You can get you one with green stamps," the woman said. "That's most likely wher he got hisn. Save you up enough, you can get you most anythang. I got me some joo'ry."

Ought to have got you a wash rag and some soap, Mrs. Turpin thought.

"I get contour sheets with mine," the pleasant lady said.

The daughter slammed her book shut. She looked straight in front of her, directly through Mrs. Turpin and on through the yellow curtain and the plate glass window which made the wall behind her. The girl's eyes seemed lit all of a sudden with a peculiar light, an unnatural light like night road signs give. Mrs. Turpin turned her head to see if there was anything going on outside that she should see, but she could not see anything. Figures passing cast only a pale shadow through the curtain. There was no reason the girl should single her out for her ugly looks.

"Miss Finley," the nurse said, cracking the door. The gum-chewing woman got up and passed in front of her and Claud and went into the office. She had on red high-heeled shoes.

Directly across the table, the ugly girl's eyes were fixed on Mrs. Turpin as if she had some very special reason for disliking her.

"This is wonderful weather, isn't it?" the girl's mother said.

"It's good weather for cotton if you can get the niggers to pick it," Mrs. Turpin said, "but niggers don't want to pick cotton any more. You can't get the white folks to pick it and now you can't get the niggers—because they got to be right up there with the white folks."

"They gonna *try* anyways," the white-trash woman said, leaning forward.

"Do you have one of those cotton-picking machines?" the pleasant lady asked.

"No," Mrs. Turpin said, "they leave half the cotton in the field. We don't have much cotton anyway. If you want to make it farming now, you have to have a little of everything. We got a couple of acres of cotton and a few hogs and chickens and just enough white-face that Claud can look after them himself."

"One thang I don't want," the white-trash woman said, wiping her mouth with the back of her hand. "Hogs. Nasty stinking things, a-gruntin and a-rootin all over the place."

Mrs. Turpin gave her the merest edge of her attention. "Our hogs are not dirty and they don't stink," she said. "They're cleaner than some children I've seen. Their feet never touch the ground. We have a pig parlor—that's where you raise them on concrete," she explained to the pleasant lady, "and Claud scoots them down with the hose every afternoon and washes off the floor." Cleaner by far than that child right there, she thought. Poor nasty little thing. He had not moved except to put the thumb of his dirty hand into his mouth.

The woman turned her face away from Mrs. Turpin. "I know I wouldn't scoot down no hog with no hose," she said to the wall.

You wouldn't have no hog to scoot down, Mrs.Turpin said to herself.

"A-gruntin and a-rootin and a-groanin," the woman muttered.

"We got a little of everything," Mrs. Turpin said to the pleasant lady. "It's no use in having more than you can handle yourself with help like it is. We found enough niggers to pick our cotton this year but Claud he has to go after them and take them home again in the evening. They can't walk that half a mile. No they can't. I tell you," she said and laughed merrily, "I sure am tired of buttering up niggers, but you got to love em if you want em to work for you. When they come in the morning, I run out and I say, 'Hi yawl this morning?' and when Claud drives them off to the field I just wave to beat the band and they just wave back." And she waved her hand rapidly to illustrate.

"Like you read out of the same book," the lady said, showing she understood perfectly.

"Child, yes," Mrs. Turpin said. "And when they come in from the field, I run out with a bucket of icewater. That's the way it's going to be from now on," she said. "You may as well face it."

"One thang I know," the white-trash woman said. "Two thangs I ain't going to do: love no niggers or scoot down no hog with no hose." And she let out a bark of contempt.

The look that Mrs. Turpin and the pleasant lady exchanged indicated they both understood that you had to *have* certain things before you could *know* certain things. But every time Mrs. Turpin exchanged a look with the lady, she was aware that the ugly girl's peculiar eyes were still on her, and she had trouble bringing her attention back to the conversation.

"When you got something," she said, "you got to look after it." And when you ain't got a thing but breath and britches, she added to herself, you can afford to come to town every morning and just sit on the Court House coping and spit.

A grotesque revolving shadow passed across the curtain behind her and was thrown palely on the opposite wall. Then a bicycle clattered down against the outside of the building. The door opened and a colored boy glided in with a tray from the drug store. It had two large red and white paper cups on it with tops on them. He was a tall, very black boy in discolored white pants and a green nylon shirt. He was chewing gum slowly, as if to music. He set the tray down in the office opening next to the fern and stuck his head through to look for the secretary. She was not in there. He rested his arms on the ledge and waited, his narrow bottom stuck out, swaying slowly to the left and right. He raised a hand over his head and scratched the base of his skull.

"You see that button there, boy?" Mrs. Turpin said. "You can punch that and she'll come. She's probably in the back somewhere."

"Is thas right?" the boy said agreeably, as if he had never seen the button before. He leaned to the right and put his finger on it. "She sometime out," he said and twisted around to face his audience, his elbows behind him on the counter. The nurse appeared and he twisted back again. She handed him a dollar and he rooted in his pocket and made the change and counted it out to her. She gave him fifteen cents for a tip and he went out with the empty tray. The heavy door swung to slowly and closed at length with the sound of suction. For a moment no one spoke.

"They ought to send all them niggers back to Africa," the white-trash woman said. "That's wher they come from in the first place."

"Oh, I couldn't do without my good colored friends," the pleasant lady said.

"There's a heap of things worse than a nigger," Mrs. Turpin agreed. "It's all kinds of them just like it's all kinds of us."

"Yes, and it takes all kinds to make the world go round," the lady said in her musical voice.

As she said it, the raw-complexioned girl snapped her teeth together. Her lower lip turned downwards and inside out, revealing the pale pink inside of her mouth. After a second it rolled back up. It was the ugliest face Mrs. Turpin had ever seen anyone make and for a moment she was certain that the girl had made it at her. She was looking at her as if she had known and disliked her all her life—all of Mrs. Turpin's life, it seemed too, not just all the girl's life. Why, girl, I don't even know you, Mrs. Turpin said silently.

She forced her attention back to the discussion. "It wouldn't be practical to send them back to Africa," she said. "They wouldn't want to go. They got it too good here."

"Wouldn't be what they wanted—if I had anythang to do with it," the woman said.

"It wouldn't be a way in the world you could get all the

niggers back over there," Mrs. Turpin said. "They'd be hiding out and lying down and turning sick on you and wailing and hollering and raring and pitching. It wouldn't be a way in the world to get them over there."

"They got over here," the trashy woman said. "Get back like they got over."

"It wasn't so many of them then," Mrs. Turpin explained.

The woman looked at Mrs. Turpin as if here was an idiot indeed but Mrs. Turpin was not bothered by the look, considering where it came from.

"Nooo," she said, "they're going to stay here where they can go to New York and marry white folks and improve their color. That's what they all want to do, every one of them, improve their color."

"You know what comes of that, don't you?" Claud asked.

"No, Claud, what?" Mrs. Turpin said.

Claud's eyes twinkled. "White-faced niggers," he said with never a smile.

Everybody in the office laughed except the white-trash and the ugly girl. The girl gripped the book in her lap with white fingers. The trashy woman looked around her from face to face as if she thought they were all idiots. The old woman in the feed sack dress continued to gaze expressionless across the floor at the high-top shoes of the man opposite her, the one who had been pretending to be asleep when the Turpins came in. He was laughing heartily, his hands still spread out on his knees. The child had fallen to the side and was lying now almost face down in the old woman's lap.

While they recovered from their laughter, the nasal chorus on the radio kept the room from silence.

> *"You go to blank blank*
> *And I'll go to mine*
> *But we'll all blank along*
> *To-geth-ther,*
> *And all along the blank*

We'll hep eachother out
Smile-ling in any kind of
Weath-ther!"

Mrs. Turpin didn't catch every word but she caught
enough to agree with the spirit of the song and it turned her
thoughts sober. To help anybody out that needed it was her philosophy of life. She never spared herself when she found somebody in need, whether they were white or black, trash or decent.
And of all she had to be thankful for, she was most thankful that
this was so. If Jesus had said, "You can be high society and have
all the money you want and be thin and svelte-like, but you
can't be a good woman with it," she would have had to say,
"Well don't make me that then. Make me a good woman and it
don't matter what else, how fat or how ugly or how poor!" Her
heart rose. He had not made her a nigger or white-trash or ugly!
He had made her herself and given her a little of everything.
Jesus, thank you! she said. Thank you thank you thank you!
Whenever she counted her blessings she felt as buoyant as if she
weighed one hundred and twenty-five pounds instead of one
hundred and eighty.

"What's wrong with your little boy?" the pleasant lady
asked the white-trashy woman.

"He has a ulcer," the woman said proudly. "He ain't give
me a minute's peace since he was born. Him and her are just
alike," she said, nodding at the old woman, who was running
her leathery fingers through the child's pale hair. "Look like I
can't get nothing down them two but Co' Cola and candy."

That's all you try to get down em, Mrs. Turpin said to herself. Too lazy to light the fire. There was nothing you could tell
her about people like them that she didn't know already. And it
was not just that they didn't have anything. Because if you gave
them everything, in two weeks it would all be broken or filthy or
they would have chopped it up for lightwood. She knew all this
from her own experience. Help them you must, but help them
you couldn't.

All at once the ugly girl turned her lips inside out again. Her eyes were fixed like two drills on Mrs. Turpin. This time there was no mistaking that there was something urgent behind them.

Girl, Mrs. Turpin exclaimed silently, I haven't done a thing to you! The girl might be confusing her with somebody else. There was no need to sit by and let herself be intimidated. "You must be in college," she said boldly, looking directly at the girl. "I see you reading a book there."

The girl continued to stare and pointedly did not answer.

Her mother blushed at this rudeness. "The lady asked you a question, Mary Grace," she said under her breath.

"I have ears," Mary Grace said.

The poor mother blushed again. "Mary Grace goes to Wellesley College," she explained. She twisted one of the buttons on her dress. "In Massachusetts," she added with a grimace. "And in the summer she just keeps right on studying. Just reads all the time, a real book worm. She's done real well at Wellesley; she's taking English and Math and History and Psychology and Social Studies," she rattled on, "and I think it's too much. I think she ought to get out and have fun."

The girl looked as if she would like to hurl them all through the plate glass window.

"Way up north," Mrs. Turpin murmured and thought, well, it hasn't done much for her manners.

"I'd almost rather to have him sick," the white-trash woman said, wrenching the attention back to herself. "He's so mean when he ain't. Look like some children just take natural to meanness. It's some gets bad when they get sick but he was the opposite. Took sick and turned good. He don't give me no trouble now. It's me waitin to see the doctor," she said.

If I was going to send anybody back to Africa, Mrs. Turpin thought, it would be your kind, woman. "Yes, indeed," she said aloud, but looking up at the ceiling, "it's a heap of things worse than a nigger." And dirtier than a hog, she added to herself.

"I think people with bad dispositions are more to be pitied

than anyone on earth," the pleasant lady said in a voice that was decidedly thin.

"I thank the Lord he has blessed me with a good one," Mrs. Turpin said. "The day has never dawned that I couldn't find something to laugh at."

"Not since she married me anyways," Claud said with a comical straight face.

Everybody laughed except the girl and the white-trash.

Mrs. Turpin's stomach shook. "He's such a caution," she said, "that I can't help but laugh at him."

The girl made a loud ugly noise through her teeth.

Her mother's mouth grew thin and tight. "I think the worst thing in the world," she said, "is an ungrateful person. To have everything and not appreciate it. I know a girl," she said, "who has parents who would give her anything, a little brother who loves her dearly, who is getting a good education, who wears the best clothes, but who can never say a kind word to anyone, who never smiles, who just criticizes and complains all day long."

"Is she too old to paddle?" Claud asked.

The girl's face was almost purple.

"Yes," the lady said, "I'm afraid there's nothing to do but leave her to her folly. Some day she'll wake up and it'll be too late."

"It never hurt anyone to smile," Mrs. Turpin said. "It just makes you feel better all over."

"Of course," the lady said sadly, "but there are just some people you can't tell anything to. They can't take criticism."

"If it's one thing I am," Mrs. Turpin said with feeling, "it's grateful. When I think who all I could have been besides myself and what all I got, a little of everything, and a good disposition besides, I just feel like shouting, 'Thank you, Jesus, for making everything the way it is!' It could have been different!" For one thing, somebody else could have got Claud. At the thought of this, she was flooded with gratitude and a terrible pang of joy ran through her. "Oh thank you, Jesus, Jesus, thank you!" she cried aloud.

Revelation

The book struck her directly over her left eye. It struck almost at the same instant that she realized the girl was about to hurl it. Before she could utter a sound, the raw face came crashing across the table toward her, howling. The girl's fingers sank like clamps into the soft flesh of her neck. She heard the mother cry out and Claud shout, "Whoa!" There was an instant when she was certain that she was about to be in an earthquake.

All at once her vision narrowed and she saw everything as if it were happening in a small room far away, or as if she were looking at it through the wrong end of a telescope. Claud's face crumpled and fell out of sight. The nurse ran in, then out, then in again. Then the gangling figure of the doctor rushed out of the inner door. Magazines flew this way and that as the table turned over. The girl fell with a thud and Mrs. Turpin's vision suddenly reversed itself and she saw everything large instead of small. The eyes of the white-trashy woman were staring hugely at the floor. There the girl, held down on one side by the nurse and on the other by her mother, was wrenching and turning in their grasp. The doctor was kneeling astride her, trying to hold her arm down. He managed after a second to sink a long needle into it.

Mrs. Turpin felt entirely hollow except for her heart which swung from side to side as if it were agitated in a great empty drum of flesh.

"Somebody that's not busy call for the ambulance," the doctor said in the off-hand voice young doctors adopt for terrible occasions.

Mrs. Turpin could not have moved a finger. The old man who had been sitting next to her skipped nimbly into the office and made the call, for the secretary still seemed to be gone.

"Claud!" Mrs. Turpin called.

He was not in his chair. She knew she must jump up and find him but she felt like some one trying to catch a train in a dream, when everything moves in slow motion and the faster you try to run the slower you go.

"Here I am," a suffocated voice, very unlike Claud's, said.

He was doubled up in the corner on the floor, pale as paper, holding his leg. She wanted to get up and go to him but she could not move. Instead, her gaze was drawn slowly downward to the churning face on the floor, which she could see over the doctor's shoulder.

The girl's eyes stopped rolling and focused on her. They seemed a much lighter blue than before, as if a door that had been tightly closed behind them was now open to admit light and air.

Mrs. Turpin's head cleared and her power of motion returned. She leaned forward until she was looking directly into the fierce brilliant eyes. There was no doubt in her mind that the girl did know her, knew her in some intense and personal way, beyond time and place and condition. "What you got to say to me?" she asked hoarsely and held her breath, waiting, as for a revelation.

The girl raised her head. Her gaze locked with Mrs. Turpin's. "Go back to hell where you came from, you old wart hog," she whispered. Her voice was low but clear. Her eyes burned for a moment as if she saw with pleasure that her message had struck its target.

Mrs. Turpin sank back in her chair.

After a moment the girl's eyes closed and she turned her head wearily to the side.

The doctor rose and handed the nurse the empty syringe. He leaned over and put both hands for a moment on the mother's shoulders, which were shaking. She was sitting on the floor, her lips pressed together, holding Mary Grace's hand in her lap. The girl's fingers were gripped like a baby's around her thumb. "Go on to the hospital," he said. "I'll call and make the arrangements."

"Now let's see that neck," he said in a jovial voice to Mrs. Turpin. He began to inspect her neck with his first two fingers. Two little moon-shaped lines like pink fish bones were indented over her windpipe. There was the beginning of an angry red swelling above her eye. His fingers passed over this also.

"Lea' me be," she said thickly and shook him off. "See about Claud. She kicked him."

"I'll see about him in a minute," he said and felt her pulse. He was a thin grey-haired man, given to pleasantries. "Go home and have yourself a vacation the rest of the day," he said and patted her on the shoulder.

Quit your pattin me, Mrs. Turpin growled to herself.

"And put an ice pack over that eye," he said. Then he went and squatted down beside Claud and looked at his leg. After a moment he pulled him up and Claud limped after him into the office.

Until the ambulance came, the only sounds in the room were the tremulous moans of the girl's mother, who continued to sit on the floor. The white-trash woman did not take her eyes off the girl. Mrs. Turpin looked straight ahead at nothing. Presently the ambulance drew up, a long dark shadow, behind the curtain. The attendants came in and set the stretcher down beside the girl and lifted her expertly onto it and carried her out. The nurse helped the mother gather up her things. The shadow of the ambulance moved silently away and the nurse came back in the office.

"That ther girl is going to be a lunatic, ain't she?" the white-trash woman asked the nurse, but the nurse kept on to the back and never answered her.

"Yes, she's going to be a lunatic," the white-trash woman said to the rest of them.

"Po' critter," the old woman murmured. The child's face was still in her lap. His eyes looked idly out over her knees. He had not moved during the disturbance except to draw one leg up under him.

"I thank Gawd," the white-trash woman said fervently, "I ain't a lunatic."

Claud came limping out and the Turpins went home.

As their pick-up truck turned into their own dirt road and made the crest of the hill, Mrs. Turpin gripped the window ledge and looked out suspiciously. The land sloped gracefully down through a field dotted with lavender weeds and at the start of the rise their small yellow frame house, with its little flower beds spread out around it like a fancy apron, sat primly in its accustomed place between two giant hickory trees. She would not have been startled to see a burnt wound between two blackened chimneys.

Neither of them felt like eating so they put on their house clothes and lowered the shade in the bedroom and lay down, Claud with his leg on a pillow and herself with a damp wash-cloth over her eye. The instant she was flat on her back, the image of a razor-backed hog with warts on its face and horns coming out behind its ears snorted into her head. She moaned, a low quiet moan.

"I am not," she said tearfully, "a wart hog. From hell." But the denial had no force. The girl's eyes and her words, even the tone of her voice, low but clear, directed only to her, brooked no repudiation. She had been singled out for the message, though there was trash in the room to whom it might justly have been applied. The full force of this fact struck her only now. There was a woman there who was neglecting her own child but she had been overlooked. The message had been given to Ruby Turpin, a respectable, hard-working, church-going woman. The tears dried. Her eyes began to burn instead with wrath.

She rose on her elbow and the washcloth fell into her hand. Claud was lying on his back, snoring. She wanted to tell him what the girl had said. At the same time, she did not wish to put the image of herself as a wart hog from hell into his mind.

"Hey, Claud," she muttered and pushed his shoulder.

Claud opened one pale baby blue eye.

She looked into it warily. He did not think about anything. He just went his way.

"Wha, whasit?" he said and closed the eye again.

"Nothing," she said. "Does your leg pain you?"

"Hurts like hell," Claud said.

"It'll quit terreckly," she said and lay back down. In a moment Claud was snoring again. For the rest of the afternoon they lay there. Claud slept. She scowled at the ceiling. Occasionally she raised her fist and made a small stabbing motion over her chest as if she was defending her innocence to invisible guests who were like the comforters of Job, reasonable-seeming but wrong.

About five-thirty Claud stirred. "Got to go after those niggers," he sighed, not moving.

She was looking straight up as if there were unintelligible handwriting on the ceiling. The protuberance over her eye had turned a greenish-blue. "Listen here," she said.

"What?"

"Kiss me."

Claud leaned over and kissed her loudly on the mouth. He pinched her side and their hands interlocked. Her expression of ferocious concentration did not change. Claud got up, groaning and growling, and limped off. She continued to study the ceiling.

She did not get up until she heard the pick-up truck coming back with the Negroes. Then she rose and thrust her feet in her brown oxfords, which she did not bother to lace, and stumped out onto the back porch and got her red plastic bucket. She emptied a tray of ice cubes into it and filled it half full of water and went out into the back yard. Every afternoon after Claud brought the hands in, one of the boys helped him put out hay and the rest waited in the back of the truck until he was ready to take them home. The truck was parked in the shade under one of the hickory trees.

"Hi yawl this evening?" Mrs. Turpin asked grimly, appearing with the bucket and the dipper. There were three women and a boy in the truck.

"Us doin nicely," the oldest woman said. "Hi you doin?" and her gaze stuck immediately on the dark lump on Mrs. Turpin's forehead. "You done fell down, ain't you?" she asked in a solicitous voice. The old woman was dark and almost toothless. She had on an old felt hat of Claud's set back on her head. The other two women were younger and lighter and they both had new bright green sun hats. One of them had hers on her head; the other had taken hers off and the boy was grinning beneath it.

Mrs. Turpin set the bucket down on the floor of the truck. "Yawl hep yourselves," she said. She looked around to make sure Claud had gone. "No. I didn't fall down," she said, folding her arms. "It was something worse than that."

"Ain't nothing bad happen to you!" the old woman said. She said it as if they all knew that Mrs. Turpin was protected in some special way by Divine Providence. "You just had you a little fall."

"We were in town at the doctor's office for where the cow kicked Mr. Turpin," Mrs. Turpin said in a flat tone that indicated they could leave off their foolishness. "And there was this girl there. A big fat girl with her face all broke out. I could look at that girl and tell she was peculiar but I couldn't tell how. And me and her mama were just talking and going along and all of a sudden WHAM! She throws this big book she was reading at me and . . ."

"Naw!" the old woman cried out.

"And then she jumps over the table and commences to choke me."

"Naw!" they all exclaimed, "naw!"

"Hi come she do that?" the old woman asked. "What ail her?"

Mrs. Turpin only glared in front of her.

"Somethin ail her," the old woman said.

"They carried her off in an ambulance," Mrs. Turpin continued, "but before she went she was rolling on the floor and they were trying to hold her down to give her a shot and she said something to me." She paused. "You know what she said to me?"

"What she say?" they asked.

"She said," Mrs. Turpin began, and stopped, her face very dark and heavy. The sun was getting whiter and whiter, blanching the sky overhead so that the leaves of the hickory tree were black in the face of it. She could not bring forth the words. "Something real ugly," she muttered.

"She sho shouldn't said nothin ugly to you," the old woman said. "You so sweet. You the sweetest lady I know."

"She pretty too," the one with the hat on said.

"And stout," the other one said. "I never knowed no sweeter white lady."

"That's the truth befo' Jesus," the old woman said. "Amen! You des as sweet and pretty as you can be."

Mrs. Turpin knew just exactly how much Negro flattery was worth and it added to her rage. "She said," she began again and finished this time with a fierce rush of breath, "that I was an old wart hog from hell."

There was an astounded silence.

"Where she at?" the youngest woman cried in a piercing voice.

"Lemme see her. I'll kill her!"

"I'll kill her with you!" the other one cried.

"She b'long in the sylum," the old woman said emphatically. "You the sweetest white lady I know."

"She pretty too," the other two said. "Stout as she can be and sweet. Jesus satisfied with her!"

"Deed he is," the old woman declared.

Idiots! Mrs. Turpin growled to herself. You could never say anything intelligent to a nigger. You could talk at them but not with them. "Yawl ain't drunk your water," she said shortly. "Leave the bucket in the truck when you're finished with it. I got more to do than just stand around and pass the time of day," and she moved off and into the house.

She stood for a moment in the middle of the kitchen. The dark protuberance over her eye looked like a miniature tornado cloud which might any moment sweep across the horizon of her brow. Her lower lip protruded dangerously. She squared her massive shoulders. Then she marched into the front of the house and out the side door and started down the road to the pig parlor. She had the look of a woman going single-handed, weaponless, into battle.

The sun was a deep yellow now like a harvest moon and was riding westward very fast over the far tree line as if it meant to reach the hogs before she did. The road was rutted and she kicked several good-sized stones out of her path as she strode along. The pig parlor was on a little knoll at the end of a lane that ran off from the side of the barn. It was a square of concrete as large as a small room, with a board fence about four feet high around it. The concrete floor sloped slightly so that the hog wash could drain off into a trench where it was carried to the field for fertilizer. Claud was standing on the outside, on the edge of the concrete, hanging on to the top board, hosing down the floor inside. The hose was connected to the faucet of a water trough nearby.

Mrs. Turpin climbed up beside him and glowered down at the hogs inside. There were seven long-snouted bristly shoats in it—tan with liver-colored spots—and an old sow a few weeks off from farrowing. She was lying on her side grunting. The shoats were running about shaking themselves like idiot children, their little slit pig eyes searching the floor for anything left. She had read that pigs were the most intelligent animal. She doubted it. They were supposed to be smarter than dogs. There had even been a pig astronaut. He had performed his assignment perfectly but died of a heart attack afterwards because they left him in his electric suit, sitting upright throughout his examination when naturally a hog should be on all fours.

A-gruntin and a-rootin and a-groanin.

"Gimme that hose," she said, yanking it away from Claud. "Go on and carry them niggers home and then get off that leg."

"You look like you might have swallowed a mad dog," Claud observed, but he got down and limped off. He paid no attention to her humors.

Until he was out of earshot, Mrs. Turpin stood on the side of the pen, holding the hose and pointing the stream of water at the hind quarters of any shoat that looked as if it might try to lie down. When he had had time to get over the hill, she turned her head slightly and her wrathful eyes scanned the path. He was nowhere in sight. She turned back again and seemed to gather herself up. Her shoulders rose and she drew in her breath.

"What do you send me a message like that for?" she said in a low fierce voice, barely above a whisper but with the force of a shout in its concentrated fury. "How am I a hog and me both? How am I saved and from hell too?" Her free fist was knotted and with the other she gripped the hose, blindly pointing the stream of water in and out of the eye of the old sow whose outraged squeal she did not hear.

The pig parlor commanded a view of the back pasture where their twenty beef cows were gathered around the haybales Claud and the boy had put out. The freshly cut pasture sloped down to the highway. Across it was their cotton field and beyond that a dark green dusty wood which they owned as well. The sun was behind the wood, very red, looking over the paling of trees like a farmer inspecting his own hogs.

"Why me?" she rumbled. "It's no trash around here, black or white, that I haven't given to. And break my back to the bone every day working. And do for the church."

She appeared to be the right size woman to command the arena before her. "How am I a hog?" she demanded. "Exactly how am I like them?" and she jabbed the stream of water at the shoats. "There was plenty of trash there. It didn't have to be me.

"If you like trash better, go get yourself some trash then," she railed. "You could have made me trash. Or a nigger. If trash is what you wanted why didn't you make me trash?" She shook her fist with the hose in it and a watery snake appeared momentarily in the air. "I could quit working and take it easy and be filthy," she growled. "Lounge about the sidewalks all day drinking root beer. Dip snuff and spit in every puddle and have it all over my face. I could be nasty.

"Or you could have made me a nigger. It's too late for me to be a nigger," she said with deep sarcasm, "but I could act like one. Lay down in the middle of the road and stop traffic. Roll on the ground."

In the deepening light everything was taking on a mysterious hue. The pasture was growing a peculiar glassy green and the streak of highway had turned lavender. She braced herself for a final assault and this time her voice rolled out over the pasture. "Go on," she yelled, "call me a hog! Call me a hog again. From hell. Call me a wart hog from hell. Put that bottom rail on top. There'll still be a top and bottom!"

A garbled echo returned to her.

A final surge of fury shook her and she roared, "Who do you think you are?"

The color of everything, field and crimson sky, burned for a moment with a transparent intensity. The question carried over the pasture and across the highway and the cotton field and returned to her clearly like an answer from beyond the wood.

She opened her mouth but no sound came out of it.

A tiny truck, Claud's, appeared on the highway, heading rapidly out of sight. Its gears scraped thinly. It looked like a child's toy. At any moment a bigger truck might smash into it and scatter Claud's and the niggers' brains all over the road.

Mrs. Turpin stood there, her gaze fixed on the highway, all her muscles rigid, until in five or six minutes the truck reappeared, returning. She waited until it had had time to turn into their own road. Then like a monumental statue coming to life, she bent her head slowly and gazed, as if through the very heart of mystery, down into the pig parlor at the hogs. They had settled all in one corner around the old sow who was grunting softly. A red glow suffused them. They appeared to pant with a secret life.

Until the sun slipped finally behind the tree line, Mrs. Turpin remained there with her gaze bent to them as if she were absorbing some abysmal life-giving knowledge. At last she lifted her head. There was only a purple streak in the sky, cutting through a field of crimson and leading, like an extension of the highway, into the descending dusk. She raised her hands from the side of the pen in a gesture hieratic and profound. A visionary light settled in her eyes. She saw the streak as a vast swinging bridge extending upward from the earth through a field of living fire. Upon it a vast horde of souls were rumbling toward heaven. There were whole companies of white-trash, clean for the first time in their lives, and bands of black niggers in white robes, and battalions of freaks and lunatics shouting and clapping and leaping like frogs. And bringing up the end of the procession was a tribe of people whom she recognized at once as those who, like herself and Claud, had always had a little of everything and the God-given wit to use it right. She leaned forward to observe them closer. They were marching behind the others with great dignity, accountable as they had always been for good order and common sense and respectable behavior. They alone were on key. Yet she could see by their shocked and altered faces that even their virtues were being burned away. She lowered her hands and gripped the rail of the hog pen, her eyes small but fixed unblinkingly on what lay ahead. In a moment the vision faded but she remained where she was, immobile.

At length she got down and turned off the faucet and made her slow way on the darkening path to the house. In the woods around her the invisible cricket choruses had struck up, but what she heard were the voices of the souls climbing upward into the starry field and shouting hallelujah.

THE MAN
OF THE WORLD

by Frank O'Connor

W HEN I was a kid, there were no such things as holidays for
me, and I have no feeling of grievance about it because,
in the way of kids, I simply played that I had them. One year,
my summer holiday was a couple of nights I spent at the house
of a friend of mine called Jimmy Leary, who lived on the other
side of the road at the end of our lane. His parents sometimes
went away for a couple of days to visit a sick relative in Bantry,
and he was given permission to have a friend in to keep him
company. I took my holiday with great gravity, insisted on the
loan of Father's old travelling bag, and dragged it myself down
the lane, past the neighbors standing at their doors.

"Are you off somewhere, Larry?" asked one.

"Yes, Mrs. Rooney. Off for my holidays to the Learys'," I
said cheerfully.

"Wisha, aren't you lucky?"

Lucky? I felt made for life. The Learys' house was a big

one, with a long flight of steps up to the front door, which was always kept shut. They had a piano in the sitting room, a pair of binoculars on a table near the window, furniture in the bedrooms, and an indoor toilet, on the stairs, which struck me as the last word in immodesty. From the window of the bedroom where Jimmy and I slept, you could see the whole road up and down, from the quarry at the foot, with the tiny houses perched on the edge of it, to the open fields at the other end, where the last gas lamp rose against the sky. I was up each morning at the first light, leaning out the window in my nightshirt and watching, through the binoculars, all the mysterious figures you never saw from our lane—policemen, railway men, and farmers on their way to market.

I admired Jimmy almost as much as I admired his house and for much the same sort of reasons. He was a year older than I, and was well mannered and well dressed, and he would not associate with most of the kids on the road at all. He had a way when any of them joined us of resting against a wall with his hands in his trousers pockets and listening to them with sort of a well-bred smile, a knowing smile, that seemed to me the height of elegance. And it was not that he was a softy, because he was an excellent boxer and wrestler, and could easily have held his own with any of them had he wished to. But he didn't. He was superior to them. He was—there is only one word that still describes it for me—sophisticated.

I envied him his sophistication, for I knew that I was always taken in by the world of appearances. I would take a sudden violent liking to some boy and, when I went to his house, would like his parents and his sisters as well, and think how wonderful it must be to have such a home; but when I told Jimmy, he would smile in that knowing way of his and say quietly, "I believe they had the bailiffs in a few weeks ago." And even though I didn't know what bailiffs were, I would see that I had been deceived again.

It was the same with fellows and girls, too. Seeing some bigger chap we knew walking out with a girl for the first time,

Jimmy would say, "He'd better mind himself; that one is dynamite." And even though I knew as little of girls who were dynamite as I did of bailiffs, his tone was sufficient to indicate that I had again been taken in by sweet voices and broad-brimmed hats, gaslight and evening smells from gardens.

Forty years later, I can still measure the extent of my admiration, for though my own handwriting is almost illegible, I sometimes find myself scribbling idly on a pad in a small, stiff, perfectly legible hand that I recognize with amusement as a reasonably good forgery of Jimmy's. My admiration still lies there somewhere, a fossil in my memory, but Jimmy's knowing smile is something I have never managed to acquire.

And it all goes back to my curiosity about fellows and girls. As I say, I only imagined things about them but Jimmy knew. I was excluded from knowledge by the world of appearances, that blinded and deafened me with emotion. The least thing could excite or depress me. The trees in the morning when I went to early Mass, the stained-glass windows in the church, the blue streets at evening, with the green flare of the gas lamps, the smells of cooking and of perfume, and even the smell of a cigarette packet that I had picked up from the gutter and crushed to my nose—all kept me on this side of the world of appearances. Jimmy, by some right of birth or breeding, was always at the other, and I wanted him to take me there.

One evening, he was listening to me talk while he leaned against the pillar of his gate, his pale neat hair framing his pale, good-humored face.

"Why don't you come over some night the family is away, and I'll show you a few things?" he asked lightly.

"What'll you show me, Jimmy?" I asked eagerly.

"Noticed the new couple that's come to live next door?" he asked.

"No," I replied in disappointment. It wasn't only that I never knew anything; I never noticed anything. And when he described the new family who had taken rooms in the house above the Learys', I realized with chagrin that I didn't know the old family, either.

"Oh, they're a newly married couple," he said. "They don't know that they can be seen from our house."

"But how, Jimmy?"

"Don't look up now," he said with a dreamy smile while his eyes strayed past my shoulder in the direction of the lane. "Wait till you're going. Their end wall is only a couple of feet from ours. You can see right into the bedroom from our attic."

"And what do they do, Jimmy?"

"Oh," he said with a pleasant laugh, "everything. You really should come."

"You bet I'll come!" I said, trying to sound tougher than I felt.

For three evenings I stood under the gas lamp at the foot of our lane, till I had identified the new couple. It was not enough for me to get behind the world of appearances. I also had to study the appearances themselves. The husband was the first I spotted. He came from his work at a regular hour, usually accompanied from the bus stop by an older man. He was tall, with jet-black hair and a big black guardsman's mustache that somehow failed to conceal the youthfulness of his face. Usually he stood for a few minutes outside his door, chatting—a black-coated, bowler-hatted figure who made large, sweeping gestures with his evening paper and sometimes doubled up in an explosion of loud laughter.

On the third evening, I saw his wife. She had obviously been waiting for him, looking from behind the parlor curtains, and when she saw him she scurried down the steps to join in the conversation. She had thrown an old jacket about her shoulders, and stood there, her arms folded as though to protect herself from the cold wind that blew down the road from the open country, while her husband rested one hand fondly on her shoulder.

For the first time, I began to feel qualms about what I had promised to do. It was one thing to do it to people you didn't know or care about, but for me even to recognize people like that was to adopt an emotional attitude toward them. That night I remained awake, thinking out the terms of an anonymous letter that would put them on their guard, till I had worked myself up into a fever of eloquence and indignation.

But I knew that they would recognize the villain of the letter and that the villain would recognize me, so I did not write it. Instead, I gave way to fits of anger and moodiness against my parents. Yet even these emotions were unreal, because on Saturday night when Mother made a parcel of my nightshirt—I had now become sufficiently self-conscious not to take a bag—I nearly broke down and said I wouldn't go. There was something about my own house that night that upset me all over again. Father was sitting under the wall lamp, reading aloud from the paper, and Mother, with a shawl about her shoulders, was crouched over the fire in her little wickerwork chair, listening, and I suddenly realized that they, too, were part of the world of appearances that I had plotted to destroy, and as I said good night, I almost felt that I was saying goodbye to them as well.

But, once inside Jimmy's house, I did not care so much. It always had that effect on me, of blowing me up to twice the size. I tried to pick out a tune on the piano with one hand, and Jimmy, having listened to me with amusement for some time, sat down and played it himself as I felt it should be played, and this, too, seemed to be part of his superiority.

"I suppose we'd better put on a show of going to bed," he said. "Someone across the road may notice and tell. *They*'re in town. I don't suppose they'll be back till late."

We had a glass of milk in the kitchen, went upstairs, and undressed and lay down, though we put our overcoats by the bed. Jimmy had a packet of sweets, but he insisted on keeping them till later. "We may need them before we're done," he said with a smile. I noticed again, with admiration, what an orderly sort of chap he was. We talked in bed for a quarter of an hour, then put out the light, got up again, put on our overcoats and socks, and tiptoed upstairs to the attic, Jimmy leading the way with an electric torch. Everything had been planned as if for a meeting. Two trunks had been drawn up to the little window to

act as seats, and there were even cushions on them. Looking out, you could at first see nothing but an expanse of blank end wall topped with chimney stacks, but gradually you could make out the outline of a single window, eight or ten feet below. Jimmy sat beside me and opened his packet of sweets.

"Of course, we could have stayed in bed until we heard

them come in," he whispered. "You can usually hear them at
the front door, but we might have fallen asleep or they might
have come in quietly. It's best to make sure."

"But why don't they draw the blind?" I asked, my heart
beginning to beat uncomfortably.

"Because there isn't a blind," he said with a chuckle. "Old
Mrs. MacCarthy never had one, and she's not going to put one
in for lodgers."

I envied him his nonchalance as he sat back with his legs
crossed, sucking a sweet, as though he were waiting in the cin-
ema for the show to begin. I was scared by the darkness and the
mystery, and by the sounds that came to us from the road with
such extraordinary clarity. Besides, it wasn't my house, and I
didn't feel at home there. At any moment I expected the front
door to open and his parents to come in and catch us.

We must have been waiting for half an hour before we
heard voices in the roadway, the sound of a key in the lock, and
a door opened and shut softly. Jimmy reached out and touched
my arm. "I think that's our pair," he whispered. "Better not
speak any more. They might hear us." I nodded, wishing I had
never come. At that moment a faint light became visible in the
great expanse of black wall: a faint, yellow stair light that was
just sufficient to silhouette the window frame below us. Suddenly
the whole room lit up. The man I had seen in the street stood by
the doorway, his hand still on the switch. I could see it all
plainly now—an ordinary small, suburban bedroom with flowery
wallpaper, a colored picture of the Sacred Heart over the double
bed with the big brass knobs, a wardrobe, and a dressing table.

He stood there till the woman came in, removing her hat in
a single gesture and tossing it from her into a corner of the
room. The man still stood by the door. He took off his tie and
struggled with his collar, his head uplifted as he made an agonized face. His wife kicked off her shoes, and then sat on a chair
by the bed and began to take off her stockings. She seemed to be
talking all the time, because her head was raised, looking at him,
but you couldn't hear a word she said. I glanced at Jimmy. The

light from the window below softly illuminated his face as he sucked with tranquil enjoyment.

The woman rose as her husband sat on the bed, with his back to us, and began to take off his shoes and socks in the same slow, agonized way. At one point he held up his left foot and looked at it with what might have been concern. She undressed in swift, jerky movements, twisting and turning and apparently talking all the time. She crouched as she took off her slip, and then pulled her nightdress over her head and finished her undressing beneath it. As she removed her underclothes, she seemed to throw them anywhere at all, and I had the feeling that she was haphazard and disorderly, while the articles of clothing her husband took off seemed to be removed in order and put where he could find them most readily in the morning. I saw him take out his watch, look at it carefully, wind it, and hang it neatly on a nail over the bed.

Then, to my surprise, she knelt by the bed, facing out toward the window, glanced up at the picture of the Sacred Heart, made a large, swift sign of the Cross, and then put her face in her hands and buried her head in the bedclothes. I looked at Jimmy in dismay, but he did not seem to be disturbed by the sight. The husband, his folded trousers in his hand, moved about the room slowly and carefully, as though out of respect for his wife's devotions, and when he pulled on the trousers of his pajamas, he turned away. Then he put on his pajama jacket and knelt beside her. He, too, glanced at the picture over the bed and crossed himself, but he did not bury his face and head, as she had done. He knelt upright, with nothing of the abandonment suggested by her pose, and with a composed expression that managed, in a curious way, to combine reverence with self-respect. It was the expression of an employee who knew that he might, like the rest of humanity, have a few little weaknesses but recognized that he was somebody who deserved well of the management. He finished his prayers before his wife, and he crossed himself again slowly, rose, and climbed into bed, glancing again at his watch as he did so.

Several minutes passed before she drew herself up, blessed herself in her wide, sweeping way, and rose. She crossed the room in a swift movement that almost escaped me, and next moment the light went out, and it was as if the window through which we had watched the scene had disappeared with it and there was nothing but a blank black wall mounting to the chimney pots.

Jimmy rose slowly and pointed the way out to me with his flashlight.

When we got downstairs, we put on the bedroom light, and I saw on his face the virtuous and sophisticated air of a collector who has shown you all his treasure in the best possible light. Faced with that look, I could not bring myself to talk of the woman at prayer. I could not have explained to him how at that moment everything had changed for me—how, beyond us, watching the young married couple from ambush, I had felt someone else, watching us, and we had at once ceased to be observers and become the observed, and the observed in such an ignominious position! I wanted to pray myself, but I found I couldn't. Instead, I lay in bed in the darkness, covering my eyes with my hand, and I think that even then I knew that I should never be sophisticated like Jimmy, never able to put on a knowing smile, because always beyond the world of appearances I would see only eternity watching.

"Sometimes, of course, it's better than that," Jimmy's drowsy voice said from the darkness. "You shouldn't judge it by tonight."

MR. ARCULARIS

by Conrad Aiken

M R. ARCULARIS stood at the window of his room in the hospital and looked down at the street. There had been a light shower, which had patterned the sidewalks with large drops, but now again the sun was out, blue sky was showing here and there between the swift white clouds, a cold wind was blowing the poplar trees. An itinerant band had stopped before the building and was playing, with violin, harp, and flute, the finale of "Cavalleria Rusticana." Leaning against the window-sill—for he felt extraordinarily weak after his operation—Mr. Arcularis suddenly, listening to the wretched music, felt like crying. He rested the palm of one hand against a cold window-pane and stared down at the old man who was blowing the flute, and blinked his eyes. It seemed absurd that he should be so weak, so emotional, so like a child—and especially now that everything was over at last. In spite of all their predictions, in spite, too, of his own dreadful certainty that he was going to die, here he was, as fit as a fiddle—but what a fiddle it was, so out of tune!—with a long life before him. And to begin with, a voyage to England ordered by the doctor. What could be more delightful? Why should he feel sad about it and want to cry like a baby? In a few minutes Harry would arrive with his car to take him to the wharf; in an hour he would be on the sea, in two hours he would see the sunset behind him, where Boston had been, and his new life would be opening before him. It was many years since he had been abroad. June, the best of the year to come— England, France, the Rhine—how ridiculous that he should already be homesick!

There was a light footstep outside the door, a knock, the door opened, and Harry came in.

"Well, old man, I've come to get you. The old bus actually got here. Are you ready? Here, let me take your arm. You're tottering like an octogenarian!"

Mr. Arcularis submitted gratefully, laughing, and they made the journey slowly along the bleak corridor and down the stairs to the entrance hall. Miss Hoyle, his nurse, was there, and the Matron, and the charming little assistant with freckles who had helped to prepare him for the operation. Miss Hoyle put out her hand.

"Good-by, Mr. Arcularis," she said, "and *bon voyage*."

"Good-by, Miss Hoyle, and thank you for everything. You were very kind to me. And I fear I was a nuisance."

The girl with the freckles, too, gave him her hand, smiling. She was very pretty, and it would have been easy to fall in love with her. She reminded him of someone. Who was it? He tried in vain to remember while he said good-by to her and turned to the Matron.

"And not too many latitudes with the young ladies, Mr. Arcularis!" she was saying.

Mr. Arcularis was pleased, flattered, by all this attention to a middle-aged invalid, and felt a joke taking shape in his mind, and no sooner in his mind than on his tongue.

"Oh, no latitudes," he said, laughing. "I'll leave the latitudes to the ship!"

"Oh, come now," said the Matron, "we don't seem to have hurt him much, do we?"

"I think we'll have to operate on him again and *really* cure him," said Miss Hoyle.

He was going down the front steps, between the potted palmettoes, and they all laughed and waved. The wind was cold, very cold for June, and he was glad he had put on his coat. He shivered.

"Damned cold for June!" he said. "Why should it be so cold?"

"East wind," Harry said, arranging the rug over his knees. "Sorry it's an open car, but I believe in fresh air and all that sort of thing. I'll drive slowly. We've got plenty of time."

They coasted gently down the long hill towards Beacon Street, but the road was badly surfaced, and despite Harry's care Mr. Arcularis felt his pain again. He found that he could alleviate it a little by leaning to the right, against the arm-rest, and not breathing too deeply. But how glorious to be out again! How strange and vivid the world looked! The trees had innumerable green fresh leaves—they were all blowing and shifting and turning and flashing in the wind; drops of rainwater fell downward sparkling; the robins were singing their absurd, delicious little four-noted songs; even the street cars looked unusually bright and beautiful, just as they used to look when he was a child and had wanted above all things to be a motorman. He found himself smiling foolishly at everything, foolishly and weakly, and wanted to say something about it to Harry. It was no use, though—he had no strength, and the mere finding of words would be almost more than he could manage. And even if he should succeed in saying it, he would then most likely burst into tears. He shook his head slowly from side to side.

"Ain't it grand?" he said.

"I'll bet it looks good," said Harry.

"Words fail me."

"You wait till you get out to sea. You'll have a swell time."

"Oh, swell! . . . I hope not. I hope it'll be calm."

"Tut tut."

When they passed the Harvard Club Mr. Arcularis made a slow and somewhat painful effort to turn in his seat and look at it. It might be the last chance to see it for a long time. Why this sentimental longing to stare at it, though? There it was, with the great flag blowing in the wind, the Harvard seal now concealed by the swift folds and now revealed, and there were the windows in the library, where he had spent so many delightful hours reading—Plato, and Kipling, and the Lord knows what—and the balconies from which for so many years he had watched the finish of the Marathon. Old Talbot might be in there now, sleeping with a book on his knee, hoping forlornly to be interrupted by anyone, for anything.

"Good-by to the old club," he said

"The bar will miss you," said Harry, smiling with friendly irony and looking straight ahead.

"But let there be no moaning," said Mr. Arcularis.

"What's *that* a quotation from?"

" 'The Odyssey.' "

In spite of the cold, he was glad of the wind on his face, for it helped to dissipate the feeling of vagueness and dizziness that came over him in a sickening wave from time to time. All of a sudden everything would begin to swim and dissolve, the houses would lean their heads together, he had to close his eyes, and there would be a curious and dreadful humming noise, which at regular intervals rose to a crescendo and then drawlingly subsided again. It was disconcerting. Perhaps he still had a trace of fever. When he got on the ship he would have a glass of whisky. . . . From one of these spells he opened his eyes and found that they were on the ferry, crossing to East Boston. It must have been the ferry's engines that he had heard. From another spell he woke to find himself on the wharf, the car at a standstill beside a pile of yellow packing-cases.

"We're here because we're here because we're here," said Harry.

"Because we're here," added Mr. Arcularis.

He dozed in the car while Harry—and what a good friend Harry was!—attended to all the details. He went and came with tickets and passports and baggage checks and porters. And at last he unwrapped Mr. Arcularis from the rugs and led him up the steep gangplank to the deck, and thence by devious windings to a small cold stateroom with a solitary porthole like the eye of a cyclops.

"Here you are," he said, "and now I've got to go. Did you hear the whistle?"

"No."

"Well, you're half asleep. It's sounded the all-ashore. Good-by, old fellow, and take care of yourself. Bring me back a spray of edelweiss. And send me a picture post card from the Absolute."

"Will you have it finite or infinite?"

"Oh, infinite. But with your signature on it. Now you'd better turn in for a while and have a nap. Cheerio!"

Mr. Arcularis took his hand and pressed it hard, and once more felt like crying. Absurd! Had he become a child again?

"Good-by," he said.

He sat down in the little wicker chair, with his overcoat still on, closed his eyes, and listened to the humming of the air in the ventilator. Hurried footsteps ran up and down the corridor. The chair was not too comfortable, and his pain began to bother him again, so he moved, with his coat still on, to the narrow berth and fell asleep. When he woke up, it was dark, and the porthole had been partly opened. He groped for the switch and turned on the light. Then he rang for the steward.

"It's cold in here," he said. "Would you mind closing the port?"

The girl who sat opposite him at dinner was charming. Who was it she reminded him of? Why, of course, the girl at the hospital, the girl with the freckles. Her hair was beautiful, not quite red, not quite gold, nor had it been bobbed; arranged with a sort of graceful untidiness, it made him think of a Melozzo da

Forli angel. Her face was freckled, she had a mouth which was both humorous and voluptuous. And she seemed to be alone.

He frowned at the bill of fare and ordered the thick soup.

"No hors d'œuvres?" asked the steward.

"I think not," said Mr. Arcularis. "They might kill me."

The steward permitted himself to be amused and deposited the menu card on the table against the water-bottle. His eyebrows were lifted. As he moved away, the girl followed him with her eyes and smiled.

"I'm afraid you shocked him," she said.

"Impossible," said Mr. Arcularis. "These stewards, they're dead souls. How could they be stewards otherwise? And they think they've seen and known everything. They suffer terribly from the *déjà vu*. Personally, I don't blame them."

"It must be a dreadful sort of life."

"It's because they're dead that they accept it."

"Do you think so?"

"I'm sure of it. I'm enough of a dead soul myself to know the signs!"

"Well, I don't know what you mean by that!"

"But nothing mysterious! I'm just out of hospital, after an operation. I was given up for dead. For six months I had given *myself* up for dead. If you've ever been seriously ill you know the feeling. You have a posthumous feeling—a mild, cynical tolerance for everything and everyone. What is there you haven't seen or done or understood? Nothing."

Mr. Arcularis waved his hands and smiled.

"I wish I could understand you," said the girl, "but I've never been ill in my life."

"Never?"

"Never."

"Good God!"

The torrent of the unexpressed and inexpressible paralyzed him and rendered him speechless. He stared at the girl, wondering who she was and then, realizing that he had perhaps stared too fixedly, averted his gaze, gave a little laugh, rolled a pill of bread between his fingers. After a second or two he allowed himself to look at her again and found her smiling.

"Never pay any attention to invalids," he said, "or they'll drag you to the hospital."

She examined him critically, with her head tilted a little to one side, but with friendliness.

"You don't *look* like an invalid," she said.

Mr. Arcularis thought her charming. His pain ceased to bother him, the disagreeable humming disappeared, or rather, it was dissociated from himself and became merely, as it should be, the sound of the ship's engines, and he began to think the voyage was going to be really delightful. The parson on his right passed him the salt.

"I fear you will need this in your soup," he said.

"Thank you. Is it as bad as that?"

The steward, overhearing, was immediately apologetic and solicitous. He explained that on the first day everything was at sixes and sevens. The girl looked up at him and asked him a question.

"Do you think we'll have a good voyage?" she said.

He was passing the hot rolls to the parson, removing the napkins from them with a deprecatory finger.

"Well, madam, I don't like to be a Jeremiah, but—"

"Oh, come," said the parson, "I hope we have no Jeremiahs."

"What do you mean?" said the girl.

Mr. Arcularis ate his soup with gusto—it was nice and hot.

"Well, maybe I shouldn't say it, but there's a corpse on board, going to Ireland; and I never yet knew a voyage with a corpse on board that we didn't have bad weather."

"Why, steward, you're just superstitious! What nonsense."

"That's a very ancient superstition," said Mr. Arcularis. "I've heard it many times. Maybe it's true. Maybe we'll be wrecked. And what does it matter, after all?" He was very bland.

"Then let's be wrecked," said the parson coldly.

Nevertheless, Mr. Arcularis felt a shudder go through him on hearing the steward's remark. A corpse in the hold—a coffin? Perhaps it was true. Perhaps some disaster would befall them. There might be fogs. There might be icebergs. He thought of all the wrecks of which he had read. There was the *Titanic,* which he had read about in the warm newspaper room at the Harvard Club—it had seemed dreadfully real, even there. That band, playing "Nearer My God to Thee" on the after-deck while the ship sank! It was one of the darkest of his memories. And the *Empress of Ireland*—all those poor people trapped in the smoking-room, with only one door between them and life, and that door locked for the night by the deck-steward, and the deck-steward nowhere to be found! He shivered, feeling a draft, and turned to the parson.

"How do these strange delusions arise?" he said.

The parson looked at him searchingly, appraisingly—from chin to forehead, from forehead to chin—and Mr. Arcularis, feeling uncomfortable, straightened his tie.

"From nothing but fear," said the parson. "Nothing on earth but fear."

"How strange!" said the girl.

Mr. Arcularis again looked at her—she had lowered her face—and again tried to think of whom she reminded him. It wasn't only the little freckle-faced girl at the hospital—both of them had reminded him of someone else. Someone far back in his life: remote, beautiful, lovely. But he couldn't think. The meal came to an end, they all rose, the ship's orchestra played a feeble fox-trot, and Mr. Arcularis, once more alone, went to the bar to have his whisky. The room was stuffy, and the ship's engines were both audible and palpable. The humming and throbbing oppressed him, the rhythm seemed to be the rhythm of his own pain, and after a short time he found his way, with slow steps, holding on to the walls in his moments of weakness and dizziness, to his forlorn and white little room. The port had been —thank God!—closed for the night: it was cold enough anyway. The white and blue ribbons fluttered from the ventilator, the bottle and glasses clicked and clucked as the ship swayed gently to the long, slow motion of the sea. It was all very peculiar—it was all like something he had experienced somewhere before. What was it? Where was it? . . . He untied his tie, looking at his face in the glass, and wondered, and from time to time put his hand to his side to hold in the pain. It wasn't at Portsmouth, in his childhood, nor at Salem, nor in the rose-garden at his Aunt Julia's, nor in the schoolroom at Cambridge. It was something very queer, very intimate, very precious. The jackstones, the Sunday School cards which he had loved when he was a child . . . He fell asleep.

The sense of time was already hopelessly confused. One hour was like another, the sea looked always the same, morning was indistinguishable from afternoon—and was it Tuesday or Wednesday? Mr. Arcularis was sitting in the smoking-room, in his favorite corner, watching the parson teach Miss Dean to play chess. On the deck outside he could see the people passing and repassing in their restless round of the ship. The red jacket went by, then the black hat with the white feather, then the purple scarf, the brown tweed coat, the Bulgarian mustache, the monocle, the Scotch cap with fluttering ribbons, and in no time at all the red jacket again, dipping past the windows with its own peculiar rhythm, followed once more by the black hat and the purple scarf. How odd to reflect on the fixed little orbits of these things—as definite and profound, perhaps, as the orbits of the stars, and as important to God or the Absolute. There was a kind of tyranny in this fixedness, too—to think of it too much made one uncomfortable. He closed his eyes for a moment, to avoid seeing for the fortieth time the Bulgarian mustache and the pursuing monocle. The parson was explaining the movements of knights. Two forward and one to the side. Eight possible moves, always to the opposite color from that on which the piece stands. Two forward and one to the side: Miss Dean repeated the words several times with reflective emphasis. Here, too, was the terrifying fixed curve of the infinite, the creeping curve of logic which at last must become the final signpost at the edge of nothing. After that—the deluge. The great white light of annihilation. The bright flash of death. . . . Was it merely the sea which made these abstractions so insistent, so intrusive? The mere notion of *orbit* had somehow become extraordinarily naked; and to rid himself of the discomfort and also to forget a little the pain which bothered his side whenever he sat down, he walked slowly and carefully into the writing-room, and examined a pile of superannuated magazines and catalogues of travel. The bright colors amused him, the photographs of remote islands and mountains, savages in sampans or sarongs or both —it was all very far off and delightful, like something in a dream or a fever. But he found that he was too tired to read and was incapable of concentration. Dreams! Yes, that reminded him. That rather alarming business—sleep-walking!

Later in the evening—at what hour he didn't know—he was telling Miss Dean about it, as he had intended to do. They were sitting in deck-chairs on the sheltered side. The sea was black, and there was a cold wind. He wished they had chosen to sit in the lounge.

Miss Dean was extremely pretty—no, beautiful. She looked at him, too, in a very strange and lovely way, with something of inquiry, something of sympathy, something of affection. It seemed as if, between the question and the answer, they had sat thus for a very long time, exchanging an unspoken secret, simply looking at each other quietly and kindly. Had an hour or two passed? And was it at all necessary to speak?

"No," she said, "I never have."

She breathed into the low words a note of interrogation and gave him a slow smile.

"That's the funny part of it. I never had either until last night. Never in my life. I hardly ever even dream. And it really rather frightens me."

"Tell me about it, Mr. Arcularis."

"I dreamed at first that I was walking, alone, in a wide plain covered with snow. It was growing dark, I was very cold, my feet were frozen and numb, and I was lost. I came then to a

signpost—at first it seemed to me there was nothing on it. Nothing but ice. Just before it grew finally dark, however, I made out on it the one word 'Polaris.' "

"The Pole Star."

"Yes—and you see, I didn't myself know that. I looked it up only this morning. I suppose I must have seen it somewhere? And of course it rhymes with my name."

"Why, so it does!"

"Anyway, It gave me—in the dream—an awful feeling of despair, and the dream changed. This time, I dreamed I was standing *outside* my stateroom in the little dark corridor, or *cul-de-sac,* and trying to find the door-handle to let myself in. I was in my pajamas, and again I was very cold. And at this point I woke up. . . . The extraordinary thing is that's exactly where I was!"

"Good heavens. How strange!"

"Yes. And now the question is, *where had I been?* I was frightened, when I came to—not unnaturally. For among other things I *did* have, quite definitely, the feeling that I *had been* somewhere. Somewhere where it was very cold. It doesn't sound very proper. Suppose I had been seen!"

"That might have been awkward," said Miss Dean.

"Awkward! It might indeed. It's very singular. I've never done such a thing before. It's this sort of thing that reminds one —rather wholesomely, perhaps, don't you think?"—and Mr. Arcularis gave a nervous little laugh—"how extraordinarily little we know about the workings of our own minds or souls. After all, what *do* we know?"

"Nothing—nothing—nothing—nothing," said Miss Dean slowly.

"*Absolutely* nothing."

Their voices had dropped, and again they were silent; and again they looked at each other gently and sympathetically, as if for the exchange of something unspoken and perhaps unspeakable. Time ceased. The orbit—so it seemed to Mr. Arcularis— once more became pure, became absolute. And once more he found himself wondering who it was that Miss Dean—Clarice

Dean—reminded him of. Long ago and far away. Like those pictures of the islands and mountains. The little freckle-faced girl at the hospital was merely, as it were, the stepping-stone, the signpost, or, as in algebra, the "equals" sign. But what was it they both "equalled"? The jackstones came again into his mind and his Aunt Julia's rose-garden—at sunset; but this was ridiculous. It couldn't be simply that they reminded him of his childhood! And yet why not?

They went into the lounge. The ship's orchestra, in the oval-shaped balcony among faded palms, was playing the finale of "Cavalleria Rusticana," playing it badly.

"Good God!" said Mr. Arcularis, "can't I ever escape from that damned sentimental tune? It's the last thing I heard in America, and the last thing I *want* to hear."

"But don't you like it?"

"As music? No! It moves me too much, but in the wrong way."

"What, exactly, do you mean?"

"Exactly? Nothing. When I heard it at the hospital—when was it?—it made me feel like crying. Three old Italians tootling it in the rain. I suppose, like most people, I'm afraid of my feelings."

"Are they so dangerous?"

"Now then, young woman! Are you pulling my leg?"

The stewards had rolled away the carpets, and the passengers were beginning to dance. Miss Dean accepted the invitation of a young officer, and Mr. Arcularis watched them with envy. Odd, that last exchange of remarks—very odd; in fact, everything was odd. Was it possible that they were falling in love? Was that what it was all about—all these concealed references and recollections? He had read of such things. But at his age! And with a girl of twenty-two!

After an amused look at his old friend Polaris from the open door on the sheltered side, he went to bed.

The rhythm of the ship's engines was positively a persecution. It gave one no rest, it followed one like the Hound of Heaven, it drove one out into space and across the Milky Way and then back home by way of Betelgeuse. It was cold there, too. Mr. Arcularis, making the round trip by way of Betelgeuse and Polaris, sparkled with frost. He felt like a Christmas tree. Icicles on his fingers and icicles on his toes. He tinkled and spangled in the void, hallooed to the waste echoes, rounded the buoy on the verge of the Unknown, and tacked glitteringly homeward. The wind whistled. He was barefooted. Snowflakes and tinsel blew past him. Next time, by George, he would go farther still—for altogether it was rather a lark. Forward into the untrodden! as somebody said. Some intrepid explorer of his own backyard, probably, some middle-aged professor with an umbrella: those were the fellows for courage! But give us time, thought Mr. Arcularis, give us time, and we will bring back with us the night-rime of the Obsolute. Or was it Absolete? If only there weren't this perpetual throbbing, this iteration of sound, like a pain, these circles and repetitions of light—the feeling as of everything coiling inward to a center of misery . . .

Suddenly it was dark, and he was lost. He was groping, he touched the cold, white, slippery woodwork with his fingernails, looking for an electric switch. The throbbing, of course, was the throbbing of the ship. But he was almost home—almost home. Another corner to round, a door to be opened, and there he would be. Safe and sound. Safe in his father's home.

It was at this point that he woke up: in the corridor that led to the dining saloon. Such pure terror, such horror, seized him as he had never known. His heart felt as if it would stop beating. His back was towards the dining saloon; apparently he had just come from it. He was in his pajamas. The corridor was dim, all but two lights having been turned out for the night, and—thank God!—deserted. Not a soul, not a sound. He was perhaps fifty yards from his room. With luck he could get to it unseen. Holding tremulously to the rail that ran along the wall, a brown, greasy rail, he began to creep his way forward. He felt very weak, very dizzy, and his thoughts refused to concentrate. Vaguely he remembered Miss Dean—Clarice—and the freckled girl, as if they were one and the same person. But he wasn't in the hospital, he was on the ship. Of course. How absurd. The Great Circle. Here we are, old fellow . . . steady round the corner . . . hold hard to your umbrella . . .

In his room, with the door safely shut behind him, Mr. Arcularis broke into a cold sweat. He had no sooner got into his bunk, shivering, than he heard the night watchman pass.

"But where"—he thought, closing his eyes in agony— "have I been? . . ."

A dreadful idea had occurred to him.

"It's nothing serious—how could it be anything serious? Of course it's nothing serious," said Mr. Arcularis.

"No, it's nothing serious," said the ship's doctor urbanely.

"I knew you'd think so. But just the same—"

"Such a condition is the result of worry," said the doctor. "Are you worried—do you mind telling me—about something? Just try to think."

"Worried?"

Mr. Arcularis knitted his brows. *Was* there something? Some little mosquito of a cloud disappearing into the southwest, the northeast? Some little gnat-song of despair? But no, that was all over. All over.

"Nothing," he said, "nothing whatever."

"It's very strange," said the doctor.

"Strange! I should say so. I've come to sea for a rest, not for a nightmare! What about a bromide?"

"Well, I can give you a bromide, Mr. Arcularis—"

"Then, please, if you don't mind, give me a bromide."

He carried the little phial hopefully to his stateroom, and took a dose at once. He could see the sun through his porthole. It looked northern and pale and small, like a little peppermint, which was only natural enough, for the latitude was changing with every hour. But why was it that doctors were all alike? and all, for that matter, like his father, or that other fellow at the hospital? Smythe, his name was. Doctor Smythe. A nice, dry little fellow, and they said he was a writer. Wrote poetry, or something like that. Poor fellow—disappointed. Like everybody else. Crouched in there, in his cabin, night after night, writing blank verse or something—all about the stars and flowers and love and death; ice and the sea and the infinite; time and tide—well, every man to his own taste.

"But it's nothing serious," said Mr. Arcularis, later, to the parson. "How could it be?"

"Why, of course not, my dear fellow," said the parson, patting his back. "How could it be?"

"I know it isn't and yet I worry about it."

"It would be ridiculous to think it serious," said the parson.

Mr. Arcularis shivered: it was colder than ever. It was said that they were near icebergs. For a few hours in the morning there had been a fog, and the siren had blown—devastatingly— at three-minute intervals. Icebergs caused fog—he knew that.

"These things always come," said the parson, "from a sense of guilt. You feel guilty about something. I won't be so rude as to inquire what it is. But if you could rid yourself of the sense of guilt—"

And later still, when the sky was pink:

"But is it anything to worry about?" said Miss Dean. "Really?"

"No, I suppose not."

"Then don't worry. We aren't children any longer!"

"Aren't we? I wonder!"

They leaned, shoulders touching, on the deck-rail, and looked at the sea, which was multitudinously incarnadined. Mr. Arcularis scanned the horizon in vain for an iceberg.

"Anyway," he said, "the colder we are the less we feel!"

"I hope that's no reflection on *you*," said Miss Dean.

"Here . . . feel my hand," said Mr. Arcularis.

"Heaven knows it's cold!"

"It's been to Polaris and back! No wonder."

"Poor thing, poor thing!"

"Warm it."

"May I?"

"You can."

"I'll try."

Laughing, she took his hand between both of hers, one palm under and one palm over, and began rubbing it briskly. The decks were deserted, no one was near them, everyone was dressing for dinner. The sea grew darker, the wind blew colder.

"I wish I could remember who you are," he said.

"And you—who are you?"

"Myself."

"Then perhaps *I* am yourself."

"Don't be metaphysical!"

"But I *am* metaphysical!"

She laughed, withdrew, pulled the light coat about her shoulders.

The bugle blew the summons for dinner—"The Roast Beef of Old England"—and they walked together along the darkening deck toward the door, from which a shaft of soft light fell across the deck-rail. As they stepped over the brass door-sill Mr. Arcularis felt the throb of the engines again; he put his hand quickly to his side.

"*Auf wiedersehen*," he said. "*Tomorrow and tomorrow and tomorrow.*"

Mr. Arcularis was finding it impossible, absolutely impossible, to keep warm. A cold fog surrounded the ship, had done so, it seemed, for days. The sun had all but disappeared, the transition from day to night was almost unnoticeable. The ship, too, seemed scarcely to be moving—it was as if anchored among walls of ice and rime. Monstrous, that merely because it was June, and supposed, therefore, to be warm, the ship's authorities should consider it unneccessary to turn on the heat! By day, he wore his heavy coat and sat shivering in the corner of the smoking-room. His teeth chattered, his hands were blue. By night, he heaped blankets on his bed, closed the porthole's black eye against the sea, and drew the yellow curtains across it, but in vain. Somehow, despite everything, the fog crept in, and the icy fingers touched his throat. The steward, questioned about it, merely said, "Icebergs." Of course—any fool knew that. But how long, in God's name, was it going to last? They surely ought to be past the Grand Banks by this time! And surely it wasn't necessary to sail to England by way of Greenland and Iceland!

Miss Dean—Clarice—was sympathetic.

"It's simply because," she said, "your vitality has been lowered by your illness. You can't expect to be your normal self so soon after an operation! When *was* your operation, by the way?"

Mr. Arcularis considered. Strange—he couldn't be quite sure. It was all a little vague—his sense of time had disappeared.

"Heaven knows!" he said. "Centuries ago. When I was a tadpole and you were a fish. I should think it must have been at about the time of the Battle of Teutoburg Forest. Or perhaps when I was a Neanderthal man with a club!"

"Are you sure it wasn't farther back still?"

What did she mean by that?

"Not at all. Obviously, we've been on this damned ship for ages—for eras—for aeons. And even on this ship, you must remember, I've had plenty of time, in my nocturnal wanderings, to go several times to Orion and back. I'm thinking, by the way, of going farther still. There's a nice little star off to the left, as you round Betelgeuse, which looks as if it might be right at the edge. The last outpost of the finite. I think I'll have a look at it and bring you back a frozen rime-feather."

"It would melt when you got it back."

"Oh, no, it wouldn't—not on *this* ship!"

Clarice laughed.

"I wish I could go with you," she said.

"If only you would! If only—"

He broke off his sentence and looked hard at her—how lovely she was, and how desirable! No such woman had ever before come into his life; there had been no one with whom he had at once felt so profound a sympathy and understanding. It was a miracle, simply—a miracle. No need to put his arm around her or to kiss her—delightful as such small vulgarities would be. He had only to look at her, and to feel, gazing into those extraordinary eyes, that she knew him, had always known him. It was as if, indeed, she might be his own soul.

But as he looked thus at her, reflecting, he noticed that she was frowning.

"What is it?" he said.

She shook her head, slowly.

"I don't know."

"Tell me."

"Nothing. It just occurred to me that perhaps you weren't looking quite so well."

Mr. Arcularis was startled. He straightened himself up.

"What nonsense! Of course this pain bothers me—and I feel astonishingly weak—"

"It's more than that—much more than that. Something is worrying you horribly." She paused, and then with an air of challenging him, added, "Tell me, did you?"

Her eyes were suddenly asking him blazingly the question he had been afraid of. He flinched, caught his breath, looked away. But it was no use, as he knew: he would have to tell her. He had known all along that he would have to tell her.

"Clarice," he said—and his voice broke in spite of his effort to control it—"it's killing me, it's ghastly! Yes, I did."

His eyes filled with tears, he saw that her own had done so also. She put her hand on his arm.

"I knew," she said. "I knew. But tell me."

"It's happened twice again—*twice*—and each time I was farther away. The same dream of going round a star, the same terrible coldness and helplessness. That awful whistling curve . . ." He shuddered.

"And when you woke up"—she spoke quietly—"where were you when you woke up? Don't be afraid!"

"The first time I was at the farther end of the dining saloon. I had my hand on the door that leads into the pantry."

"I see. Yes. And the next time?"

Mr. Arcularis wanted to close his eyes in terror—he felt as if he were going mad. His lips moved before he could speak, and when at last he did speak it was in a voice so low as to be almost a whisper.

"I was at the bottom of the stairway that leads down from the pantry to the hold, past the refrigerating-plant. It was dark, and I was crawling on my hands and knees . . . *Crawling on my hands and knees! . . .*"

"Oh!" she said, and again, "Oh!"

He began to tremble violently; he felt the hand on his arm trembling also. And then he watched a look of unmistakable horror come slowly into Clarice's eyes, and a look of understanding, as if she saw . . . She tightened her hold on his arm.

"Do you think . . ." she whispered.

They stared at each other.

"I know," he said. "And so do you . . . Twice more—three times—and I'll be looking down into an empty . . ."

It was then that they first embraced—then, at the edge of the infinite, at the last signpost of the finite. They clung together desperately, forlornly, weeping as they kissed each other, staring hard one moment and closing their eyes the next. Passionately, passionately, she kissed him, as if she were indeed trying to give him her warmth, her life.

"But what nonsense!" she cried, leaning back and holding his face between her hands, her hands which were wet with his tears. "What nonsense! It can't be!"

"It is," said Mr. Arcularis slowly.

"But how do you know? . . . How do you know where the—"

For the first time Mr. Arcularis smiled.

"Don't be afraid, darling—you mean the coffin?"

"How could you know where it is?"

"I don't need to," said Mr. Arcularis . . . "I'm already almost there."

Before they separated for the night, in the smoking-room, they had several whisky cocktails.

"We must make it gay!" Mr. Arcularis said. "Above all, we must make it gay. Perhaps even now it will turn out to be nothing but a nightmare from which both of us will wake! And even at the worst, at my present rate of travel, I ought to need two more nights! It's a long way, still, to that little star."

The parson passed them at the door.

"What! turning in so soon?" he said. "I was hoping for a game of chess."

"Yes, both turning in. But tomorrow?"

"Tomorrow, then, Miss Dean! And good-night!"

"Good-night."

They walked once round the deck, then leaned on the railing and stared into the fog. It was thicker and whiter than ever. The ship was moving barely perceptibly, the rhythm of the engines was slower, more subdued and remote, and at regular intervals, mournfully, came the long reverberating cry of the foghorn. The sea was calm, and lapped only very tenderly against the side of the ship, the sound coming up to them clearly, however, because of the profound stillness.

" 'On such a night as this—' " quoted Mr. Arcularis grimly.

" 'On such a night as this—' "

Their voices hung suspended in the night, time ceased for them, for an eternal instant they were happy. When at last they parted it was by tacit agreement on a note of the ridiculous.

"Be a good boy and take your bromide!" she said.

"Yes, Mother, I'll take my medicine!"

In his stateroom, he mixed himself a strong potion of bromide, a very strong one, and got into bed. He would have no trouble in falling asleep: he felt more tired, more supremely exhausted, than he had ever been in his life; nor had bed ever seemed so delicious. And that long, magnificent, delirious swoop of dizziness . . . the Great Circle . . . the swift pathway to Arcturus . . .

It was all as before, but infinitely more rapid. Never had Mr. Arcularis achieved such phenomenal, such supernatural, speed. In no time at all he was beyond the moon, shot past the North Star as if it were standing still (which perhaps it was?), swooped in a long, bright curve round the Pleiades, shouted his frosty greetings to Betelgeuse, and was off to the little blue star which pointed the way to the unknown. Forward into the untrodden! Courage, old man, and hold on to your umbrella! Have you got your garters on? Mind your hat! In no time at all we'll be back to Clarice with the frozen time-feather, the time-feather, the snowflake of the Absolute, the Obsolete. If only we don't wake . . . if only we needn't wake . . . if only we don't wake in that—in that—time and space . . . somewhere or nowhere . . . cold and dark . . . "Cavelleria Rusticana" sobbing among the palms; if a lonely . . . if only . . . the coffers of the poor—not coffers, not coffers, not coffers. Oh, God, not coffers, but light, delight, supreme white and brightness, and above all whirling lightness, whirling lightness above all—and freezing—freezing—freezing . . .

At this point in the void the surgeon's last effort to save Mr. Arcularis's life had failed. He stood back from the operating table and made a tired gesture with a rubber-gloved hand.

"It's all over," he said. "As I expected."

He looked at Miss Hoyle, whose gaze was downward, at the basin she held. There was a moment's stillness, a pause, a brief flight of unexchanged comment, and then the ordered life of the hospital was resumed.

THE SCHREUDERSPITZE

by Mark Helprin

IN MUNICH are many men who look like weasels. Whether by
genetic accident, meticulous crossbreeding, an early and puz-
zling migration, coincidence, or a reason that we do not know,
they exist in great numbers. Remarkably, they accentuate this
unfortunate tendency by wearing mustaches, Alpine hats, and
tweed. A man who resembles a rodent should never wear tweed.

One of these men, a commercial photographer named
Franzen, had cause to be exceedingly happy. "Herr Wallich has
disappeared," he said to Huebner, his supplier of paper and
chemicals. "You needn't bother to send him bills. Just send them
to the police. The police, you realize, were here on two separate
occasions!"

"If the two occasions on which the police have been here
had not been separate, Herr Franzen, they would have been here
only once."

"What do you mean? Don't toy with me. I have no time
for semantics. In view of the fact that I knew Wallich at school,
and professionally, they sought my opinion on his disappearance.

They wrote down everything I said, but I do not think that they will find him. He left his studio on the Neuhausstrasse just as it was when he was working, and the landlord has put a lien on the equipment. Let me tell you that he had some fine equipment —very fine. But he was not such a great photographer. He didn't have that killer's instinct. He was clearly not a hunter. His canine teeth were poorly developed; not like these," said Franzen, baring his canine teeth in a smile which made him look like an idiot with a mouth of miniature castle towers.

"But I am curious about Wallich."

"So is everyone. So is everyone. This is my theory. Wallich was never any good at school. At best, he did only middling well. And it was not because he had hidden passions, or a special genius for some field outside the curriculum. He tried hard but found it difficult to grasp several subjects; for him mathematics and physics were pure torture.

"As you know, he was not wealthy, and although he was a nice-looking fellow, he was terribly short. That inflicted upon him great scars—his confidence, I mean, because he had none. He could do things only gently. If he had to fight, he would fail. He was weak.

"For example, I will use the time when he and I were competing for the Heller account. This job meant a lot of money, and I was not about to lose. I went to the library and read all I could about turbine engines. What a bore! I took photographs of turbine blades and such things, and seeded them throughout my portfolio to make Herr Heller think that I had always been interested in turbines. Of course, I had not even known what they were. I thought that they were an Oriental hat. And now that I know them, I detest them.

"Naturally, I won. But do you know how Wallich approached the competition? He had some foolish ideas about mother-of-pearl nautiluses and other seashells. He wanted to show how shapes of things mechanical were echoes of shapes in nature. All very fine, but Herr Heller pointed out that if the public were to see photographs of mother-of-pearl shells contrasted with photographs of his engines, his engines would come out the worse. Wallich's photographs were very beautiful—the tones of white and silver were exceptional—but they were his undoing. In the end, he said, 'Perhaps, Herr Heller, you are right,' and lost the contract just like that.

"The thing that saved him was the prize for that picture he took in the Black Forest. You couldn't pick up a magazine in Germany and not see it. He obtained so many accounts that he began to do very well. But he was just not commercially-minded. He told me himself that he took only those assignments which pleased him. Mind you, his business volume was only about two-thirds of mine.

"My theory is that he could not take the competition, and the demands of his various clients. After his wife and son were killed in the motorcar crash, he dropped assignments one after another. I suppose he thought that as a bachelor he could live like a bohemian, on very little money, and therefore did not have to work more than half the time. I'm not saying that this was wrong. (Those accounts came to me.) But it was another instance of his weakness and lassitude.

"My theory is that he has probably gone to South America, or thrown himself off a bridge—because he saw that there was no future for him if he were always to take pictures of shells and things. And he was weak. The weak can never face themselves, and so cannot see the practical side of the world, how things are laid out, and what sacrifices are required to survive and prosper. It is only in fairy tales that they rise to triumph."

Wallich could not afford to get to South America. He certainly would not have thrown himself off a bridge. He was excessively neat and orderly, and the prospect of some poor fireman handling a swollen bloated body resounding with flies deterred him forever from such nonsense.

Perhaps if he had been a Gypsy he would have taken to the road. But he was no Gypsy, and had not the talent, skill, or taste for life outside Bavaria. Only once had he been away, to Paris.

355

It was their honeymoon, when he and his wife did not need Paris or any city. They went by train and stayed for a week at a hotel by the Quai Voltaire. They walked in the gardens all day long, and in the May evenings they went to concerts where they heard the perfect music of their own country. Though they were away for just a week, and read the German papers, and went to a corner of the Luxembourg Gardens where there were pines and wildflowers like those in the greenbelt around Munich, this music made them sick for home. They returned two days early and never left again except for July and August, which each year they spent in the Black Forest, at a cabin inherited from her parents.

He dared not go back to that cabin. It was set like a trap. Were he to enter he would be enfiladed by the sight of their son's pictures and toys, his little boots and miniature fishing rod, and by her comb lying at the exact angle she had left it when she had last brushed her hair, and by the sweet smell of her clothing. No, someday he would have to burn the cabin. He dared not sell, for strangers then would handle roughly all those things which meant so much to him that he could not even gaze upon them. He left the little cabin to stand empty, perhaps the object of an occasional hiker's curiosity, or recipient of cheerful postcards from friends travelling or at the beach for the summer —friends who had not heard.

He sought instead a town far enough from Munich so that he would not encounter anything familiar, a place where he would be unrecognized and yet a place not entirely strange, where he would have to undergo no savage adjustments, where he could buy a Munich paper.

A search of the map brought his flying eye always southward to the borderlands, to Alpine country remarkable for the steepness of the brown contours, the depth of the valleys, and the paucity of settled places. Those few depicted towns appeared to be clean and well placed on high overlooks. Unlike the cities to the north—circles which clustered together on the flatlands or along rivers, like colonies of bacteria—the cities of the Alps stood alone, *in extremis,* near the border. Though he dared not cross the border, he thought perhaps to venture near its edge, to see what he would see. These isolated towns in the Alps promised shining clear air and deep-green trees. Perhaps they were above the tree line. In a number of cases it looked that way—and the circles were far from resembling clusters of bacteria. They seemed like untethered balloons.

He chose a town for its ridiculous name, reasoning that few of his friends would desire to travel to such a place. The world bypasses badly named towns as easily as it abandons ungainly children. It was called Garmisch-Partenkirchen. At the station in Munich, they did not even inscribe the full name on his ticket, writing merely "Garmisch-P."

"Do you live there?" the railroad agent had asked.

"No," answered Wallich.

"Are you visiting relatives, or going on business, or going to ski?"

"No."

"Then perhaps you are making a mistake. To go in October is not wise, if you do not ski. As unbelievable as it may seem, they have had much snow. Why go now?"

"I am a mountain climber," answered Wallich.

"In winter?" The railway agent was used to flushing out lies, and when little fat Austrian boys just old enough for adult tickets would bend their knees at his window as if at confession and say in squeaky voices, "Half fare to Salzburg!," he pounced upon them as if he were a leopard and they juicy ptarmigan or baby roebuck.

"Yes, in the winter," Wallich said. "Good mountain climbers thrive in difficult conditions. The more ice, the more storm, the greater the accomplishment. I am accumulating various winter records. In January, I go to America, where I will ascend their highest mountain, Mt. Independence, four thousand metres." He blushed so hard that the railway agent followed suit. Then Wallich backed away, insensibly mortified.

A mountain climber! He would close his eyes in fear when

looking through Swiss calendars. He had not the stamina to rush up the stairs to his studio. He had failed miserably at sports. He was not a mountain climber, and had never even dreamed of being one.

Yet when his train pulled out of the vault of lacy ironwork and late-afternoon shadow, its steam exhalations were like those of a man puffing up a high meadow, speeding to reach the rock and ice, and Wallich felt as if he were embarking upon an ordeal of the type men experience on the precipitous rock walls of great cloud-swirled peaks. Why was he going to Garmisch-Partenkirchen anyway, if not for an ordeal through which to right himself? He was pulled so far over on one side by the death of his family, he was so bent and crippled by the pain of it, that he was going to Garmisch-Partenkirchen to suffer a parallel ordeal through which he would balance what had befallen him.

How wrong his parents and friends had been when they had offered help as his business faltered. A sensible, graceful man will have symmetry. He remembered the time at youth camp when a stream had changed course away from a once gushing sluice and the younger boys had had to carry buckets of water up a small hill, to fill a cistern. The skinny little boys had struggled up the hill. Their counsellor, sitting comfortably in the shade, would not let them go two to a bucket. At first they had tried to carry the pails in front of them, but this was nearly impossible. Then they surreptitiously spilled half the water on the way up, until the counsellor took up position at the cistern and inspected each cargo. It had been torture to carry the heavy bucket in one aching hand. Wallich finally decided to take two buckets. Though it was agony, it was a better agony than the one he had had, because he had retrieved his balance, could look ahead, and, by carrying a double burden, had strengthened himself and made the job that much shorter. Soon, all the boys carried two buckets. The cistern was filled in no time, and they had a victory over their surprised counsellor.

So, he thought as the train shuttled through chill half-harvested fields, I will be a hermit in Garmisch-Partenkirchen. I will know no one. I will be alone. I may even begin to climb mountains. Perhaps I will lose fingers and toes, and on the way gather a set of wounds which will allow me some peace.

He sensed the change of landscape before he actually came upon it. Then they began to climb, and the engine sweated steam from steel to carry the lumbering cars up terrifying grades on either side of which blue pines stood angled against the mountainside. They reached a level stretch which made the train curve like a dragon and led it through deep tunnels, and they sped along as if on a summer excursion, with views of valleys so distant that in them whole forests sat upon their meadows like birthmarks, and streams were little more than the grain in leather.

Wallich opened his window and leaned out, watching ahead for tunnels. The air was thick and cold. It was full of sunshine and greenery, and it flowed past as if it were a mountain river. When he pulled back, his cheeks were red and his face pounded from the frigid air. He was alone in the compartment. By the time the lights came on he had decided upon the course of an ideal. He was to become a mountain climber, after all—and in a singularly difficult, dangerous, and satisfying way.

A porter said in passing the compartment, "The dining car is open, sir." Service to the Alps was famed. Even though his journey was no more than two hours, he had arranged to eat on the train and had paid for and ordered a meal to which he looked forward in pleasant anticipation, especially because he had selected French strawberries in cream for dessert. But then he saw his body in the gently lit half mirror. He was soft from a lifetime of near-happiness. The sight of his face in the blond light of the mirror made him decide to begin preparing for the mountains that very evening. The porter ate the strawberries.

Of the many ways to attempt an ordeal perhaps the most graceful and attractive is the Alpine. It is far more satisfying than Oriental starvation and abnegation precisely because the European ideal is to commit difficult acts amid richness and overflowing beauty. For that reason, the Alpine is as well the most demanding. It is hard to deny oneself, to pare oneself down, at the heart and base of a civilization so full.

Wallich rode to Garmisch-Partenkirchen in a thunder of proud Alps. The trees were tall and lively, the air crystalline, and radiating beams spoke through the train window from one glowing range to another. A world of high ice laughed. And yet ranks of competing images assaulted him. He had gasped at the sight of Bremen, a port stuffed with iron ships gushing wheat steam from their whistles as they prepared to sail. In the mountain dryness, he remembered humid ports from which these massive ships crossed a colorful world, bringing back on laden decks a catalogue of stuffs and curiosities.

Golden images of the north plains struck from the left. The salt-white plains nearly floated above the sea. All this was in Germany, though Germany was just a small part of the world, removed almost entirely from the deep source of things—from the high lakes where explorers touched the silvers which caught the world's images, from the Sahara where they found the fine glass which bent the light.

Arriving at Garmisch-Partenkirchen in the dark, he could hear bells chiming and water rushing. Cool currents of air flowed from the direction of this white tumbling sound. It was winter. He hailed a horse-drawn sledge and piled his baggage in the back. "Hotel Aufburg," he said authoritatively.

"Hotel Aufburg?" asked the driver.

"Yes, Hotel Aufburg. There is such a place, isn't there? It hasn't closed, has it?"

"No, sir, it hasn't closed." The driver touched his horse with the whip. The horse walked twenty feet and was reined to a stop. "Here we are," the driver said. "I trust you've had a pleasant journey. Time passes quickly up here in the mountains."

The sign for the hotel was so large and well lit that the street in front of it shone as in daylight. The driver was guffawing to himself; the little guffaws rumbled about in him like subterranean thunder. He could not wait to tell the other drivers.

The Schreuderspitze

Wallich did nothing properly in Garmisch-Partenkirchen. But it was a piece of luck that he felt too awkward and ill at ease to sit alone in restaurants while, nearby, families and lovers had self-centered raucous meals, sometimes even bursting into song. Winter took over the town and covered it in stiff white ice. The unresilient cold, the troikas jingling through the streets, the frequent snowfalls encouraged winter fat. But because Wallich ate cold food in his room or stopped occasionally at a counter for a steaming bowl of soup, he became a shadow.

The starvation was pleasant. It made him sleepy and its constant physical presence gave him companionship. He sat for hours watching the snow, feeling as if he were part of it, as if the diminution of his body were great progress, as if such lightening would lessen his sorrow and bring him to the high rim of things he had not seen before, things which would help him and show him what to do and make him proud just for coming upon them.

He began to exercise. Several times a day the hotel manager knocked like a woodpecker at Wallich's door. The angrier the manager, the faster the knocks. If he were really angry he spoke so rapidly that he sounded like a speeded-up record: "Herr Wallich, I must ask you on behalf of the other guests to stop immediately all the thumping and vibration! This is a quiet hotel, in a quiet town, in a quiet tourist region. Please!" Then the manager would bow and quickly withdraw.

Eventually they threw Wallich out, but not before he had spent October and November in concentrated maniacal pursuit of physical strength. He had started with five each, every waking hour, of pushups, pull-ups, sit-ups, toe-touches, and leg-raises. The pull-ups were deadly—he did one every twelve minutes. The thumping and bumping came from five minutes of running in place. At the end of the first day, the pain in his chest was so intense that he was certain he was not long for the world. The second day was worse. And so it went, until after ten days there was no pain at all. The weight he abandoned helped a great deal to expand his physical prowess. He was, after all, in his middle twenties, and had never eaten to excess. Nor did he smoke or drink, except for champagne at weddings and municipal celebrations. In fact, he had always had rather ascetic tendencies, and had thought it fitting to have spent his life in Munich—"Home of Monks."

By his fifteenth day in Garmisch-Partenkirchen he had increased his schedule to fifteen apiece of the exercises each hour, which meant, for example, that he did a pull-up every four minutes whenever he was awake. Late at night he ran aimlessly about the deserted streets for an hour or more, even though it sometimes snowed. Two policemen who huddled over a brazier in their tiny booth simply looked at one another and pointed to their heads, twirling their fingers and rolling their eyes every time he passed by. On the last day of November, he moved up the valley to a little village called Altenburg-St. Peter.

There it was worse in some ways and better in others. Altenburg-St. Peter was so tiny that no stranger could enter unobserved, and so still that no one could do anything without the knowledge of the entire community. Children stared at Wallich on the street. This made him walk on the little lanes and approach his few destinations from the rear, which led housewives to speculate that he was a burglar. There were few merchants, and, because they were cousins, they could with little effort determine exactly what Wallich ate. When one week they were positive that he had consumed only four bowls of soup, a pound of cheese, a pound of smoked meat, a quart of yogurt, and two loaves of bread, they were incredulous. They themselves ate this much in a day. They wondered how Wallich survived on so little. Finally they came up with an answer. He received packages from Munich several times a week and in these packages was food, they thought—and probably very great delicacies. Then as the winter got harder and the snows covered everything they stopped wondering about him. They did not see him as he ran out of his lodgings at midnight, and the snow muffled his tread. He ran up the road toward the Schreuderspitze, first for a kilometre, then two, then five, then ten, then twenty—when finally he had to stop because he had begun slipping in just before the farmers arose and would have seen him.

By the end of February the packages had ceased arriving, and he was a changed man. No one would have mistaken him for what he had been. In five months he had become lean and strong. He did two hundred and fifty sequential pushups at least four times a day. For the sheer pleasure of it, he would do a hundred and fifty pushups on his fingertips. Every day he did a hundred pull-ups in a row. His midnight run, sometimes in snow which had accumulated up to his knees, was four hours long.

The packages had contained only books on climbing, and equipment. At first the books had been terribly discouraging. Every elementary test had bold warnings in red or green ink: "It is extremely dangerous to attempt genuine ascents without proper training. This volume should be used in conjunction with a certified course on climbing, or with the advice of a registered guide. A book itself will not do!"

One manual had in bright-red ink, on the very last page: "Go back, you fool! Certain death awaits you!" Wallich imagined that, as the books said, there were many things he could not learn except by human example, and many mistakes he might make in interpreting the manuals, which would go uncorrected save for the critique of living practitioners. But it didn't matter. He was determined to learn for himself and accomplish his task alone. Besides, since the accident he had become a recluse, and could hardly speak. The thought of enrolling in a climbing school full of young people from all parts of the country paralyzed him. How could he reconcile his task with their enthusiasm? For them it was recreation, perhaps something aesthetic or spiritual, a way to meet new friends. For him it was one tight channel through which he would either burst on to a new life, or in which he would die.

Studying carefully, he soon worked his way to advanced treatises for those who had spent years in the Alps. He understood these well enough, having quickly learned the termi-

nologies and the humor and the faults of those who write about
the mountains. He was even convinced that he knew the spirit in
which the treatises had been written, for though he had never
climbed, he had only to look out his window to see high white
mountains about which blue sky swirled like a banner. He felt
that in seeing them he was one of them, and was greatly encouraged when he read in a French mountaineer's memoirs:
"After years in the mountains, I learned to look upon a given
range and feel as if I were the last peak in the line. Thus I felt
the music of the empty spaces enwrapping me, and I became not
an intruder on the cliffs, dangling only to drop away, but an
equal in transit. I seldom looked at my own body but only at the
mountains, and my eyes felt like the eyes of the mountains."

He lavished nearly all his dwindling money on fine equipment. He calculated that after his purchases he would have
enough to live on through September. Then he would have
nothing. He had expended large sums on the best tools, and he
spent the intervals between his hours of reading and exercise
holding and studying the shiny carabiners, pitons, slings, chocks,
hammers, ice pitons, axes, étriers, crampons, ropes, and special-
ized hardware that he had either ordered or constructed himself
from plans in the advanced books.

It was insane, he knew, to funnel all his preparation into a
few months of agony and then without any experience whatever
throw himself alone onto a Class VI ascent—the seldom climbed
Westgebirgsausläufer of the Schreuderspitze. Not having driven
one piton, he was going to attempt a five-day climb up the
nearly sheer western counterfort. Even in late June, he would
spend a third of his time on ice. But the sight of the ice in
March, shining like a faraway sword over the cold and absolute
distance, drove him on. He had long passed censure. Had anyone known what he was doing and tried to dissuade him, he
would have told him to go to hell, and resumed preparations
with the confidence of someone taken up by a new religion.

For he had always believed in great deeds, in fairy tales, in
echoing trumpet lands, in wonders and wondrous accom-

plishments. But even as a boy he had never considered that such things would fall to him. As a good city child he had known that these adventures were not necessary. But suddenly he was alone and the things which occurred to him were great warlike deeds. His energy and discipline were boundless, as full and overflowing as a lake in the mountains. Like the heroes of his youth, he would try to approach the high cord of ruby light and bend it to his will, until he could feel rolling thunder. The small things, the gentle things, the good things he loved, and the flow of love itself were dead for him and would always be, unless he could liberate them in a crucible of high drama.

It took him many months to think these things, and though they might not seem consistent, they were so for him, and he often spent hours alone on a sunny snow-covered meadow, his elbows on his knees, imagining great deeds in the mountains, as he stared at the massive needle of the Schreuderspitze, at the hint of rich lands beyond, and at the tiny village where he had taken up position opposite the mountain.

Toward the end of May he had been walking through Altenburg-St. Peter and seen his reflection in a store window—a storm had arisen suddenly and made the glass as silver-black as the clouds. He had not liked what he had seen. His face had become too hard and too lean. There was not enough gentleness. He feared immediately for the success of his venture if only because he knew well that unmitigated extremes are a great cause of failure. And he was tired of his painful regimen.

He bought a large Telefunken radio, in one fell swoop wiping out his funds for August and September. He felt as if he were paying for the privilege of music with portions of his life and body. But it was well worth it. When the storekeeper offered to deliver the heavy console, Wallich declined politely, picked up the cabinet himself, hoisted it on his back, and walked out of the store bent under it as in classic illustrations for physics textbooks throughout the industrialized world. He did not put it down once. The storekeeper summoned his associates and they bet and counterbet on whether Wallich "would" or "would not," as he moved slowly up the steep hill, up the steps, around the white switchbacks, onto a grassy slope, and then finally up the precipitous stairs to the balcony outside his room. "How can he have done that?" they asked. "He is a small man, and the radio must weigh at least thirty kilos." The storekeeper trotted out with a catalogue. "It weighs fifty-five kilograms!" he said. "Fifty-five kilograms!," and they wondered what had made Wallich so strong.

Once, Wallich had taken his little son (a tiny, skeptical, silent child who had a riotous giggle which could last for an hour) to see the inflation of a great gas dirigible. It had been a disappointment, for a dirigible is rigid and maintains always the same shape. He had expected to see the silver of its sides expand into ribbed cliffs which would float over them on the green field and amaze his son. Now that silver rising, the sail-like expansion, the great crescendo of a glimmering weightless mass, finally reached him alone in his room, too late but well received, when a Berlin station played the Beethoven Violin Concerto, its first five timpanic D's like grace before a feast. After those notes, the music lifted him, and he riveted his gaze on the dark shapes of the mountains, where a lightning storm raged. The radio crackled after each near or distant flash, but it was as if the music had been designed for it. Wallich looked at the yellow light within a softly glowing numbered panel. It flickered gently, and he could hear cracks and flashes in the music as he saw them delineated across darkness. They looked and sounded like the bent riverine limbs of dead trees hanging majestically over rocky outcrops, destined to fall, but enjoying their grand suspension nonetheless. The music travelled effortlessly on anarchic beams, passed high over the plains, passed high the forests, seeding them plentifully, and came upon the Alps like waves which finally strike the shore after thousands of miles in open sea. It charged upward, mating with the electric storm, separating, and delivering.

To Wallich—alone in the mountains, surviving amid the

dark massifs and clear air—came the closeted, nasal, cosmopolitan voice of the radio commentator. It was good to know that there was something other than the purity and magnificence of his mountains, that far to the north the balance reverted to less than moral catastrophe and death, and much stock was set in things of extraordinary inconsequence. Wallich could not help laughing when he thought of the formally dressed audience at the symphony, how they squirmed in their seats and heated the bottoms of their trousers and capes, how relieved and delighted they would be to step out into the cool evening and go to a restaurant. In the morning they would arise and take pleasure from the sweep of the drapes as sun danced by, from the gold rim around a white china cup. For them it was always too hot or too cold. But they certainly had their delights, about which sometimes he would think. How often he still dreamed, asleep or awake, of the smooth color plates opulating under his hands in tanks of developer and of the fresh film which smelled like bread and then was entombed in black cylinders to develop. How he longed sometimes for the precise machinery of his cameras. The very word *"Kamera"* was as dark and hollow as this night in the mountains when, reviewing the pleasures of faraway Berlin, he sat in perfect health and equanimity upon a wicker-weave seat in a bare white room. The only light was from the yellow dial, the sudden lightning flashes, and the faint blue of the sky beyond the hills. And all was quiet but for the music and the thunder and the static curling about the music like weak and lost memories which arise to harry even indomitable perfections.

A month before the ascent, he awaited arrival of a good climbing rope. He needed from a rope not strength to hold a fall but lightness and length for abseiling. His strategy was to climb with a short self-belay. No one would follow to retrieve his hardware and because it would not always be practical for him to do so himself, in what one of his books called "rhythmic recapitulation," he planned to carry a great deal of metal. If the metal and he reached the summit relatively intact, he could make short work of the descent, abandoning pitons as he abseiled downward.

He would descend in half a day that which had taken five days to climb. He pictured the abseiling, literally a flight down the mountain on the doubled cord of his long rope, and he thought that those hours speeding down the cliffs would be the finest of his life. If the weather were good he would come away from the Schreuderspitze having flown like an eagle.

On the day the rope was due, he went to the railroad station to meet the mail. It was a clear, perfect day. The light was so fine and rich that in its bath everyone felt wise, strong, and content. Wallich sat on the wooden boards of the wide platform, scanning the green meadows and fields for smoke and a coal engine, but the countryside was silent and the valley unmarred by the black woolly chain he sought. In the distance, toward France and Switzerland, a few cream-and-rose-colored clouds rode the horizon, immobile and high. On far mountainsides innumerable flowers showed in this long view as a slash, or as a patch of color not unlike one flower alone.

He had arrived early, for he had no watch. After some minutes a car drove up and from it emerged a young family. They rushed as if the train were waiting to depart, when down the long troughlike valley it was not even visible. There were two little girls, as beautiful as he had ever seen. The mother, too, was extraordinarily fine. The father was in his early thirties, and he wore gold-rimmed glasses. They seemed like a university family —people who knew how to live sensibly, taking pleasure from proper and beautiful things.

The littler girl was no more than three. Sunburned and rosy, she wore a dress that was shaped like a bell. She dashed about the platform so lightly and tentatively that it was as if Wallich were watching a tiny fish gravityless in a lighted aquarium. Her older sister stood quietly by the mother, who was illumined with consideration and pride for her children. It was apparent that she was overjoyed with the grace of her family.

The Schreuderspitze

She seemed detached and preoccupied, but in just the right way. The littler girl said in a voice like a child's party horn, "Mummy, I want some peanuts!"

It was so ridiculous that this child should share the appetite of elephants that the mother smiled. "Peanuts will make you thirsty, Gretl. Wait until we get to Garmisch-Partenkirchen. Then we'll have lunch in the buffet."

"When will we get to Garmisch-Partenkirchen?"

"At two."

"Two?"

"Yes, at two."

"At two?"

"Gretl!"

The father looked alternately at the mountains and at his wife and children. He seemed confident and steadfast. In the distance black smoke appeared in thick billows. The father pointed at it. "There's our train," he said.

"Where?" asked Gretl, looking in the wrong direction. The father picked her up and turned her head with his hand, aiming her gaze down the shimmering valley. When she saw the train she started, and her eyes opened wide in pleasure.

"Ah . . . there it is," said the father. As the train pulled into the station the young girls were filled with excitement. Amid the noise they entered a compartment and were swallowed up in the steam. The train pulled out.

Wallich stood on the empty platform, unwrapping his rope. It was a rope, quite a nice rope, but it did not make him as happy as he had expected it would.

Little can match the silhouette of mountains by night. The great mass becomes far more mysterious when its face is darkened, when its sweeping lines roll steeply into valleys and peaks and long impossible ridges, when behind the void a concoction of rare silver leaps up to trace the hills—the pressure of collected starlight. That night, in conjunction with the long draughts of music he had become used to taking, he began to dream his dreams. They did not frighten him—he was beyond fear, too strong for fear, too played out. They did not even puzzle him, for they unfolded like the chapters in a brilliant nineteenth-century history. The rich explanations filled him for days afterward. He was amazed, and did not understand why these perfect dreams suddenly came to him. Surely they did not arise from within. He had never had the world so beautifully portrayed, had never seen as clearly and in such sure, gentle steps, had never risen so high and so smoothly in unfolding enlightenment, and he had seldom felt so well looked after. And yet, there was no visible presence. But it was as if the mountains and valleys were filled with loving families of which he was part.

Upon his return from the railroad platform, a storm had come suddenly from beyond the southern ridge. Though it had been warm and clear that day, he had seen from the sunny meadow before his house that a white storm billowed in higher and higher curves, pushing itself over the summits, finally to fall like an air avalanche on the valley. It snowed on the heights. The sun continued to strike the opaque frost and high clouds. It did not snow in the valley. The shock troops of the storm remained at the highest elevations, and only worn gray veterans came below—misty clouds and rain on cold wet air. Ragged clouds moved across the mountainsides and meadows, watering the trees and sometimes catching in low places. Even so, the air in the meadow was still horn-clear.

In his room that night Wallich rocked back and forth on the wicker chair (it was not a rocker and he knew that using it as such was to number its days). That night's crackling infusion from Berlin, rising warmly from the faintly lit dial, was Beethoven's Eighth. The familiar commentator, nicknamed by Wallich Mälzels Metronom because of his even monotone, discoursed upon the background of the work.

"For many years," he said, "no one except Beethoven liked this symphony. Beethoven's opinions, however—even regarding his own creations—are equal at least to the collective pronouncements of all the musicologists and critics alive in the West during any hundred-year period. Conscious of the merits of the F-Major Symphony, he resolutely determined to redeem and . . . ah . . . the conductor has arrived. He steps to the podium. We begin."

Wallich retired that night in perfect tranquillity but awoke at five in the morning soaked in his own sweat, his fists clenched, a terrible pain in his chest, and breathing heavily as if he had been running. In the dim unattended light of the early-morning storm, he lay with eyes wide open. His pulse subsided, but he was like an animal in a cave, like a creature who has just escaped an organized hunt. It was as if the whole village had come armed and in search of him, had by some miracle decided that he was not in, and had left to comb the wet woods. He had been dreaming, and he saw his dream in its exact form. It was, first, an emerald. Cut into an octagon with two long sides, it was shaped rather like the plaque at the bottom of a painting. Events within this emerald were circular and never-ending.

They were in Munich. Air and sun were refined as on the station platform in the mountains. He was standing at a streetcar stop with his wife and his two daughters, though he knew perfectly well in the dream that these two daughters were meant to be his son. A streetcar arrived in complete silence. Clouds of people began to embark. They were dressed and muffled in heavy clothing of dull blue and gray. To his surprise, his wife moved toward the door of the streetcar and started to board, the daughters trailing after her. He could not see her feet, and she moved in a glide. Though at first paralyzed, as in the instant before a crash, he did manage to bound after her. As she stepped onto the first step and was about to grasp a chrome pole within the doorway, he made for her arm and caught it.

He pulled her back and spun her around, all very gently. Her presence before him was so intense that it was as if he were trapped under the weight of a fallen beam. She, too, wore a winter coat, but it was slim and perfectly tailored. He remembered the perfect geometry of the lapels. Not on earth had such angles ever been seen. The coat was a most intense liquid emerald color, a living light-infused green. She had always looked best in green, for her hair was like shining gold. He stood before her. He felt her delicacy. Her expression was neutral. "Where are you going?" he asked incredulously.

"I must go," she said.

He put his arms around her. She returned his embrace, and he said, "How can you leave me?"

"I have to," she answered.

And then she stepped onto the first step of the streetcar, and onto the second step, and she was enfolded into darkness.

He awoke, feeling like an invalid. His strength served for naught. He just stared at the clouds lifting higher and higher as the storm cleared. By nightfall the sky was black and gentle, though very cold. He kept thinking back to the emerald. It meant everything to him, for it was the first time he realized that they were really dead. Silence followed. Time passed thickly. He could not have imagined the sequence of dreams to follow, and what they would do to him.

He began to fear sleep, thinking that he would again be subjected to the lucidity of the emerald. But he had run that course and would never do so again except by perfect conscious recollection. The night after he had the dream of the emerald he fell asleep like someone letting go of a cliff edge after many minutes alone without help or hope. He slid into sleep, heart beating wildly. To his surprise, he found himself far indeed from the trolley tracks in Munich.

Instead, he was alone in the center of a sunlit snowfield, walking on the glacier in late June, bound for the summit of the Schreuderspitze. The mass of his equipment sat lightly upon him. He was well drilled in its use and positioning, in the subtleties of placement and rigging. The things he carried seemed part of him, as if he had quickly evolved into a new kind of animal suited for breathtaking travel in the steep heights.

His stride was light and long, like that of a man on the moon. He nearly floated, ever so slightly airborne, over the dazzling glacier. He leaped crevasses, sailing in slow motion against intense white and blue. He passed apple-fresh streams and opalescent melt pools of blue-green water as he progressed toward the Schreuderspitze. Its rocky horn was covered by nearly blue ice from which the wind blew a white corona in sines and cusps twirling about the sky.

Passing the bergschrund, he arrived at the first mass of rock. He turned to look back. There he saw the snowfield and the sun turning above it like a pinwheel, casting out a fog of golden light. He stood alone. The world had been reduced to the beauty of physics and the mystery of light. It had been rendered into a frozen state, a liquid state, a solid state, a gaseous state, mixtures, temperatures, and more varieties of light than fell on the speckled floor of a great cathedral. It was simple, and yet infinitely complex. The sun was warm. There was silence.

For several hours he climbed over great boulders and up a range of rocky escarpments. It grew more and more difficult, and he often had to lay in protection, driving a piton into a crack of the firm granite. His first piton was a surprise. It slowed halfway, and the ringing sound as he hammered grew higher in pitch. Finally, it would go in no farther. He had spent so much time in driving it that he thought it would be as steady as the Bank of England. But when he gave a gentle tug to test its hold, it came right out. This he thought extremely funny. He then remembered that he had either to drive it in all the way, to the eye, or to attach a sling along its shaft as near as possible to the rock. It was a question of avoiding leverage.

He bent carefully to his equipment sling, replaced the used piton, and took up a shorter one. The shorter piton went to its eye in five hammer strokes and he could do nothing to dislodge it. He clipped in and ascended a steep pitch, at the top of which he drove in two pitons, tied in to them, abseiled down to retrieve the first, and ascended quite easily to where he had left off. He made rapid progress over frightening pitches, places no one would dare go without assurance of a bolt in the rock and a line to the bolt—even if the bolt was just a small piece of metal driven in by dint of precariously balanced strength, arm, and Alpine hammer.

Within the sphere of utter concentration easily achieved during difficult ascents, his simple climbing evolved naturally into graceful technique, by which he went up completely vertical rock faces, suspended only by pitons and étriers. The different placements of which he had read and thought repeatedly were employed skillfully and with a proper sense of variety, though it was tempting to stay with one familiar pattern. Pounding metal into rock and hanging from his taut and colorful wires, he breathed hard, he concentrated, and he went up sheer walls.

At one point he came to the end of a subtle hairline crack in an otherwise smooth wall. The rock above was completely solid for a hundred feet. If he went down to the base of the crack he would be nowhere. The only thing to do was to make a swing traverse to a wall more amenable to climbing.

Anchoring two pitons into the rock as solidly as he could, he clipped an oval carabiner on the bottom piton, put a safety line on the top one, and lowered himself about sixty feet down the two ropes. Hanging perpendicular to the wall, he began to walk back and forth across the rock. He moved to and fro, faster and faster, until he was running. Finally he touched only in places and was swinging wildly like a pendulum. He feared that the piton to which he was anchored would not take the strain, and would pull out. But he kept swinging faster, until he gave one final push and, with a pathetic cry, went sailing over a drop which would have made a mountain goat swallow its heart. He caught an outcropping of rock on the other side, and pulled himself to it desperately. He hammered in, retrieved the ropes, glanced at the impassable wall, and began again to ascend.

As he approached great barricades of ice, he looked back. It gave him great pride and satisfaction to see the thousands of feet over which he had struggled. Much of the west counterfort was purely vertical. He could see now just how the glacier was riverine. He could see deep within the Tyrol and over the border to the Swiss lakes. Garmisch-Partenkirchen looked from here like a town on the board of a toy railroad or (if considered only two-dimensionally) like the cross-section of a kidney. Altenburg-St. Peter looked like a ladybug. The sun sent streamers of tan light through the valley, already three-quarters conquered by shadow, and the ice above took fire. Where the ice began, he came to a wide ledge and he stared upward at a sparkling ridge which looked like a great crystal spine. Inside, it was blue and cold.

He awoke, convinced that he had in fact climbed the counterfort. It was a strong feeling, as strong as the reality of the emerald. Sometimes dreams could be so real that they competed with the world, riding at even balance and calling for a decision. Sometimes, he imagined, when they are so real and so important, they easily tip the scale and the world buckles and dreams become real. Crossing the fragile barricades, one enters his dreams, thinking of his life as imagined.

He rejoiced at his bravery in climbing. It had been as real as anything he had ever experienced. He felt the pain, the exhaustion, and the reward, as well as the danger. But he could not wait to return to the mountain and the ice. He longed for evening and the enveloping darkness, believing that he belonged resting under great folds of ice on the wall of the Schreuderspitze. He had no patience with his wicker chair, the bent wood of the window-sill, the clear glass in the window, the green-sided hills he saw curving through it, or his brightly colored equipment hanging from pegs on the white wall.

Two weeks before, on one of the eastward roads from Altenburg-St. Peter—no more than a dirt track—he had seen a child turn and take a well-worn path toward a wood, a meadow, and a stream by which stood a house and a barn. The child walked slowly upward into the forest, disappearing into the dark close, as if he had been taken up by vapor. Wallich had been too far away to hear footsteps, and the last thing he saw was the back of the boy's bright blue-and-white sweater. Returning at dusk, Wallich had expected to see warmly lit windows, and smoke issuing efficiently from the straight chimney. But there were no lights, and there was no smoke. He made his way through the trees and past the meadow only to come upon a small farmhouse with boarded windows and no-trespassing signs tacked on the doors.

It was unsettling when he saw the same child making his way across the upper meadow, a flash of blue and white in the near darkness. Wallich screamed out to him, but he did not hear, and kept walking as if he were deaf or in another world, and he went over the crest of the hill. Wallich ran up the hill.

When he reached the top he saw only a wide empty field and not
a trace of the boy

Then in the darkness and purity of the meadows he began
to feel that the world had many secrets, that they were shattering
even to glimpse or sense, and that they were not necessarily unpleasant. In certain states of light he could see, he could begin to
sense, things most miraculous indeed. Although it seemed self-
serving, he concluded nonetheless, after a lifetime of adhering to
the diffuse principles of a science he did not know, that there was
life after death, that the dead rose into a mischievous world of
pure light, that something most mysterious lay beyond the en-
folding darkness, something wonderful.

This idea had taken hold, and he refined it. For example,
listening to the Beethoven symphonies broadcast from Berlin, he
began to think that they were like a ladder of mountains, that
they surpassed themselves and rose higher and higher until at
certain points they seemed to break the warp itself and cross into
a heaven of light and the dead. There were signs everywhere of
temporal diffusion and mystery. It was as if continents existed,
new worlds lying just off the coast, invisible and redolent, waiting for the grasp of one man suddenly to substantiate and light
them, changing everything. Perhaps great mountains hundreds
of times higher than the Alps would arise in the sea or on the
flatlands. They might be purple or gold and shining in many
states of refraction and reflection, transparent in places as vast as
countries. Someday someone would come back from this place,
or someone would by accident discover and illumine its remarkable physics.

He believed that the boy he had seen nearly glowing in the
half-darkness of the high meadow had been his son, and that the
child had been teasing his father in a way only he could know,
that the child had been asking him to follow. Possibly he had
come upon great secrets on the other side, and knew that his
father would join him soon enough and that then they would
laugh about the world

When he next fell asleep in the silence of a clear windless

night in the valley, Wallich was like a man disappearing into the warp of darkness. He wanted to go there, to be taken as far as he could be taken. He was not unlike a sailor who sets sail in the teeth of a great storm, delighted by his own abandon.

Throwing off the last wraps of impure light, he found himself again in the ice world. The word was all-encompassing—*Eiswelt*. There above him the blue spire rocketed upward as far as the eye could see. He touched it with his hand. It was indeed as cold as ice. It was dense and hard, like glass ten feet thick. He had doubted its strength, but its solidity told that it would not flake away and allow him to drop endlessly, far from it.

On ice he found firm holds both with his feet and with his hands, and hardly needed the ice pitons and étriers. For he had crampons tied firmly to his boots, and could spike his toe points into the ice and stand comfortably on a vertical. He proceeded with a surety of footing he had never had on the streets of Munich. Each step bolted him down to the surface. And in each hand he carried an ice hammer with which he made swinging cutting arcs that engaged the shining stainless-steel pick with the mirrorlike wall.

All the snow had blown away or had melted. There were no traps, no pitfalls, no ambiguities. He progressed toward the summit rapidly, climbing steep ice walls as if he had been going up a ladder. The air became purer and the light more direct. Looking out to right or left, or glancing sometimes over his shoulders, he saw that he was now truly in the world of mountains.

Above the few clouds he could see only equal peaks of ice, and the Schreuderspitze dropping away from him. It was not the world of rock. No longer could he make out individual features in the valley. Green had become a hazy dark blue appropriate to an ocean floor. Whole countries came into view. The landscape was a mass of winding glaciers and great mountains. At that height, all was separated and refined. Soft things vanished, and there remained only the white and the silver.

He did not reach the summit until dark. He did not see the

stars because icy clouds covered the Schreuderspitze in a crystalline fog which flowed past, crackling and hissing. He was heartbroken to have come all the way to the summit and then be blinded by masses of clouds. Since he could not descend until light, he decided to stay firmly stationed until he could see clearly. Meanwhile, he lost patience and began to address a presence in the air—casually, not thinking it strange to do so, not thinking twice about talking to the void.

He awoke in his room in early morning, saying, "All these blinding clouds. Why all these blinding clouds?"

Though the air of the valley was as fresh as a flower, he detested it. He pulled the covers over his head and strove for unconsciousness, but he grew too hot and finally gave up, staring at the remnants of dawn light soaking about his room. The day brightened in the way that stage lights come up, suddenly brilliant upon a beam-washed platform. It was early June. He had lost track of the exact date, but he knew that sometime before he had crossed into June. He had lost them in early June. Two years had passed.

He packed his things. Though he had lived like a monk, much had accumulated, and this he put into suitcases, boxes, and bags. He packed his pens, paper, books, a chess set on which he sometimes played against an imaginary opponent named Herr Claub, the beautiful Swiss calendars upon which he had at one time been almost afraid to gaze, cooking equipment no more complex than a soldier's mess kit, his clothing, even the beautifully wrought climbing equipment, for, after all, he had another set, up there in the *Eiswelt*. Only his bedding remained unpacked. It was on the floor in the center of the room, where he slept. He put some banknotes in an envelope—the June rent—and tacked it to the doorpost. The room was empty, white, and it would have echoed had it been slightly larger. He would say something and then listen intently, his eyes flaring like those of a lunatic. He had not eaten in days, and was not disappointed that even the waking world began to seem like a dream.

He went to the pump. He had accustomed himself to bathing in streams so cold that they were too frightened to freeze. Clean and cleanly shaved, he returned to his room. He smelled the sweet pine scent he had brought back on his clothing after hundreds of trips through the woods and forests girdling the greater mountains. Even the bedding was snowy white. He opened the closet and caught a glimpse of himself in the mirror. He was dark from sun and wind; his hair shone; his face had thinned; his eyebrows were now gold and white. For several days he had had only cold pure water. Like soldiers who come from training toughened and healthy, he had about him the air of a small child. He noticed a certain wildness in the eye, and he lay on the hard floor, as was his habit, in perfect comfort. He thought nothing. He felt nothing. He wished nothing.

Time passed as if he could compress and cancel it. Early-evening darkness began to make the white walls blue. He heard a crackling fire in the kitchen of the rooms next door, and imagined the shadows dancing there. Then he slept, departing.

On the mountain it was dreadfully cold. He huddled into himself against the wet silver clouds, and yet he smiled, happy to be once again on the summit. He thought of making an igloo, but remembered that he hadn't an ice saw. The wind began to build. If the storm continued, he would die. It would whittle him into a brittle wire, and then he would snap. The best he could do was to dig a trench with his ice hammers. He lay in the trench and closed his sleeves and hooded parka, drawing the shrouds tight. The wind came at him more and more fiercely. One gust was so powerful that it nearly lifted him out of the trench. He put in an ice piton, and attached his harness. Still the wind rose. It was difficult to breathe and nearly impossible to see. Any irregular surface whistled. The eye of the ice piton became a great siren. The zippers on his parka, the harness, the slings and equipment, all gave off musical tones, so that it was as if he were in a place with hundreds of tormented spirits.

The gray air fled past with breathtaking speed. Looking away from the wind, he had the impression of being propelled upward at unimaginable speed. Walls of gray sped by so fast that they glowed. He knew that if he were to look at the wind he would have the sense of hurtling forward in gravityless space.

And so he stared at the wind and its slowly pulsing gray glow. He did not know for how many hours he held that position. The rape of vision caused a host of delusions. He felt great momentum. He travelled until, eardrums throbbing with the sharpness of cold and wind, he was nearly dead, white as a candle, hardly able to breathe.

Then the acceleration ceased and the wind slowed. When, released from the great pressure, he fell back off the edge of the trench, he realized for the first time that he had been stretched tight on his line. He had never been so cold. But the wind was dying and the clouds were no longer a great corridor through which he was propelled. They were, rather, a gentle mist which did not know quite what to do with itself. How would it dissipate? Would it rise to the stars, or would it fall in compression down into the valley below?

It fell; it fell all around him, downward like a lowering curtain. It fell in lines and stripes, always downward as if on signal, by command, in league with a directive force.

At first he saw just a star or two straight on high. But as the mist departed a flood of stars burst through. Roads of them led into infinity. Starry wheels sat in fiery white coronas. Near the horizon were the few separate gentle stars, shining out and turning clearly, as wide and round as planets. The air grew mild and warm. He bathed in it. He trembled. As the air became all clear and the mist drained away completely, he saw something which stunned him.

The Schreuderspitze was far higher than he had thought. It was hundreds of times higher than the mountains represented on the map he had seen in Munich. The Alps were to it not even foothills, not even rills. Below him was the purple earth, and all the great cities lit by sparkling lamps in their millions. It was a clear summer dawn and the weather was excellent, certainly June.

He did not know enough about other cities to make them out from the shapes they cast in light, but his eye seized quite easily upon Munich. He arose from his trench and unbuckled the harness, stepping a few paces higher on the rounded summit. There was Munich, shining and pulsing like a living thing, strung with lines of amber light—light which reverberated as if in crystals, light which played in many dimensions and moved about the course of the city, which was defined by darkness at its edge. He had come above time, above the world. The city of Munich existed before him with all its time compressed. As he watched, its history played out in repeating cycles. Nothing, not one movement, was lost from the crystal. The light of things danced and multiplied, again and again, and yet again. It was all there for him to claim. It was alive, and ever would be.

He knelt on one knee as in paintings he had seen of explorers claiming a coast of the New World. He dared close his eyes in the face of that miracle. He began to concentrate, to fashion according to will with the force of stilled time a vision of those he had loved. In all their bright colors, they began to appear before him.

He awoke as if shot out of a cannon. He went from lying on his back to a completely upright position in an instant, a flash, during which he slammed the floorboards energetically with a clenched fist and cursed the fact that he had returned from such a world. But by the time he stood straight, he was delighted to be doing so. He quickly dressed, packed his bedding, and began to shuttle down to the station and back. In three trips, his luggage was stacked on the platform.

He bought a ticket for Munich, where he had not been in many many long months. He hungered for it, for the city, for the boats on the river, the goods in the shops, newspapers, the pigeons on the square, trees, traffic, even arguments, even Herr Franzen. So much rushed into his mind that he hardly saw his train pull in.

He helped the conductor load his luggage into the baggage

car, and he asked, "Will we change at Garmisch-Partenkirchen?"

"No. We go right through, direct to Munich," said the conductor.

"Do me a great favor. Let me ride in the baggage car."

"I can't. It's a violation."

"Please. I've been months in the mountains. I would like to ride alone, for the last time."

The conductor relented, and Wallich sat atop a pile of boxes, looking at the landscape through a Dutch door, the top of which was open. Trees and meadows, sunny and lush in June, sped by. As they descended, the vegetation thickened until he saw along the cinder bed slow-running black rivers, skeins and skeins of thorns darted with the red of early raspberries, and flowers which had sprung up on the paths. The air was warm and caressing—thick and full, like a swaying green sea at the end of August.

They closed on Munich, and the Alps appeared in a sweeping line of white cloud-touched peaks. As they pulled into the great station, as sooty as it had ever been, he remembered that he had climbed the Schreuderspitze, by its most difficult route. He had found freedom from grief in the great and heart-swelling sight he had seen from the summit. He felt its workings and he realized that soon enough he would come once more into the world of light. Soon enough he would be with his wife and son. But until then (and he knew that time would spark ahead), he would open himself to life in the city, return to his former profession, and struggle at his craft.

THE MARRIAGE FEAST

by Pär Lagerkvist

Jonas and Frida were to be married at four o'clock in the afternoon, and the guests were beginning to collect at the little house on the outskirts of the village by the railway where the ceremony was to take place. Ponies and traps came from the surrounding countryside, where one or two distant relatives of Frida lived—Jonas hadn't any—and there were also several people from the village itself. It seemed they would be about fifteen, all told.

It was a lovely day and the men were outside, strolling in the little garden, shaking hands with each other, standing talking, or taking a turn around the house as though they were looking it over. On the east gable was a faded sign over a small doorway:

Frida Johansson
Harberdasher

Hm. Well, well, so Frida was getting off today. Aha. That was all they said, but their tone implied a lot.

The Marriage Feast

Hm, it was a funny thing about this wedding, but there would be the usual food and drink anyway, and they might just as well be there, seeing they were invited. So they thought about going in.

The bridegroom was standing on the steps. He was a thick-set, insignificant little man, with a fair, drooping moustache and a continual happy smile—he was always smiling. He had clear, kind, almost grateful eyes, and he blinked a lot, almost as though to keep out of the way. He was apt to hold his head rather on one side, as if he were listening. He had a very pleasing appearance, he had indeed. His real name was Jonas Samuelsson; but he was usually called Jonas Gate, owing to his habit of always hanging about down by the level-crossing gate in his younger days, in case anyone off the train wanted a hand with the luggage. It had thus been quite some time before he had turned his hand to any steady job, but he had been porter at the hotel for a long time now, so his standing down by the level-crossing gate was all in order. It was his profession. As to that, of course, he was going to marry Frida today, so it was harder now to say what he was, or thought of being: whether he would help her in the shop if need be, or even give up work altogether. There was no telling what Frida's plans were, or how much she had been able to scrape together. No one had any idea. Maybe it was quite a tidy sum. But she might just as well let him stay on down there, it suited him somehow. He wasn't a particularly go-ahead chap.

The relatives didn't really like the idea of Frida's going and getting married in this way, and it wasn't surprising. Not that they cared what she let herself in for—that was her lookout. But there was no need to go and get married at her age; it was un-necessary, they thought. And she had always been one to save a bit—not that *they* knew anything about that, it was nothing to do with them. But now that she *was* going to at last, she might have chosen someone other than Jonas. Not that there were so many to choose from, of course. However, Frida was one of them, after all, and came of quite good family, so it did seem strange that she could put up with him. Well, well, that was her business; she wanted it that way, well and good. He was certainly a nice, good-natured sort of chap, that he was. No one could say he wasn't.

Jonas was standing on the porch receiving the guests and looking around obligingly as though wondering if there were something he could carry. And if someone arrived with a coat that he had had on in the gig, or with anything at all, he was delighted to help carry it in. It was something he could do, and on a day like this a man is only too glad to show what he is capable of. It was worse once all the guests had arrived, for no one spoke to him and he just stood there, still smiling, with his arms hanging beside his new black suit, which Frida had had made for the occasion. He had nothing in particular to do, but as usual he looked contented all the same.

It was better after a while when it was time for coffee and he could find chairs for everyone and beamingly invite them to sit up to the table. He said nothing; he preferred only to speak when he had to. He did think of asking them to be sure and have more buns and cakes, but he thought better of it; they were Frida's, after all. The guests helped themselves, all the same, and over their second cups began talking and feeling more at home. Jonas was delighted; he stood beside the mantelpiece with his cup of coffee, listening to all that was said with the most heartfelt good-will; ran out into the kitchen to fill up the coffee-pot, handed round the sugar to the women at the tables by the window, and generally made himself useful. Of course, it wasn't usual for the bridegroom to do the waiting like that, but he probably didn't know. They smiled at him in their own way, and he gave them his sweet smile in return. They may have thought he was rather silly with that smile of his, but one couldn't say that, because it was both wise and kind. It was just that he never stopped smiling. Well, that was his way. He was thinking now how well it was all going—it was too, there wasn't a hitch.

Up in the attic Frida was sitting being dressed as a bride. Agnes Karlsson, her best friend as they say, was pinching Frida's thin hair around the tongs so that there was a smell of burning right out through the window. It was the first time Frida had had her hair curled, but then it was the thing to do. She hardly recognized herself as she looked in the bureau mirror that she had had moved up. She was not very like the old Frida, which was as it should be on such a festive day.

Oh, just think of its being today! Today that she and Jonas were to stand in front of the altar and be joined in matrimony forever and ever before their God. To think that that day was really here, and that it was to happen soon, in a little while.

"I hope they have arranged the flowers properly down there, as I said, beside the stools. Do you think they have, Agnes?"

"Oh yes, they'll have done that all right."

"And do you think the wedding cake has arrived safely, the one with our initials?"

"Yes, it's sure to have come. I saw Klas arriving with a cake box—that was probably it."

"Supposing you were to go down just to make sure?"

"Good heavens, we must get this finished."

"Yes, of course, that's very important. Everything is important on a day like this; one must think of everything."

Oh, if only everything goes off all right, and it's the kind of festival she has hoped for, that she has dreamed about so much. If only it's all as the great solemnity of the occasion demands.

What is there on earth greater than two people being made one, meeting before God to have their compact sealed at the throne of the Eternal One? Alas, there were no doubt many who never gave a thought to what kind of festival this really was, looked on it as a gay party where they could dance and laugh. Which it was as well; of course, she herself was so happy that she was dancing inside. No bride could be happier than she, and none had more reason to be. No, none.

And yet, in spite of everything, in spite of all this joy—it was nevertheless the solemnity she felt most of all. The great solemnity that lay over this day of theirs. What they were now faced with was the most momentous thing that could happen to her and Jonas. Their lives were to be united, they were to be made one, their souls were to be joined together for ever. Neither of them would be lonely any more, neither she nor Jonas. How strange it was, never to be lonely any more. She knew what it meant, she who had been alone ever since her parents died when she was a child. She had been made to know so well what it was, every day of her life. No, it is not good for man to live alone.

Was it strange then, that at this glorious moment she wanted everything to be as worthy and beautiful as possible?

"Take a look in the mirror and see what you think," Agnes said.

And Frida leaned forward and looked at her reflection, stroked her forehead, touched her unfamiliar hair.

How small and thin her face was; she looked like a girl with anaemia. But her features were worn and her cheeks were sunken. The years had put their mark on her, she had so many wrinkles; but it was all so delicate and fine, it all seemed to have been carefully done. Even a scar on her neck seemed small and delicate, like everything else about her. Only her eyes were large, infinitely gentle and artless, and strangely wide open. Her mouth looked like a thin line, as though she had been a very determined and enterprising woman, but that was only because it was so thin and just as pale as the rest. It was when she smiled that it became transformed. It was extraordinary; her whole face lit up at once. Also she had the nicest false teeth in the whole district; there were many who thought so if it came to that. They fitted so well.

No, she was not beautiful. She never had been and now it was no longer to be expected. But there was something unusually pure about her, as is often the way with seamstresses and laundresses. She had done sewing for many years before setting up her shop, and there, too, she always had to do with clean and delicate things. She was so well suited to them, which is probably why she had taken to it. Her hands were quite white, since she had never had to do any rough work, but she had worked hard with them just the same; one could see that.

"What about trying on the coronet," Agnes said, "so that we can see if the hair suits it? You say you want to have it."

"Yes, Agnes dear, do."

So Agnes fastened it on to the top of Frida's head with hairpins, a little coronet of myrtle which Frida had woven so neatly out of a myrtle she had inherited from her mother, who had used it when she was a bride. Three times it had died out, but she had taken cuttings, so it was the same tree really. The inside of the coronet was filled with white tulle, which billowed out in a lovely veil.

Frida stood up to see herself properly in the mirror. She had not yet put on her petticoat and dress, in order not to crease them, but her drawers were snow white and trimmed with the finest lace in the whole shop; the veil fell light and airy down her back, right to her knees. She was really very sweet standing there admiring herself, so thoughtful and happy. She looked at her reflection with dreamy eyes, seeing herself for the first time as a bride.

"You've nothing on but your drawers!" Agnes exclaimed, and burst out laughing.

She hadn't, either. Frida smiled gently as she realized it, then held the veil aside and carefully sat down again.

Agnes thought the coronet was too flat on the head.

"No, do you think so? I hadn't thought of it. Yes, perhaps it's not quite right."

"Supposing we curled the hair a bit more, so that it sits a little higher? But it's not so easy to get it up any higher, you see."

"No, it's so thin, isn't it?"

"Yes, that's just the trouble, but I'll have a try."

So Agnes very kindly started all over again; she took hair from the sides and got it up on top, although it wouldn't really reach, and then had the idea of putting the knot up there, too, for it didn't matter where it was, seeing that the veil would hide it anyway. She was so kind and helpful.

And during all this Frida sat there in a dream, which was not strange. . . .

She was thinking of how she and Jonas had met, how their destinies had been linked together, their steps guided forward to this great and glorious hour. They had been fond of each other for a long, long time, goodness knows how many years. It was a secret harmony of their souls, without words, without their being aware of it themselves. It had not blossomed into real love until later on, but they had, as it were, come closer to one another, even so. She remembered how he had taken her suitcase once when she had come off the train from town. They had walked along the street and he had said, "I suppose you have been in to do some shopping," and she had said, "Yes, I have," but as she said it she had happened to look into his eyes. That was four years ago now, but she remembered as though it were yesterday. That was when it had started in earnest.

Yes, how strange everything is, people's destinies—what is it that guides us? What had brought her and Jonas together to this sacred feeling that they would never be parted again?

But still a long time passed before there was anything said between them. That's the way of it. Oh, this deceptive game of love, this sweet game of hide-and-seek played by two people in love. The feelings of both are the same, but neither will admit it. Their souls are drawn to each other, reach out to each other in ardent longing, call to each other like twittering birds, like animals in their stalls in the evening.

And mixed up with it all a constantly disquieting uneasiness, in spite of everything. I suppose he does love me. Perhaps he doesn't. And do I really love him, with all my heart, deep down inside, as one should? As one must? Is it ordained by God that we are two souls meant to meet during our wandering here, to enter into the shining abode of love? Are we chosen and fitted for it? Yes, yes, I will believe, I will believe!

Yes, she believed. She knew. She sat gazing in front of her in tranquil rapture, transported by happiness.

No, no two people on earth could have met in a nicer, more beautiful way than they had, she and Jonas. Her eyes grew moist

as she thought of it, and her gaze grew remote as though she were looking at a far-off land.

Was she right? Yes, that's how it was; what they felt for each other was love. She had accepted him because she was fond of him. She loved for the sake of loving. And Jonas? He had said yes because he thought it was so boundlessly good of her to accept him. He had never imagined it; but as soon as he was allowed to, he loved her more than words can say. He had never loved anyone before because no one had asked him, and it wasn't really the sort of thing he could bring himself to ask. But to repeat, once given permission, he was the most ardent lover imaginable. He looked up to her as to something divine, something inconceivably good and beautiful. He could not imagine a more perfect being. She was as providence itself to him.

He had not bothered much about the fact that she had a little money, because he didn't understand much about that kind of thing. He used it so seldom. But of course it was very nice, seeing that everyone talked about it. He himself felt a kind of reverence at the thought of these things. It made everything even more wonderful, if possible.

As long as it didn't mean that he would no longer be able to stand down by the level-crossing gate, because he would certainly miss that. He was used to it, and once one has got used to something, it's hard to go without. That was his profession, as it were. But if Frida thought it was beneath him to go on working he would just have to put up with it. It would probably be all right, even so. That was something he had not liked to ask her about in so many words. Time enough for that. He loved her, that was the main thing; he loved her more than he could say, and there was nothing he wouldn't do for her. He loved Frida for her own sake, and because it was *she* who had been good enough to bother about him.

That's how it was. It amounted to love on both sides.

Jonas, yes . . . She thought of him, and the kind of man he was. Thought of when he had thrown his arms around her out in the woods last spring, and said that she was his most beautiful flower. He could indeed say so much that was remarkable, things that no one else could have thought of. He had great gifts, that was certain, which no one but she knew anything about.

Agnes stopped combing.

"There now, Frida, we won't do better than that," she said.

"Oh, my dear, it's lovely! Thank you so much."

They looked at the hair from all angles, and found that it now sat much better and as prettily as they could wish.

"Now I think we ought to hurry up and get your dress on."

"Yes, I suppose it's nearly time. . . . Oh, Agnes dear, you've no idea how strange it feels."

"Yes, it must."

"Just imagine being dressed as a bride—it's all like a dream. I can't really believe it's true."

"If I might suggest it," Agnes said, "you ought to wear your nice black dress instead, it suits you so well."

"Agnes dear, how can you! You're not serious!" Frida looked at her in amazement, quite distressed that she could say anything so thoughtless. "A bride must have white, you know that; it's an occasion for joy."

"Yes, yes, I only meant—that's *my* opinion—but of course you must do just as you like."

So Frida had her way. It would have been strange if she hadn't, after getting herself the dress for this very moment, sitting up sewing it night after night. And all the dreams she had put into it. Agnes helped her put it on. It was all so beautifully ironed and mustn't be creased at all, and all the lace had to hang properly. But the petticoat was showing at the back. What were they to do— they would have to pin it up.

Agnes stopped to listen.

"The pastor must have come."

"Oh, it's not possible," Frida said softly, feeling herself grow pale.

"You can hear he has, no one's saying a word."

"Then we must get ready," Frida said very quietly. Jonas knocked gently on the half-open door.

"The pastor has come," he whispered reverently.

"Jonas dear, is that you? You can't see me, not yet. In just half a minute, we're just fastening this up. The pastor is here, you said. The time has come then—fancy its hanging down like that—it's funny, isn't it? Dear Agnes, do try and hurry."

"Well, stand still then, so that I can get at it!"

"Yes, yes, of course I will. . . . What did the pastor say, Jonas?"

"The pastor—what did he say? Oh, he didn't say anything."

"Didn't you say how do you do to him?"

"No, I left the room when he arrived."

"Did you?"

"Yes, I thought I would come up here."

"Yes, it was good of you to come and tell me. Now I'll just put the coronet on, then I'm ready. Jonas dear, are you sure everything is as it should be down there?"

"Yes, Frida dearest, I think everything's all right; it all looks so nice."

"Are the flowerpots in the right place?"

"Yes."

"And the lace cloths on the stools—Hulda won't have forgotten them?"

"No, they're there."

"And the cake? The cake, Jonas! Do you know definitely if it has come?"

"Well, I can't say for sure, but I did see Klas arrive with a cake box; I should think that was probably it."

"Yes, that must have been it. Oh, I hope everything will be all right, and just as it should be, on this great and wonderful day in our life. They did get something to eat with their coffee, Jonas?"

"Yes, indeed."

"You did ask them to help themselves?"

"There was no need, Frida dear."

"Now I think you're ready," Agnes said, giving her a final critical look of inspection.

The Marriage Feast

"Am I! Oh, thank you, Agnes dear. You can come in now, Jonas dear, there's no need for you to go on standing there behind the door."

So Jonas came in. He stood dumbfounded with admiration at this radiant vision in the middle of the room, dazzlingly white and lovely; at his own darling Frida, the sight of whom filled him with an almost dizzy joy. He looked and looked at her with shining eyes, unable to believe it was true.

"Am I all right, dear?"

"Yes," he said, his voice thick and his eyes filling with tears, poor fellow. He couldn't say any more, just pressed and pressed her hand as though to thank her—over and over again.

"Then everything's all right," Frida whispered with a sob. "We can go down together." And she dried her eyes, holding her handkerchief in front of them so as not to show her emotion and how touched she was.

"The bridal bouquet!" cried Agnes, getting it out of the vase and drying it on a towel. It was of pink carnations and greenery.

"Oh, dear Agnes, thank you so much. Fancy forgetting! One forgets everything at a time like this."

And so down they went. Side by side, tightly pressed against each other. The coronet slipped a little to one side going down the stairs, but otherwise all was well. Their eyes were shining as they entered the bridal room, the little room with the sun shining in through the curtains. As they advanced between the guests, the women stared hard at them and the men cleared their throats. Up by the stools the pastor was waiting for them, severe and dignified. They stood in front of him like simple-hearted children, full of devout expectancy. He eyed them over his pince-nez, then opened the book and began to read.

"In the name of God the Father, God the Son, and God the Holy Ghost . . ."

They hung on his words. There could not have been two more attentive listeners, so afraid were they of missing a single word, so moved by the solemnity of the moment. Jonas did in-

deed smile as usual, but it was merely out of inexpressible reverence. He kept his head a little on one side in order to hear everything, and his hands were clasped together in implicit reliance
on what was being said to him. Frida, too, held her hands tightly
together with the bouquet between them, and looked at the pastor with trusting, humble gratitude.

Presently, when they had to kneel down, they thought that
was the loveliest of all. The sun shone on them, on Frida's lovely
white dress with the veil all around it that seemed to be made of
light, and on Jonas in his brand-new clothes. They were kneeling
right in front of the window, and so their eyes shone with an almost supernatural radiance. Around them were all the flowerpots. It was a moment full of light and beauty.

The others, of course, could not feel it in the same way.
They were only there because they were invited. But God's word
was being read out, so of course it was a solemn occasion. The
women were a little weepy, as they always are at weddings, and
everyone listened to the trembling voices answering the time-
honoured questions. It was certainly nice being there when they
knew them both so intimately—because up to a point they knew
Jonas very well, too.

The pastor gave no address for them, nor was there any
need for one. But he read Our Father and the Benediction, and
they thought it had never sounded so beautiful; they were like
two completely new prayers with memorable new words that applied only to them. Then he closed the book, and the moving
ceremony was at an end. Frida and Jonas were wedded to each
other for always.

Wine was handed around, and everyone drank with them;
first the pastor, who wished them happiness, then all the others
according to age and position or relationship. The sun shone on
the glasses, they clinked and sparkled all at once, the entire little
room had something so festive about it. In the middle of the
guests, entirely surrounded, stood the bride, radiant with happiness. And beside her stood Jonas, smiling with every wrinkle of
his kind face. They drank to him, too, and he held his glass ex-

tended between his fingertips as though he were holding out an extraordinary kind of flower. Everywhere were kindly eyes that must be thanked, and he kept bowing incessantly. A wave of warmth and cordiality flowed toward him such as he could never have imagined. Then it grew a little quieter, they all sat down at the window tables or over on the sofa and began talking among themselves, and he was left to himself in the middle of the floor, quite a lot to himself.

But the women took hold of Frida by the arm to say a few words more heartfelt than the mere congratulations.

"Well, Frida dear, now you have got what you wanted, so I suppose you are happy, aren't you?"

"Oh yes, thank you, Mrs Lundgren, I am indeed. I am as happy as it is possible for anyone to be."

"Yes, I suppose you are, Frida dear."

And all the relatives had to go up and talk to her for a moment.

"So you're married, Frida dear."

"Yes, Emma dear."

"Oh well, you never know how things will turn out."

"Yes, who would have thought it would be like this? But then we don't really know what's ahead of us."

"Oh," put in Miss Svensson from the tobacconist's, "I always thought that Frida would get married. I said many times that it's a wonder Frida Johansson doesn't get married. She could easily."

"Yes, that's just what I thought. My old man always used to say as we sat talking about the family, 'No, Frida will never get married.' But I thought, no, it's always best to wait and see, one never really knows for sure. Well, good luck, Frida dear, we are all so *glad* that you've managed it."

"Thank you, thank you, dear Matilda."

So the talk went on, Frida smiling and happy. After all, she had Jonas. They nodded at each other secretively, their gaze still obscured, the sacred words resounding within them. They were now a little apart from each other, but that didn't matter, it was only for a little while. And it was all going so well—she could see he thought so, too. Oh yes, everyone was so nice and kind. Some of them had come a long way in order to be present on this, their great day. Strange that there were so many gathered here just for their sake. There were so many conversations going on that it was hard to follow them, and one didn't know whom to listen to. And just think how festive it was when they had all come up and drunk their health.

Now there was the smell of cooking from the kitchen, and the women began wondering what it was they were going to have; it was sure to be roast meat, as was customary. Frida was sure to have only the best, and she could no doubt afford it. What her income was from the little shop no one could say. And Hulda was going to do the waiting, ah yes. And she had a lace apron, well I never.

The pastor came up and said he must be going. There was nothing much to wait for at a wedding like this, and he had so much work to do at home, routine office work as it is called. No, of course he didn't know who Frida was, and what she had to offer. How should he know?

Frida had hoped that he would stay. He is sure to, she had thought. It would make it all so festive. But he was obliged to go. Yes, of course, when he had such an awful lot to do; one can imagine a clergyman who is responsible for all that is most important in life, for the souls of so many people. Yes, there must be a lot of work, a lot that is not apparent. She thanked him for making this moment so sacred, for all the beautiful words he had read. Both she and Jonas went to the door with him, and Jonas helped him on with his coat and opened the gate leading out into the road, where he stood bowing until the pastor had disappeared through the trees.

Dinner was ready now, and they all sat down, the bridal pair in the principal seats in the centre of one side, and the others gathered around them for this banquet in honour of the newly married. The men were talking of a sewer which emptied out into the lake too near the village; they had been discussing it and were going to finish the subject, for the farmers didn't know what a fuss there had been about it at the meeting. But now they got their smörgåsbord and an aquavit and began to think about eating. There was plenty to choose from, dishes of every kind, and there was nothing wrong with the aquavit either, so they had another. They began to feel nice and cheery, as was fitting at a wedding. Now that old Frida was getting married, they must see that it was done properly, and eat and drink as much as they could when it was offered for once in a while.

"Come on, Jonas, have a stiffener, it won't hurt you."

"What, isn't he drinking?" shouted Emil of Östragård, Frida's second cousin, across the table. "I should think he needs one! Go on, have one, it'll put a tongue in your head."

And Jonas smiled and took it, though he didn't usually touch that kind of thing, but of course he must when they wanted him to join them.

"Well, to think it's come to a wedding. Who would have thought it!"

"Oh, more surprising things than this can happen. Sometimes they're in such a hurry that it makes you wonder what's wrong. No question of that in this case!"

"No, Julius, that it isn't! Cheers! You were always a wag!"

"No, by Christ, if they want to swap bullocks with me, then they'll have to bring along the best they have and still pay the difference. I told him so, too. No, it was the rottenest cattle-market I've ever been to."

"Didn't you even get a drink?"

"No, the place was shut."

"Oh well, then, of course you couldn't do any business."

"Hey there, Emil, fill them up here! You can't keep it all down your end!"

They went on drinking after the roast meat was brought in, and Jonas had to join in, though he didn't want to. "You're a damn queer sort of chap, not drinking." He was to have a drop in him, same as they. So Jonas drank, though he tried to have as little as possible. He was one of those people who just couldn't say no. And they all meant so well, wanting him to join in.

"Take a stiff one and get your strength up; you've got a

good day's work ahead of you such as you never did in your life before, I'll bet!"

"You must at least have a good strong breath if Frida's to be satisfied with you."

"Well, you're in for a good time now, Jonas. No need for you to go and overwork in any way."

"Are you going to give up your job at the hotel? Oh, you don't know. Hasn't she said anything yet?"

"Perhaps you'll be selling embroidery in your old age. Well, not so bad either, a nice dainty job. And I suppose you'll have to go poking about here with all these flowers. Frida's got a frightful lot of flowerpots, that she has."

"What's the idea; is Jonas going to help in your shop, or what are you going to make him do?"

There was no need for Frida to answer; they were all talking at once and there was a terrific hubbub. She sat looking straight in front of her with her big, gentle eyes, the bridal coronet slightly askew, but dignified and calm in her white dress, which really suited her very well when you came to think of it. Now and then she would squeeze Jonas's hand under the table, and she would light up with a blissful smile as they looked at each other with secret joy. Then she would grow serious again, almost melancholy.

It was twilight now, and Hulda had to light the lamps. The sweet was brought in. It had turned out very well, but Frida could not eat much; she just tasted it to see that it was all right. Yes, of course, it was all right; they'd taken such trouble with it. And then came the cake. It was certainly very handsome. In the middle was a J and an F in bright red jam, but no one noticed it, and besides the letters were all intertwined. But she and Jonas saw it, and they gave each other a happy, tender look, and held each other's hand under the table. Wine was served with the cake. If the pastor had been able to stay he would probably have made a speech for them now, he would indeed. He could make a very good speech when he had to. But it all went very well notwithstanding and the cake was eaten up.

Afterwards there was to be coffee. They all got up from the table and spread out over the room, the men talking and booming, a little unsteady on their feet. Cigars were handed around and the coffee was poured out.

"Haven't you any brandy, Frida?" asked Emil.

No, that's something she had forgotten. It hadn't really occurred to her that they would drink so much on an occasion like this.

"Well, that's stingy when we're celebrating like this," Emil said. "It *is* a wedding, you know, so there ought to be some brandy, see! I've got a bottle out in the trap that I went and bought, so we can have that." And he lumbered out through the door, returning in a minute with the bottle.

"Now for a drop in the coffee!"

They started drinking. They shouted everything they said, as though they were standing out in the fields yelling across at each other from one farm to the next, and they all swore as though they were going to kill each other when they met, though they were firm friends standing close together, all talking at once. They became more and more drunk as the evening wore on, swaying against each other and sitting down heavily so that the chairs creaked. The ones from the village were a little more dignified—they had grown rather more superior—but those farmers were really too awful. The room was filled with fumes from the liquor and the warm smell of billowing smoke.

The women were having a nice time on their own. They had gathered in one corner and were talking about people who were not there, and what had happened in the district—there was quite a lot since last time, for there were not so many parties nowadays. Then they spoke their minds, shaking their heads, pursing their lips, whispering and listening and repeating things, whatever it happened to be. Frida sat with them for a while, then cast an eye into the kitchen, rearranged the flowers that had not been put back as they should, and saw to the lamp. Finally she just stood in the middle of the floor with her hands clasped, looking in front of her and listening to the noise all around her.

"Silly little thing, decking herself out in white," she heard someone say behind her. Then she went over and sat by Jonas, and as she sat down she burst into tears.

But she wasn't really crying, the tears ran so gently and quietly down her cheeks. No one noticed them except Jonas. He got really frightened; he patted her and took her hand, holding it tenderly in his, asking over and over again what was wrong and why she was crying. Then she looked at him so warmly and smiled so sweetly, as she always did when they spoke to each other.

"It's nothing, Jonas dear, it's only tears of joy."

Then he was reassured, because he could see that it was true.

"Dear Jonas," she said then, "we'll go upstairs now."

And so they did. They said good-bye to everybody, happily and affectionately, like the bridal pair they were, and went up to their room.

It had all been got ready just as Frida had arranged, the bed nicely made up with the sheets with lace insertions, the widest in the shop; there were fresh-cut flowers on the table, and a clean white cloth with hemstitching, and the same on the chest of drawers. The window was open to the silence of the late summer night with its clear stars shining in.

How quiet and peaceful it was here. They threw their arms around each other, overwhelmed with bliss. They stood there, entirely filled with their happiness, for a long while, so long that they were not aware of time. Downstairs the noise went on, but it was strange how they didn't hear it. It was strange not being able to hear anything like that, anything at all.

They undressed and got into bed, caressing each other and whispering. They thrilled to each other, and felt the most wonderful feeling that they had never known before, which was like nothing else—nothing.

She had never thought that love could be so great. She had thought a lot about all this, but had never really been able to imagine it. It was as though she had lived her life just for this moment when she and Jonas became one. He held her in his arms, strong from all he had carried in his life, and she gave herself to her beloved; it was so unspeakably lovely to give him all she had, so really wonderful. She bit him with her false teeth so that he was quite dizzy. She, too, felt a little stupefied soon afterwards, but it was love speaking, that great, divine love, the incomprehensible miracle which made everything sacred.

Afterwards they lay side by side, tired and blissful, just holding each other's hand, as though that were even more tender than being caressed. They were almost numbed by the perfection of their happiness.

Jonas fell asleep, replete with his day. He was so handsome and good as he lay there beside her on the pillow; she stroked his hair and arranged it. She, too, felt a little exhausted, but she lay listening in the semi-darkness with open eyes.

How quiet it was, how extraordinarily quiet. Were they still there, or had they gone? She heard nothing but the great, unfathomable night, and the loved one at her side, snoring softly. Otherwise nothing.

She crept down beside him and she, too, fell asleep, his hand tightly clasped in hers. They lay there together in the darkness, near each other, with burning cheeks and their mouths half-open for a kiss. And like a heavenly song of praise, like a hosanna of light around the only living thing, the stars rose around their bed in mighty hosts, their numbers increasing with the darkness.